Our Daughter:
Our Love,
Our Light,
Our Joy,
Our Pleasure,
Heart of Our
Hearts Forever

Our Daughter:
Our Love,
Our Light,
Our Joy,
Our Pleasure,
Heart of Our
Hearts Forever

❖

Beth Carol Solomon

Library of Congress Control Number:		2021901527
ISBN:	Hardcover	978-1-6641-5489-6
	Softcover	978-1-6641-5487-2
	eBook	978-1-6641-5488-9

Print information available on the last page.

Rev. date: 01/29/2021

To order additional copies of this book, contact:
Xlibris
844-714-8691
www.Xlibris.com
Orders@Xlibris.com
824656

Contents

PART 1

Brooklyn, 8:00 p.m., 2000.. 1
Seven Years Later 3
The next day 5

PART 2

Two Years Later, Saturday Afternoon 17
Sunday Morning.. 23
Monday, 6:00 p.m... 29
Two Months Later: Francine's Thirteenth Birthday 31
A Month Later.. 32
Six Months Later, Friday, 4:00 p.m. 34
Saturday, 10:00 a.m.. 36
Sunday, 9:00 a.m. 39
While at the Mall.. 49
One Month Later: Francine's Fourteenth Birthday 60
Sunday 9:00 a.m.. 73
Two Weeks Later: Saturday 9:00 a.m.. 86
Sunday, After Breakfast, 10:00 a.m... 93
Saturday, One Week Later, 11:00 a.m. 95
Friday, 3:00 p.m.. 109
Monday, 7:00 a.m. 112
Tuesday, 8:00 a.m. 135
Wednesday, 4:00 p.m.. 141
Thursday, 5:00 p.m... 146
Friday, 9:00 a.m. 150
Mother's Day Morning.. 153
A Month Since Mother's Day: Six Weeks Since Francine's Hospital Stay...... 155

Sunday Morning.. 158
A Week Later, Father's Day, 8:00 a.m... 164
Burlington Psychiatric Center for Women.....................................174
Washington Heights Psychiatric Facility for Men 176
The End of June, Beginning of Summer...178
The Big Day, 9:00 a.m.. 183
While Upstairs... 188
Sunday, 9:00 a.m. 199
The Next Day, 7:00 a.m. 209
A Week Later: Monday, Lunch Break 12:00 p.m. 219
Monday Night, 8:00 p.m. 220
Sunday Afternoon: The Homecoming.. 221
While at the Marsowe Residence.. 224
Monday Morning 226
Sunday Afternoon: The Homecoming.. 229
While on the Way to the Cemetery.. 232
Farmingdale Cemetery... 234
Crestville Nursing Home, 7:00 p.m. 236
The Night before the Big Day 239
The Big Day in August... 241
September: The First Day of High School.................................... 244

About the Author.. 247

To my Mom and Dad who taught me what love and family are all about.

Part 1

Brooklyn, 8:00 p.m., 2000

The little girl, just three years old, crouched into the corner of the hallway, covering her ears, trying relentlessly to block out the yelling and screaming and the banging and throwing of pots and pans across the room. They were fighting. *Again*. Her parents. Practically every single night. Clad in a green flannel pajama top, urine flowing from her underpants, she felt her head would burst open. She cried out continually, "Mommy, I'm hungry!" She had growling pains in her stomach. No one paid any heed. As usual.

"Philip," she addressed her husband adamantly, "I work three fuckin' jobs just to pay the rent and food and your tuition so you can become a doctor. A psychiatrist! And what do you do? Nothing! Not a damned thing! I ask you to buy milk and pork chops for dinner. Also, you can't even pick up after yourself and see that your daughter is fed and cleaned!" Her mother screamed day after day after day. Nada! Nada! She slammed the cabinet doors while kicking her husband's legs again and again, pounding on his back with her fists. And he never retaliated. He was used to his wife's ungovernable temper tantrums. He was calm and patient while watching her usual rages escalate.

He would try to explain to her, "Leonora, honey, I have a dissertation that's due in two weeks, an oral next week, and a meeting with a new patient. I do understand you are tired, but do try to see what I have been going through. I am busy, too. And I do try, I do. I love you and our daughter."

She stood there in the middle of the kitchen—drippings on the drawers, chunks of dirt on the plates and utensils, food on the counters, grease, grime, and garbage strewn around everywhere. It was useless. His face resigned and weary. She refused to cave in, feeling she was always the martyr. No one cared how she felt. *Poor me, the victim, the scapegoat.*

"Get out of this house, now!" she demanded angrily. "And don't come back. Ever! You shiftless piece of shit!"

Then he put his hands on her shoulders, "Please, honey, do try to understand," he said in his usual soothing demeanor.

No one said anything for a while.

Their daughter's piercing, deafening screams bolted into her parents' ears.

Philip walked over to the little girl and picked her up while gently patting her back.

"Francine, my princess." He gazed into his daughter's large dark eyes with love and gentleness. "I'll make you eggs and clean you up, okay?" he comforted her.

Leonora watched with fury, hands on her hips, indignant, her eyes blazing, doing and saying nothing.

Suddenly, she blurted out, "Do what you have to do. And go and do not come back. We do not need you here. We'll manage just fine."

Seven Years Later

Late evening, Francine bolted up from her bed, mattress torn and filled with bugs, clad in a ripped, dirty nightdress. It was her mother and a new boyfriend laughing hysterically, slobbering each other with kisses. Her mother held a cigarette in one hand and an almost-empty bottle of whiskey in the other hand. Her shoulder-length dark hair was greasy and disheveled. Also, she was clad in tight black shorts and a dirty T-shirt with a short leather jacket.

The man, practically bald, was clad in a short-sleeved undershirt and ragged baggy pants hanging from his waist. He pushed her down on the couch. Still laughing and making kissing noises.

Every day, the same thing—a new man on top of her, both drunk, but without a care.

Papers, bottles, cans, plates, and cups strewn around the apartment; drippings from the kitchen counter; and crumbs scattered on the floor.

Francine was very hungry. *Again*. Hardly any food in the refrigerator.

Her stomach was growling. Her face, thin and wan. Her body covered with filth and practically all bones.

Her face was tear-stained. Her dark, large eyes nearly bolted out of their sockets. Her nose was running.

Every single day.

Tonight, Francine dared to leave her room, watching her mother and new boyfriend screwing, unaware that she was watching them with disgust. The man's hands were all over her body, then under her shirt, and into her pants. Leonora was giggling uncontrollably. She enjoyed it.

"I'm hungry," Francine cried out plaintively, holding her stomach tightly. It hurt like hell.

Leonora turned toward her daughter, pointing to her bedroom with anger. "Get into your bed, now!" Francine still sobbed painfully, telling her she was hungry, but Leonora ignored her request. Neither caved in. The man watched them then laughed under his breath with a wicked smile. He was enjoying the moment.

"I'll get her to bed," he offered, bounding off the couch. Then, grabbing Francine's arm, he pushed her into her bedroom. She cried hysterically. The man threw her down on the bed and smacked her around and then kicked her between her legs, paying no heed to her pain.

"Shut the fuck up, you stupid, moronic idiot brat! And not another word!" he threatened menacingly, his beady eyes glaring.

Then, it was quiet. He left the room grinning gleefully and satisfied while watching her lying on her right side, sobbing silently. She looked out her window. There was darkness, but stars shone in the sky. She thought, one day, someone would love her. It made her feel good thinking that.

The next day

Francine dragged herself to school. Her clothes torn, dirty, and ragged. Her head was down and sullen. She sluggishly pushed her backpack by its strap on the sidewalk. Girls were walking in groups watching her. They always did, smirking and taunting her, throwing pebbles at her, while pointing at her.

"Ha, ha!" one girl piped up, "Where's your daddy? Or better yet, who is your daddy? Bet your mama doesn't even know."

Another girl chimed in, "Look at that ragamuffin. Don't your mother feed you? Maybe one day you will have a roasted turkey with stuffing and potatoes fit for a king?!"

Then one more girl grinned. "Anything fashionable at the Goodwill? Perhaps we will check it out. There might be something for me to wear to the King's Ball!"

"Her mother's a two-bit whore," some girl jeered wickedly. "She got a boyfriend for you? Or maybe she could find one for our mothers."

Francine continued walking, saying nothing to the girls, who resumed their merciless taunting, their eyes wide and bright, smirks of satisfaction on their faces.

9:00 a.m.

The school bell rung. Everyone was in their classrooms, ready to start the day.

Francine went to her seat in the back of the room. Sluggishly and mournfully she sat, her arms clasped on her desk, her face teary-eyed and tired, just staring into space. Her classmates were jumping around her desk, throwing balls of paper at her, kicking her backpack, and then emptying its contents on the floor, making grueling faces while pushing the back of her chair with their feet. Everyone screamed out with laughter. No one did a damned thing to help her.

"Class!" Ms. Lorme, their fifth-grade teacher, shouted as she entered the classroom. Stunned, the students froze in their spots, eyes blazed and shaking.

Ms. Lorme stumped her feet toward Francine's desk. She wagged her finger at the children and spoke with an angry, high-pitched voice, "You all, clean all this mess up at once. Then you are all to go back to your seats and stay there. Do not move a muscle. You will all be punished, and your parents will be notified. The punishment will be two weeks' detention and no after-school activities. I'm ashamed of all of you."

The children mournfully nodded, their faces drooping, and began their teacher's instructions. She again stated, "Not a peep out of any of you! Do I make myself clear?"

They went on with their teacher's orders, not uttering a sound.

Ms. Lorme turned to Francine and put her arm around her, but she jumped away in a flash.

"Everything will be all right, honey," she assured her.

Every day, Ms. Lorme noticed her tattered, uncleaned, too-big clothes, emaciated body, tear-stained, grimy face, and greasy, stringy dark hair on her shoulders. She tried to find out about her home life and at times would comfort her, but she would say nothing. She was always frightened and often shook with fear when her teacher would initiate a hug or friendly pat. Francine had trust issues. Ms. Lorme had written letters home but never received a reply. The telephone was disconnected, and there was no Internet, email, or text access. She did not know anything about Leonora's employment status, so there was no work number available to contact her mother. Still, Ms. Lorme refused to be deterred. She was going to help Francine and be there for her regardless of all these obstacles. Nothing was going to stand in her way, she promised herself. For Francine.

Ms. Lorme was a new young teacher. All her life, she wanted to teach children for she loved them. She had six nieces and nephews that she thought of as her own children, and they thought of her as their second mother. She was a comely young woman with short, dark curly hair and large opal eyes framed with black-rimmed oval-shaped lensed glasses. Her nose was tiny but cute and pert; her lips small but perky. She always wore a smile. She encouraged her students to do their best and was patient with the challenging ones, never raising her voice or losing her temper. Except for today. For it disturbed her deeply to see Francine teased, tormented, and abused. She decided to take matters into her own hands.

"Willow," she called to a girl with long, straight, light brown hair from the front row. The girl rose from her seat and turned to her teacher, who instructed, "Please, watch the class. There is to be no talking whatsoever. I want every student to write one hundred times. 'I was very mean and cruel to my classmate and I am very ashamed of myself. I promise never to be unkind to her again and am deeply sorry for my behavior.' Your parents are to sign it, and I want it on my desk first thing tomorrow morning. Also, when Francine comes back to class, you are all going to apologize to her for the way you treated her, and you will be nice to her for now on. Is that understood, class?" They mumbled and nodded solemnly.

"I'm taking Francine to the children's shelter now. I want every boy and girl in this class to think about what you all did." Then, she added, "I am extremely appalled by your conduct. Each one of you. Okay, Willow? I'm depending on you and leaving you in charge."

"Yes, ma'am," she complied, assuring with a smile. "I'll see that everything is under control. Don't worry."

Ms. Lorme turned toward Francine, smiled, and extended her hand, "Come with me. I'm taking you to a place where there are other children in similar situations and circumstances as yourself."

Tears filled Francine's eyes and she hysterically cried, clenching her stomach, backing away. "No! My mother will yell and whip me with an extension cord! And her boyfriend, too. He'll hurt me badly with a belt!" she blurted out, protesting bitterly.

"Calls will be made that your mother cannot and will not be in contact with you. She broke the law and will be taken into custody. So I am taking you where you will be protected and safe. And, perhaps, you will be placed with a foster family. You will be treated the way you deserve and are entitled to. You will be bathed, cleaned, and washed, and have nice, presentable clothes, eat proper meals, play games, and watch television with the other children. No one will hurt you, and if someone does, you call a social worker, okay, honey?"

Francine nodded silently and took her teacher's hand after collecting all her belongings into her backpack. They exited the classroom.

11:00 a.m.

They rode in the car in silence. Every so often, Ms. Lorme would turn and face Francine with a smile and try to initiate conversation, but Francine would not utter a sound for she did not know what to say. She was not used to love and kindness. Her teacher knew that, but still, she refused to admit defeat. Her goal was to get her student to trust the people who only had her best interests at heart. So far, no one took a stand.

"We're here," Ms. Lorme pronounced, facing Francine with a pleasant grin.

They got out of the car, with Ms. Lorme extending her hand, and Francine slowly clasped it into hers. They entered the building and walked to the front desk.

"Excuse me," Ms. Lorme began to the receptionist, "I'm Urva Lorme, and this is Francine Hawes, my student. Mrs. Playne is expecting us."

The girl smiled pleasantly and stated, "Of course, I'll go get her now." She left her desk.

Ms. Lorme turned to her student, "You'll be taken care of properly. Mrs. Playne will show you to your room and tell you what to do. She is very good with children, especially those who have been abused. Okay?"

Again, Francine said nothing, but she nodded, slowly facing her teacher.

Finally, an acknowledgment, though still no verbal communication. "It's a start," Ms. Lorme satisfactorily agreed.

A few minutes later, Mrs. Playne appeared. Tall, with short, light brown hair in a bob, and with her eyes gleaming, she smiled at Francine, who said nothing. She went up to the girl and extended her hand. Francine jumped backward.

"Don't be afraid, honey," Ms. Lorme assured her. "She's going to help you."

Then she faced Mrs. Playne and mentioned, "She's been severely abused and hurt most of her life. She doesn't trust anyone," she spoke quietly and apologetically.

Mrs. Playne was not perturbed by her behavior. "It's all right. I understand. A lot of abused and neglected children have trouble with trust and attachment to people, for they never really felt kindness from the people who are supposed to love them the most. But she will be fine. Hopefully, she will adjust, but let me warn you. It does take time, perhaps a lot of it, so we'll just have to be patient."

Ms. Lorme nodded in agreement. She then turned to Francine and spoke quietly, "I'm going to leave you here. Tomorrow morning, I will pick you up and bring you to school. You do everything Mrs. Playne says. She's going to take care of you, all right?"

Again, Francine did not speak, but she nodded an agreement to her teacher.

Ms. Lorme left, and Mrs. Playne smiled and again extended her hand, but this time, she took it. Another small miracle.

Hand in hand, they walked into a room with other children who were playing games or watching television.

"Children," she called out, her hands on Francine's shoulders, "This is Francine Hawes. She is going to be staying with us. Please make her feel welcome." Some children looked up, murmuring "Hello." Others nodded by rote.

"First," Mrs. Playne stated to Francine, "we will get you out of these dirty, filthy clothes. You will be getting new and different clothes afterward. These rags will be discarded. Then, you'll take a bath and clean yourself up."

Francine looked fearfully at Mrs. Playne, who understood. "You probably never had a bath before, so the aide will help you while you're in the tub, okay?"

Another nod, but with complete trust.

"Later, you'll have lunch in the cafeteria down the hall. Afterward, Ms. Lin, an aide, will take you shopping for some new clothes. Then, we will show you your own room and get settled, okay?"

"Yes, ma'am," the girl suddenly blurted out. Mrs. Playne sighed gleefully. Finally, verbal acknowledgment. Fine for now.

Francine obediently walked with Mrs. Playne to the bathroom.

Francine glanced around at her new surroundings. She could not believe it. *Warm, loving kindness*, she thought to herself in silence. It was a lot to take in, but she did not want to get so happy for it may not last long. *Only time will tell*, she thought hesitantly, but she did everything she was told without question. She knew that children were to do what they are told or there would be consequences. She aimed to please. Perhaps, one day, she will be loved unconditionally. She thought again as she did when she lived with her abusive, neglectful, drug-addicted, and alcoholic mother and her endless stream of good-for-nothing boyfriends who hurt her as well. She reveled in this dream for it made her feel good and proud. No one could stop her from this reverie. No one, she would think to herself, pleased with happiness. It kept her wanting to go on living, something to hold on to. Her secret pleasure. Hers and hers alone. Not to be shared.

Today was the start of a new beginning for Francine. No more beatings, whippings, neglect, filth, dirt, poverty, hunger, or ragged, torn clothing. Still, Francine was on edge and doubtful. Today was too good to be true. She did not want to believe in a new start. *Perhaps*, she pondered to herself.

The aide washed her tangled, matted, greasy hair, which was a very difficult job, but it needed to be done. The aide put shampoo and conditioner on her hair, swishing it around. Francine felt gleeful, the feeling of having her hair cleaned, for her mother never took the time, and when she did, she was mean and cruel, smacking, slamming, and banging her around.

After her bath, Francine insisted on drying herself with a towel. She was still leery of physical contact. The aide understood completely but offered help if she asked for it.

As for her hair, she attempted to dry it but was not sure if she was doing it correctly, for no one ever showed her, so the aide did it and then blow-dried it. Francine was startled, but she liked the coolness of the dryer. The aide brushed her hair, which was fluffy and shiny. Her thick, wavy dark-brown hair hung on her shoulders. She parted it on the right side.

"Look in the mirror!" the aide insisted excitedly, posing her to face herself. "You're so pretty!"

Francine did as the aide said. Her eyes lit up brightly. She was very pleased and cheerful.

When she went to the cafeteria and saw the other children eating, she quickly looked for a seat away, fearful of being hurt. And also when she saw her lunch—chicken soup with a tuna fish sandwich and an apple, cookies, and milk—she dived in voraciously, wolfing down her meal. The other children saw and were perplexed. They did not know she would be so starved for food. Thus, a monitor saw her and did not berate or yell at her, but gently explained and showed her the proper way to eat and use her utensils for no one taught her. Afterward, Francine, a little teary-eyed, gulped as she spoke, "I am sorry. I won't do it anymore. I will be good. I promise." The monitor smiled and patted her on the shoulder. "It's all right. You didn't know. You are a very good girl." Francine smiled—smiled. She would be all right.

Francine had been given a long-sleeved pink dress to wear. It was a little worn but in good condition. Ms. Lin and she planned to go shopping for new clothes for Francine. She would be getting a new wardrobe. With the shelter's high-limit credit card and funds, Francine was amazed at all the stores that sold children's clothing. She was mesmerized and felt like a princess.

Early Evening

Francine ate her supper as a lady was supposed to, though she was hungry. She made sure she did as the monitor instructed her. Supper consisted of a hamburger, french fries, a pickle, coleslaw, Jell-O, milk, and cookies. It felt like a feast and she was a princess.

Then an aide took her to the playroom. The children were watching cartoons or playing games. Francine was not interested in either, so she asked the aide for any books for she loved to read. The aide pointed to a bookcase near the window in the back of the room. Francine dashed off in a flash. She was genuinely happy. Still, she made no attempt at befriending the other children. But all in all, it was a good day.

8:00 p.m.

Francine was escorted to her room. It was small with a chest of drawers, a twin bed, a table with a lamp on it next to the bed. Pictures of colored flowers were posted on the walls. There was a closet for hew new clothes. Everything was clean and spotless. Francine could not believe her eyes. Her own room and private space. She glanced out the window near her bed and saw the dark sky filled with twinkling stars. She managed a smile. Hopefully, her dream would come true. To be loved for herself. No more abuse.

"Are you all right, honey?" Mrs. Playne asked, standing by her door, watching Francine in her long pink nightdress reading a book.

Francine looked up and answered, staring into Mrs. Playne's eyes, "Yes, ma'am."

"Very good. I heard you had a very good day and are starting to feel at ease and comfortable and that you are talking a little. Do not worry, you will be fine. Your teacher will pick you up tomorrow at 7:30 a.m. Have a good night," she offered.

Francine put her book down on the table and climbed into bed. She slipped the comforter over her, laid her head on the pillow, which was soft and fluffy, and replied to Mrs. Playne, "You, too." She closed the light, smiling as she shut the door.

Morning

Francine tossed around in her bed, still mesmerized and wondering, but was jubilant. She still felt she was in a dream and would suddenly awaken to her old reality. She wanted to believe her new reality but was hesitant.

She plopped out of bed and ran to the window. The sun was out, the sky, a clear blue. She smiled, a first in a long time.

It was 6:00 a.m. She was up early, still taking in her new surroundings, sighing and breathing pleasantly.

She opened her closet and saw all her new clothes. It was hard for her to decide what to wear. She was in a dilemma, but a good one. So many choices.

She picked out a pair of light brown denim jeans with a matching vest and a long-sleeved, swooped-neck white shirt. She wore brown moccasins. So excited, she put on her new apparel. She smiled to herself. She felt just fine. Ready to begin the day.

Mrs. Playne appeared at her door. "Good morning," she greeted Francine. "Are you ready for breakfast? Everyone is waiting for you." She extended her hand, which Francine took at once and smiled, "Yes, ma'am."

They went downstairs to the cafeteria. Francine saw the other children who looked at her with wide-opened mouths. One little girl remarked, "You look nice today. Why don't you sit next to me?" she patted the seat near her.

Francine nodded happily and sat down next to the girl. Everyone started digging into their breakfast. Francine took her napkin and placed it on her lap and began her meal that consisted of scrambled eggs, two slices of bacon, orange juice, three oatmeal cookies, and a container of milk. Everybody ate while chattering with each other. Some of the girls giggled among themselves. Francine observed but did not say much at first. Her large dark eyes sparkled as captive stars; her hair, in two ponytails, hung down her shoulders.

7:45 a.m.

Francine packed her books and school supplies into her new backpack. Then she grabbed her new brown leather jacket and hastily put it on.

"Ms. Lorme is waiting for you," Mrs. Playne mentioned. "Are you ready?"

Francine looked up and briefly acknowledged her, "Yes, ma'am," she answered.

She grabbed her belongings and extended her hand to Mrs. Playne. They left.

Ms. Lorme was waiting in the reception area and smiled at her student, her eyes bright.

"Good morning, honey," her teacher greeted her.

Francine walked up to her and grinned enthusiastically. "Good morning," then hesitantly continued, "Ms. Lorme."

Both, cheerfully nodding at each other, turned to Mrs. Playne and in unison greeted, "Goodbye, and thank you, Mrs. Playne. Have a good day!"

They turned as Mrs. Playne smiled and reciprocated. "You, too, ladies." She watched them wave as they exited the building.

9:00 a.m.

All the students were babbling among themselves while sitting at their desks. Ms. Lorme and Francine entered the classroom but stood in the doorway.

"Class," their teacher announced with her hands on Francine's shoulders.

The class turned and faced them in silence.

"Remember what I said yesterday morning?" she prompted them firmly but gently.

In unison, they replied solemnly, "Yes, Ms. Lorme."

"Go on," she pushed her students.

The class agreeably began their speech. "We're very, very sorry for the way we treated you and we are deeply ashamed of our behavior. Will you forgive us?" they pleaded earnestly.

Francine smiled and responded, "Yes, I do forgive you all."

Willow and two other girls, Arlene and Stephanie, stood beside her. Arlene had thick, shoulder-length, fluffy, ash-blond hair and large, light brown twinkling eyes. Stephanie's hair was of a chestnut brown color cut in a short bob. Her eyes bright and hazel. Both smiled at Francine.

Willow notedly remarked to Francine, "I love your new outfit. It's awesome."

"You look very nice," Stephanie added.

Willow offered, "Would you like to join us for lunch later? We'd like you to sit with us," she resumed.

Francine gleamed, "Yes, oh yes, thank you. I'd love to."

Ms. Lorme smiled at her and then at the girls and at the rest of the class, "All right, class. Now, let us begin with our math lesson on page 52."

The class did as instructed. Francine went to her seat at the back of the room, sat down, and opened her book. Everything was fine.

For the next two years, Francine grew and seemed to be adjusting well. She made friends with Willow, Arlene, and Stephanie and continued their friendship. She lived at the children's shelter and mostly kept to herself. But she loved to read and did so voraciously, hungry for knowledge. She never spoke of her wretched past and was blossoming into a lovely, sweet young lady.

Still, a foster home had not yet been found for her since most people wanted babies or young children, being they would not likely remember their turbulent past, and Francine, an older child, did so quite vividly. Thus, foster homes might not be equipped to deal or handle her excess baggage even though they knew it was not the child's fault.

This did not faze her. Hopefully, sooner or later, one might be. But for now, Francine lived each day, one at a time, fiercely savoring in and enjoying each moment with relish and pleasure. Perhaps her dream of being unconditionally loved might very well materialize. But she was jubilant and satisfied. She was going to be all right.

Part 2

Two Years Later, Saturday Afternoon

Francine, clad in a scooped-neck red tank top and blue denim jeans and wearing opened-toe sandals, sat curled up in a chair in the playroom, reading a book. Her hair was shorter, below her ears, still soft and fluffy, wavy and earthy brown.

"Francine!" called Mrs. Playne, standing by the doorway.

Francine looked up and put her book to the side, saying nothing at first. She was still a little edgy when someone called her, thinking she did something wrong and would be punished harshly.

"It's all right, Francine," Mrs. Playne assured her. "You didn't do anything wrong. In fact, I have good news for you."

At that, she got off her chair and walked up to Mrs. Playne, who put her arm around her shoulder. They walked down the corridor and turned right to an office. The administrator of the shelter was sitting behind a large desk. She motioned for Francine to sit down in front. Hesitantly, she obeyed but had a tense look on her face.

"Relax, dear," she said comfortably.

She began, hands clasped on her desk, papers surrounding.

"We found you a foster mother. Usually, we have foster couples, but this woman is a widow. Her husband and daughter, who was your age, were killed in a car accident two months ago. As you know, generally foster parents want a child who has little or no recall of a turbulent past, thus they feel they could handle such a child. Older children usually have extremely vivid recollections of very abusive and neglectful backgrounds. Thus, most of these families, though they do not blame the child, feel they are not sure they could help such a child who may be beyond help for they may be too damaged or traumatized. But this bereaved young woman specifically requested a twelve-year-old girl regardless of her history. I told her about you, and she is interested in meeting you."

Francine said nothing but bounced out of her chair, clapping her hands in the air, her eyes sparkling.

"She owns her own flower shop a few miles away. She says she will come over this evening after 6:00 p.m. I told her supper is around that time. She promised to come and take you to her home. In the meantime, you will get ready. An aide will be there to assist you, okay?"

"Yes, ma'am," Francine agreed politely, though somewhat leery. A foster mother, she thought pleasantly to herself. She dared not think too much. It may happen, she pondered to herself. She will be loved and cared for unconditionally.

7:00 p.m.

She stood there—tall, erect, with creamy, ivory skin, her wavy blond hair carefully styled below her earlobes, her large eyes, sharp and deep brown, twinkling as captive stars, her nose medium and straight, her lips, just right. Her smile showing her pearly white teeth. She was dressed in a paisley red tank top, with long red slacks. She wore dangling earrings and a cameo around her neck. She gazed at Francine, with sparkling, gleaming eyes. Francine wanted to reciprocate but got tense and unsure, so she just stood at her spot, motionless, unable to respond. But she was not deterred and extended her arms out for a hug. Still, Francine knew not how to react to this woman's kindly gestures. They stood there, both wanting some interaction. Then she introduced herself.

"Hello, Francine. My name Bettye Jo. You could call me that if you want."

Francine began breathing heavily, her hands shaking, still saying not a word.

Mrs. Playne looked at her and said gently, "Honey, this is your foster mother. She is dying to get to know you. She really wants to. Don't be afraid," she added.

Francine walked up to Bettye Jo and extended her hand, "Pleased to meet you," she managed hesitantly.

Bettye Jo continued to smile and took her hand. "Let's go home now, all right, honey?"

Francine nodded slowly. An aide took her belongings and walked with them to Bettye Jo's car.

While in the car, Bettye Jo spoke. Francine listened.

"We'll be home in about a half hour. I will show you your room. It was my daughter's room. I fixed it up for you. I am very happy to meet you. My daughter was your age when she died," she spoke softly and calmly, still tensely.

Bettye Jo went on. "I heard your birthday is two months from now. You'll be thirteen, right?"

Francine answered with a nod.

Bettye Jo surmised, "Let's say you and I celebrate it any way you want—a movie, restaurant, you name it, okay, honey?"

"All right," she responded plaintively.

Then Francine apologetically remarked, "I am very sorry for your loss." Finally, she spoke with a little more ease, for she was becoming comfortable. A good start and sign.

Bettye Jo desperately wanted Francine to believe she would never hurt her and that she could confide, talk, or ask her anything, and she would not be angry or abuse her in any way. But she knew just plain talking was not feasible. Talk is cheap, and saying and doing were totally different. Furthermore, actions speak louder than words. Another person would give up, but not Bettye Jo. She was not that kind of person. She knew Francine had a wretched, turbulent childhood, thus she had trouble trusting people, especially those adults who were supposed to love her the most. Francine was beaten and whipped for wanting Leonora's love. For asking, for craving. It was hard. Bettye Jo knew well. She would keep plunging, no matter how long it took.

When they entered her house, Bettye Jo led her to her daughter's bedroom and told her to make herself comfortable and if she needed anything, to just ask. Francine looked up with a small smile and acknowledged, "All right." She was about to address her by her name but became tongue-tied. Maybe another time soon.

"Afterward, would you like ice cream and cookies?" she offered.

"Yes, please," Francine still smiling at Bettye Jo, who returned it to her. Things were looking up.

Bettye Jo left the room. While Francine put her belongings on the bed, she gazed around with awe. The walls were of a pinkish color. They had pictures of actors and singers. Shelves were filled with a lot of books. Porcelain dolls stood on the white furniture. An outdated computer rested on the side of a chest of drawers. There was a vanity table and an oval-shaped mirror in front. Pink, flowery curtains draped the window. The bedspread was covered with a floral print quilt and two fluffy pillows. Two end tables flanked the sides of the bed. On table had a clock with a dancing ballerina. The lamps were placed on both tables. "Wow," she thought to herself. Bettye Jo really loved her daughter—to give her all this, her own bedroom. It was hard to believe, but it was real, she was finally convinced. Perhaps Bettye Jo was a loving mother. Still hoping her dream to be loved will come about. As for a second thought, it could be, not maybe, but. She was feeling more confident and at ease. She jumped up, clasping her hands in the air, smiling brightly. She went to put her belongings away. She was dancing, feeling like a princess, loving and being loved. Happy as a lark. It was not a dream anymore. Reality, a new one, occurred. She was no longer scared, hesitant, or doubtful. This was all hers. Perhaps, Bettye Jo wanted to love her. She would not be surprised if she did want her, despite her vituperative childhood. Everything was going to be different. She could not wait to tell Willow, Arlene, and Stephanie. They might be envious, but still happy for her. That is what true friends are for.

Francine changed into her reddish purple, floral nightgown that reached the floor. Pink terry-clothed slippers were on her feet. She walked out of the bedroom. Bettye Jo waited, seated at the kitchen table. A plate of chocolate ice cream with three Oreo cookies and a napkin were placed on the table across. Francine sat down. Bettye Jo brought over a glass of milk and set it down on the table. Accidentally, Francine moved her hand and knocked the glass of milk, which splattered on the table. Francine jumped up with terror, her eyes wide and blazed. She screamed with all her lung power and flung herself on the floor, crouching in the corner of the kitchen. Her face was beet red with rage and then she put her arms in front of her face, sobbing uncontrollably. A horrifying memory surfaced into her mind. Being beaten with a strap for that same infraction. "You bad, bad girl," that woman screamed repeatedly. Francine covered her ears, sobbing, her head down. "Why do you make me do it?" She would not stop crying. "Shut the hell up, you fuckin' brat!"

Bettye Jo watched with such terror. That poor child. Her piercing screams bolted through her whole body. What did that horrible woman do to her? She felt so helpless. Then, she said gently, "It is all right, darling. It was only an accident. Don't cry."

Francine could not stop gulping; tears streamed down her face. She was crying so bitterly. Bettye Jo walked up to her, her hands out, wanting to comfort her, but Francine was so frightened and terrorized. Bettye Jo knew this quite well. This poor little girl. She felt like crying herself. She did not know what she could do. Words were useless. But she would not give up.

Bettye Jo stood looking at her mournfully, pain in her stomach.

"I'm not angry with you. You did nothing wrong. You are a very, very good girl. Everything is fine. I am not going to hit you. I promise. I would never do that. I have no reason to."

She paused for a minute, then she went on. "She, that woman, she was wrong, so terribly wrong to hurt you so cruelly. She was very sick, mentally sick. She did not know how to love or show it. She had no right. You are a very special little girl. That is why I chose you. I want to help you and for you to believe I would never hurt you for any reason. I promise never to intentionally cause you any pain or harm. I love you very much. I do. I want you to know that I will always be here for you, all right? No one will ever hurt you. I'll make sure of it and if they do, they'll answer to me."

She looked into Francine's face. She stopped crying and put her arms down on her lap. She picked her head up but said nothing.

Bettye Jo extended her hand to her. Francine slowly got up from the floor and with both her arms out, walked up to her and gave her a hug. Bettye Jo did so back. They held each other tightly. Neither one uttered a sound.

Bettye Jo led her to the sink, sat her down on a stool, took a damp cloth and patted her face gently. Then she took a towel to dry her face. Both felt better and relieved. Bettye Jo took her hand and led her to the table.

Francine looked at Bettye Jo. "I'm sorry. I'll help you clean it up."

Bettye Jo said calmly while touching her arm gently, "It's all right. Everything is going to be fine. You just sit and have your ice cream and cookies. I will take care of it."

The doorbell rang. Bettye Jo turned her head and walked to the window, pushing the curtain aside. Two policemen stood there. She opened the door, stunned, but greeted flatly, "Yes?"

"We received a telephone call from one of your neighbors. They heard screaming here. Is everything all right?" The policemen looked inside and saw Francine at the table eating her ice cream and cookies.

Bettye Jo noticed and calmly with assurance stated, "Everything is fine, Officers." Gazing at Francine, she mentioned quietly, "That's my foster daughter. This is her first day with me. And if you think I was beating her, Officers, you couldn't be more wrong." She continued explaining adamantly, without conviction. "She was having a flashback. Her birth mother physically abused her continually with a belt. But that is all over now, Officers. She's with me now, safe and sound, and she knows that." Then she turned to Francine and smiled at her, "Isn't that right, sweetheart? Would I ever hurt you?" she asked, quite knowing her response.

"No, never," she grinned happily and then resumed eating her ice cream with relish.

The policemen listened and seemed to believe her. They wanted to. But they knew if they were wrong, their jobs could be in jeopardy.

"All right, ma'am. The child seems fine and calm and not at all frightened. We are going to take your word for it. Sorry, but you do understand, we must take precautions. Child abuse is a very serious issue in today's times."

Bettye Jo nodded slowly, "I do, sir and if you want, I'll give you the social worker's business card from the children's shelter. You could call her." She reached into her pocketbook and handed the card to him. "Here."

He took it, but said, "Thank you, but I don't think it will be necessary. Good day, ma'am," and to Francine, "Bye, honey." She nodded and the officers left.

Bettye Jo went to the sink and took some paper towels and then wiped up the spilt milk. She took the empty glass and put it in the sink. Then she sat down, facing Francine. Both had loving smiles on their faces. Francine vowed to be good, do what she was supposed to do, and be a valuable young lady to this woman, believing that she now loved her and took her to her heart. She was going to be just fine and was no longer afraid.

As Francine, slowly and daintily, ate her ice cream, she remarked, "Your daughter's room is simply mesmerizing and breath-taking. It's so beautiful and cheerful."

Bettye Jo listened attentively. Francine was finally opening up. She no longer needed prompting.

Then she complied, "It's now your room. If you want anything changed, just ask me."

"Oh, no," she answered quickly. "It's more than I can ever hope for. It is perfect. And," she said as an afterthought, "is it really mine, forever and ever?"

Bettye Jo nodded with a smile, her eyes bright. "Yes, my precious angel, forever and ever."

Francine finished her ice cream then took the plate and spoon, got up, and went to the sink to start washing them.

Bettye Jo then stated hastily as she rose from her chair, "You don't have to do that."

"But I want to," she insisted, firmly but gently.

Bettye Jo shrugged but gleefully gave in. "All right." Then she added, "Thank you, honey. You're a wonderful little girl."

9:00 p.m.

Both Francine and Bettye Jo sat at the table, making small talk—a new one for Francine who never knew what that was.

Bettye Jo quipped up, "How's about if we spend the whole day together tomorrow? You can do whatever you want. It's your day especially."

Francine bounced up in her chair, clapping her hands with joy. "Oh, yes!"

Then, with great hesitation, heart pounding heavily, she got up and gave her foster mother a hug. Bettye Jo was taken by surprise but with a happy, excited smile, she returned the hug and softly and gently patted her back.

"Good night," Francine, enlightened, greeted. Then with some trepidation, she managed, "Bettye Jo."

She smiled at her foster daughter, gazing at her with love. "You, too."

Francine wanted to tell her she loved her, but though she was feeling more confident, she still needed a little more time. Bettye Jo did not push. She understood. Francine headed toward her new bedroom. It was a very good first day. A good start; slowly but surely wins the race.

Sunday Morning

Francine shot up in bed, gazing around, sinking in her new environment, and attempting to imbibe the last two days of events. It felt more and more real. She was not so tense or unsure anymore. Maybe, just a little, she tried to put that thought out of her mind. She hardly thought of her horrible, terrible childhood. Bettye Jo did not encourage it. She figured if she wants to, she will. She was in no hurry. But she loved her, she knew it. But it was too soon and premature, she knew quite well. Patience and time. Time and patience. She did not want to jump the gun. They decided to give each other space and get to know each other. Still, they loved each other. They felt it in their hearts. But not a word was uttered or said. No use rushing. For now, anyway.

Francine threw the covers off, leapt out of bed, and dashed to the window. The sun was very bright, the sky a clear blue. She looked up and smiled. *A good day*, she pondered to herself. She rushed to the closet and pulled out a puffed-sleeved blouse with stars on its white background and a pair of blue denim jeans with holes in its knees. Excitedly, she got dressed. She could hardly wait for her day with Bettye Jo. Just Bettye Jo and herself. Their day together.

Bettye Jo knocked on her door. Francine, just finishing buttoning her blouse and putting her belt around her waist, looked up and called out, "Yes, Bettye Jo?" she asked.

"Are you ready? Breakfast is on the table," she informed her.

"In a minute," she acknowledged as she adjusted her clothes accordingly. Then she bounded down the stairs. Bettye Jo stood by the bottom of the staircase, smiling.

"Good morning," she greeted enthusiastically, putting her arm around her shoulder.

"You, too," the girl reciprocated.

As Francine sat down, she saw her breakfast—scrambled eggs, two slices of toast with grape jelly smeared on them, a glass of orange juice, another of milk with three Oreo cookies. She took her napkin and placed it on her lap. She waited for Bettye Jo to sit down before beginning her meal.

Bettye Jo watched her while she sat not touching her food and pointed out,

"You don't have to wait for me. I am only having coffee. And besides, you don't want your food to get cold."

Then, Francine stated plainly that it is not good manners to eat before everyone has their food in front of them. She learned this at the children's shelter.

Bettye Jo smiled. Such a sweet and polite young lady, always helpful, willing to please. She was still a little tense, but she is coming along nicely.

"Tell me about your daughter," she inquired with curiosity.

"She was very shy and quiet and loved to read," she began.

"I know," Francine stated, "I saw she had a lot of books. I love to read also," she volunteered.

"She aimed to please people, especially me. Her teachers remarked on what a bright student she was. She always handed in her assignments on time and the first to raise her hand when a teacher asked a question. She really was not socially oriented. Some of her classmates antagonized her, but she would smile and turn away quietly. She would bring me flowers on Mother's Day and my birthday. She was always looking up information on her computer for she was curious about everything. She loved country music. She never put her back up or sass or talk back to me when I would ask her to do her chores or if things did not pan out as planned. She always told me and her father she loved us but was timid about physical demonstrativeness. She took everything in stride with a grain of salt. Not a mean bone in her body."

Francine listened attentively. Her daughter been a wonderful little girl.

"What was her name? What did she look like?" Francine continued to seek more information about her "sister."

"Sherry, Sherry Jo," Bettye Jo replied instantly. "She had dark, fluffy, wavy hair on her shoulders. Her eyes, wide and brown, like opals; her nose, perky; her lips a pale pink; and perfect white teeth. She was slender and fine boned; her skin, soft and of an olive color."

Francine tried to envision Sherry Jo. She sounded beautiful and asked if she could see a photograph of her and her husband, William.

She delightedly agreed, but since today was beautiful out weather-wise, she suggested they wait until tonight. They planned to go out for the day.

"May I call my friends later? I want them to meet you and you meet them, okay?"

"I'd love to meet your friends but perhaps tomorrow after I come home from my florist shop. You could invite them here for dinner," she offered pleasantly.

"Oh, thank you, thank you!" She threw her arms around her neck. Bettye Jo was startled but ecstatic at her sudden display of affection.

"Let's get our jackets," Bettye Jo suggested gleefully.

Francine went to get her shiny black leather jacket, and Bettye Jo chose her black suede one. Together, they left.

While in the car, Francine asked, "May I see your florist shop? Mrs. Playne said you owned one."

"Of course, honey, if you'd like. But it will take a few minutes," she pointed out while driving.

Both sat enjoying each other's company. Bettye Jo was patient, letting Francine have time getting used to her new life. Slowly, but surely, she was opening and did not appear anxious anymore. Still, she never spoke of her past and Bettye Jo did not inquire. She did know certain aspects of it—being beaten and abused and living in filth and garbage with Leonora and her boyfriends, always hungry, clad in rags, shut off from beauty and love.

Francine knew that was all water under the bridge. She did not want to relive it. Someday, she will forgive Leonora, perhaps. But she did not think about that now. Bettye Jo was in the here and now, hopefully forever.

"Would you like to go to the mall?" Bettye Jo inquired Francine.

She was puzzled and said she had never heard of a mall. So Bettye Jo explained it to her—all the different kinds of stores and all the eating places. Francine's eyes brightened. It sounded awesome and mesmerizing. She agreed to Bettye Jo's suggestion with a sparkle.

As Bettye Jo turned the car to the right, she pointed and said to Francine, "That's the florist shop that I own."

Francine turned her head in that direction. It had a green canopy with all different kinds and colors of flowers and plants. However, being today was Sunday, the shop was closed. Maybe another time Francine would be able to go inside and look around.

"It's so big!" she remarked.

Bettye Jo smiled, and she drove away.

"The mall is a few blocks down the next corner," she mentioned methodically.

When they arrived and stopped, Bettye Jo fished into her purse and handed Francine her credit card. She was puzzled, trying to figure out what it was for since she never heard of one before.

Bettye Jo started to explain, "You use it to purchase merchandise and at the end of each month, the credit card company bills the consumer who pays them."

Francine tried to understand, but she nodded slowly, trying to figure out what Bettye Jo said.

"Since today is a special day, I am going to give it to you, and you can pick out anything you want. The clerk at the register will swipe it and charge every item you buy. You have to sign the receipt slip."

Surprised, "Me?!" Francine exclaimed excitedly.

"That's right," Bettye Jo replied firmly with a smile.

"I think I'd like some books, that's all. I have enough clothes," Francine mentioned.

"Anything you want, honey," she offered with pleasure in her voice.

Bettye Jo parked her car and they got out. Francine bounced up to a store entrance. She could hardly wait.

So went the day. They browsed around in many of the stores with curiosity. Naturally, they located a bookstore. Francine found a few books that she thought looked interesting. She went on line to pay, and as Bettye Jo instructed, the cashier swiped the card and Francine signed the slip. The cashier, with a smile, handed the receipt to her. She accepted it but did not know what else she had to do, so she gave it to Bettye Jo.

"It's a receipt. You get one every time you make a purchase."

Francine nodded. She understood.

As they left the store, Bettye Jo asked if she was hungry and what she would like to eat.

"A hamburger with tomato, onions, and lettuce. Also, french fries and a Coke."

"Wow!" Bettye Jo remarked, "You must be very hungry!"

They went to the food court, where Francine witnessed so many kinds of eateries. She could not believe there was so many choices.

As they sat down at a table, Bettye Jo reached into her handbag for money. She told Francine to order what she wanted. Bettye Jo said she only wanted black coffee with sugar and cream.

"Remember to get the correct change after you order your food. I gave you more than enough."

"Okay!" Francine's eyes lit up as she skipped up to the eatery waiting her turn. She looked around. So many people talking, eating, laughing, and smiling, all having a good time and enjoying themselves. It was simply breath-taking for she was never in such an environment in her life.

Later, both sat and ate. Happy and excited. Bettye Jo sipped her coffee. Francine consumed her meal delicately, taking small bites of her hamburger. She offered Bettye Jo some french fries. Bettye Jo took a few and dipped them in ketchup. She said she loved their taste. Then Francine put a straw in her Coke and asked Bettye Jo if she would like a sip. She politely declined with a smile.

After they were through with their lunch, they strolled down the mall corridor. Francine hopped ahead and twirled around with a gleaming smile at Bettye Jo, who simply could not believe this was the same frightened girl she met Friday night at the children's shelter. She was a totally different girl, without a worry in the world. No one would believe she had a tortured, painful childhood. Bettye Jo was ecstatic and amazed at her foster daughter's transformation.

As they headed out to the car, Bettye Jo put her arm around Francine's shoulder who then looked up at her face.

"You're my girl," she announced joyfully as they strolled down the parking lot heading home.

Francine bounded up the stairs to call Willow. Bettye Jo put her purse down on the table, removed her jacket, and headed toward the kitchen. She heard Francine chattering delightedly on the telephone, giggling and laughing like a normal adolescent girl. Bettye Jo was pleased. She really loved her—and vice versa. Still, both did not yet feel ready to say it though they wanted to. *Time will tell*, they both thought to themselves. There was no hurry. It was just the second day. But they knew, they did know how they felt.

Francine pounced down the stairs after dinner wearing her long, puffed-sleeved pink nightdress. Bettye Jo observed her from downstairs.

"Let us look at your albums. I would like to see the photographs. You said we would," she reminded her foster mother with sparkles in her eyes.

They went into the living room and sat on the couch. The albums lay on the table in front of it.

Bettye Jo reached for one and as she opened it, she pointed to a photo of Sherry Jo on her twelfth birthday. Francine looked in awe.

"She was very pretty," Francine remarked.

"She was so happy and full of life that day," Bettye Jo stated. Suddenly, she became quiet, unable to say more. Her eyes got teary. Francine watched her. Suddenly, she put her hand on her shoulder.

"Don't be sad, Bettye Jo. It's all right. I know you miss her very much."

Bettye Jo managed a smile while wiping the tears with the back of her hand.

"I'm here now and forever," Francine stated. "I'll always be here for you," she added quietly but sincerely.

"I know," Bettye Jo struggled to blurt out, while trying to control the gulping in her throat. Then she attempted to smile at her foster daughter.

"I just can't help it sometimes," she mentioned.

"She'll always be in your heart," Francine reasoned.

"I know," Bettye Jo still hiccupping, "I know, honey."

Then she took the album and showed her other photographs of Sherry Jo. She seemed to be more composed. Also, there were photographs of her husband, William. He had thick, dark, wavy hair. His eyes dazzling, gleaming. He had thick lips and straight, pearly white teeth. His face melted Bettye Jo's heart with love. He and her daughter were the loves of her life for they loved her, and she loved them. But they were gone. Then Bettye Jo thought afterward as she faced her foster daughter and with a wink said, "I've got you now."

Francine then thought logically, "I'm sure Sherry Jo and William would want you to be happy. Their deaths were not in vain. You know, I just thought of something. Not that I am religious, but when God closes a window, God opens a door. Open your heart, Bettye Jo, to me." She put her hand on Bettye Jo's shoulder again. Bettye Jo did smile, with a struggle, but one, nonetheless.

"I'll be here for you, too," Bettye Jo staunchly spoke those words.

She placed the album back down on the table.

"Let's go into the kitchen and have some cake, okay?" she offered and

Francine obliged her suggestion. They rose from the couch with their arms wrapped around each other's shoulders.

"My girl," she announced lovingly. Both looked up into each other's eyes, smiling brightly.

8:00 p.m.

It had been a long and good day. However, it was getting late and it was a school night, thus Francine got ready for bed. Before she headed upstairs, she turned and threw her arms around Bettye Jo's neck. She was very surprised. Her eyes blazed. She returned the hug and patted her on her back softly and gently. Francine reminded her about her friends coming to dinner the next day at 6:00 p.m. Bettye Jo was pleased for she desired to meet these friends and they wanted to meet her as well. Francine gave glowing reports about Bettye Jo, her foster mother whom she loved and loved her.

"Tomorrow," Bettye Jo instructed, "make sure you call me the minute you arrive home. I want to make sure you're safe and sound." Spoken like a true and real mother, which she was.

Francine nodded agreeably and bid her a good night. She turned and dashed upstairs. Bettye Jo watched her; her face was glowing. Francine was becoming a very lovely, mature, and happy young lady just as her peers. No one would ever think she was an abused and neglected victim. She was adjusting just fine. No sign of a scar. Just like other girls. Quite a girl, she surmised pleasantly.

Monday, 6:00 p.m.

Willow, Arlene, and Stephanie sat around the dinner table, chattering and giggling, poking each other's arms playfully.

Bettye Jo made spaghetti and meatballs. Francine was helping her serve her three guests. She took two plates and handed them to Willow and Arlene. Then, she handed the third to Stephanie. Each took their plates gracefully, set them down in front of them, and as they looked down, their eyes lit up with delight.

"This looks delicious, Mrs. Pennington," Willow complimented her.

"Simply scrumptious," Arlene offered.

Then Stephanie chimed in and remarked, "You are such a gourmet cook, Mrs. Pennington."

Bettye Jo turned and faced the girls with a smile. "Thank you, girls. It is no problem. Glad you are enjoying your dinner." Then she turned and handed Francine a plate for Francine and herself.

When all five persons were seated, everyone began eating while glancing gleefully at each other.

"Dinner was simply delicious, Mrs. Pennington," Willow cheerfully remarked as the girls took their plates to the sink.

Bettye Jo smiled. "Why, thank you, girls," she graciously replied.

"You're a good cook," Arlene added.

"Yeah, that was the best meatball and spaghetti dinner I have ever eaten," Stephanie quipped up.

"It was a pleasure to serve you girls. Francine is lucky to have such nice friends as you. You've all have been very nice to her."

"No problem," Willow stated. "She's a terrific kid!"

Then Arlene stated, "Francine speaks very highly of you, Mrs. Pennington."

"She's a fortunate girl. I am glad to be her foster mother. She's a joy to be around and helpful, too!" Bettye Jo turned and smiled at Francine, who started rinsing the dishes and utensils in the sink.

Bettye Jo turned to her and said, "No, you go show your friends your room. I'll take care of this," she insisted. "Have a good time, girls."

Francine excitedly motioned to her friends. "Let us check out my room. It's got such cool stuff."

She and her friends eagerly dashed up the stairs, giggling vivaciously and jabbing each other's elbows playfully.

Bettye Jo heard the door slam. Francine put on her digital tuner, and the girls were dancing around and around the room, laughing uncontrollably but very happy. They were having a good time. Bettye Jo sighed pleasantly.

8:00 p.m.

"Bye, guys." Francine waved as her friends grabbed their jackets and replied, "See you in school tomorrow!"

Then Bettye Jo called out, "Nice meeting you all."

"Bye, Mrs. Pennington. Thank you for such a nice dinner." They graciously thanked her while heading out the door.

Two Months Later: Francine's Thirteenth Birthday

"How's the birthday girl?" Bettye Jo asked with delight.

"All right, I guess." She knew not what to say for this was all so new to her. "Could we go to the library? I would like to check out the books. Then we could have lunch in the mall," she suggested.

Bettye Jo nodded, her hand on her arm. "Okay, if you wish." Then, Bettye Jo added, "We'll have your favorite chocolate layer cake tonight, okay?"

She smiled, her eyes gleaming with joy. She was ecstatic for she never had a birthday celebration before. No one ever sent her a card or gave her gifts or a cake or a party or even greetings. It was unbelievable but true.

She also had no one to give a Mother's Day or Father's Day card or present to. She told herself she would give Bettye Jo a card although she was just her foster mother, but she was a mother figure, nonetheless. Hers—the only one in her whole life, for she took care of her and looked out for her as a mother is supposed to, regardless of a lack of a biological tie. A dog could give birth.

A Month Later

"Is everything okay?" Francine asked with a bit of hesitation in her voice. She had not been anxious or tense lately and was feeling quite content and at ease with Bettye Jo and knew Bettye Jo loved her, but still, she was a little queasy. She did not want to sound too eager or enthusiastic for in the past she was not able to bank on anything for good reason though she knew now somewhat her dream would come true.

"Yes, honey!" Bettye Jo responded adamantly. "In fact, everything is more than all right. I know we have only known each other for three months, and perhaps I am being a bit premature and hasty. But I knew when I first met you that Friday night at the children's shelter, I wanted you to be in my life permanently." She paused and tried to catch her breath, then she blurted out with excitement in her voice, "How would you like to be my real and true daughter?"

Francine listened intently, saying nothing at first. It was a lot to take in. Her eyes lightened up wide and clear, and a smile crossed her face. She could not believe it. Then she jumped out of her chair, nearly knocking it over, while clapping her hands together in the air.

"Really!" she exclaimed, her heart palpitating.

"Yes, oh, yes," she jumped and danced around the kitchen, arms flying around and around in the air.

Bettye Jo watched her. Her new daughter with a gleam in her eyes.

"I want to adopt you. And I will. Definitely. But a lot of paperwork and meetings with case workers and social services must be taken care of for me to legally adopt you. But you are my daughter. For real!"

Then as an afterthought, Bettye Jo quietly but adamantly resumed, "And most important, I want you to know you are not a replacement for Sherry Jo. She was a very good girl. And you are, as well. But you are not Sherry Jo. And that is fine. I do not want you to think you are a substitute or a reincarnation for my deceased daughter. She is gone but will always be in my heart. But you are in my life now. And I love you for yourself and I always will."

Tears of joy filled Francine's eyes. She cried out with happiness. She threw her arms around Bettye Jo's neck and gave her a kiss on her cheek—the first time, but not the last.

"I love you; I love you," she reiterated.

Bettye Jo laughed and smiled at her daughter. She took her hands and put them on the sides of Francine's face and kissed her on both of her cheeks.

Both were in ecstasy. It was real. She was loved unconditionally. Forever and always.

Six Months Later, Friday, 4:00 p.m.

"Everything is in order, Mrs. Pennington. Now all you must do is come down Monday afternoon to sign some papers. Then, it will be legal. Francine is now your adopted daughter."

Bettye Jo smiled while on the telephone. "All right, yes, thank you. We'll be there Monday afternoon. Bye, now. You, too, have a good weekend."

Francine sat at the kitchen table listening to Bettye Jo's telephone conversation with her case manager.

Francine jumped out of her chair and ran up into her new mother's arms, hugging each other and twirling around and around in the hallway.

"Mama!" Francine exclaimed.

"Daughter!" Bettye Jo addressed gleefully.

Forever and ever.

"May I call my friends tonight to tell them the news? Also, may I invite them over for a slumber party tomorrow . . . Mama?"

She smiled. "Yes, my darling daughter! My precious angel!" she consented joyfully. Then Bettye Jo with delight suggested, "Let us go out for dinner tonight to celebrate. You pick the restaurant." She looked lovingly at her daughter with sparkling eyes.

"Chinese!" Francine replied brightly.

"Fine," her mother agreed.

Mother and daughter grabbed their jackets and headed out the door with their arms around each other, smiling and looking into their gleaming eyes.

They held hands as they skipped to the car and drove off to the mall where their favorite Chinese restaurant was located. They put on a rock-and-roll station and sang off-key but with high-pitched voices at the top of their lungs. Francine was swinging back and forth, her arms out leading the back and swaying to the music. They stopped in the parking lot near the mall. Still singing, they got out of the car and joined hands. Bettye Jo had her arms around her and vice versa. Giggling aloud, while entering the mall, they skipped to their restaurant, sat at a table, and picked up their menus to decide on what to order. A waiter came over, pen and pad in his hands, and began, "Are you ready to order, ladies?" Bettye Jo smiled and said, "In a minute." She pleasantly replied. He smiled and bowed and walked away.

9:00 p.m.

Mother and daughter entered their house, very tired but very happy. It was a very good day. All was well.

"Good night, darling," she addressed her daughter, who threw her arms around her neck, giving her a kiss on her cheek then adding, "I love you, Mama. All the way to Pluto and back."

Bettye Jo reciprocated. "I love you, too," she stated without hesitation, stars in her eyes. Then Francine bounded up the stairs. Bettye Jo watched as she entered her bedroom and closed the door behind her. Bettye Jo sighed with pleasure.

Saturday, 10:00 a.m.

Francine was just finishing up her breakfast. Bettye Jo made her three slices of french toast, three strips of bacon, a glass of orange juice, and a cup of tea. She knew her daughter loved that.

Francine remarked while putting her fork and knife down, "That was very delicious, Mama. Thank you."

Bettye Jo smiled at her daughter but said nothing at first.

"Mama," she began, "They are having a two-hour book discussion at the library. May I go, please?" she implored quietly and gently. "I promise to be home by 1:00 p.m."

"Yes, darling," Bettye Jo consented agreeably, "but today I have to go to the shop to take care of some business matters. So, when you return home, please call me so I do not worry. I just want you to be safe and sound, all right?"

"Oh, yes, oh, yes, Mama. Oh, thank you so much." She arose from her chair and threw her arms around Bettye Jo's neck.

"Okay, okay, sweetheart," she giggled.

Then Francine reminded her mother, "Remember, Willow, Arlene, and Stephanie are coming over at 7:00 p.m."

"I didn't forget. Don't worry." Then she added, "I love you," as Francine grabbed her jacket and pocketbook and waved to her mother. "Bye, now. Have a good day!"

Bettye Jo waved back, "You, too, honey!"

She was out the door. Bettye Jo cleared the dishes off the table and put them in the sink and rinsed them while humming to herself.

7:00 p.m.

Francine and her friends were dancing around the living room. Her digital tuner was on playing rock-and-roll music. All four of them were clad in their nightgowns. Bettye Jo brought them a big bowl of popcorn. They dug into the bowl at one time. Gently, Bettye Jo ordered them, "One at a time, girls." They calmed down and plopped on the couch. "Want some punch, girls?" Bettye Jo offered. They jumped up with cups in their hands while she poured the drink into each of their cups.

"Thanks," the three girls stated graciously as they bounced down on the sofa. Three throw pillows lay on it.

Francine took one and said, "Catch." It hit the back of Willow's head. She turned and laughed. Then the two other girls took another one and they began pillow fighting with laughter.

"All right, girls," Bettye Jo suggested. They stopped in their tracks. And she continued, "I don't want anyone to get hurt or break anything, okay?"

Francine obediently said, "Yes, Mama."

Her friends complied, "Yes, Mrs. Pennington." She smiled and then went into the kitchen.

"Let us watch *Rock and Roll High School*. I have the DVD," Francine suggested.

She put on the television and slid the DVD into the player. Suddenly, she clutched her stomach; her face cringed.

"What's wrong, Francine?" Willow asked, concerned.

Without answering, Francine ran up the stairs, her hand on her stomach. Bettye Jo walked into the living room.

"What happened?" she asked them.

Arlene replied, "I don't know. She was putting a DVD into the player. Then suddenly, she got a pain in her stomach."

Bettye Jo did not answer at first, but she was worried. Suddenly, she heard uncontrollable screaming.

"Mama! Mama!" Francine cried hysterically. Bettye Jo turned and rushed up the stairs. The girls watched, upset and worried.

Francine stood near the toilet, holding up the bottom of her nightgown. Blood was dripping from her leg. She was frightened and thought she was dying. Bettye Jo saw her daughter was terrified, but she smiled at her.

"Remember what we spoke about a few months ago? Where babies come from? You do remember the book I showed you about your reproductive organs and the part boys play in it? I showed you photographs."

Francine said nothing at first. She let her mother talk. Yes, she remembered their talk but was still scared. She did not think it would occur. Not now, anyway.

"Yes," she slowly nodded.

"You wait right here," her mother instructed. "I'll just be a minute." She did so and was not too scared anymore.

Her mother brought a box of Kotex pads with a pair of underpants. She told Francine she will learn to clean herself up and showed her what to do.

"Mozel tov, darling. You're a woman now," she informed her daughter as she wiped off the blood and put her padded underpants on. She smiled and was no longer tense or frightened. *A woman*, she thought pleasantly.

She heard the girls muttering among themselves downstairs.

Arlene called out, "Is Francine, okay, Mrs. Pennington?"

Stephanie added, "We were worried. She was so upset."

Bettye Jo called from the upstairs, "Francine is just fine. I'll let her tell you herself." She motioned to her daughter with her arm around her shoulder, leading her out of the bathroom to the stairs where her friends were standing, eyeing her with concern.

"I'm a woman. A woman now," she announced.

The girls gaped, their eyes enlarged.

Willow exclaimed, "Wow! Cool!"

Arlene and Stephanie smiled gleamingly. They were relieved that Francine was just fine. Although they had not begun menarche yet, they were happy for their friend.

"Are you all right, honey?" Bettye Jo asked her daughter.

"Yes, Mama. I am very fine. Can we watch the movie now?"

Bettye Jo smiled contentedly, "Yes, you may. You go join your friends now." Then to the girls, "She's all right," she surmised. Francine quickly walked down the stairs to join her friends in the living room. She put on the movie, a musical. The girls sat in front of the screen, swaying back and forth, swinging their arms about and singing off-tune to the music. They were having a good time.

Bettye Jo went into the kitchen to get the girls a bowl of potato chips.

"Here you go, girls." They turned as she handed them the bowl. They took it gingerly and passed it around to each other, digging in voraciously, still engrossed in their movie.

"Anyone want something to drink? Soda, water, cocoa?" she offered.

"No, thanks, Mrs. Pennington," Willow declined quite pleasantly.

"We're good," Arlene chimed in.

"Fine, girls. If you need anything, I will be in the kitchen." She turned back.

The girls continued watching the movie, enjoying themselves and each other.

10:00 p.m.

The movie was over. Everyone was yawning and stretching out on the couch.

Bettye Jo announced, "It's late, girls. Why don't you all get your sleeping bags from the closet where you put them when you arrived. Let's call it a night. You're all very tired." Then turning to her daughter, she contentedly mentioned, "It's been a big day."

The girls obediently got their bags and rolled them out in the living room. They went upstairs to brush their teeth and wash their faces. At last, they fell asleep. Bettye Jo cleared the table of food and drinks, closed the lights, and headed to the kitchen.

Sunday, 9:00 a.m.

The girls were heading out the door. Francine and Bettye Jo watched and waved at them.

"Goodbye, girls. Thank you for coming," Bettye Jo stated.

Willow then piped up, "Goodbye, Mrs. Pennington, thanks for having us."

"We had a very good time," Arlene added.

"See you in school tomorrow," Stephanie announced.

Francine smiled. "You're the greatest, guys," she amicably complimented her friends.

Bettye Jo closed the door after they left.

"How do you feel, honey?" her mother asked, turning toward her.

"I'm fine, Mama," she replied gleefully.

"Good, but in case you don't, you could lay down later. After all, you are quite a young lady now. And you are such a pretty girl. Boys will be lining up down the block to date you."

Francine stood, saying nothing to her mother. Her hair hung down on her shoulders. She was wearing a full-length lacy slip with a pink cardigan over it.

"Are you hungry? I will make you french toast and bacon. How does that sound, darling?"

"Okay," she replied without a second thought.

Both went into the kitchen. Francine sat down at the table. Her mother began preparing breakfast. She took three eggs out and beat them furiously. She reached for three slices of white bread and three strips of bacon. She took a tab of butter and put it in the frying pan.

"You want some orange juice?" her mother offered.

Francine nodded but then offered, "I'll get it. You seem to be very busy, so the least I could do is get it myself. I don't want to give you more work than you can handle."

Bettye Jo smiled. "It's no bother to make my lovely, sweet daughter—who though is now a young woman—her favorite breakfast. It is never too much trouble to do anything with pleasure for you. You are my daughter now and for always, and I am honored to be your mother, for that is what mothers are for—to be there no matter what for their daughters, especially one who is as lovely as you." She put her arm around Francine's shoulder and with a grin stated, "You're my girl."

10:00 a.m.

Breakfast was over. Francine and Bettye Jo cleared the dishes and brought them to the sink. Bettye Jo began rinsing them, and Francine offered to stack them in the dishwasher.

Then the doorbell rang. Both wondered. Who can that be on a Sunday morning? A day of rest. People slept in on a Sunday.

Francine put the plates in the dishwasher. She offered, "I'll see who it is." She peeked out the window. A man was there. He stood tall and erect as a soldier. His dark hair neatly combed, eyes, dark and wide. He was clad in a long overcoat. *Who is he?* Francine wondered while watching by the window. Reluctantly, she opened the door. The man gazed at Francine, who said nothing. She was perplexed. *Why is he staring at me like that?* she thought to herself. He did not say a word, but he smiled slightly at her with a wink. He had a gleam in his eyes. For a long while, neither spoke nor moved.

"Francine?" he addressed her.

She still said not a word. She began to quiver.

"Princess?" he addressed her as he reached to stroke her cheek. She backed away for she still was unable to utter a sound. She could not. Who was he? This man? And how did he know her name? And why did he call her princess?

Bettye Jo called from the kitchen, "Who is it?" She turned to Francine.

Finally, he announced, "I'm your father."

Francine gaped. Her eyes wide opened. Bettye Jo stood behind her, with her hands on her shoulders. Both were speechless.

Bettye Jo turned to Francine, stroking her hair. "Please go on upstairs for a little while. Okay, darling? I will be up to tell you when to come down. If you are not feeling well, you could'lay down on your bed. I will give you aspirin later if you need it. This man and I need to talk a bit. Do not worry. Everything is fine," she assured her with a twinkle in her eyes.

Francine hugged her around her neck with a kiss on her cheek, which she reciprocated. "Yes, Mama." She obediently headed upstairs.

"Would you like some coffee, sir?" she offered him.

"My name is Dr. Philip Marsowe. I'm a psychiatrist," he stated a matter-of-factly. "And as for coffee, that would be nice, Mrs. Pennington," he added.

He sat at the table while Bettye Jo prepared the coffee. "I didn't come here to make trouble," he affirmed.

While putting on the kettle, Bettye Jo avowed frankly, "I just want you to know I plan to adopt Francine and I am not going to break that promise. All her life she has suffered abuse and neglect and had no one to trust, turn to, or depend on. I have no intention of hurting her or taking anything I gave her away. If I must fight tooth and nail, I will. Francine is my daughter and always will be. I love her and she loves me. I want you to understand, I am not going to back down. I do not know what your game is or what you are trying to pull, Doctor. But you have some nerve showing up at my doorstep thinking you could claim Francine after all these years. And now that Francine is in a place where she is loved, safe, stable, and well-adjusted, I am not going to allow you to yank her away from me or this home. It is her home, too. And where were you all these years thinking you have rights?" She could not stop, being she was quite overwhelmed with this abrupt and rather disruptive situation. Bettye Jo was very angry at this man proclaiming to be her daughter's biological father and could just come in out of the blue demanding to see her. Bettye Jo was Francine's mother now and forever. Francine never knew her father or remembered him for he never abused her, and he took care of her when Leonora continually neglected and hurt her without any mercy.

Dr. Marsowe just sat, listening intensively to Bettye Jo. He said nothing for he did not know what to say. He knew Bettye Jo was right and agreed with her. He had no intention of upsetting Francine and disrupting her life. It was not his fault he never got to see or know Francine. All he wanted was a chance to get to know her.

"Mrs. Pennington, I completely understand how you feel. I have no intention of hurting Francine. She loves you, and you love her. I just would like to get to know her," he assured her.

"Okay," Bettye Jo agreed with hesitation. "I will make a deal with you, Dr. Marsowe. You could see her a few times this week. You and she can become acquainted. She could get to know you and you could get to know her. But she must be home early on school nights and is to call me to check in. She knows that. Also, if you hurt her in any way, you will never have any contact with her. I am going to let Francine decide. It is her decision and hers alone. I will not have anything to do with her choice. Do you understand, Dr. Marsowe?"

"Of course, Mrs. Pennington," he assured her. "Just she and I getting to know one another." Then he resumed, "I know you are wondering why I never got to see her after she was three years old. I think it's only fair for me to explain it to you and Francine."

"That's fine," Bettye Jo confirmed. "I'll go upstairs and discuss this with her. Then I will have her come down, so you could explain everything to her. I promise to understand, but it is up to her, okay, Dr. Marsowe?"

He agreed with a nod, and Bettye Jo went upstairs to speak to Francine. He watched her with awe, his eyes gazing, his mouth watering, his heart palpitating furiously, his breathing heavy. He could not take his eyes off her. He was unable to help it. Her long, slender legs; deep, dazzling dark eyes; curvy hips; wavy blonde hair; ivory soft skin. Wow! Although she had been sharp and adamant with him for, she loved his daughter dearly. She was a goddess. Their daughter, that is. Is it possible? Nah! But one can never tell. But he was in heaven. In a daze. In a trance.

They came down the stairs. Bettye Jo behind her daughter. Philip got out of his chair and smiled at them. "Ladies," he addressed them. He pulled a chair out for Bettye Jo, and then for Francine. They grinned cheerfully at him, nodding "Thank you." *He is a gentleman*, Bettye Jo thought to herself.

All three sat around the kitchen table. No one said a word for a while or knew how to begin.

Philip turned toward Francine, choosing his words carefully. He did not want to say the wrong thing to upset her or Bettye Jo. Both sat, intensively waiting.

"I always loved you. You were my princess. But you probably do not remember, do you?" he asked his daughter with understanding. Francine nodded slightly but did not make a sound.

"Your mother . . .," he began, but Francine tartly retorted, her face glaring angrily, "Bettye Jo is my mother."

Bettye Jo then grabbed her hand and said gently, "He knows, darling."

"I'm sorry, you're right," he apologized.

"Leonora was a very disturbed and unhappy woman. Nothing I ever did was good enough. She was always flying into rages, and she would kick my behind and sock me in the mouth saying I never did anything. I would tell her over and over that I loved her, but she would not listen. She worked three jobs and agreed to pay for medical school for me to become a psychiatrist. However, nothing I said or did made a dent. She was frustrated and took it out on you. One night, she demanded I get out of her house. She threw all my belongings out of the apartment. I was very frightened and worried about what she was going to do. But I did love you. I took care of you. I was between a rock and a hard place. She would not stop. So, I went to live with my parents and younger brother and continued to attend medical school on a scholarship." He paused and took a deep breath before resuming. Francine and Bettye Jo sat listening and waited for him to continue. They seemed to understand and did not appear angry.

"I never forgot you. I sent you cards, letters, and presents on your birthday. Everything came back to me 'Return to Sender.' For she would evade paying the rent and fled from one shithole of an apartment to another. No landlord was ever able to track her down. At times, she lived in the streets and prostituted her body. And Social Services was at a loss. The minute they thought they had caught up with her, she was off. People were afraid of her temper and worried about their safety. She lived off many men who were no better. They were all dregs of society. I knew and really wanted to find you. But no one was able to help me. I did get in touch with the elementary school you attended. Your fifth-grade teacher, Ms. Lorme, still teaches there. She remembered you and took a stand. I was able to contact her and she told me you were at the children's shelter for two years. Then,

I called them and that led me here to you." He looked down while spreading his hands across the table. He said what needed to be said.

Quietly, Francine stated, "I understand. I believe you. But I am sorry, I do not remember you. Leonora never mentioned you and I never asked. I was afraid of what she might do."

Philip went on, "I know. Leonora was very disturbed. She hurt you. It was my job to protect you."

Francine nodded slowly. "I'm not angry with you," then she added, "I'm very grateful for Ms. Lorme. She was very supportive and caring."

Philip was not through. "I want you to know, honey, I know Bettye Jo plans to adopt you, which is very kind and that will not change. I know Bettye Jo has been loving and wonderful to you and is very determined, and I will not stand in her way. She loves you and you love her. She made that quite clear. But I would like to get to know you. Perhaps, you would like me to visit you from time to time. Bettye Jo agreed to it. But she told me it is up to you, and she will not stand in the way. Would you like to try and see what happens?" he questioned her gently.

Francine agreed and consented. "All right, if it's all right with you, Mama." She faced Bettye Jo, who smiled and nodded firmly.

"Good," Philip stated. Then, he looked at his watch. "It's almost 12:00 p.m. Would you like to go to the mall and spend the afternoon with me to become better acquainted? We will do anything you like. Today is your day," he avowed.

Francine agreed and turned to her mother, who winked gleefully at her.

"I'd like to get ready now. I'll be down in five minutes, okay?" She turned to Philip. Then, she dashed upstairs to change her clothes and fix her hair.

Both Philip and Bettye Jo watched her. Then they faced each other.

"She's quite a girl, Bettye Jo. You are doing a good job with her. And for that, I'm eternally grateful."

"It's a pleasure, Dr. Marsowe."

"Call me Phil, please. After all, we will be seeing quite a lot of each other."

"All right," she confirmed, "and please call me Bettye Jo."

They both smiled in agreement. Philip was gazing at Bettye Jo, looking into her eyes. His heart was melting. She was so beautiful, he mused, but said nothing. He wanted to but was unable. *Am I wrong?* he questioned to himself. *Should I tell her how I feel? Would that be too presumptuous for I just met the mother of my little girl? Does she feel the same? What if she does not?* He did not want to make a fool of himself if Bettye Jo was not interested in him. What if she thought he was a jerk? He felt awkward and inadequate. He fidgeted while playing with his fingers on the table. He surmised, leave it for now. He knew he was being premature. He just met her. It was only a few hours. Still, his heart pounded. She is a goddess!

Saying nothing, Bettye Jo got up and offered, "Do you want more coffee?" He declined her offer, still gazing into her eyes, heart beating furiously, breathing heavily, a lump in his throat.

A few minutes later, Francine daintily walked down the stairs clad in a long, puffed-sleeved pink dress. A pink headband was placed in her hair.

"Hey, guys," she called, and Bettye Jo and Philip turned.

Francine asked anxiously, "Do I look all right?"

"You look lovely," her mother replied with a gleam in her eyes.

"You're quite a young lady," Philip remarked.

Then Bettye Jo asked hesitantly, "Honey, is there something you'd like to tell Phil, you know, about last night?"

Francine wanted to. She did. Though Philip seemed to be a great and nice guy who always loved her, and she believed it, she was still shy, unsure, and hesitant.

"No need to be embarrassed," Philip remarked. "Bettye Jo said it was up to you." Then he looked at her, "Isn't that right?"

"Yes, it is," she affirmed carefully.

"Perhaps later," Francine decided.

Philip looked at his watch while rising from his chair. He attempted to put his hand under her chin, but she jumped away for she was ashamed of herself for rebuffing him by her rudeness and offensive behavior. Deep down she knew Philip was nothing like Leonora's male friends, but flashbacks still serviced. She wanted to control them, make them disappear and go away forever. Philip knew about Leonora's boyfriends abusing her and no one helping or supporting her. Still, she was leery and hesitant. Philip understood for he dealt with patients having issues dealing with their past traumas. He would tell them to put such thought into proper prospective and to forgive their abusers and that even their horrible, wretched childhoods could build character. They could also learn how not to hurt others as they were and become better people, because they knew how it felt to be hurt by those who should love them the most. But this was his daughter. Not one of his patients. Sometimes, it is easier to help complete strangers or others one has no bond or feelings for than it is with someone very close to them. It can be hard taking your own advice because it is personal especially within one's own family. Being objective is hard. He knew that constant reinforcing and reassuring her of his love and good intentions were just trite, common, daily platitudes. Thus, he decided to give it time. Let him get to know her and she to know him. He surmised, patience and time. Never giving up. He did not believe this was a lost cause. This was his daughter whom he loved dearly. Francine believed that. She told herself that one day, she will be fine. Just like with Bettye Jo, her mother forever.

"Sorry, I did not mean to be impolite," she said mournfully. "Please, do not be angry." She hung her head sullenly.

Bettye Jo piped in and put her hand on her arm, "Don't worry, honey. Phil understands. He knows you know his intentions are kind and loving. Isn't that right, Philip?" She looked at him, knowing his response.

"Of course," then to Francine, "You want to go now?"

Bettye Jo added, "Francine knows to call me when she arrives and is ready to leave. You do have a cell phone, right, Philip?" she confirmed.

"Certainly," he replied to Bettye Jo and then to Francine, "Are you ready?"

Francine got her leather jacket from the closet. Philip helped her put it on. She was surprised but pleased. She turned toward Bettye Jo with a wink. They both nodded in agreement. Philip was indeed a gentleman.

Bettye Jo walked up to Francine and asked, quite knowingly the answer, "Do I get a kiss from you?" Francine obliged and her mother reciprocated.

"Have fun, you two," she called out pleasantly.

Both turned toward Bettye Jo with smiles on their faces, their eyes gleaming like captive stars. They waved. "Love, you," said her daughter, and "Bye, Bettye Jo," Philip said, still gazing into Bettye Jo's eyes.

They were out the door. Bettye Jo watched, while standing still a bit. Philip was indeed a kind and loving man, tolerant and understanding, she mused and smiled to herself. *Does he like me?* She pondered. She knew she liked him but did not want to appear too forthright for she did not even know him for a whole day. Would he think she was being too forward and eager, too pushy and demanding? Should she play hard to get and wait for him to make the first move as all girls are told when they are young and in love? What if she does, and he is not interested, and nothing happens? She was not a brazen woman or particularly shy and introverted. She had good people and communication skills, being she owned a business that required her to have these attributes to deal with the public. For the last year or so, she was alone. Her parents died young from cancer. She did have a sister, but they were not close and did not speak to each other in years. She was a photojournalist who travelled to foreign countries to conduct business projects. She never did settle down, for she liked lots of men but not serious with any one of them. Bettye Jo, on the other hand, though she owned her own florist shop, married William, who was a good provider and supporter to his wife and daughter. But they were killed in a car accident. Bettye Jo took their deaths very hard and was inconsolable for she had no one to love or to love her back, so she decided to become a foster mother. She specifically asked for a twelve-year-old girl. It did not matter what the girl's background entailed. Now, she had a daughter to love and who returned her love to her. So, she wanted to adopt her, and nothing was going to deter her from that promise. But this morning, Francine's birth father shows up. At first, she was furious and abrupt with him. He was not going to prevent her from adopting his daughter. She told him he had some nerve claiming a daughter he has not seen in ten years. But he did say he understood and all he wanted was to become acquainted with her and perhaps he could get visitation rights. But it was Francine's decision alone. Everyone agreed. Now, she thought to herself. She was in love. She did not expect to have romantic feelings for him, but she did not know how to handle it. It had been a while for she never went out or dated any man. In her mind, William was the only man she gave her heart to. But he was dead. Gone forever. Then, she pondered, "He'd want me to be happy." She knew that is what he would want. He would approve of Philip. He really loved his daughter, and he was determined. And so was she. They did like each other a lot, but both did not know how the other felt. They were in a quandary. But they did know one thing. They both loved Francine, their daughter, and wanted her to be happy and secure.

And as for Philip, he never did have any serious relationships with women since Leonora threw him out of the apartment. He did love her and did tell her that, but she did not pay any heed or acknowledge it. She was a deeply disturbed woman whom he felt sorry for. She needed serious psychiatric help due to her lack of impulse control, violent temper, and being prone to abrupt rages and abusing their daughter, and no one could help her. People were frightened and did not know what she was capable of doing. After that, his parents agreed to let him come home and stay with them while attending medical school. When he graduated, he started his own practice and developed a clientele. His patients, young and old, did not matter the situation, for they really liked him. He was a good listener and was patient with each of them by getting to know and understand their issues. However, he lacked a social life, though he did want to meet someone to love and to love him back. He had a younger brother, Paul. He liked him, but they were not close. He worked as an assistant in a hardware shop. He dated many women; some were just teenagers, but he knew nothing would ever come of it. At least, Paul was honest and admitted he was not into anything long-term. After work, he would join his friends for a beer, and they would ogle, flirt with, and whistle at any girl passing in the street. That was not Philip's style, for he was responsible, hardworking, and honest. He always did what he had to do, whatever it was. When their parents reached their fifties, Philip had to put them in a rest home. His father became afflicted with dementia, and his mother developed serious arthritis in her legs and hands. She was unable to walk or do anything for herself. She was in deep pain. When they were not able to take care of themselves, Philip did the most caregiving for them. Paul did visit at times but was not very on top of what was going on. It did not bother Philip. He accepted his brother as he was and never complained or got angry with him. It did not pay. He was what he was, Philip surmised. Occasionally, Paul would call him to invite him over for a beer with his buddies, but he always declined. He was busy, he would state, and he meant it. Paul did know it as well. Philip had obligations. He was not carefree or flighty as Paul was. But still Philip harbored no grudges. He loved him as he was. That was the kind of man Philip was. He took everything in stride. Now, he thought, enough of Paul. He was getting to know his daughter whom he had not seen in ten years. God, he knew, how much he wanted to be with her, to be there for her through thick and thin. He was her father and was very proud of it and her foster mother, Bettye Jo, who loved her dearly and planned to adopt her. He was all for it. Though he knew he could not get legal custody, the most, perhaps, he might get were visitation rights. He would settle for that. He did not want to ruin Francine and Bettye Jo's lives by asking for more. He did want to be able to raise her, but *get real*, he mused to himself. He went on and on, pondering his love for Francine in his mind, playing the same tapes continually. He could not get it out of his head. And Bettye Jo, she was dazzling. So beautiful inside and out. His heart beat heavily as he thought to himself. He was like a schoolboy in love, but he was not one anymore. He was a man, a man in love, not a crush, or a passing fancy, or an infatuation. It was real. However, he would then think, does she feel the same? What is the worst that could happen? She did not feel the same, but as she did promise him, he could get visitation privileges and see her at certain times—legally, that is. *I want to be part of both their lives.* He was determined. He loved both, and to be in their lives forever.

Slowly, Francine reached out and touched his arm. "Are you all right? You seem to be in a daze," she pointed out.

At once, he quickly answered, "Yes, honey, I'm fine. Really."

Francine was not deterred, "You seem deep in thought," she went on.

Philip continued driving, staring straight ahead. What could he say? How could he tell his daughter that he is in love with her foster mother? And he wants him and Bettye Jo to raise their daughter together? And that he does not know how or what to do and is afraid Bettye Jo will reject him, and he will feel like a fool and that Bettye Jo would call him a jerk. He had been smiling ever since he was at their home. He and Bettye Jo sat and talked. His eyes gleamed and were doing so now. Still, he said nothing and watched the road. His hands were shaking, just as when he was back home.

"Bettye Jo is very pretty, isn't she?" he tried to make small talk. Still, his breath was heavy; his heart pounding. "She loves you very much." Then he added, "You love her, too. I can tell, and why shouldn't you? Her eyes are deep and dark as opals. Her hands, soft and gentle. Her legs, slender. She is simply devoted to you. She's been wonderful . . ."

Francine jumped up almost out of her seat and exclaimed with excitement, "You're in love with her, aren't you? I could tell. I watched you and she wink. You did not stop. Your eyes were watery." She kept bouncing in her seat. "I can't believe it! You love my mother!" She paused to catch her breath for a few seconds. Then she settled down, but still quite hyper and gleefully continued, "Tell her," she insisted, poking his arm. "Tell her! Tell her when we get back. Tell her," she was persistent.

Philip was stunned, unable to speak. Francine knew all along. She is not even fourteen yet. What does she know about romantic love between two people? It took him a while, then he admitted with a smile, "Yes, yes, I do!"

Francine clapped her hands in the air. "I knew it!" she said, still bouncing in her seat, jumping up and down joyfully. She stopped herself for she did not know how to address him. The subject never came up. She wanted to call him "Daddy" as little girls usually do. And he wanted to be her "Daddy," but it still seemed premature. She loved him. Still, she felt things should take a little time.

"I'd like to call you Daddy," she mentioned, "but it seems too early in our relationship," she carefully pointed out.

"Okay, honey, I'd like that, but you're right. We should take things slowly and not rush. Why don't you call me Phil for now?" he suggested.

"Fine," she consented, "Phil."

They continued their ride to the mall, both very excited, smiling and happy and in love.

"By the way, honey," he said as he reached under his seat. He had a wrapped package and card, which he handed to Francine. "I know I missed your birthday, and I am sorry. This is your belated present from me. You could open it later," he mentioned.

Francine thanked him; her eyes lit up. She put the present on her lap.

Then they silently continued the ride to the mall.

When they arrived at the mall, Philip gently informed Francine not to say anything to Bettye Jo about their conversation. It would be hard since they both were trying to contain their present joy and gleefulness. They were both extremely excited, their hearts pounding furiously, both breathing heavily and uncontrollably.

Philip took out his cell phone and dialed. Bettye Jo picked it up at the first ring. She knew who it was.

"Bettye Jo," he addressed, "We're at the mall. You want to speak to Francine?" He handed her the phone, and she took it eagerly. "Mama?" she addressed.

"Yes, honey?" Bettye Jo heard excited voices. "Is everything all right? You both sound giggly."

"Yes, yes," Francine answered, but Bettye Jo would not relent.

"What's going on?" she asked.

"Nothing, Bettye Jo," he tried reassuring her, still with heaviness in his voice.

"Everything is fine, Mama," she insisted, still with a giggle in her voice.

"All right," she stated resignedly. "Enjoy your day."

"Love you, Mama," she said matter-of-factly.

"We'll call you later, Bettye Jo," Philip affirmed.

All three said "Goodbye" at once and to each other.

Francine and Philip felt relieved afterward.

"That was close," Philip remarked with relief.

"We did it. It was difficult, but we did it," Francine added contentedly.

Bettye Jo looked at her telephone after hanging up. She was in a quandary. *What were they up to?* she pondered to herself. She could not get it out of her mind. *What was it?* she continued musing, in a daze, a dream. Finally, she stopped and then took the newspaper and sat down at the kitchen table, sipping her coffee, and began reading, but she could not concentrate. She was thinking pleasantly. She sighed to herself with a smile, her eyes wide and bright.

While at the Mall

Philip and Francine walked casually in the mall for a while. Neither knew what to say. Philip said he loved Bettye Jo, Francine's soon-to-be adoptive mother, and Francine knew this. She had been watching him ogling Bettye Jo, looking into her eyes at the kitchen table. She said nothing then, but she knew. It was not a dream or wishful thinking. It was real. Also, she noticed Bettye Jo staring at this man who at first was adamant, firm, and acidic toward him, for she thought he was going to demand custody and yank Francine away from her. But he did not want to do that for he saw Francine was happy with Bettye Jo, who loved her, and Francine loved her back. Both were very concerned for Francine's happiness, security, and safety.

Francine looked at Philip and remarked, "You're very quiet, Phil. You have not said one word since the phone call."

He turned and smiled at Francine. "I'm just thinking, honey," he replied justifiably. He was in love and Francine knew it.

They passed the food court and decided to have lunch.

"Let's sit down." Philip guided Francine to a seat. He pulled a chair out for her and took off her jacket.

Once they were seated, Francine began, "Phil, something happened last night at my slumber party. I know I should not be embarrassed since you are my father, but I am. I am sorry that I feel this way."

Philip put his hand on hers. She did not flinch.

"I want you to know that it is all right to feel as you do. We are just getting acquainted, so you can take your time. I'm not going to force you to do or say anything . . ."

Suddenly she blurted it out, "I got my period!"

Philip smiled. "You're a woman now. Congratulations, honey!" Then he went on, "Now boys will be interested in you. You are very pretty and sweet, so boys will be lining up down the block to go out with you. I am sure Bettye Jo explained everything to you, to be careful and not let boys take advantage of you, because that is what boys do at that age. Their hormones rage. So do not do anything you do not want to do or feel uncomfortable with, okay?"

"Mama already told me that. Don't worry," she reassured Philip.

"Well, congratulations again! You're a woman now!" he exclaimed gleefully.

"Yeah," Francine agreed. Then she decided to change the subject.

"What do you do?" she asked Philip.

"I'm a psychiatrist," he replied flatly.

"What does a psychiatrist do?" She inquired.

"I help people deal with and come to terms with their feelings and thoughts. I help them sort out any issues in their lives that they are struggling with. I try to help them make wise choices," he explained.

"I heard you deal with what a lot of people call 'crazy.' People that do not act right."

Philip pondered for a while without answering. He wanted to choose his words carefully so Francine could understand.

"That's a myth. Crazy is not really a word. People who use it are not aware and do not understand and do not know any better, so they are quick to judge others. A lot of famous and highly educated and brilliant people see a psychiatrist. And most people who do not see one usually do need help, but refuse to. They consider it a stigma—something bad—but it is not a sign of weakness to ask for help."

"Oh," Francine sighed, "I do understand now." Then she resumed, "Do you help a lot of people?"

"I hope and I do try to. It is not always easy, but patience is a virtue, especially in this occupation. A lot of my patients feel better after a session. Some patients feel hopeful. I'd like to think and feel that."

"Do you ever encounter patients that you cannot help?" she inquired.

"I keep in mind that all my patients are treated with respect regardless of their issues and progress in therapy. But unfortunately, there are some challenging patients, but I treat them just as anyone else. Just like in any profession or occupation, there could be hard-to-reach patients. It is sad but true. I do wish them well and try to understand. It can be difficult at times. Fortunately, most of my patients do benefit from my services," he affirmed a matter-of-factly. Then he went on, "And I happen to enjoy what I do, regardless of any negativity or failures. As a matter of fact, to appreciate success and positivity, people can learn and grow from failures and setbacks."

"Your profession sounds interesting. I'd like to do that one day," she decidedly professed. She then mused to herself, *I am only thirteen and have not known Philip for not even a day. And I have an idea on what to do when I grow up.* She sounded pleased with herself.

Then she felt hunger pains in her stomach and suggested they eat.

"What would you like to have?" Philip asked his daughter.

"I love their hamburgers with onion and french fries and a Coke," she replied. "We could share the Coke. It's a very big cup."

"I think I'll have that, too," he decided. He took out his wallet and gave her a ten-dollar bill. "You could keep the change," he asserted. She smiled as he gave her the bill. Then she went to purchase their lunch. He sighed as he watched her—his daughter—with love.

His eyes gazed around the food court—so many eatery places to pick out. People were interacting with each other, enjoying themselves, talking to their friends and families while taking bites of their food, smiling, laughing. Philip was deeply mesmerized by all of it, and most important, he felt joy. Being with his daughter whom he had not seen in ten years, wondered what her life was like. He did know that she lived in filth and grime, being abused and neglected by Leonora whom he did love at first and even when she would go into one of her rages, he loved her and told her, but she would ignore him. He could not reason with her. He was relieved when Francine's fifth-grade teacher came along and changed her life. She reported Leonora to the authorities and had Francine admitted to a children's shelter. For that, he was grateful. Of course, more importantly, Bettye Jo wanted to be her foster mother. Later, she wanted to adopt her. He was truly happy that his daughter finally found love and security. All of this made him eager to get to know Francine. And to think he came into her life when she began menarche. She became a woman, a lovely, sweet young lady whom he was proud to have as his daughter. He was going to treasure and savor every single moment with her and not take time for granted even if it meant just having visitation rights. He would settle for that for he wanted to be in her life. Then, his thoughts turned to Bettye Jo. He would tell her tonight, he adamantly planned. Meanwhile, Francine came to the table with their lunch on a tray.

"Are you all right, Phil? You seem in a dream," she pointed out.

He turned toward her with a joyous smile, "I'm just fine, honey." And he was.

They started their hamburgers. A tall glass of Coke with two straws stood in the middle of the table. They each took a sip and sighed pleasantly to each other.

"Tell me about your friends. I really want to know," he inquired of her eagerly.

She told him that Willow, Arlene, and Stephanie were in her fifth-grade class and were friends ever since. They witnessed their classmates tormenting her. Thus, they invited her to join them for lunch at their table. They were always there by her side, making sure those cruel, mean children never bothered her again. Ms. Lorme chose Willow to be in charge while she took Francine to the shelter, which Willow took seriously. Finally, Francine had friends. She never did before.

"I can't wait to tell them about you. I am going to call them tonight. I want them to meet you," she stated staunchly.

"I'd be delighted," Philip said to his daughter.

She told him she loved to read and went to the library frequently. She always had her nose in a book. Mostly, she spoke of the tragic death of Bettye Jo's husband and daughter, who was the same age as Francine. Thus, Bettye Jo specifically asked for a twelve-year-old girl. It did not matter what her background entailed. She said Bettye Jo now had someone to love and to give her love to in return.

Bettye Jo was very patient and understanding of Francine, for she never pushed her to talk or do anything she did not feel comfortable with. She had plenty of time.

"How do you like your hamburger, Phil?" she asked.

He took a bite before answering, "It's scrumptious. I see why you like them, especially when they are covered with onions, lettuce, and tomato sprinkled with ketchup. All that makes it extremely tasty and savory."

They continued eating their lunch daintily, but with relish. Then, they picked up a french fry and dipped it in the ketchup. Philip remarked about the french fries, "They are delicious, too."

Francine nodded as she picked up another one. They were enjoying themselves, sharing a favorite meal and talking and getting to know each other. They sipped the Coke happily, blowing bubbles, giggling and smiling.

"I'd like to open my present now, Phil, okay?" He consented, "Of course."

She furiously ripped off the wrapping paper. She saw a box and opened its lid. "It's a charm bracelet. It is beautiful. I love it. Thank you so much." She read the card: "To a very special girl on her thirteenth birthday."

"Oh, my God!" She was so happy. "Thank you again." Philip smiled at her, saying nothing.

"Let us take each other's pictures." Philip reached for his cell phone. "Smile!" he instructed, and she did while holding up a french fry. *Click, click*, he snapped. "Now, you take one of me."

Francine smiled sweetly. "Certainly," she said, as she took the cell phone. "Smile," she ordered with a giggle. Philip took a bite of his hamburger. *Click, click, click*, she went.

"Now let's take a selfie," he advised. And they did, smiling brightly into the camera.

"Let's go get them developed in the photo store down the aisle," Philip suggested.

Francine agreed.

"We'll show them to your mother." He had it planned out.

They resumed their meal, gazing at each other. Philip winked at his daughter, her eyes large and bright as shining stars.

A half hour later

Francine and Philip were through with their meal. They wiped their hands and faces with their napkins.

"Let's go, honey," he stated pleasantly.

Philip went behind Francine, pulling her chair from under her. Then he put her jacket around her shoulders. She looked up at her father, thanking him for his chivalry.

Philip asked a man at the next table in a kind voice, "Would you please take a picture or two of me and my daughter?" he said, his hands on her shoulders.

"Sure," the man consented.

Francine and Philip, with their arms around their waists, posed with smiles as the man clicked the button. Both changed poses and Philip inquired, "Would you please do one more, sir? My daughter and I would appreciate it."

The man agreed and did so.

"You have a beautiful daughter, sir," he complimented him and Francine.

"Thanks a lot, sir, and have a good day," Philip graciously said to the man.

Philip turned to Francine and went on, "I'd like to take one of you near the railing," he pointed, and she obliged consented. *Click, click*. Philip pushed the camera button a few times.

Then Francine also asked Philip to stand by the railing, and he willingly did so. *Click, click* again and again.

Then they walked down the aisle. Philip had his hand on her shoulder. Suddenly they wrapped each other's arms closely on their shoulders. Francine looked up and smiled at her father, eyes sparkling. Philip gazed at his daughter, and he smiled as well. They continued their stroll with their hands clasping, swinging back and forth. Francine skipped a head and turned to Philip, twirling around and around, arms out flying, her eyes on her father's eyes. Then, she turned ahead and pointed to Mike's Photo Shop.

"Let us go in and get these pictures developed. I can't wait to show Mama," she excitedly and gleefully remarked. "Won't she be surprised!" she added.

They entered the shop. They could hardly wait for they were eager to share them with Bettye Jo.

"She'll simply flip when she sees them," Francine cried out happily.

3:00 p.m.

Philip and Francine were carrying shopping bags filled with books, posters, DVDs, jeans, sundresses, hats, and T-shirts. They were very tired, but it was a very good day for both father and daughter.

Philip handed her his phone to inform Bettye Jo that they were on their way home.

"Mama, Mama," Francine addressed into the phone with enthusiasm. "I can't wait to see you and show you what Phil bought me! We had the greatest time ever!" She was ecstatic. "And furthermore, he bought me a charm bracelet for my thirteenth birthday. It is really beautiful, Mama. I can't wait to show it to you!" She was filled with joy.

"That's wonderful, darling," she brightly exclaimed. "I'm so happy you and Philip had a good day!"

Then she asked, "Let me speak with him."

Francine handed the phone back to her father. He could hardly contain his composure. He was going to speak to Bettye Jo, but he was tongue-tied and breathless.

"Hi, Bettye Jo," he addressed into the phone. He could not go on. He was not ready to tell her his feelings. Not yet anyway.

"Philip?" she questioned, "Are you okay? You sound jittery."

"I'm fine, Bettye Jo," he tried, but stuttered again. What else could he say?

"We had a good time today. We cannot wait to get home and tell you everything that occurred today and to show you the birthday gift I gave Francine. Sorry, it was late, but better late than never. You, no, I mean, we have a wonderful, lovely daughter," he concluded. That was all he was able to say.

"That's terrific, Philip," she remarked sincerely. Then she had an afterthought. "How about we order in Chinese food for dinner tonight? The three of us."

"Fine," he agreed. Then he turned to Francine, "Would you like Chinese food for supper? Your mother suggested we should all have dinner tonight."

Francine smiled brightly, "Yes, oh, yes, Phil!"

Philip then continued to Bettye Jo, "It's a date!"

"Great!" shouted Francine and Bettye Jo in unison.

"Bye," he said to Bettye Jo, who smiled into the phone.

They left the mall, skipping along happily, swinging their bags back and forth to the car, giggling and laughing. They were so eager to get home. Such excitement, and the day was not yet over. *There was more to come*, both thought with great anticipation.

6:00 p.m.

The three sat around the kitchen table eating their Chinese food delicately but with relish and enjoyment. Francine would, on occasion, observe Philip stealing glances at her mother. Every now and then he would stop eating to sneak a peek at her. He was waiting for her to face him, trying to get her attention. When he caught Francine watching him, he would quickly return to his food. Francine knew his intentions and Philip knew this. But he still hesitated. He did not want to appear as a jerk to Bettye Jo.

Then Bettye Jo turned toward him and offered while picking up a container of fried rice, "Would you like some more fried rice, Philip?" She was smiling at him, her dark eyes bright.

Stuttering, he answered, "Y-Yes, B-Bettye Jo, thank you, I would." He was unable to say more though he wanted to.

She still smiled and looked at him pleasantly and scooped out some fried rice and placed it on his plate.

"T-Thanks," he said, still bumbling under his breath. He resumed eating, eyes on his food.

Bettye Jo watched him. She, too, knew not what to say or do, but she did want to. And so did he. Both felt awkward. No one was sure how to proceed. Francine observed them with awe, thinking to herself, *Tell her, Phil, tell him, Mama*. She thought of blurting it all out. But she did not want to appear presumptuous. *Come on, come on, both of you, say something, do something,* she continued impatiently. *Tell her, tell him*. They went back to their meal in silence. Francine still hoped one of them would be the first one. Her heart pounded heavily. Reluctantly, Francine resumed eating, but every now and then, she would look up at them. It was useless, she thought defeatedly at first, but she refused to give up hope. They loved each other and they knew it. She was screaming inside of herself. The three were silent. No one knew what to do next. *Mama, Phil, please, one of you, make the first move already. You both know you love each other. Do it already!* she demanded inside of herself.

Finally, after about twenty minutes, they wiped their hands and put their napkins on their plates.

They had finished their meal, still saying nothing.

Bettye Jo turned toward Francine and asked gently, "Please help me clear the table. Then stack the dishwasher." Francine obediently did so, still staring at Philip and Bettye Jo, who still felt queasy, still saying not a word, but stealing gleaming glances at each other. *Are they smiling at each other?* she pondered hopefully while grinning to herself. *It is a start*, she still hoped. *Finally, at last, smiling!*

"Would you like some ice cream?" Bettye Jo offered.

"Yes, please," Francine answered brightly.

Philip said nothing, but a minute later, glancing at Bettye Jo, he replied, grinning delightedly, "Yes, Bettye Jo," with love in his eyes. And with love in her eyes, as well, she answered, "All right, Philip, gladly." Their mouths opened and wide, gaping with joy. They could not take their eyes from each other.

Bettye Jo turned and motioned gladly for Francine to help her. They stood by the counter, scooping out the ice cream. Francine smiled at her mother and she did so as well. Bettye Jo was humming under her breath. Francine looked at her, eyes shining, her mouth grinning lovingly. *Finally,* Francine thought with much elatedness. Philip sitting sideways at the table, watching her, Bettye Jo, his daughter's mother, with love and mesmerizing wonder. He just sat and stared, heart beating heavily—*boom, boom, boom*. Francine with a scooper in her hand, watched Philip, her father, in love with her mother, Bettye Jo, who just kept scooping out the ice cream, still singing in a lilting voice, smiling to herself though her back was to him. She did not want to seem brazen or impetuous. But her heart beat faster. Still, she scooped chocolate on top of vanilla in the bowl. Then, she took the bowl with both hands and handed it to Philip, who reached for it. Both hands touching hers. They bolted, as though shocked, and jumped away as the bowl of ice cream splattered on the floor. Both cried out in aghast, "I'm sorry," Philip pleaded. "No!" Bettye Jo cried. They began picking up the pieces from the floor carefully, so as not to touch each other, but they could not help themselves any longer. They faced each other, unable to say anything, though they had the desire to do so. Francine came up to them, volunteering, "Let me clean this up, okay, guys?" They smiled at her. Then, suddenly, they clasped each other's hands tightly, looking into each other's eyes for a very long moment, longing for the other to finally say how they felt. Philip put both his hands on the sides of her face. Then, Bettye Jo took her hands and put them on the sides of his face. Their lips met. Hungrily with passion, they kissed voraciously, never stopping. Both sighed heavily, "Ah!" they both moaned and caught up in the moment. At last. Francine, while holding the shattered pieces and dropping them into the garbage disposal, her eyes blazed, arms wide out, exclaimed joyfully, "Way to go, guys!" Then she clapped her hands together while jumping up and down, then with her arms outstretched, she twirled as a ballerina around the kitchen. "Finally!" she excitedly chanted. "Finally!" Her eyes were filled with tears of glistening stars. She was crying. She was so happy. Her mother and father finally let it all out. Each knew how and what the other felt. It was mutual. No more wondering. They both knew. No more mind games or second-guessing.

Bettye Jo and Philip stood. He, holding her waist and she, his arms. Both faced their daughter. All smiles.

Suddenly, she remembered Philip's belated 13th birthday present. She got up and walked over to a little table in the foyer where she set it down. She brought it over to her mother and piped up with glee, "Mama, look what Phil bought me." She dangled it in front of her. Bettye Jo's eyes lit up and reached for it. "It's so lovely." Then turning to Philip, she remarked, "You're quite a gentleman." Then Philip said, "Anything for my special girl." He winked at Francine. Bettye Jo placed the bracelet on the table.

Francine then asked, "May I be excused? I would like to call Willow now and tell her everything. Is that all right?" she was polite and direct.

"Sure, honey," Bettye Jo consented.

"I'll be down later to say good night," she mentioned as an afterthought.

Both agreed and Francine ran up the stairs in haste, eager to tell her friend the wonderful news. She slammed the door behind her.

Bettye Jo and Philip laughed as they watched her. Then they faced each other.

"Can I get you anything?" Bettye Jo asked.

"Nothing, dear. Let us just sit here for a little while longer and talk." Then, as he tapped his fingertips on the tabletop, he added, "I'd like to take you out some time this week. Just the two of us, okay?"

"That will be lovely," she answered brightly.

Then she remembered that tomorrow was Monday, and she had an appointment to sign some papers finalizing Francine's adoption. She knew what she was going to say and was not worried. Unforeseen circumstances always come up. However, in this case, they were good ones.

Bettye Jo and Philip heard Francine's excited voice on the telephone. She could hardly contain herself.

"Would you believe it?" Francine remarked, "Not only did he show up unexpectedly this morning saying he was my birth father, but he is actually in love with my mother. And she is, with him. At first, she was uptight and leery, worrying that he was to come and yank me away demanding full custody. But they love each other. And it has only been one day! Would you believe it! They kissed each other, really and truly! I am so excited. I would like you, Arlene, and Stephanie to meet him. He is wonderful and handsome and smart. You will like him! And you know what he does for a living? He is a psychiatrist. He helps people solve their problems, and he tries to understand his patients and their issues and situations. I think I want to be one someday. Most important, he does not use labels such as crazy or abnormal. To him, each patient is special and treats them accordingly, as such."

Bettye Jo stood by Philip's chair, facing Francine's bedroom. She was smiling. Philip glanced up also with a wide grin. Both said nothing for a while. They were engrossed in listening to Francine's telephone call.

"She's so happy," Bettye Jo noticed and pointed out.

"She has a right to be. She has two parents who love her dearly," Philip reasoned.

Then Bettye Jo mentioned to Philip, "You know her fourteenth birthday is next month. Why don't we do something special for her?"

Philip agreed but added, "Let us make it a surprise. How about we take her to Seabreeze Amusement Park? She loves rides and arcade games," he offered.

Bettye Jo went on, "I'll call her friends. We could all go. But I would like to ask their parents for approval."

"At night, we'll get a cake and have a party with presents, okay?" Philip pointed out.

"Splendid!" she consented happily.

Suddenly, Francine walked down the stairs. Both Bettye Jo and Philip jumped up, startled, and faced her,

Francine asked, "What's going on?"

Both said nothing. They thought she heard them and quickly stated, "Nothing, honey, we're discussing some plans, nothing serious," Bettye Jo answered nervously with a gleaming grin. She turned to Philip, also smiling, "Isn't that right, Philip?" she said, waiting for him to support her answer.

"Yes, dear," he supported Bettye Jo.

Francine stood on the stairs for a while, saying nothing. *What is going on?* she thought to herself. Anyway, she decided not to pursue the matter, whatever it was. It is between them. She shrugged it off with a sigh and let it go. *Whatever?* she concluded.

She resumed walking down the stairs. It was getting late—almost 8:00 p.m. There was school tomorrow.

"It was a simply wonderful day, guys," she remarked, "but I am tired now. I'd like to say good night."

Bettye Jo held her arms out to embrace her. Francine ran into them kissing her, bidding her a good night.

Then she turned to Philip, and he began, "Good night . . .," then she stopped.

Philip piped up, "Good night . . . princess," he addressed his daughter.

Suddenly, Francine froze and said nothing, her mouth ajar, standing as a statue, her mind having a flashback. She started thinking, still not uttering a sound.

Bettye Jo walked over to her.

"What's the matter, darling?" She put her hand on her shoulder.

Francine did not reply. She stood there. She remembered it quite well. That night when Leonora, in one of her rages kicking and screaming, threw Philip out of the apartment. Francine not quite three years old, filthy, and dirty, urinating on the floor, crying aloud, and Leonora yelling at her to shut up. And then Philip quietly and lovingly walked over to her as she squatted in a corner against the wall, picking her up, smoothing her hair, telling her not to cry and that she was a very good girl, and everything will be all right. Then, she remembered. He called her princess. It all came back to her.

Remembering this, she covered her ears and shut her eyes tightly, trying to block out the horror she experienced as a child. She began sobbing relentlessly, letting it all out.

"I-I-I r-remember," she stuttered tearfully. She turned to Philip, "Daddy, you used to call me that. It just came back to me. I remember now, vividly." She paused.

Bettye Jo and Philip stared at her, saying nothing but looking at each other.

"I-I'm sorry," Francine sobbed, tears streaming down her face. Bettye Jo turned her around to face her. "It's okay," she affirmed. "You did not do anything wrong," Bettye Jo hugged her closely to her breast, patting her back, then stroking her hair gently, comforting her.

"You remembered. You did," Bettye Jo assured her, managing a smile. "That's wonderful." Neither uttered a word. Francine stopped crying and looked up at her and Philip, still watching his daughter.

"She remembers now," Philip asserted. Then to Francine, "You are free now, honey. You are safe. You're going to be just fine."

Francine looked back at her father, then with a forced smile. She remembered him. Still shaking, she calmly called him, "Good night, Daddy!" it finally came out after all these years. She finally called him Daddy. She always did. But now, she remembered Philip quite vividly and that he always loved her, though through no fault of his own, was not able to have any contact with her. Francine completely understood and did not blame him.

All three said nothing for a little while. It was a lot to take in all at once, they smiled at each other.

Francine a firmly stated, "I love you, guys."

Philip extended his hand to her, which she grasped lovingly. He squeezed it, and she reciprocated and smiled; her eyes lit up as captive stars.

Bettye Jo watched them. She was quite pleased.

Philip looked up at Bettye Jo.

"We love you, too," Bettye Jo stated. Philip chimed in, "All the way to Pluto and back."

While dashing up the stairs, she turned around, "Good night, Mama, Daddy!" she called out joyfully. Then she was in her bedroom. She flopped down on her bed. She was going to be okay.

One Month Later: Francine's Fourteenth Birthday

Francine pranced down the stairs in her duster. Bettye Jo and Philip were in the kitchen. They turned as they heard her footsteps.

"What's going on?" Francine inquired.

Bettye Jo shook her head hastily.

"Nothing, honey," she replied quickly. Then as an afterthought, she suggested, "Why don't you put on your best clothes. Then you could come down for breakfast. We are making you french toast and bacon. Your favorite, all right?" she asserted pleasantly.

Francine did not respond at first. She was puzzled. She knew something was going on. But what? Everyone was behaving mysteriously and secretively. She was in the dark. Even her three best friends were acting peculiarly. When she would walk up to them at school, she would see them giggling coyly and when they saw her, they stopped abruptly, pretending innocence. She did not stop wondering.

She was clad in a pair of blue denim bell-bottom dungarees with embroidered flowers on them. She wore a long-sleeved, white T-shirt with the word "Love" across the top. Each letter sparkled with different colors. She had beaded black moccasins on her feet. She put her hair in a bun with a scrunchie around it. Her necklace consisted of multicolored beads strung together, lying flat down on the front of her T-shirt and reaching her belly button. On both her wrists were various colored beaded bracelets. Lastly, she had a mood ring on her index finger on her right hand.

She heard the doorbell ring. There were voices, excited, gleeful ones. Everyone was laughing, Again, she was in a quandary. What is happening? She stood by her bedroom door, leaning against the frame, for a bit. Doing and saying nothing. She went back to look at herself in the mirror. She pranced around, smiling, admiring herself moving to and for posing in different positions, swaying back and forth.

She was very pleased with herself. She liked what she saw. Herself. *I am special, I am a wonder.* She mused brightly, smiling to herself. She was loved and supported by Bettye Jo and Philip. And she had three best friends. All five of them stood by her through thick and thin. What more could one say? She was doing all right. She has not at one time spoke of her viperous, wretched childhood devoid of love, warmth, and beauty. She had it all now. Friends and family. Hers forever, not ever to be taken away from her.

"Francine!"

She heard her name. Everyone shouted it all at once.

"Francine!" they called again.

She left her bedroom and ran down the stairs. Everyone stood at the bottom, smiling, laughing, and shouting. Francine saw a large sign near the front door.

HAPPY BIRTHDAY!

Tears of happiness filled her eyes. She was speechless.

They began singing the birthday song, off-key, but with ardency.

"Oh my God!" Francine cried out. Everyone went up to her with hugs and kisses. She was jubilant. She did not believe it.

Then Francine saw her breakfast on the table. She quickly but daintily sat down and ate it. "Take your time, honey," Bettye Jo stated carefully. "We'll all be in the living room, okay?" Francine agreed. And they left her to her breakfast.

They shuffled around while Francine ate her breakfast.

An Hour Later

"Get your jacket, birthday girl," Philip addressed her gleefully.

"Where are we going?" Francine inquired awesomely.

No one answered her.

Bettye Jo walked over to her without responding to her question. She smiled at her and just flatly said, "Just get your jacket." Then she turned to the others, "Let's go, guys!"

Everyone still had smiles on their faces as they opened the front door.

Philip helped Francine put her jacket on. He and Bettye Jo stood behind her, leading her out, their hands on her shoulders.

All went out the door and piled into the car. All four girls were laughing and giggling, nudging each other's arms. Philip got into the driver's seat. Francine sat between her mother and father. They were off.

The sky was a clear blue without a cloud. The sun shone brightly. Francine slid in a country/Western CD. Everyone sang loudly and off-key while swaying to the music leading the band and bouncing up and down in their seats, giving each other playful high-fives.

"Girls, do please try to control yourselves," Bettye Jo asked firmly with a smile. "Philip needs to concentrate on his driving."

The girls became quiet and sat down. Still the music played, and they sang softly among themselves.

The ride was peaceful and uneventful. The girls made some small talk, chattering away. Bettye Jo smiled at them, Francine's friends. She was so lucky to have such good girlfriends for they were always there for her and they planned her birthday with her parents.

Luckily, the sun was out. It was not too hot nor too cold. It was simply a perfect day for Francine's birthday. Francine deserved a good birthday, since all her life she never had a party or presents or friends to bond with. She had no one during those years, but she did now. Also, the girls thought Francine was very fortunate to have Bettye Jo as her adoptive mother, and Philip, her birth father, as loving parents who happened to have fallen in love with each other a few hours after they first met. It was hard to believe, but true. These two people wanting to raise Francine as their own. Francine was indeed fortunate, everyone thought to themselves. And they were also fortunate to have Francine in theirs. She was such a sweet and lovely girl, hardly showing any signs of her terrible and horrible childhood.

As they rode, they saw a large, colorful, bright sign that read "Seabreeze Amusement Park."

Francine gleefully pointed, "We're here!" she exclaimed brightly. She turned toward her friends, who agreed in harmony. Philip drove the car into a spot in the parking lot. "This is it, everybody," he announced. He turned off the ignition, got out of the car, and opened the door first for Bettye Jo and Francine. He held his hand out for both and they gladly took it. Afterward, he let Francine's friends out one at a time graciously. The girls skipped and twirled themselves around and around, laughing and giggling. Bettye Jo and Philip, his arm around her, followed them. Bettye Jo put on her sunglasses, as did Philip. The sun was very bright.

All five of them looked around, gazing at all the sites. They were so mesmerized by their surroundings. There was so much to take in, they could hardly breathe. Each of them pointed to different sites in amazement. They could not decide what to do first for there was so much to choose from.

Francine pointed to the cyclone and excitedly suggested, "Let's go on that, guys!" The girls agreed in unison.

"And Daddy, why don't you try to win a prize for Mama, okay?"

Philip and Bettye Jo smiled at their daughter's thoughtful suggestion. Philip took out his wallet and gave the girls money for whatever activities they wanted to try out and do. Then, he turned toward Bettye Jo and said, "Let's go to that stand over there," he pointed on his right. "I'll try to win a prize for you, but I cannot promise, all right, honey? I'll give it my best shot," he warned. Bettye Jo gleefully replied, "That is so sweet and thoughtful of you," she said sincerely.

"Afterward," Philip went on, "Let us all agree to meet us in the park near the confection stand for lunch at 1:00 p.m. All right, girls?" Everyone nodded in agreement. They were off and running. Such excitement. Philip and Bettye Jo watched the girls heading toward the cyclone with intense awe. Then, they walked toward the stand where all the prizes of different colored stuffed animals were displayed. The game involved hitting a row of moving ducks with a ball. Philip was hesitant for he was not sure of his aim, but he promised Bettye Jo he would try and go for it. He knew she would not be insulted if he lost, but still, he did want to try.

The girls piled into the seats of the cyclone ride, all excited with great anticipation. The cyclone clerk made sure everyone was safe and secure in their seats. He made certain they were buckled in and the handles were tight. They were rearing to go. The clerk put the switch on. And they were off, flying and screaming with their hands in the air. The wind was blowing their hair across their face. They were so full of joy and without a care in the world. The ride was a little scary at first, but it did not deter them. They were on air. The ride hardly took five minutes, but they were still breathless with joy. The ride was thrilling and surprising. The girls were so hyper after it that they could hardly contain themselves.

They walked on, observing other people laughing and talking with their friends and families and in groups eating popcorn and cotton candy. Others were carrying stuffed animals, balloons, toys, and souvenirs. They were having a good time. The girls planned on having fun, too, especially for Francine who never had such a great experience in her life. This trip was the first one Francine had. It was a novelty for her. She never encountered such joy. And, also, she had her three best friends and a mother and father who loved her and shared themselves with her. Indeed, Francine had a very good time. She did not want the day to end. But she knew it would, but her memories will always stay with her and that she would have many more days as wonderful as today. They were hers forever. No one could or would ever deny her pleasures and joys. Everyone was definite about that. And so was she.

As the four of them strolled, Francine came across a man doing card tricks on a table. A crowd gathered. They were also interested, and thus, they decided to check it out. The magician asked for a volunteer. At once, Francine raised her hand, and he motioned for her to come up and assist him. Her friends shouted out, "Today's her birthday, sir!" He smiled at Francine and asked amicably, "How would you like to do a card trick with me?" Then he offered, "You'll receive a free gift from me, my birthday present to you!" Francine joyfully grinned and nodded. He instructed her on what to do with the cards, and she obediently followed his orders. Everyone clapped at the end. He gave her a deck of "magic" cards, and she profusely thanked him and bid him a good day.

"Let's all take pictures of each other," Willow thought of while taking out her smart phone. All of them took pictures, all with different poses and grimaces. People were looking, but they did not care.

"Let's go on the carousel," Arlene pointed to it.

Again, they dashed off and hopped on the mechanical horses for a chance to grab the brass ring. Whoever was able to obtain the most rings had a choice of prizes—trinkets, costume jewelry, keychains, Rubik's cubes, seashells, small stuffed animals, etc. Thus, when they were securely on the ride, it went around and around faster and faster. Francine happened to have grasped the most rings. However, her friends were not successful. She felt badly, so she gave each friend a gift she won. Willow got a beaded bracelet, Arlene got a keychain, and Stephanie, a red plaid small-change purse.

After they were off the ride, they saw Bettye Jo and Philip on a horse carriage ride. Bettye Jo had a pink fluffy dog on her lap and Philip, a purple stuffed rabbit on his lap as well. Philip told the driver to please take their pictures. Some of them were of Philip and Bettye Jo kissing each other on their lips. The girls were watching and shouting, "Way to go, guys!" Bettye Jo and Philip, startled, jumped up and saw them. They embarrassedly giggled but were pleased as punch. Philip handed Francine the purple stuffed rabbit he won. She took it graciously.

Francine pointed to a hotdog stand. "Let us eat, it's almost 1:00 p.m." They eagerly went and bought hotdogs, french fries, and sodas. They brought their food to a wooden table and sat down, enjoying their meal. They spoke cheerfully with each other about their day's events. Then Francine wanted pictures of her parents and friends together. She went over to an employee of the stand and requested him to please take some pictures. He cheerfully consented with a small grin. First, the girls, then her parents, then all five of them in one picture. Lastly, she asked him to take one of her parents kissing each other. They were a little hesitant and blushed, but they consented. It was Francine's day. So, they concurred with each other that she could have and do anything just for her special day. She was the birthday girl, her parents told the young man. Again, he consented with a smile and did it. Everyone thanked him. "No problem," he commented. "It was a pleasure." He walked away toward his post at the stand.

The five of them resumed their meal.

Afterward, Philip mentioned while looking at his watch, "It's almost 2:00 p.m. We will stay for about an hour and then meet at the admissions stand. Since a lot of traffic is expected, we will leave, okay? You do understand." They did in accordance.

"Bettye Jo and I will stroll down by the bridge near a pond with waterfalls. If we have time, we will go for a boat ride. You girls stick together and have a good time. You deserve it," he added pleasantly.

The girls smiled and left. Philip and Bettye Jo smiled agreeably. They were off. Philip put his arm around Bettye Jo, and they gazed at each other lovingly.

The girls skipped down the path leading to the gift shop. Francine planned to buy her parents presents. She chose a necklace with a red heard for her mother and a brown pencil holder for her father. Bettye Jo loved hearts, and Philip needed a place to put his pens and pencils in. She chose a flowery headband for herself. Willow bought a mood ring. Stephanie picked a cameo pin. And Arlene, a small music box with a ballerina.

They continued their walk along the path. They spotted a clown juggling balls in the air. People gathered around, and they joined them with delight. The clown was smiling and winking at them.

Afterward, they chose to just stroll down the walkaway, observing people enjoying themselves for they were getting tired. Unbeknownst to Francine, her friends and parents had another surprise for her.

Meanwhile, Philip and Bettye Jo crossed the bridge to watch the waterfalls slide off a brook. They took a picture of it. They did have time for a boat ride. So, Philip paddled, and Bettye Jo sat enjoying the scenery—green trees, colorful flowers, the glistening dark water, the sun shining, the sky, a bright blue. It was quite breathtaking. All of it. They reached the end of their ride. Philip helped her out by taking her hand. Then hand in hand they walked back. It was nearly 3:00 p.m. The girls were waiting for them, as planned. All had smiling faces when they saw each other. They were eager to discuss their wonderful afternoons together.

6:00 p.m.

They all entered the house with much joy and happiness.

"Girls," Bettye Jo turned to them, "please take Francine up to her bedroom and do whatever you like. Philip and I will be here downstairs. We will let you know when we need you, all right?"

Willow nodded assertively, "Yes, Mrs. Pennington."

Bettye Jo then thought afterward, "Also, girls. You do not have to call me Mrs. Pennington anymore, since we all know each other very well and are on friendly terms. Call me Bettye Jo," then she faced Philip and resumed, "And you could call Francine's father Philip," she stated firmly. "Is that right, honey?" she asked looking at him.

"Yes, dear," Philip agreed with Bettye Jo.

Stephanie nodded, "Of course."

Arlene chimed in, "Certainly."

Both Bettye Jo and Philip grinned like a Cheshire. "Good," they said in unison.

The girls ran up the stairs and into Francine's bedroom, plopping down on her bed and bouncing on it, giggling ecstatically with each other, hitting each other playfully on their elbows.

Francine took a John Denver CD and inserted it into her digital tuner, then she pushed the power button on.

The girls got up and wildly danced around the room to the music, arms flying around and around up in the air, jumping and twirling their bodies in time to the music, singing loudly with gaiety, but off-key.

Suddenly they got tired and breathless and pounced backward onto the bed, still singing but in a lower octave. Francine shut the digital tuner off and plopped down beside them while shaking the bed. "Whew!" she brushed her hand across her brow. She flopped on her back. The girls were exhausted but in a happy mood. It might be early evening, but the day was not over yet, not by a long shot. There was more to come. Francine was clueless and wondered. *What is next?* Her friends glanced with smiles to each other secretively. *What were they thinking?* Francine questioned to herself. She did not think to ask, though she was tempted to, and if she did, how would they react. She did not want to know. Surely soon, she would be, she surmised. After all, they were her best friends now and always. She knew that quite well. They would not betray her, she told herself convincingly. It was true. Definitely. She had nothing to dread or worry about. Then, she stopped herself. Pause. She was not going to beat herself up about it anymore.

Suddenly, Willow piped up and suggested, "Francine, why don't you show us those 'magic' cards you got at the fair?"

Stephanie continued, "Yeah, let's try some magic tricks." She turned to Willow and Arlene, "Okay, guys?"

They nodded with harmonious excitement. Francine went to her dresser and took out the deck. Willow reached for it. Arlene and Stephanie grabbed the instructions and fought over who should begin. Willow piped up. They assorted and glanced at each card. Francine watched them awesomely. Then the cards fell on the bed. Quickly, they tried to gather them in their hands but were unable to.

"Let me," Francine offered.

Then they heard voices from downstairs.

"Girls!" It was Bettye Jo.

"It's your mother," Arlene mentioned. Then she nudged Willow and Stephanie and spoke, "Guys, it's time now."

"What do you mean?" Francine was curious. "Why? What?" she kept questioning her friends.

Stephanie tapped her hand. "Never mind. Not you, you stay here and freshen up. Your parents want us to do something."

Arlene added, "We'll be back, we promise." She eyed Stephanie and Willow with a wink.

The three friends motioned to each other while waving their hands at Francine. Then they dashed out of the room, pouncing down the staircase. Francine stood there watching, saying nothing at first, but shrugged her shoulders.

She picked up the cards from the floor and put them away. She decided to change her clothes, comb her hair, and wash her face. She thought, *In the meantime.*

She chose a long-puffed-sleeve dress with flowers against a white background. She put on her white sandals. She pulled the scrunchie out of her hair, letting it fall down her shoulders. She brushed it furiously and put a pink headband on. Then she went to the bathroom sink and scrubbed her face with a washcloth, squeezing soap out of a dispenser and smoothing it over her face. Lastly, she splashed cold water and patted her face gently while drying it with a towel. Afterward, she looked at herself in the mirror. Her face sparkled. She smiled. She was pleased with herself.

Then she grabbed a book off the shelf, flopped down on her bed, and began reading. Still, she mused, "What's happening?" Time stood still. She went back to her book. She tried to stop racking her brain and thinking about whatever it was. She will know soon enough. She was sure of it. For it was just a matter of time. She had to be patient. She knew patience was a virtue and good things come to those who wait, she continued telling herself. *Think happy, positive thoughts. Again, and again and again.*

About ten minutes later, she heard heavy footsteps clamping up the stairs. She stood in wonder, saying and doing nothing. Breathless with anticipation. Then she heard loud pounding on the door. It flew open. Francine's eyes practically bolted out of their sockets, her arms and hands nearly touching her chest in fists.

Willow mentioned while motioning with her hand, "Come with us." She started to lead her down. Stephanie put a blindfold around her eyes. She was shaking and giggling. Arlene took her other hand. The three friends escorted her downstairs very cautiously. No one said a word, but they were laughing among themselves. "He he he," they went on. Francine was still clueless but said nothing. They led her into the living room. Stephanie tore off the blindfold. Francine's eyes grew larger and bright, and her hands flew out away from her sides. She was speechless. Then she went, "Oh, my God!" A large colorful sign above the television read, "HAPPY BIRTHDAY, FRANCINE!"

Everyone began singing in high-pitched loud voices.

"HAPPY BIRTHDAY TO YOU!"

"HAPPY BIRTHDAY TO YOU!"

"HAPPY BIRTHDAY, DEAR FRANCINE!"

"HAPPY BIRTHDAY TO YOU!"

"AND MANY, MANY MORE!"

A Pepperidge Farm chocolate layer cake sat on the table saying in pink icing, "HAPPY 14TH BIRTHDAY, FRANCINE!" Fifteen different colored lit candles shone brightly. Francine clasped her hands together with a gleeful expression on her face.

Bettye Jo took the camera and instructed her to blow out the candles while she snapped a picture.

Francine did so obediently, and everyone clapped in unison.

Bettye Jo walked over to her daughter to hug her and she did so back.

"Happy birthday, darling!" she exclaimed.

Francine saw colorfully wrapped packages on the couch and was surprised, "Is this all for me?" she questioned.

"Yes," Bettye Jo replied, "it certainly is. It's your day, sweetheart!"

Then she mentioned, "I will get a knife, plates, forks, and napkins. And you will cut the cake and give each of us a piece, okay?" She looked at her daughter. Then she asked Philip to help her serve. He obliged and followed her into the kitchen. The girls were alone together. Willow asked if Francine wanted to start opening her presents. "Wait till you see what we got you," Willow stated impatiently but with a joyful grin. Arlene affirmed, "We can't wait to see the expression on your face." Francine smiled at her friends. They were all hopping around, clapping their hands and high-fiving each other. Then they became quiet. Bettye Jo and Philip were talking in the kitchen. The girls were trying to hear what they were discussing.

"I want her to have all my cards, letters, and presents I have sent her all these years. She is entitled to know. I always loved her. I did, you know, Bettye Jo," Philip mentioned.

"You're right, Philip," Bettye Jo acknowledged, "she should."

The girls looked at each other with puzzled expressions on their faces. They were excited, especially Francine. *He had presents and cards for me*, she thought pleasantly to herself. "Oh! I can hardly wait to see them." All these years. So much time wasted, always believing she did not have a father, one that always loved her anyway. Years and years. But he appeared at her house, suddenly wanting to get to know her. He did. Today is her birthday and he was willing to give her all the presents and cards that had accumulated all these years. She could hardly wait.

Then Bettye Jo and Philip came into the living room with plates, forks, and cups for a big bottle of Coke that they set on the table.

"Here," Bettye Jo said, handing a knife to Francine "You could begin cutting pieces of your cake for your friends, and then, for us," indicating her and Philip.

Francine did so with a pleasant expression on her face. Bettye Jo and Philip were not aware that Francine heard their conversation in the kitchen. But everyone went about eating their food and drinking soda. No one said anything for a while. They knew not what to say, yet each person would steal a glance to each other, all waiting for someone to begin, to start to speak, to say something, anything, each thought to themselves eagerly with great anticipation.

Philip began, "I'm very happy to be here. I found my daughter whom I've always loved though it was unbeknownst to her and for that I am sorry. But she knows and understands that I was not the one to blame. Fortunately, though I cannot change the past, if I could, I would. However, she is in my life, and me, in hers, now and forever," then he glanced a smile at Bettye Jo and continued, "And most important, without any intentions, I fell in love with Bettye Jo, her mother, though I had not known her for even a day when I showed up unexpectedly on her doorstep that I met her. I am quite delighted that Bettye Jo is my daughter's mother, for she loves her dearly and vice versa." He took a cup of his drink and paused to catch his breath for a few seconds. Then he resumed, turning to Bettye Jo with a gleam in his eyes, "I know today is Francine's birthday, but I have an announcement to make. I've wanted to for some time now, and it is a happy and good one."

He then got on his bent knee, reaching into his pants pocket, and took out a small box and opened its lid. "Bettye Jo," he said hesitantly, his heart heavy, "will you marry me?" Time stood still. Everyone was in awe, surprised but happy.

"Say yes," the girls demanded joyfully. "Say it, say it," they insisted repeatedly.

Bettye Jo, motionless but with a gleeful smile, finally answered delightedly with her hands clasped together, "Yes, yes, of course I'll marry you, Philip!"

He slid the ring on her finger. Then he put his hands on the sides of her face. They kissed for a very long minute.

The girls watched, their hands together. "Way to go!" they excitedly proclaimed, jumping and hopping around the living room.

Bettye Jo and Philip laughed as they saw the girls' reaction to their news. Francine went up to her parents, hugging them and kissing their cheeks. "Congratulations, Mama, Daddy." She pronounced, "I love you both forever and ever!"

Bettye Jo looked at Francine. "We love you, too." Then she faced Philip and asked, "Isn't that right, honey?"

Philip nodded, smiling. "Certainly, of course, sweetheart," he answered sincerely as they looked at their daughter with delight.

"Now for the presents," Bettye Jo indicated, facing toward the corner table with wrapped packages. She reached toward the table and chose a gift and glanced at its top and read the card, "This is from Willow." She handed it to Francine who took it. She ripped the wrapping paper off eagerly and picked up a book entitled *An American Girl* by Ella Johnson. She screeched for joy, her eyes wide and bright. "I can't believe it. She is my most favorite author," she announced and turned toward her friend with a hug. "Thank you so very much." Then she turned to the others, showing the book gleefully. Everyone nodded happily.

Then Philip reached for another present and read the card. "This is from Stephanie." He handed it to Francine. Again, she furiously ripped off the wrapping, and her eyes lit up brightly. "Doodling Basics for Beginners Kit," she read its title. She turned to Stephanie and hugged her. "How did you know?" she asked eagerly.

Stephanie replied, "We all heard you speak of afterschool classes in it to a staff member the other day."

"Oh!" Francine exclaimed, "You son of a gun." She laughed with her friends, then put it on the table.

Then Bettye Jo reached for another gift. "And this is from Arlene." She handed it to her daughter. Again, she took it and ripped off its wrapping, "Oh!" Her eyes blazed—a thick book entitled *Penny House Variety Puzzles*. "Oh my, God," she exclaimed again.

Arlene then remarked, "We also knew you enjoy doing puzzles."

"Oh, you guys, you're all the greatest, my best friends." She hugged Arlene, then smiled at the others.

Then Willow handed her a card. "Here's a card we all signed. It read, 'Happy birthday to our best friend ever.'" Francine took it and exclaimed gleefully, "It's simply beautiful. Thank you, guys." She hugged them again.

But it was not finished. There was more.

Bettye Jo and Philip stood together with gleaming smiles and their faces. They held a small box. "Here, sweetheart," Bettye Jo announced. Francine took it and opened its velvety lid. It was a necklace with a heart-shaped locket. She then opened it. It had a photo of Bettye Jo and Philip with bright smiles. "It's beautiful!" she remarked breathlessly. "I knew you would like it," Philip stated.

"I do, I do," she responded. She hugged Bettye Jo, then Philip.

"There's more," Bettye Jo mentioned. Francine pounced up and down on her heel and toes in her spot, eyes blazing, hands clasped together excitedly. Philip took a big box and gave it to his daughter. Unwrapping it and opening its lid, she saw ten different colored scarfs. "We know you love scarves," Philip said matter-of-factly.

"Oh, thank you," Francine graciously said enthusiastically. "Look, guys." She showed the scarves to her friends, who reached into the box, each grabbing one and parading it around the room, waving it in the air. Everyone laughed.

"I wonder what this is," Philip mused as he gave Francine another present, which she took gingerly, but with awe. She saw it was a journal with a colorful floral cover.

"Oh my, oh my," she exclaimed.

Bettye Jo added, "I know you love to write, so we bought it for you to write whatever you like and feel. All right?" she nodded.

"Oh yes, oh yes." She was in heaven, still rocking back and forth on her heels. Then Bettye Jo reached for a thin envelop. Everyone wondered what it could possibly be, except for Bettye Jo and Philip who handed it to her while smiling and winking at each other. Francine was stumped. She simply had no clue as to what its contents were. They handed it to her, and she unsealed the envelop and looked at a small card that said, "A year's subscription to *American Teen Girl*." She gently took a card out of the envelope saying, "To a very wonderful, loving daughter on her birthday." It was signed, "Lovingly, Mama and Daddy. Our loving, darling daughter forever." She hugged them tightly. "I cannot believe it, all this," she looked around.

Philip remarked, "I know you have been pining for this magazine, but you felt it was too expensive, so you said nothing. But we knew, didn't we, honey?" he faced Bettye Jo, who nodded pleasantly in agreement.

"Yes," she said, winking at Philip. Both she and Philip leaned down, facing their daughter, their hands clasped, eyes lit up. "Happy birthday, darling," they announced happily.

Then Philip glanced at his watch. "It's almost 8:00 p.m. I would like to leave now to avoid traffic. It is usually heavy on a Saturday." To his daughter, he leaned over, facing her, "Happy birthday, princess." They hugged each other.

"Thanks, Daddy." She smiled.

Then he turned to her friends, "Thanks for being my daughter's friends and making her birthday special."

Willow piped up while glancing at Stephanie and Arlene, "It was a pleasure, Doctor, I mean, Philip." Then as an afterthought, she stated, "My mother will be picking us up soon. We will wait until she arrives."

Philip nodded at the girls. Then he faced Bettye Jo and kissed her on her cheek. "I'll call you tomorrow, darling," he promised.

Then he turned and waved, "Good night, everybody. It was a great day."

Everyone waved back at him. "You, too!"

He was out the door.

Bettye Jo turned toward Francine and her friends. "Girls," she suggested pleasantly, "why don't you wait in the living room while I clean up, okay?"

"I'll help you, Mama," Francine offered, but Bettye Jo touched her hand gently. "No, you're the birthday girl. It is your special day. I can manage." She reached for the plates and utensils and left. The girls sat on the couch, giggling and poking each other's arms.

"Thanks, guys, thanks again for my birthday and all these unexpected gifts. I simply could not imagine this day for it is simply more than I ever dreamed possible," she graciously told her friends.

"It was a pleasure," Arlene stated.

"For you have always been a good friend to us," Stephanie added.

Then they got silent and yawned. They heard honking outside.

"That's Mom!" Willow piped up. The girls went to get their jackets.

"Thanks, Bettye Jo," and to their friend, "See you in school Monday." They waved to Bettye Jo and Francine, returning their greetings, "Bye, everybody." They waved back as they left.

Both mother and daughter stood facing each other.

"It was a wonderful day, so very wonderful," Bettye Jo stated while staring at her engagement ring.

"He proposed, Mama, he did. I am so glad he did. He loves you, Mama, he always did. And you love him. I am so happy, Mama," she kept repeating, "And on my birthday yet. It is beyond my wildest dreams. Oh, I am so happy, Mama." She threw her arms around her, giving her a kiss on her cheek. Bettye Jo smiled and reciprocated. Francine continued, "I am quite tired now. But it was quite a day."

Bettye Jo agreed, "Yes, darling, it was."

Francine turned toward the staircase. "Good night, Mama. I love you all the way to Pluto and back." She kissed her mother again.

"Me, too." She watched her daughter ascending the stairs, turning to and from her mother, eyes gleaming and with a smile.

It was the end of a very pleasant and wonderful day.

Sunday 9:00 a.m.

Bettye Jo was busy in the kitchen, her back to the stove. Francine pranced down the stairs clad in a long-sleeved white T-shirt and denim jeans, her hair up in a messy bun with a scrunchie around it.

"Good morning, Mama!" she greeted her mother in a cheerful, lilting voice, eyes bright, a smile on her face.

Bettye Jo turned to her and returned her greeting while standing over the stove holding a frying pan and a spatula in her hands.

"Good morning, sweetheart. I'm making you your favorite—french toast and bacon," she announced.

Francine's hands clasped together as she skipped over to her chair at the table.

"Thanks, Mama, you're the best."

Bettye Jo smiled. "Anything for my girl."

She turned back to the stove, preparing breakfast. Francine sipped her orange juice. They were silent for a while for yesterday was quite eventful, especially for Francine. She never had a birthday as she had yesterday. She never received any gifts, or a cake, or a card, or a party. Nothing at all. Her birthday was always another day in her life. Nothing special or eventful. An insignificant day in her life until yesterday, which was beyond her wildest dreams.

The woman who gave her life, supposed to love her the most, did nothing for her birthday. No acknowledgments, nothing, nada. All she cared about was alcohol, getting high, and screwing a different man every day. Men who abused her and that woman let it happen. *No more.* Francine thought pleasantly. *No one. It was going to end—finally!* She mused at the thought.

Also, this woman starved her, clad her in rags, let her live in filth and dirt for she did not bathe her or comfort her. Instead, she abused her for wanting what every child is entitled to—unconditional love, which she denied her and was incapable of giving to her.

In addition to her birthday, most important was that Philip proposed to Bettye Jo right in front of her and her friends. The two most wonderful events occurring in one day. It was simply amazing, too good to be true. Her parents, Bettye Jo, her foster/adoptive mother, and Philip, her birth father falling in love with each other being they knew each other for barely one day. Stranger than fiction. Francine was in a reverie, smiling at herself. This was not a dream or fantasy or wishful thinking.

"Honey?" Bettye Jo leaned toward her while tapping her shoulder. Francine's head was gazing about when her mother called her. Francine faced her.

"Are you okay? I was calling you. Daddy's on the phone," she stated.

"I'm sorry, Mama," she apologized. "I was just thinking—thinking wonderful, happy thoughts."

Bettye Jo smiled at her. "That's all right. You want to speak to him?" She handed her the telephone.

"Hi, Daddy!" she greeted her father brightly.

"Hi, princess!" he returned her greeting.

They spoke for a while as Bettye Jo continued preparing breakfast. After a few minutes they said goodbye and hung up.

"Breakfast is ready," Bettye Jo announced.

Francine sat in her seat. Bettye Jo handed it to her. Then she sat down across her daughter. They began eating slowly, but with daintiness. Bettye Jo began to speak, "Daddy is coming over at 12:00 p.m. to discuss the wedding. Also, he has boxes of gifts, cards, and letters he sent you, which came back to him. He saved them and wants you to have them. You do understand, don't you? At your leisure, you could sort through them and read everything he always wanted you to know, but as you already are aware, it was not his fault you never knew him. All these years, he has thought of you, wanting you to know he always loved you, and that someday, hopefully, you will get to know and meet him."

"Okay," Francine replied flatly. "I knew that since the day he appeared on our doorstep. He explained everything to me."

Bettye Jo patted her hand. "That's good, sweetheart." She was pleased with her daughter's attitude and understanding.

They resumed their meal in pleasant silence, but they were jubilant. Things were looking up for both.

12:00 p.m.

Francine and Bettye Jo were clearing the breakfast dishes from the table and stacked them in the dishwasher. The doorbell rang. Both turned from the kitchen.

Bettye Jo turned toward her daughter and asked her, "Could you please get that? I would like to freshen up for Daddy. Okay?"

Francine nodded with understanding. Bettye Jo headed upstairs.

She went to get the door. Philip smiled and had two bouquets of colorful flowers, one for Francine, and the other for Bettye Jo. Francine took them into the kitchen and laid them on the counter by the sink. She wanted to greet her father.

"Hi, Daddy!" She put her arms around him, and he swung her around by her hands. She squealed with delight. She never had that happen to her before.

"How's my princess?" he asked cheerfully, his pearly white teeth showing.

"Never better," she replied. "Mama went upstairs to fix herself up. She wants to look her best for you."

"Your mother always looks beautiful to me," he affirmed.

At that, Bettye Jo walked quietly down the steps. Her blonde hair fluffy and wavy around her face. She put on pearl button earrings and a cameo necklace. She was clad in a white halter top with black, flimsy slacks. She wore opened-toed sandals. Philip gazed up at her while Francine faced her mother.

Philip, with his arms out, walked up to her and gently put his hands on her face, kissing her passionately on the lips. Then she put her hands on his face. They did not move. They stood for like over a minute in that position. Francine observed them with awe, a smile, and her eyes lighting up with wonder.

"Come on, you guys," she giggled playfully.

Both turned to their daughter and laughed.

Francine motioned to them with her hand. "Look what Daddy got us, Mama," she indicated to where she put the flowers.

Bettye Jo saw the flowers. She walked over to the counter and smelled them. She sighed pleasantly, "Ah!"

"I'll tend to these," she mentioned. "In the meantime, why don't you two just sit and talk. You both have a lot to discuss."

Francine and Philip sat, facing each other.

Philip began, "I have a lot stuff for you that has accumulated these past ten years. I'm sure Mama told you."

Francine nodded agreeably but said nothing at first. Then she blurted out, "I cannot wait to see all of it. I am so happy."

Then Philip went on, "There is a lot of it, so I brought a few dollies. Do you want to help me, princess?"

Francine popped out of her chair, clapping her hands in the air. She wanted to so badly. "Yes, oh yes."

Philip got up and took his daughter's hand. As they headed out the door, he told Bettye Jo, "We'll be back soon, honey."

Bettye Jo turned and grinned. "All right, you guys." She went back to tend the flowers. Philip and Francine were already out the door. Bettye Jo smiled pleasantly as she put the flowers into vases and filled them with water. She placed them on the windowsill over the sink. *They are so beautiful*, she thought to herself.

Then she watched them from her kitchen window. Francine was skipping around and around on the sidewalk, her arms flying out in the air. Philip opened the trunk and took out some dollies and opened the trunk and emptied the boxes on the dollies. Francine gazed in wonder. So many of them, she mused with joy. So many presents all these years, and she had not known. But that was all in the past. This is the present, she surmised. She was speechless but joyful. She could hardly wait to open the boxes and read all the cards and letters. She knew it would take time, but she did not care. She was grateful and willing to be patient though everything was happening so fast. She needed a chance to imbibe everything in. She was his princess and to Bettye Jo, her girl. What more could she ask for?

Bettye Jo continued observing by the window. Francine was still jumping up and down with her hands together. Philip was piling the boxes on the dollies as though they were as light as a feather. Finally, he was finished and rubbed his brow with the back of his hand. "Woof," he stated breathlessly. He was tired but jubilant. He finally gave all his daughter's return-to-sender accumulated presents, cards, and letters to her to cherish. His mementos for her, expressing his deep love for her, which she was convinced of. She had all of it now to read, play with, use, collect, cherish, and enjoy for the rest of her life. Then he and Francine started wheeling the dollies in, one at a time, naturally. It would take a while, but that was fine with them. Though they were hot and exhausted, they were thrilled. Philip did what he intended to do. He put his arm around his daughter, and she did so, likewise smiling up at him as they entered the house. Bettye Jo was standing in the hallway greeting them.

"You poor dears," she noticed. "You must be exhausted. Here, let me give you fresh cold water." She offered them with concern.

Before they could answer her, they left the boxes by the door and walked into the kitchen. Philip had his hand on Francine's shoulder. As they sat down, Bettye Jo took out a pitcher of cold water and poured it into two glasses. They took their glasses and gingerly drank the water, which was very refreshing since they were outside doing all that lifting, carrying, and moving around. They thanked Bettye Jo for the water. She observed them with all her love, and they loved her in return.

"Thanks, honey," Philip graciously said as he winked at her. Then he turned to his daughter, "Mama and I have some issues to discuss now. But later, we will call you to come downstairs to inform you of our plans for you and us. You could, if you want, take any boxes upstairs so you could occupy yourself. I'll help you with the rest later, okay?" He put his hand on hers as she rose from her chair. Francine piped up with a smile, "You don't have to help me with them, Daddy. I will come down and get the rest of them when I am finished with the ones I now have. I do not mind taking several trips up and down the stairs. I would be delighted to use the dollies. Thanks, anyway. See you both later, you guys."

Philip replied, "Fine, princess."

Francine sorted through the boxes, trying to decide which ones to pick first. She did, and then pranced up the stairs like a gazelle, eager to see what Philip had for her all these years. Her heart bounded with joy. Philip and Bettye Jo watched her with amazement as she went into her bedroom and shut the door quietly. She plopped on her bed and began opening the boxes fervently.

"She's quite a girl," Philip remarked agreeably.

"That she is," Bettye Jo affirmed.

They turned and faced each other with sparkling eyes melting together.

Bettye Jo rose from her seat and offered, "Philip, would you like some coffee? I'll put the kettle on."

Philip nodded, still watching her every movement, completely mesmerized by this woman who loved his daughter—no, their daughter. Bettye Jo gazed at him, smiling, as she prepared the coffee. Philip leaned his chin with his arm on the table unmoving.

Meanwhile, Francine was in her bedroom furiously and eagerly opening the boxes. She reached inside a carton and saw a Chatty Cathy doll, a Betsy Wetsy doll, a Thumbelina doll, a Tressy doll with a hair setting and styling kit, a Tammy doll, Barbie and Ken dolls with clothes for them, a tea set, Nancy Drew and the Bobbsey Twins book series, a magic set, and a jewelry-making kit.

Then she realized, there are more boxes downstairs. She skipped out of her room and galloped down the stairs as she breathed heavily, dragging the dolly in front of her. She saw her parents sitting at the table drinking coffee. "Hi, guys!" she greeted breathlessly with a wave of joy and excitement. She went to get some more boxes with some struggle, yet she managed to get them up the stairs to her bedroom. Philip observed her and offered again to help her, but Francine was insistent, adamant, determined, perseverant, and a go-getter. Graciously, she declined his offer with a gleeful smile and continued up the stairs. The boxes slipped off the dolly, but she was so eager and impatient. Her heart was beating like a drum, but she managed.

"Stubborn just like her father," Bettye Jo remarked, shaking her head gleefully at Francine and then to Philip.

"I know," Philip agreed. "That she is. But, also, very loving and sweet just as her mother." He patted Bettye Jo's hand with love.

They both laughed seeing their daughter so happy and excited. Their pride and joy. Then they resumed drinking their coffee, discussing the future for their daughter and each other. There was a lot of arrangements and decisions to be made. Thus, they needed time for themselves.

While in her bedroom, she zealously ripped opened more boxes. One box contained a concentration game, word-for-word game, Jeopardy game, and a password game. There was a doll house, a weaving set, jigsaw puzzles, a mosaic tile set, follow-the-dots and crossword puzzle books, paper dolls set, colored pencils, fairy-tale books, and a perfume kit. There was still more, she sighed breathlessly but quite contentedly—colored barrettes, bows, and headbands.

Among the boxes, she found bunches of letters and cards. *So many*, she thought to herself. *It will take forever for me to read them all. That is all right*, she continued to think. She was not in any hurry. She did sort through some of the greeting cards, which were bright and cheerful. They had pictures of little girls smiling brightly. "To My Princess," the cards always began. And they ended, "With love always,

Daddy." Francine read it over and over, each card practically. She smiled to herself pleasantly—all this accumulated over the past ten years of her life. So much catching up had to be done. And it will, she surmised, convincingly to herself. No one and nothing will ever come between Francine, Philip, her birth father, Bettye Jo, her foster/adoptive mother. They were the team. Together they stood, always and forever. Francine wanted the world to know how happy and loved she was. She gazed around her bedroom at all her stuff. So much to take in and absorb, but it did not matter. She was a very fortunate young lady. She knew that. She always was, but now, she was sure. She loved and was loved, she sighed continually to the air, looking up, then out her bedroom window. The sun shone brightly from the clear blue sky, just for her, she mused cheerfully. Yes, indeed, as she leaned on her hands on the windowsill gazing at the breath-taking scenery with much awe and pleasure.

Suddenly, Francine heard knocking on her bedroom door. She skipped with hands swinging back and forth at her sides as she opened the door. It was Bettye Jo. "Honey, how are you doing? You must be quite overwhelmed with all the gifts and cards Daddy sent you."

Francine jumped up, clasping her hands playfully. "Oh yes, Mama. I am."

Bettye Jo grinned happily and extended her hand. "Let us go downstairs now. Daddy and I want to speak to you about arrangements for the future. Okay?"

Francine affirmed with a nod and then she took her mother's hand, and they went down the stairs, hand in hand. Philip looked up at them from his chair with amazement on his face. They winked and smiled at him.

When they reached the bottom of the staircase, Philip got up and led them to their chairs. He pulled them out, first to Bettye Jo, and then, Francine. He wanted to make sure they were comfortable. They all sat around the table saying nothing at first and just stared at each other. No one knew how to start. Philip fidgeted with his hands on the table. His head was down. Bettye Jo nudged him. "You go." Then he looked at her, "All right, sweetheart." She nodded agreeably. He turned toward Francine and began hesitantly with his hands clasped, "About your . . ." He stopped himself by covering his mouth with his hand, realizing his mistake, then went on, "Leonora was a very sick woman. She never knew her father. Her mother and she were trailer trash. She brought home good-for-nothing men who were abusive to her. Leonora was abused by her mother as well. Her mother smoked weed and pot and took other drugs. Leonora lived in filth and barely ate. When Leonora was sixteen, she dropped out of school and ran away. She never saw or heard from her mother again. I met her at a public dance. She was beautiful, fun, cheerful, and lively, always smiling. I loved her and I thought she loved me. We got married. I told her I planned to go to medical school to become a psychiatrist. She was willing to work three jobs to pay for it in addition to rent, food, clothes, and utilities. At first, everything was fine. Then, she became pregnant with you. She said it was a very painful delivery, and she was in agony all the time. The shit hit the fan. She would accuse me of doing nothing to help with the apartment and you and that all I cared about was medical school. She would kick and punch me, but I did not do anything. I tried to explain that being a psychiatrist was very important to me. It was to be my career, and I had to work hard, but she was not listening. She abused and neglected you, and I was unable to protect or support you. She threw all my stuff out while physically assaulting me. I was helpless. I tried to contact you, but Leonora was always moving around from one shit hole to another, avoiding the landlords." He paused while drumming his fingers on the table. Francine listened attentively. Now she understood why Leonora was the way she was. She felt sorry for her. She did not hate her or hold any bitterness in her heart. She was mentally ill and needed help.

"Well, that is all in the past," Philip stated. Then he resumed, "Mama and I want to get married in the summer after you finish the eighth grade. A lot of preparations need to be made, and we want to make sure everything is done right and being taken care of correctly. We do not want to rush, and we want you to know that you will always come first with us and that you are happy, okay, princess?"

Francine smiled and nodded. "Of course, Daddy."

Philip and Bettye Jo affirmed in agreement.

"You know we both love you and that will never change. You are the reason for all of this. Your mother and I love each other, but you already know that, of course. We did not mean for it to happen, but it did, and we are happy it did. We were very lucky."

Bettye Jo put her hand on Philip's arm gently, and then she spoke, "I think it is about time we spoke of our families. I do not think Francine really knows anything for she never asked, and we did not think to volunteer any information or be pushy or forceful and to wait for the right time when she was ready. But, Philip, I think now is as good as time as any," she staunchly stated.

Philip agreed, "Right, dear." He looked at Bettye Jo and then he turned toward Francine. She said nothing for a while but was willing to hear about her parents' families. After all, they were her families, too. She had a right to know.

"You were named after my mother, your grandmother. Her name is Frances. She and my father, thus, your grandfather, are alive but live in a nursing home. Your grandfather has dementia. He does not remember who you are. I am sorry to say. He would have loved you. Your grandmother has severe arthritis and is unable to take care of herself. She does know about you. After all, you are her namesake. If you would like, I could take you there to meet them. My mother does love you and always had, though, she has not seen you since you were a baby. She would love to see you. Would you like to, princess?" he offered.

Francine listened carefully. *Why not?* she thought. It has been years. She affirmed with a nod. Philip was pleased. He wanted his daughter to meet his parents, her grandparents, even if they were incapacitated and may not have much longer to live. Francine was their only grandchild.

"Yes, Daddy, I would be delighted."

Philip nodded and agreed. "All right, fine." Then he paused and turned from his daughter and continued to drum his fingertips on the tabletop. "There's more," he resumed. "Also, you have an uncle, my younger brother, Paul." He hesitated for he really did not have anything positive to tell her. He did not want Francine to know that Paul was irresponsible, self-centered, and cared nothing about his family and that he was not interested in meeting his only niece and his new to-be sister-in-law. Bettye Jo knew this and accepted it. It did bother her a little, but she acted nonchalantly. She hardly thought about the brother Philip never really had a tight bond with. How would Francine feel and react? Would she go back into her shell, being she was just getting to know and trust people again? Or would she be accepting and understanding, as was her nature. Bettye Jo and Philip hoped her new uncle's demeanor would not set her back. Would she want to have some sort of a bond with a reckless and self-absorbed uncle? They pondered this situation for a while. Everyone was silent, not knowing what to say or do next. Francine sat at the table, watching her parents gaze at each other, saying not a word. But she was curious about her father's brother, her uncle, whatever he was. Was he horrible, bad, or abusive? Did he kill someone or was he a drug addict or an alcoholic, or did he do harm to anyone? She considered all these questions. Still, she wanted to know, whatever her uncle was, she will try to accept it. She will understand and not make judgments.

"Tell me," she leaned forward, speaking softly. "I'll understand. No matter what it is. I won't be upset," she promised earnestly. "I do have a right to know. He is my uncle, your brother. We are family."

"Paul is not a bad or horrible person. He never harmed anybody," he went on carefully but firmly. "But he is not a responsible person. He is very reckless and impulsive. He could be very charming. But he only cares about himself. He hardly visits or contacts me or our parents. He would never ask about his family and was never concerned that our parents might not live much longer. All he thinks about is going to bars and drinking with his buddies who are no better than he is. He picks up girls just for a laugh and a good time. He never had a serious relationship with any one girl. At least, he is honest about that. I did tell him about you and Mama, but he paid me no heed and showed no interest. I do not want you to take this personally. It has nothing to do with you or Mama. It is about him. That is just his nature and he does not know what he is missing out on. You and your mother mean the world to me. I love both of you. I do not dislike my brother, but I do not approve of his behavior and self-absorbed attitude. I tried at times to help him see the errors of his ways. At every time, he would laugh aloud, shrug it off, grin, and slap me on the back playfully, as though life was a lark. He would say I was no fun to be with and that I should get a life and not be so serious. I resigned

myself to the situation. He was and is what he is. I am not angry just disappointed.
I hope you understand."

Francine was listening and still not responding.

"I feel very bad, Daddy. I do. But if you and Mama can accept it without upset
or judgment, I can, too. Still, I would like to meet him anyway. I really do." She
pointed out plaintively. "Even if he is not especially concerned and interested, I
would like to see him, just once, okay, Daddy? Technically, he is my uncle. We
are family—by blood, anyway."

Philip listened to his daughter. Such a mature, caring young lady and at her
age. He was proud of her and was honored to be her father. He patted her hand.

"I will see what I can do, okay? I cannot promise you anything, but I will do
the best that I can," he stated firmly.

She patted his hand back and smiled, eyes sparkling as stars. "All right."

Everyone was satisfied.

Philip then turned to Bettye Jo and began, "Now, it is your turn." She
consented and started. She leaned over to her daughter, and she began, "Let
us talk in your bedroom. All right?" Francine consented, and Bettye Jo turned
toward Philip, "Francine and I will be upstairs, okay, dear?"

Philip replied while drumming his fingertips on the tabletop, "Yes. Also, I
think I will make some coffee while you ladies talk."

Both mother and daughter smiled at him as they headed up the stairs. Bettye
Jo closed the bedroom door. They lay back on the bed to get comfortable. Bettye
Jo began, "My parents—your grandparents—died a while ago. They were in their
fifties and were not married even thirty years, but they loved each other dearly.
They had a good marriage. I am sorry you never got to know them. They would
be so proud of you and would have loved you as I do, but unfortunately, that did
not happen or turn out the way it was meant to be. That was very unfortunate for
they succumbed to cancer. They died peacefully in their sleep. Their suffering
ended. No more pain. They died within months of each other. They were in
hospitals and doctors' offices all the time. At home, they were bedridden and
could not tend to their own needs. I went to their house a lot and had nurses care
for them. They were good, decent people, especially to me and my sister, whom I
never spoke about. We were never close. She was three years younger than I was.
I do not hate her, but I can, sadly but honestly, say we had nothing in common.
She claimed I was the favorite child, and she did not get a fair deal. That was not
true, but I could never tell her anything, for she would get her back up and stamp
her feet, slam things, and yell and cry out that she was not loved. She always
demanded her own way and refused to see the error of her ways. She was unable
to understand that other people could have an opinion that is right for them even
if she disagreed. She had no empathy and was always obstinate and demanding.
So, giving in to her was easier than dealing with her temper tantrums, raging
outbursts, and ungovernable disposition. No one could reach her, and she would

shut everybody out. She was in her little orbit and content with that. She happened to be a very pretty girl, but too bad, she had a personality disorder. Our parents took her to doctors, but that did not seem to help her or those around her. As of now, she is a photojournalist and gets to travel to different places around the world. She happens to be very good and successful at her career. I could practically say I am happy about that. As for her personal relationships, she never had any girlfriends, and as for men, she used them for her own selfish pleasures. I really am embarrassed and hate to say it since she is my sister, but she was and still is sexually active, to phrase it in a nice way, gently and kindly without bitterness. I do not remember the last time we spoke. I do not think I would even recognize her if I passed her in the street," she concluded.

Again, Francine listened to what her mother had to say about her sister. It was a shame, she pondered, to not be close with your own sister, but she did insist that she meet this aunt who was completely oblivious to everyone and everybody, except herself. But Francine was curious. This was her aunt, her family. She stood her ground firmly.

Bettye Jo hated to disappoint her daughter, but she honestly did not know how to go about her request. She did not even have a clue to where her sister was and had no contact information or a way to find her.

"Tell me her name, Mama," she asked firmly, but quietly. "I would like to try. I could go online in the library. Please, Mama," she implored softly.

"Ellen Clarke," Bettye Jo answered matter-of-factly, though reluctantly. Then she added, "I do not want you to get hurt. She may very well upset or intimidate you. I am sure of it, and I am afraid for you. She always had such a violent temper. I do not believe she has changed," Bettye Jo stated firmly. "But I do hope she has for your sake." She was not convinced or believed it. Still, she prayed hard that it would be true.

"I know you do not want me to get upset or be unhappy, and I do appreciate your concern and that you do love me and want me to be happy. But Ellen, as well as Paul, are my family, technically speaking. She is your sister despite everything. I will be careful; I can handle myself. I am practically a woman now, Mama. I could do this. I am sure of it."

"I know, honey," she confirmed. "I know you are, but you have been through so much. And I do not want to see all that hard work go to waste. Your progress in dealing with your life at this point is amazing and surprising. You are a very sweet and lovely girl, but I am just being a mother, your mother, and I have the right to worry. That is my job. You do understand?"

"And you do it very well. Too well, in fact," she said with a small giggle. "And yes, Mama, I know it very well, and appreciate it. But let me do this, please, Mama. For you and for me."

Bettye Jo resigned herself but was so pleased with her daughter. She is growing up. She mused, smiling at herself and then at Francine.

"Okay, honey," she put her hand on her shoulder.

Then afterward, she brought up Philip's presents, cards, and letters. "What do you think of all the stuff Daddy brought you? Were you surprised? How did you feel? You must be overwhelmed with joy," she surmised.

"I was so gleeful with happiness. I simply could not believe it. All these years!" she cried out, her eyes lit as captive stars, her hands together, pressing against her chest.

"I bet you are!" Bettye Jo stated agreeably.

"However," Francine thought, "a lot of them, such as all the dolls, tea set, and doll house—do not get me wrong. I love them, but I do feel I am a little too old for them. Then, I thought, I would like to donate them to the children's shelter where I used to live. The children would make good use of them," she reasoned brightly. "A lot of them do not really have many playthings, so I feel they would be very surprised and happy to get them."

Bettye Jo ran up to her daughter and gave her a hug. "Oh, honey, I am so proud of you. You are such a wonderful girl to donate your playthings to children who are less fortunate than you. Giving away toys that you are too old for, doing it for a worthy cause—poor, needy children having what they never had in their young lives. I cannot believe what a lovely young girl you are! I am raising the best daughter ever! I am so lucky!" she exclaimed with enlightenment.

Francine was surprised, though she returned her mother's embrace. She was speechless but elated. She put her personal but wonderful situation to good use. Benefiting and helping the unfortunate as she was, but now it was her time to reciprocate. She knew how these children felt. She wanted their lives to be joyful, just as hers is now filled with love.

Both mother and daughter stood in their embracing positions, happy and loved. Then, they stepped back and held each other's hands clasped together, their eyes interlocking joyfully at each other.

"Let's go tell Daddy about your plan, all right, honey?" she turned to her daughter. "He will be so pleased with you. What a fine young lady you are," she affirmed proudly. Then she took her hand and let her go downstairs, her arm around her shoulder. As they headed down the stairs, Philip looked up at them, and they winked at him with grinning faces. *What are you two up to?* he wanted to ask them. *What is happening?* No one spoke for like a minute or so until they reached the bottom step. Philip rose from his chair. Bettye Jo had both her hands on Francine's shoulders and nudged her to start. "Go on." She looked at Francine with a bright smile. "Tell him what you told me upstairs," she gently prodded her.

"Daddy," Francine began, "I simply love all the presents you got me through these past ten years. But I feel some might be too juvenile. Some I feel are for little girls, and I am a big girl, a woman, but you already know that. So, I decided to give them to the children at the shelter where I used to live. I do not want them to be deprived of having their own playthings just because they are poor orphans.

They deserve a chance at a good life filled with happiness and love as I am. What do you think?" she asked her father.

Philip's eyes blazed open, and he smiled at his daughter. "That is a simply terrific idea: donating toys you are too old for those unfortunate children who have hardly anything. You are a wonderful young lady to help children who need love and caring as you once did, but do not anymore. You want them to experience joy and pleasure as you are doing now. How did I ever get such a terrific daughter?" he asked rhetorically.

Bettye Jo chimed in, "I practically said the same things you did, Philip." They both gazed lovingly at their daughter, who hugged both her parents, and they did so, in return.

7:00 p.m. After Supper

Bettye Jo and Francine cleared the table and brought the plates, glasses, and utensils to the sink to rinse and put into the dishwasher. Philip sat and glanced at his watch.

"It is getting late, ladies," he addressed them pleasantly. "It has been a great day, but I am getting tired and think I should start for home before I hit traffic." He got up and kissed Bettye Jo on the lips. "Good night, honey."

And to his daughter whom he patted on the head as they hugged, he addressed with love, "Good night, princess."

Then he looked up at both mother and daughter and said, "I love you both all the way to Pluto and back." They nodded and smiled as they bid him good night. He got his hat and coat from the closet, waved as he opened the front door, and they waved back. It was the end of a wonderful day.

Bettye Jo and Francine went back to finish cleaning up after supper. They stacked the dishes, glasses, and silverware into the dishwasher, and then pressed the "start" button and the wash cycle started. They wiped their hands in dish towels. They were through for the day. So much excitement happening all at once to take in. But it was a simply enlightened weekend for the three of them.

Bettye Jo went into the living room to pick out a DVD movie. She felt like relaxing with a movie to watch. She asked Francine if she wanted to watch one with her for she wanted company as well as mother/daughter time. Francine was heading upstairs. She was exhausted from the last two days. She did not want to hurt her mother's feelings, but she really wanted to go to her bedroom and start reading her father's letters and cards.

"Do not be offended, Mama," she assured her. "It would be nice for us to watch a movie together, but I am very tired from this weekend, though it was the best. But I really would like to start reading Daddy's cards and letters for there are so many of them. I hope you are not upset. That is the last thing I would ever do to you," she sincerely stated.

Bettye Jo smiled while sitting on the couch. "No I am not insulted. No offense taken, honey. I would like for you to read Daddy's letters and cards. I know you are eager to do so, being there are so many of them, so it will be best if you started now. We could always watch a movie together anytime," she stated a matter-of-factly without feeling resentful or neglected. And she did not. Not at all.

"I am glad, Mama. It was such a joyous weekend." Francine yawned and covered her mouth. "I will say good night now, okay, Mama?" she offered with kindness and sincerity. Then she walked up to her and they embraced and kissed each other's cheeks. Bettye Jo patted her back gently. "That's my girl!" she announced with pride and joy.

"I love you, honey," Bettye Jo said adamantly, but with joy.

"Me, too, Mama," she said in return.

Each bid the other good night.

Bettye Jo chose a movie while Francine headed upstairs to her bedroom and closed her door quietly.

Two Weeks Later: Saturday 9:00 a.m.

Bettye Jo and Francine were clearing the breakfast dishes. Everything was rinsed and stacked into the dishwasher.

Francine went to the library to search for Bettye Jo's sister. Bettye Jo gave Francine her credit card that was only to be used for important expenses though she knew and had confidence that her daughter would not take advantage of it or squander it on frivolous pursuits. She trusted her completely, so she gave her permission to use it online to find her sister. Francine felt great and very happy for her mother completely understood her desire to find an aunt, her sister, whom she was sorry to say she was did not have a tight bond. But Francine was determined and stubborn, meant as a compliment.

She had made some progress. She was determined. Already she saw a photograph of her aunt—blonde hair in a shoulder-length pageboy, large brown eyes, button nose, perky lips. She was very pretty, just as Bettye Jo described her. Hopefully, she had changed. Also, she saw a list of her work credentials. She was indeed talented. And that was enough for now.

Bettye Jo left to open her flower shop to let her employees in to start the day's business. Philip promised to call them tonight to inform them of his plans to visit his parents. Also, he was not intending to give up on his laid-back brother as he had done in the past. He was going to visit their parents and meet his daughter and soon-to-be wife. No more, Philip meant it this time. Paul was not going to spoil it for anyone ever again as he did in the past where Philip always let it slide. That is all over now. Never again.

Also, more important, Philip called the children's shelter this morning informing them that Francine had a lot of playthings for the children, and he and his daughter offered to drive over and bring them. The staff was delighted. Mrs. Playne was still there, and luckily, she planned to stay this evening to receive the playthings. She remembered Francine very well and could not wait to see her. Philip told her she was growing up to be a very well-adjusted, mature young lady of whom he and Bettye Jo were very proud. He told her about their upcoming wedding plans. Perhaps, she will attend the wedding this summer.

2:00 p.m.

Francine came home from the library very excited. She found an address in Greenwich Village where all the starving artists and writers lived working menial jobs to support their supposed careers, trying to become well-known and famous.

Luckily, Ellen was not starving waiting tables or working temp jobs. She happened to be very successful as a photojournalist. Francine was unable to get a landline telephone number because her telephone was always disconnected or out of order and she was hardly home. She did have a smart phone, but she often had it turned off and very rarely checked her voice mail. Ellen did have an email address at the Internet cafe, and she did check it a few times a week where she always ate her breakfast.

Francine decided to send her an email and to write a letter sent via certified mail to her home address. She could hardly wait. She included her home and cell phone numbers. She began enthusiastically, her heart pounding.

In the meantime, Philip was in his apartment at his desk sorting papers. He found his brother's telephone number and began dialing. He knew exactly what he wanted to say. There was no turning back now, and he had no intention of backing down. He knew that for sure. "Here goes," he decided adamantly. *Ring, ring, ring.* "Come on, you son of a bitch," he murmured to himself. *Ring, ring, ring.* Then he got the machine. In a laughing, stupid, frivolous voice, he heard his brother's voice—that voice again, he stated disgustedly, "Hello," the high-pitched voice started, "sorry to have missed your call, ha ha. I am not available to take your call. Very busy, ha! ha! Well, what can I say? Please leave a message," he said, still laughing hysterically without a care. "Hope to hear from you," he said, giggling uncontrollably. "Bye now." Philip refused to be deterred, so he annoyingly began, "Listen, you son of a bitch. I know you are doing nothing useful. And I do not want to hear any stories of your latest twelve-year-old bimbos. I know you do not give a good goddamn about anyone but yourself, but you listen to me, and you listen well. I am only going to say this one time and one time only, and you are going to oblige by it. I plan to visit Mom and Dad in the nursing home next Saturday. They are getting on in years and might not have much time left, so try to be a human being for once in your life and you better be there. For them, if not for me. Also, you have a niece, my daughter, Francine, who for some strange reason wants to meet you, being she knows about you. You just better understand that. I am not going to disappoint her or let you hurt her. She has been through a lot. She is a wonderful young lady, a sweet, sensitive person, I am proud to call my daughter. Lastly, Bettye Jo, her foster mother, and my soon-to-be wife, wants to meet you. She, too, knows about you and accepts your selfish, arrogant attitude, but I want you to meet her nonetheless and you will. I will not let you upset the two most precious, important people I love the most in the world. And if you do not show up at the home next Saturday by 7:00 p.m., I plan to take a drive down to your shithole of an apartment and I am going to grab you by your ear as Mom did when you deliberately disobeyed her when you were a little boy and bodily shove your sorry ass into my car. I do not care about making a scene. Let everyone know what you are. It serves you right, you son of a bitch," he reiterated on the telephone. He left his telephone number and hung up. He smiled victoriously. He was pleased with himself. Finally! He said what he had to say. Then he thought, "I should have done this years ago. But unfortunately, I did not. Those days are over and gone for good. No more Mr. Nice Guy," he sighed as he looked up at the ceiling. He got up away from his desk and went into his bedroom to fix himself up. He washed his face and hands and combed his hair. He put on fresh clothes. He was going out to buy flowers for Bettye Jo and Francine and have them delivered tonight. He planned to surprise them with his good news. Knowing she was at her flower shop, he called the house. Francine was home. He would tell her himself that he will be there tonight for dinner. He said nothing more, and she promised herself she would not share her news about Bettye Jo's sister. She wanted to surprise her mother and so did he. He ended the call by reminding his daughter about their 6:00 p.m. appointment to donate the toys to the children's shelter. She could hardly wait until it was 5:00 p.m. He was coming over, and they would spend time together. She was not able to contain her excitement over today's events. She started on her letter to Ellen Clarke. On Monday, after school, she planned to take her letter to the post office and send it certified receipt and then go to the library and send her an email. She wanted to get the ball running. She was so eager.

5:00 p.m.

Bettye Jo and Philip were sitting at the kitchen table, waiting for Francine to come down the stairs. She and Philip were just about to head to the children's shelter. Philip had helped her bring the toys downstairs. They were stacked near the front door. Francine gallantly pounced down the stairs, clad in a long-sleeved pink T-shirt with the word "Love" across it and in denim jeans. Her hair was in a messy bun with a pink scrunchie around it. She and Philip shared a smile. Bettye Jo was oblivious to it. After Philip and Francine came back from the children's shelter, they planned to order in pizza for everyone was tired from their long but exciting and joyful day.

Philip stood up when she was downstairs. She grabbed her jacket and put all the toys on the dollies while heading out the door. They smiled at Bettye Jo, who was watching them, and they bid each other goodbye. Bettye Jo sighed pleasantly and went to the window and saw them fill the trunk and then head off in the car. *What are they up to?* she wondered. *What could it be? Probably something nice*, she mused convincingly with a gleam in her eyes. Then she walked away from the window and sat down and reached for today's newspaper and started reading though her mind really was not into it. She took a pencil and worked on the crossword puzzle to pass the time. A few minutes later, she heard the doorbell. *Who could it be?* She questioned herself. She was not expecting anybody. She went to push the curtain away and saw a deliveryman holding two colorful bouquets of flowers. She smiled to herself. The man announced, "Delivery for Bettye Jo and Francine."

"Oh!" she exclaimed quietly as she took them and thanked him. She shut the door. She put her nose to them. "What a pleasant aroma." She took each card and read them. One was for her, the other for Francine. "Oh, how wonderful." Bettye Jo was joyful. She took them to the sink, took out two vases, and filled them with cold water. She cut their bottoms and gently put each bouquet in a vase. She placed them on the kitchen table and glanced lovingly at them. "How thoughtful of him. What a wonderful, loving man he is." The cards read: "To My Very Lovely Ladies, Forever and Ever." They were in Philip's handwriting. Then, she surmised, "So this was the surprise." She again figured it out. *Well, it sure is a pleasant one,* she continued, thinking pleasantly to herself.

While in the car, Philip turned to his daughter, "She will be really surprised later."

Then she acknowledged, "Yes, she will, definitely."

Both smiled, agreeing with each other. Then, Francine popped up, "And the day is not yet over."

Philip nodded with a grin as he resumed his driving. Both father and daughter rode in silence, smiling to themselves while stealing glances at each other.

As Philip turned right, Francine excitedly said while pointing her finger, "There it is!"

"Yes, princess, we are here!"

They drove into the parking lot. Francine jumped out of the car and ran to the trunk. Philip opened it, and they eagerly got all the playthings set on the dollies. They simply could not wait to donate Francine's toys to the children. She wanted them to be happy and enjoy themselves. Thus, she and Philip rushed to the entrance and rang the bell. A lady holding a broom greeted them.

"Is Mrs. Playne on? She is expecting us."

The lady smiled and let them in. Indeed, Mrs. Playne stood by a desk with a pleasant greeting.

"Francine!" she exclaimed, her arms out. She gave her a hug. "You have grown so much. You are so pretty!" Then she saw Philip and stated, "And you are her father." She extended her hand, and they shook.

Philip smiled. "It is a pleasure to meet you. My daughter spoke very highly of you."

Then Mrs. Playne noticed the two dollies filled with the toys and exclaimed, "How wonderful of you both to donate all this stuff. We will have some men come and fetch it. The children will be so happy. A lot of them hardly have anything in their lives, so it is so good that people as yourselves are kind and generous to the less fortunate."

"It was Francine's idea," he mentioned, glancing at his daughter lovingly.

"Yes, she is quite a young lady, so mature and loving for someone of her age. Most girls her age is self-centered and only care about themselves. But not Francine. You must be so proud, Dr. Marsowe, to have such a wonderful daughter."

Philip nodded and smiled and then glanced at his watch.

"Yes, I am. But it is getting late. Bettye Jo is expecting us. We are having pizza. We have a lot to discuss."

Mrs. Playne understood. "Yes, I am sure you do, Dr. Marsowe." She extended her hand again and again they smiled at each other. "It was a pleasure," and to Francine, she patted her shoulder gently, "Goodbye and good luck, honey."

Francine smiled back to her and bid each other pleasantries. Francine and Philip exited the building.

7:30 p.m. After Dinner

Francine and Bettye Jo cleared the table and threw all the paper plates and plastic knives and forks and discarded them into the garbage disposal. Bettye Jo smiled at Philip, "Thank you so much, Philip. Those flowers are beautiful. Francine and I were very surprised and overjoyed."

"Anything for my sweet, special, lovely ladies," he remarked gleefully.

A few minutes later, the three of them sat around the table, each coaching each other to begin their news.

Philip piped up, "Ladies, I called the Crestville Nursing Home this morning. I informed the staff that I plan to visit my parents and that you two will there at 7:00 p.m. next Saturday."

Both Bettye Jo and Francine sat listening to him and agreed to go with him to visit his parents. They could hardly wait for they have never met any of Philip's family.

"But," he continued with slight hesitation and caution, "I tried reaching Paul, but naturally he did not pick up. As you know, that is to be expected of him.

However, I left an extremely terse, adamant message on his machine stating that he is to be at the nursing home next Saturday night, and that I will no longer stand for any of his shenanigans or lame, hollow excuses." He said to Francine, "I told him about you wanting to see him since I told him you knew about him, but you were very insistent and that I will not let him disappoint you and that you are a great daughter. I will not cave into him any longer. That is over. I also warned him that if he does not show up, I will drive down to his crumby rack shambled pitiful excuse for an apartment and bodily drag him to see our parents. I am not kidding. No more. I am through." He paused to catch his breath, but was feeling triumphant.

Francine gleamed and jumped out of her chair and gave Philip a high-five. "Way to go, Daddy!"

He laughed and turned toward his daughter. "And what have you been up to today, young lady?" he asked with pleasant anticipation.

Francine started, her hands clasped on the table. "I found Ellen's email and postal addresses. It took some time online. I sent an email to her while I was in the library. When I got home, I wrote to her home address in Soho. Monday, after school, I am going to the post office to send the letter certified receipt. I did make copies of Ellen's accomplishments. There was a photograph of her. Would you two like to see it?" She reached into her pants pocket and handed it to Bettye Jo, then to Philip.

They looked at it, and Bettye Jo admittedly remarked, "She was always very pretty, and she still is." Then sadly, she mused aloud, "For your sake, Francine, I hope she has changed. To be frank, I would not really bank on it, but you wanted to know her, and I do not want you to be hurt. You know I love you, and I allowed this for that very reason, but I cannot help having reservations. You understand, honey?"

"I know, Mama," she acknowledged, reassuring her. "I am a big girl now I am not a kid anymore."

Bettye Jo smiled proudly at her daughter and patted her hand. "I know that you are, but I am just doing my motherly job of worrying. If she does or says anything to intimidate you, you tell me, okay?"

"Yes, Mama, I promise." Bettye Jo patted her hand. "That's my girl."

Philip watched their encounter then looked at his watch. "My lovely ladies," he addressed them. "It is getting late and I would like to get going before the traffic and I am tired, but a good tiredness. It was a lovely evening." He rose and kissed Bettye Jo on her lips, and naturally, she reciprocated. Then to Francine, who was observing them, "Good night, princess."

She grabbed his hand. "You, too, Daddy." He opened the door, turned, and waved and they did so likewise. He was gone.

Bettye Jo turned to her daughter and offered, "Would you like to watch a movie together—spend some mother/daughter quality time?"

Francine gleefully replied, her eyes lighting up and her hands together, "Oh yes, Mama. I would love to!"

Bettye Jo took her by the hand and headed toward the living room. Francine plopped down on the couch. Bettye Jo selected a movie entitled *Family Holiday*. They both agreed. Bettye Jo inserted it into the DVD player. Then she sat down on the couch. Bettye Jo put her arms on Francine's shoulder, patting it lovingly as she clicked on the remote. Francine leaned back on her mother's bosom. "My girl," she sighed enlightened as her daughter smiled up at her. They watched the movie.

Sunday, After Breakfast, 10:00 a.m.

Francine, clad in a puffed long-sleeved floral peasant blouse, with light blue denim jeans, pounced gallantly down the stairs, her hair in a messy bun surrounded with a red scrunchie, grinning gleefully as Bettye Jo watched her.

"Willow's mother is picking me, Stephanie, and Arlene up soon. We are going to the mall. They are having a sale on some cool DVDs," she announced.

"Fine, honey," she consented. Then she went on, "Daddy called while you were upstairs after you finished your breakfast. He is coming over this afternoon. He is taking me to a Broadway show and dinner afterward. We will be home late. You and your friends could eat whatever you want. But please, call me every so often so I will know you are all right and where you are, okay, honey?"

"Yes, Mama, certainly," she replied with gaiety.

They heard a honk outside. Francine walked to the window. It was Willow's mom, who waved at her, which she acknowledged, "Be right there, guys," she informed them. Then she turned toward her mother. "Bye, Mama." She hugged and kissed her mother's cheek, and her mother then gently touched her shoulder and smiled. "Have a good day. Love you all the way to Pluto and back."

"Me, too, Mama!" She flew out the door.

Bettye Jo watched her, smiling and sighing joyfully. She went back to the table and opened the newspaper, looking for the crossword puzzle and began doing it with zealousness. It was her pasttime for she had read that all puzzles made the brain active and alive. She got very absorbed in the puzzle that she nearly forgot that Philip will be picking her up, and she wanted to be ready for him. She looked at the wall clock and gasped, her hand to her mouth. *I must get ready and look my best for Philip. He will be here shortly.* She laid the newspaper on the table and went upstairs. She had lots to do to make herself special for her fiancé and soon-to-be husband.

She breezily but flippantly ran her fingers through her closet, searching for something appropriate to wear on her date with Philip. She wanted it to be special for both, so she had to look her best. Finally, she found a hot pink crepe flowing pants suit with a halter top that showed off her cleavage. She gazed at it with awe, her eyes blazingly bright. "He will love this!" she thought, shaking with excitement. She pulled it off the hanger for she could not wait. Hastily, she tore off her housecoat and flung it on the bed. She was so jubilant. *Wait till Philip sees this*, she thought as she gazed into her long wall mirror, fixing and straightening the front down flat. She posed, hands on her hips, and turned from side to side, eyes gleaming, smiling, very pleased with herself. "Ah!" she sighed quite contently, swaying back and forth, twirling around and around. She chose white sling-back, medium-heeled shoes that she slid on her feet. "This is it," she announced silently. Then she saw her hair needed touching up. She gently ran a brush through it, making sure each strand was combed perfectly and all fluffed up surrounding her face. She turned to see if the back was puffed in place. Satisfied, she sprayed it. *Perfect!* she mused. Just as if she came from the beauty parlor.

Now for her face—she considered as she sat at her vanity table reaching for her foundation that she dabbed on and smoothed around her face. She took blush and patted each part of her face. She glowed in the mirror. As for her eyes, she brushed blue eye shadow on her lids. Afterward, she eye-lined the bottom of her lids carefully. Then with her eyelashes, she curled them until they fluttered up and down. Lastly, she chose a light pink lipstick and smeared it slowly and gently on her lips, which she smacked together and with tissue, patted them daintily. Her face was perfectly made up as a glamor girl.

Lastly, for jewelry, she reached for her jewelry box and picked pearl earrings that she snapped on her earlobes. Then, she chose a pearl necklace that belonged to her grandmother and clasped it behind her neck. For her wrist, she decided on a charm bracelet, a birthday gift from her mother. Then, at last, she wanted to wear her engagement ring from Philip.

As for her fingernails, she took pink nail polish and brushed each nail slowly and carefully. She waited a few minutes for them to dry.

Then she gazed into her mirror sighing happily, *Philip, here I come.* She was content and pleased. She was beautiful. She got up, took her beaded bag, and walked down the staircase with grace, just as a queen. The doorbell rang.

Her heart pounded with joy. *It's him! It's Philip!* she mused gladly. "It's open," she called. She had decided to keep the door unlocked. She did not want the hustle and bustle of running to let him in. He entered, clad in a white starched shirt with a black vest and shiny, crispy black pants. He wore black suede oxfords on his feet. His wavy, dark hair was parted neatly on the side. He was freshly shaven and his smile, wide, showing his pearly teeth.

His sharp eyes lit up with glee, his mouth open and watery as he watched her descending the stairs. "My lovely lady, you are a vision of loveliness!"

And then she remarked brightly, "You are quite dapper yourself, my handsome man." He walked up to her and took her hand. Seeing her wrap on the doorknob, he took it and put it around her shoulders. He opened the front door and motioned her out. "After you, my dear." She smiled at him. They left.

Saturday, One Week Later, 11:00 a.m.

After helping her mother clear the breakfast dishes, Francine headed toward the stairs. She stated, "Mama, I am going to get ready for Willow's mother is coming over. She is taking us to the movies. We are planning to see *Summer Vacation*."

Bettye Jo turned from the sink and smiled. "Fine, honey!"

Francine dashed up the stairs. She decided on a purple puffed-sleeved top and gray denim dungarees. As always, her hair was in a bun, surrounded with a purple scrunchie. She had wisps of hair strands around her face. She investigated her mirror, making sure she looked presentable. She grabbed the locket her parents gave her for her birthday and she eagerly put it around her neck. Again, she faced the mirror. *You are beautiful*, she smiled at herself. She took her paisley-colored bag and swung it around her neck over her shoulder. She was ready and burst out the door running down the stairs.

Bettye Jo saw her and warned, "Be careful. Do not run. You will fall," she cautiously but lovingly stated.

Francine ran up to her mother and gave her the usual hug and kiss and of course, she reciprocated, as normal, but with sincere love.

"Remember, honey, about tonight. Daddy will come before 6:00 p.m. We are seeing your grandparents," she reminded her.

"Yes, Mama, of course I remember," she acknowledged her mother.

They bid each other goodbye and stated the magic, loving words, "I love you all the way to Pluto and back."

"Enjoy your day," she said with joy, and she waved, and Francine did so back. "Thanks, Mama." She was out the door, skipping along, swinging her bag around. Bettye Jo watched with eyes wide open and bright as she entered the car with her friends. She went back to the kitchen, still clearing the table and putting the dishes in the sink and rinsing them and then piling them into the dishwasher. She dried her hands with a towel, then flung it aside on the counter. Then she sat at the table, intending to read the newspaper, and began her usual crossword puzzle activity with gusto.

A few minutes later, she heard the doorbell. Bettye Jo looked from her puzzle and wondered, "Who could that be?" she questioned to herself. She was not expecting anybody. It rang again. Bettye Jo put the newspaper down and went to push the curtain aside to see who it was. She saw a very pretty woman with long blonde hair in a page boy on her shoulders. Her eyes were large and bright as opals. She did not look pleasant or friendly or nice. Her face scowled with anger. No sign of glee or joy. She carried a big tote bag on her shoulder. She rang the bell again with much force and impatience. She was haughty and arrogant. Bettye Jo could not believe it. But it was true. She opened the door. The sisters stood facing each other, saying nothing at first.

Then Bettye Jo quietly addressed her sister, "Ellen?"

Neither one volunteered a hug or a kiss or a joyful greeting.

She has not changed, Bettye Jo surmised to herself. *Still the same*, she continued under her breath.

Ellen still scowled but began, "Is that the way to greet your sister?"

Quietly, Bettye Jo stated, "You were supposed to call before showing up. Now is not a good time."

Sullenly, Ellen retorted with fury, "I did call. I did so many times, but you never answered," she smirked.

"Don't start with me, Ellen. Don't you dare even try. You know you are a liar and always have been since we were little girls. If you did call, we would have known about it. I have caller ID and an answering machine that shows me every telephone call that comes in. And you know that very well. It is just like you to show up unannounced where you are not welcomed or invited."

Ellen continued pouting. Tears formed in her eyes and she screamed bitterly in her sister's face, clenching her fists, "You never loved me. You were always the favorite. Mom and Dad loved you best and gave you whatever you needed and wanted!"

"Don't you ever think of provoking me. It will not work anymore. You are not five years old anymore. At least, not physically, but emotionally you are—no, not five, more like a little baby, an infant who demands to be constantly coddled and pacified to get her own way 24/7. So stop with the waterworks. I am not up to it. Not today, not ever. I am through and finished with your temper tantrums and ungovernable behavior. You only care about yourself and think you are the center of the universe. But—news flash—you are not," she finally proclaimed.

Both sisters stood facing each other, saying not a word. Bettye Jo was drenched out but managed to compose herself. Ellen continued to glare at her sister, her dark eyes burning and piercing with anger. Her mouth sulking.

Then Bettye Jo motioned with her hand. "You can come in and stay for a while. I will put up some coffee. And then afterward, I want you to leave and go back to wherever you are staying. I will not have you upset my future husband or my daughter. It is not even afternoon yet, and you are not even here five minutes, and already you have attempted to get the better of me. Francine and Philip know about you, and furthermore, the only reason you were contacted was, not because of me, but because it was my daughter's idea. She is determined and adamant to meet you. I love that girl, and I will not allow her to be intimidated by you. She has had a very wretched, horror-filled childhood and has suffered enough, and I will not let you abuse or harm her in any way. She loves me and her father and we in return love her dearly. She is very precious to us, and we are very honored to be her parents. She is a very sweet and loving young lady, and you will not spoil it for her or for us. Do you understand?"

Ellen sat mournfully at the table and nodded, glumly. She replied in a whisper, "Yes."

Bettye Jo then satisfied, affirmed, "Good. Now I will make the coffee." She put the kettle on and set out two cups with saucers and sugar and cream. Ellen sat watching Bettye Jo, her long-lost sister, feeling she was preferred and always loved and had everything handed to her. She, on the other hand, was second to none, neglected and ignored. Bettye Jo thought, *Still as bitter as ever, thinking the world owed her a living, thinking I was the daughter with the benefits. Little does she know, I worked for everything I needed and wanted. I had a loving husband and daughter; God rest their souls. Sadly, they are gone, and did Ellen once support me when they died? Not even with a card or a telephone call.*

Afterward, Bettye Jo took the kettle and poured the coffee in both cups, then laid it down on the counter and sat across from her sister. They sipped their cups slowly, staring at each other.

Ellen piped up, looking around. "You did very well for yourself, I must say," she said, struggling to be amicable. Then she returned to her sulkiness. "But then you always got to be the best and have it all."

Bettye Jo was about to retort, seeing that Ellen still tried to get her goat, so she just let her sister ramble her hurtful, nonsensical accusations relentless at her. But she was not up to her fits of anger or outbursts. Bettye Jo just sat quietly, not acknowledging her sister. She felt sorry for her for she never knew how to love or knew the meaning of the word or how to give it, and all she was interested in was herself and her selfish pleasures. She said nothing, but just sat there thinking all this about Ellen. She wanted to love her and have a tight bond with her, but it was impossible for Ellen never made it easy or even tried to connect with her or anyone else. But Francine wanted to see her anyway. Hopefully, perhaps, for Francine's sake, things will work out with her sister. Still, she was doubtful and tried to dismiss these thoughts from her mind. She gained her composure for herself and Francine.

With her cup in her hands, Bettye Jo began softly, but firmly, "I am sorry you felt inferior to me though I kept telling you, that was not true. Still, you claimed our parents gave me more than they did you. Such as the money for my flower shop. Though they said it was their present to me, I paid them back. It took a while, but I did it. Luckily, it was a success. Do you think it was easy for me? Not in the least. I must deal with creditors harassing me about them getting paid for haphazard services and customers who wanted and felt entitled to special privileges when they do not pay for my merchandise and services. That is a lot to contend with, but I never gave up. It was worth all the effort, but I love it."

Ellen listened intensively, saying nothing and not making contorted facial grimaces.

Bettye Jo continued, "About the car Mom and Dad gave me as a graduation present. I showed them I was responsible for its upkeep. I had a minimum-wage job in a shop to pay for its expenses.

"Mom and Dad always worried about and your lack of ambition, and they could not trust you for you never showed any responsibility for your actions. They told me these things and they tried to get you the help you needed to sort out your life issues. I know they did it because they loved you. But all you did was complain that no one liked you. For others to like you, you must like them back and show interest in others so they would be interested in you. I am not saying it is easy. But anything good comes with a price. You must try and work to have friends and be successful in life. All it takes is effort on your part, and in the long run, you will realize it was worth your energy and while. I always wanted us to be close, but you must put in effort by giving and showing empathy for others to have successful relationships. I want to, but I cannot do it by myself. Relationships are a two-way street. I will help you along the way, and I will be patient and understanding. But you must be that, as well. I never hated you. I am not that kind of a person. I believe in the good of everyone regardless of the challenges that come about. I always pitied you because of your hurtful behaviors and that you did not know how to love or what love was. It is a beautiful gift from God. But you must work to earn it and it is hard at times, but believe me, it is the most precious gift in creation. I would not lie to you. I promise you that." Bettye Jo paused to catch her breath. Ellen still sat, saying not a word, but she was not scowling or muttering unpleasant retorts under her breath.

Bettye Jo hoped her talk made an impact on her sister. It seemed to since Ellen was not acting out or having screaming fits. Ellen looked down; her hands faced down on her lap.

"I am sorry." Ellen was barely audible. Then she lifted her head, facing her sister. "Forgive me. For everything," she added. She extended her hand and hesitantly touched Bettye Jo's hand. It felt very awkward for both. But Bettye Jo smiled and grasped her hand back. It was a start, a new beginning for both.

They heard a car door slam outside. They turned toward the window.

"Francine's home. She is back from the movies," she gleefully told her sister, who smiled amicably.

Francine burst through the door, "Mama! Mama!" she exclaimed elatedly, running up to embrace and kiss her.

"What, darling?" She took her daughter into her arms.

Francine turned and saw Ellen.

She greeted her, "Hello!" She was puzzled.

Bettye Jo smiled and stated, pointing to her sister, "This is your Aunt Ellen."

Francine's eyes lit up. She knew Ellen was supposed to have called first before coming. Bettye Jo told Francine about her talk with Ellen, who seemed agreeable and pleasant.

Bettye Jo stated, "I think your Aunt Ellen will be just fine. We had a talk," she paused and turned to her sister. "She would like to get to know you." Then she faced Ellen and asked rhetorically, "Isn't that right, Ellen?"

Ellen affirmed with a cheerful grin, "Certainly."

Francine extended her hand to her aunt. She was not too sure of how to greet her. Ellen shook her hand back though she was not too familiar on how to greet people. Her social skills were poor, but there was hope for her yet. Bettye Jo thought hopefully as she observed Francine and Ellen interact.

Ellen faced her and said, "Frannie, uh, Francie," with uncertainty. Bettye Jo tried to interject, but Francine reassured her, "It is all right, Mama."

"Francine," she corrected her affirmatively. "Don't worry." She brushed it off.

"Hi, Aunt Ellen!" she greeted her aunt. "It is so nice to meet you. Would you like to see my bedroom?" she motioned at the staircase.

Ellen smiled, nodding her head. "Of course," she replied. Then she looked up at Bettye Jo for approval. "Is it all right?"

Bettye Jo consented pleasantly, then added, "Don't be too long. Remember, tonight is going to be a big one."

Francine and Ellen headed upstairs. Francine directed her to her bedroom. Bettye Jo watched them. She was pleased. *Is she really trying to change?* she mused hopefully to herself.

4:30 p.m.

The three of them were sitting at the kitchen table pondering over the day's events. There were no upset voices or fits of anger. In fact, they spoke pleasantly. Bettye Jo sincerely hoped her sister had changed. She wanted it. Ellen and Francine seemed to hit it off and admired her bedroom that Francine showed her. Ellen made no snide remarks about anything. She apologized for not being there for her sister when her husband and daughter were killed in a car accident and was very remorseful at not being supportive when their parents got sick and died. She told her sister, her hand on hers, "I would like to make it up to you. I want us to be close," she stated softly.

Bettye Jo patted her hand. "I do so, also." Then she got up from her chair and asked, "Would you all like to have frankfurters and mashed potatoes for supper? It is no bother, for I am not really feeling up to preparing anything else now. Philip will be here soon to join us," she announced. "As you know, Ellen, we are going to visit Philip's parents. I do not want to be rude, but we were not expecting you. I do not know what to tell you, you do understand, don't you?" she asked.

Ellen said nothing at first, but then said agreeably, "Of course, I was the one in the wrong." Then she stopped when Francine interjected, holding her hand up, "Why can't Aunt Ellen come with us, Mama?" she strongly suggested. "She is your sister and part of this family. I would like her to meet Daddy's parents." Then as an afterthought, "Paul will be there, Daddy's brother. We could all meet and get to know each other."

Bettye Jo smiled at her daughter. "Just like you to be so kind and loving, always making everything wonderful. You are so thoughtful." She patted her daughter's hand. Then she faced her sister. "What can I say, Ellen? I have such a wonderful daughter who does not want to hurt anyone's feelings and is always trying to make everything right and wants everyone to be happy."

Ellen remarked, "Yes, she definitely is such a lovely girl. You must be so proud of raising such a daughter. But still, I do not want to put anyone on the spot. I should have called first and I am sorry for that."

"Nonsense, Ellen," Bettye Jo remarked. "You did show up unexpectedly, but Francine is right. We would love for you to come with us. It is what Francine wants, and I do not want to disappoint her. She's the one who brought us all together," she concluded.

Ellen threw her hands up in the air and smiled at the ceiling. "All right, girls," she confirmed. "I would love to meet the family," and to her niece, patting her hand. "Thank you again. I love you all." She got up and embraced her sister, who, though surprised at her gesture, gleefully returned the hug. Then she hugged Francine, who reciprocated it.

"It's all set," Bettye Jo stated firmly. "Now, I will prepare dinner in the meantime while waiting for Philip to arrive. He will be so surprised. Even though he knew about Ellen's past, he will welcome her into the family, and I will tell him about our talk and that Ellen is trying to change herself."

She turned to the counter and took out the frankfurters to defrost and reached for the mashed potato mix. Ellen and Francine watched her, and they offered to help her. She pleasantly declined it and suggested they go into the living room to watch television. They did.

5:00 p.m.

Ding-dong. The doorbell. All three turned toward the door. Bettye Jo announced, "That's him! That's Philip!" She took a dish towel and wiped her hands and dashed to open the door. *There he is,* Ellen thought. *Wow, he is a living doll. I wonder what his brother looks like.*

Philip smiled at Bettye Jo and put his hands on the sides of her face and gently kissed her lips. Francine and Ellen watched them, their eyes lit up gleamingly. Ellen ran up and Francine followed. They both stopped in their tracks. Philip saw Ellen, and Bettye Jo announced, "Philip, this is my sister, Ellen," she introduced, then put a hand up to Philip, "But do not worry. She is fine. We had a talk." Then turning to Ellen, she confirmed, "Isn't that right, Ellen?"

Ellen nodded pleasantly. "Yes, it is, Bettye Jo, I promise to behave."

Bettye Jo remarked, "Good, so it is all set. Francine suggested that Ellen accompany us to the nursing home, and I agreed. Is that all right, Philip?"

She faced him, waiting for his approval, and he spoke, "Certainly, any relation of Bettye Jo's and Francine's are relations of mine." He faced Ellen and they shook hands eagerly. "I will be delighted for your company."

Everyone nodded in agreement. Then Bettye Jo announced, "I am almost finished making supper. It is just frankfurters and mashed potatoes." Then all three sat down, and Bettye Jo began serving dinner. Everyone was all smiles as they resumed their meal.

7:00 p.m., Crestville Nursing Home Waiting Room

Philip glanced at his watch, grinding his teeth, seething. "Damn that son of a bitch!"

Bettye Jo watched him and put her hand on his shoulder. "Do not get excited, honey."

He ignored her, teeth chattering. He dialed his brother's number, hearing that stupid, ludicrous, flippant, idiotic voice on his machine. He yelled into the telephone, "Pick up, you son of a bitch. I know you are there." He paused, then resumed, "Last warning, pick up now. You hear me! Okay, you asked for it. I am driving down to your rat hole as I warned you I would. I am not fooling around. I am leaving, and I will be there and if I must, I will forcibly drag you to visit our parents. You son of a bitch. This is your last warning. I am on my way." He clipped his telephone shut and put it in his pocket.

Bettye Jo came over and quietly said, "Be careful, okay? I do not want you to get hurt. I am worried because you are very tense and uptight."

He turned to her. "I will be fine," he reassured her. With that, he left.

He drove down the dark street, looking around garbage-slewed, dirty sidewalks, broken-down buildings, used cars in junkyards, dilapidated stores, and broken streetlights. *This is where he lives*, Philip observed. *I would not put it past him. I know what to expect. I always did.* He found an empty parking space in front of the building where Paul lived. After he parked his car, he furiously got out and slammed the door and dashed into the building. There were cockroaches on the stairs, paint peelings off the doors, stench from urine, broken toys in the hallway, and cracks on the ceiling. It all reproached him, but this was Paul, his brother, who caused the family nothing but heartache all these years. *No more*, Philip convinced himself adamantly. *No more, brother, dear. It is over. I have had it with your selfishness and nonsense.*

He banged furiously on the door. He heard silly, inane giggly voices, but continued relentlessly for about five minutes. "Open this door, right now. I am not leaving until you do, you good-for-nothing poor excuse of a human being. I am not kidding." He went on banging.

The neighbors' doors opened, and they peeked out, "What is all that racket?" They looked at one another.

Philip turned to them. "Nothing for you to worry about. I am handling it," he calmly reassured them, and they went back inside their apartments. He got back, still pounding on the door. "You better come out or I will break the door down and drag you out!"

Suddenly, the door opened. There he was, the prodigal son, in an undershirt and boxers, his hair muffled, his eyes glazy, and his mouth open with a stupid smirk on his face, holding a can of beer. He was laughing, "Chill out, bro, take it easy."

There were two scantily dressed, baby-faced girls with hardly any breasts showing, prancing around. They looked no older than fourteen years old trying to act like thirty-year-old bitches in heat. They saw Philip and attempted to put their arms around his neck, smiling sensuously, their lips on his cheeks. One was blonde, the other a brunette. They put their hands on his chest and gazed up at him, batting their eyes. He roughly pushed them away. "Get out of here, you two-bit tramps. Put your clothes on, right now. This is between my brother and me."

"That's my brother, ladies," Paul announced. "He is such a killjoy. What he needs is to get a life. He does not know how to have a good time. Do not let him offend you." He giggled hilariously while gulping down his beer.

Philip ignored him and threw the girls' clothes at them. "And you two little girls, get out of here now. Go home to your mommy and daddy. They are probably worried sick about you since it is way past your bedtime." He took out his wallet and handed them cash. Then he called for a taxi. "Here, take it. It is money for a cab, now go!"

They sullenly put their clothes on, grabbed their bags, and to Philip, they sneered haughtily. "What a grump! What a grouch!" He ignored them, and they left.

Paul started, "Why did you go and do that for, spoiling my fun?"

Philip did not respond and stood in his spot. "You have five minutes to clean yourself up and get dressed. You hear me? You are going to visit our mother and father as a good son should. All these years, you have hurt them, but not anymore. And I am not going to tell you again—get clean and dressed. You are coming with me, and do not make me get physical. But I will if I must. You leave me no choice. I do not care if there is a scene. I am going to wait right here. Remember, five minutes." He held his hand up, showing five fingers. "I do not want to have to repeat myself. Try being and acting as a grown man for once in your pathetic life. Last warning. And furthermore, you should be ashamed of yourself. Engaging underaged girls for your own selfish pleasure. Girls barely your niece's age. What kind of example are you setting for her? I can have you arrested for that, but right now, I do not care about what you do. Just try to force yourself to be a man, a responsible human being."

Paul said nothing. He looked down mournfully on the floor and mumbled, barely audibly, "Okay." He turned to his bedroom and washed up and combed his hair and put-on decent clothes. He was ready. Philip did not have to do or say anything more. They were out the door.

While in the car, Philip took out his cell phone and punched in Bettye Jo's number and waited for her to reply. When she did, he informed, "He is with me, okay? Everything is fine. I am on my way, honey." He paused then said, "I love you, too." He snapped his telephone shut and put it in his pocket. He turned on the ignition and they were off.

"What is my niece's name again?" Paul attempted conversation. "Felicia, Florry, Fern," he tried to guess.

Philip, his eyes on the road, replied, "Francine."

"Ah, ha, nice name," Paul remarked. "You say she is named after our mother."

Philip, still staring ahead, acknowledged flatly, "That is right."

"How about your lady friend? What is her name?"

He tried to compose himself though he was feeling tense and annoyed, his blood rising, his heart racing furiously, though he managed to suppress himself and retorted staunchly, "Bettye Jo is not my lady friend, and you know that quite well, and you would if you did not always think about yourself all the time. She is my fiancée, Francine's mother."

"I thought Leonora was," Paul stated flippantly.

"Leonora gave her life. Bettye Jo is and will be her mother, her foster/adoptive mother who loves her. We plan to legally and formerly adopt after we get married this summer." He explained, not facing him.

Paul looked down, his hands on his lap. He said nothing for a minute. Both were silent. Neither knew what else to say.

Paul leaned toward Philip and put his hand on his shoulder. "Look, I am trying, okay?" Philip did not answer.

"I am sorry. Don't be mad at me," he protested and pleaded.

Philip reluctantly, without facing his brother, quietly stated with strained patience, "Don't start with that again, just like when you were a little boy and you upset our mother with your nonsense. I am not up to it. I have not got the time or the patience for that anymore." He paused and continued, "I am not angry with you, Paul, all right?"

"Good," Paul pleaded dully, "Let us have a good time," he suggested. "Okay, bro?"

Still watching the road, Philip responded agreeably and calmly, "All right."

They spent the rest of the drive in silence.

It was getting dark as they headed into the parking lot of the nursing home. They went into the waiting room and saw Bettye Jo, Francine, and Ellen talking among themselves. Philip and Paul walked up to them. Philip began the introductions. "Ladies, this is my brother, Paul," who nodded at them with a smile. Philip continued and pointed first to Bettye Jo, then to Francine, and lastly, Ellen, Bettye Jo's sister. All three of them shook his hand and said, "Pleased to meet you."

Paul did so. "Likewise."

A nurse walked over to Philip and announced, "Your parents are waiting for you. Would you all like to go in and see them now?"

Everyone affirmed with a nod. The nurse led the way down the corridor and stopped at an opened door, and with her hands, she pointed, "There they are," she stated. "Have a good visit." The nurse left them.

Philip's father sat in a chair near his bed. His eyes stared straight ahead. He did not move or respond to his family.

Philip's mother was bedridden, but her eyes lit up when she saw her family. She attempted a smile.

"Hi, Mom," Philip started with a peck on her cheek. "Look who's here." He motioned to Paul, who, with a wide grin, greeted his mother, "How are you doing, Mom?" He, too, kissed her cheek.

She gazed at her sons. "What two wonderful sons I raised," she said, overlooking the fact that Paul was selfish, irresponsible, uncaring, and a disappointment to the family all these years. She did not think to say anything negative for she wanted the visit to be a pleasant and happy one for everyone.

Philip led Francine toward her grandmother. "Mom," Philip started, "this is Francine, your namesake."

Francine went up to her and kissed her. "I am so glad to finally meet you." She paused. She did not know how to address her for this was the first time she got to face and talk with her.

"You could call me Grandma; I would be thrilled since you are my only grandchild. The last time I saw you, you were a baby, so naturally you do not remember," she affirmed brightly.

"Okay, Grandma," she confirmed.

Then Philip led Bettye Jo to her bed. "This is Bettye Jo, Francine's soon-to-be adoptive mother and my fiancée. We are getting married in the summer."

Bettye Jo took the old lady's hands in hers and smiled. "I am so happy we finally met. I have been looking forward to it."

The female senior citizen smiled back. "Such a lovely lady you are. I know you will make my son very happy." And to Francine, "You are such a pretty and sweet young lady. I feel honored to be your grandmother," she affirmed.

Lastly, Philip introduced Ellen. He started to explain slowly, "She showed up unexpectedly at Bettye Jo's house this afternoon. So, we did not know what to do in this situation. You see, Mom, Bettye Jo and she had not spoken or been in contact for years. But Francine," he proudly winked at his daughter, "strongly determined and adamantly insisted Ellen come and meet you though, she was aware of their estrangement, but Bettye Jo had a talk with Ellen, who promised to make an effort to change her past behavior and she is willing to try hard to be pleasant and kind."

Ellen smiled at the elderly lady and extended her hand. Then she realized she had arthritis and apologized profusely. "It is all right, dear," she gleamed with a smile. "You are very pretty." She patted her hand and complimented her and smiled back.

Then everyone went over to Philip's father, knowing his mind was no longer in this world. They attempted conversation, but it was futile. However, Francine walked up to him with a sweet smile. "Hi, Grandpa, remember me? I am your granddaughter, Francine. I am glad to see you." She was bright and cheerful though she knew his mind was gone. She did not care. She had heard that verbal stimulation and tone of voice with people in his condition seemed to help keep him alive even though they are not able to verbally communicate. Touch was another tactic used for dementia patients. Thus, she took his hand in hers and held it for a while. She smiled at him. "I love you, Grandpa." She pecked his cheeks.

Then she walked over to the others who were watching her interaction with her grandfather. What a lovely, wonderful daughter Bettye Jo and Philip were raising. So, caring, kind, understanding, and empathetic. Paul and Ellen were especially astonished at their newfound niece, whom they just got to meet a few hours ago. They were interested in getting to know her after all these wasted years of estrangement. They then looked at each other.

"She's a wonderful girl," Ellen stated to Paul, who profusely agreed with her. "I have to say it. I am glad to have met her. I hope you are, too."

"Of course," Ellen affirmed, "I am."

Paul turned to Philip and pointed out, "You have got quite a daughter there, bro."

"Thank you," Philip politely agreed as he turned to Bettye Jo, waiting for her reply. "She definitely is. Isn't that right, sweetheart?"

"Certainly," she affirmed. "She is the heart of our hearts."

Philip squeezed her hand.

Francine piped up, "You know, guys, I am kind of thirsty. It has been a long day, though a very joyous one. I would like a Coke." She looked around and offered. "Does anyone else want something to drink?"

Philip and Bettye Jo declined her offer, but Philip reached for his wallet and took out a $10.00 bill and handed it to his daughter. "Here, go have a good time," and looking up at Paul and Ellen, he added, "go get to know your new aunt and uncle in the meantime. Mama and I will be here with Grandma and Grandpa, okay, princess?"

He lovingly smiled at her and she affirmed elatedly, "Sure, Daddy."

She took the bill and dashed to the door, motioning for Paul and Ellen to come along. And they did.

She skipped and turned around ahead of them. "Let's go, guys!"

Ellen and Paul walked together talking. Francine knew not what, but they seemed to be deeply engrossed in their conversation.

"Guys!" she stated again. "The cafeteria is here on the left," she indicated, still twirling and hopping around as a gazelle.

The three of them sat at a round table near the vending machines.

"What will it be, guys?" she asked.

They looked up at her. Paul announced, "I would like a Sprite."

Then Ellen piped up, "A Doctor Pepper."

"I am having a Coke," she stated decisively. "I'll go get you your drinks, okay, guys?"

Ellen nodded in agreement with Paul, then they went back to their discussion.

Francine skipped up to the vending machines and made her selections.

"Here you go, guys," she said as she set each soda can down. She sat down and opened her Coke.

Ellen graciously thanked her. So did Paul. They resumed their talk. Francine watched them as she sipped her soda. They then stopped and opened their sodas, put in their straws, drinking slowly while still in deep discussion. *They seem to be enjoying each other's company.* Francine surmised to herself. They had not really said anything to her, but she was not insulted. *Do they like each other? That would be interesting, but not surprising. It might even be nice for them and for everybody. For they both were their families' disappointments, cloudy kinfolk, the black sheep. They would be perfect for each other,* she smiled at her surmising own conclusive conjectures. She said nothing, but that did not stop her from thinking and pondering these inferences in her mind. They seem to be making attempts to be civil and to overcome their past behaviors, and to act as decent and respectable people. Though they did not say much to her, Francine was jubilant and pleased. Her idea worked. Perhaps, it is a miracle getting her parents' siblings to visit, know, and meet them was the best suggestion she felt she made in her young life, and at her age, where all her peers cared or thought about were boys or clothes or some television program or movie star or singer. Not Francine. That is all she wanted—to know her aunt and uncle. She expected nothing more. Now, she sees her new relatives interacting as though they were lifelong friends. She had not planned that far, but it could happen. She sighed hopefully, but she kept those thoughts to herself. *Do not rock the boat*, she warned herself. She did not want to read too much into this situation. Still, she was unable to help it. Thus, she decided to leave it alone.

What will be will be, she reasoned. *It is in God's hands. Let go and let God*, she decided. *Let it play out by itself*, she sighed silently.

Francine turned her head to the huge glass window on her right. It was pitch black outside, but in the darkness were millions of twinkling stars. She was mesmerized. So many stars out. She felt fine for she always loved the stars ever since she was a little girl, alone, unloved, and abused. But no more. Staring at the stars was all she ever had to hold on to. Now her wish became reality, so she no longer needed them. She loved and was loved. She smiled at the thought. It made her happy, gazing at them.

Suddenly she felt two taps on her shoulders and turned around. Ellen and Paul stood behind her.

"It's time to get back, honey, it is getting late," Paul informed her.

"Yes, it is," Ellen confirmed.

Francine was startled, but she agreed. "I'm sorry. I was in a daze. The stars are very mesmerizing."

Ellen and Paul looked at each other in accordance.

"They are," both agreed with each other.

The three of them turned and left the cafeteria and headed toward her grandparents' room. Bettye Jo and Philip turned from their chairs. They were all smiles, all five of them.

"You were gone a while," Philip remarked.

"What were you doing all this time?" Bettye Jo was concerned.

Francine wanted to tell them about that her new aunt and uncle were in deep conversation all this time and seemed to be enjoying each other's company as though they were lifelong friends and her conjectures about them liking each other a lot. But she did not. She could not. What if she mistook their encounter? She looked up and smiled at them. They sat nothing. Philip and Bettye Jo also said not a word.

Ellen tapped Paul on his shoulder playfully, and he winked at her. Both gazed into each other's eyes; still neither made a sound. Francine watched them, her eyes blazed and bright, her mouth open but no sound came out.

"Come on, guys," she looked at her aunt and uncle. "Spill."

Philip and Bettye Jo sat in their chairs. "What is going on?" Philip urged.

"Tell us," Bettye Jo insisted.

Suddenly, Francine brazenly announced, "Uncle Paul and Aunt Ellen like each other. Really, I am not kidding!"

Ellen and Paul tried to suppress their silly laughing and stuttered, unable to say a word. They were embarrassed, their faces beet red. Then they smiled. First at each other, then to Bettye Jo and Philip, their eyes gleaming, but uttered not a syllable.

"Isn't it wonderful?" Francine stated. "I mean it. My new uncle and aunt actually interested in one another."

Paul conjured up admittedly, "Guys, I know I will never win a prize for loving one woman seriously. I am not a choir boy. My track record sucks. I am fully aware of it. But maybe, now will be a new beginning."

Then Ellen piped up, "And I know I am not Mother Teresa or the Virgin Mary. He knows I am not lily white and my past is nothing to brag about." She turned toward him. "But we would both like to try to take things slowly."

"It will be a long journey," Paul admitted. "Ellen and I would like to see how it works out. I hope it will and so does Ellen." He winked at her.

"Let us give it a whirl," Ellen suggested. "All right, Bettye Jo?"

Then Paul to Philip, "Okay with you, bro?"

Bettye Jo and Philip were stunned and speechless for a while.

"I want to believe you, Paul, I really do want you to be happy. But it will be hard at first." He turned to Bettye Jo, who also agreed and stated, "I do want nothing but the best for you two and as Philip said, it will not be an easy journey. I hope you both mean what you say you feel and what to do. As Philip says, we want to have faith in both of you."

Then Philip resumed, "We have been estranged for many years, and I hope you both are willing to change your previous behaviors and are cordial and respectful."

Then Bettye Jo added, "You are both part of our family and we would like to be close to each other. But not only in the good times. You must be supportive when bad things occur. That is what a family does, stick together through thick and thin." Both Philip and Bettye Jo were finished. Everyone was in accordance. Then Bettye Jo piped up as an afterthought. She looked at her daughter with love and announced, "Thanks to you, Francine, we are a family. Together we stand!" Everyone raised their arms up and looked toward the ceiling, shouting, "Way to go." They all high-fived each other. "Way to go, Francine!"

It was getting late. They all got up and bid Francine's grandparents goodbye with pecks on their cheeks. Philip shook his brother's hand and slapped him on the back. Bettye Jo hugged Ellen, and all kept saying "I love you" to one another. Francine watched them. Her family. Her eyes as captive stars beaming. Her face broke out into a wide smile. "Let's go, Francine." Bettye Jo extended her hand to her and she took it gingerly. They went out the door, heading home. The end of a very wonderful day.

Friday, 3:00 p.m.

Bettye Jo decided to close the shop early. Business had been very slow, so she let her staff leave with the promise that they would be still receiving their regular wages nonetheless.

Francine was already at home. It was the start of the Easter holiday. No school for ten days. She took a glass of milk and Oreo cookies and sat down at the kitchen table.

Philip planned to come over to take Bettye Jo out to a drive-in movie.

Francine would be home alone. Bettye Jo trusted her to use good judgment, and she gave her instructions on what to do in case of an emergency and a list of telephone numbers she may need to use.

Francine said she might call her friends, but assured Bettye Jo she would not be on the telephone for long periods, in case her parents or someone needed to call the house.

Francine heard Bettye Jo's car pull up in the driveway. She ran to open the front door to let her in. She threw her arms around her neck in a tight embrace, giving her a kiss on her cheek. Bettye Jo smiled and patted her back.

They grabbed each other's hands and went into the kitchen. Bettye Jo put her bag down on the table and removed her hat and jacket and placed them on the chair next to hers.

Bettye Jo glanced at the caller ID on her telephone screen. She saw a number she did not recognize, so she pressed the button on her answering machine and listened.

"Mrs. Pennington, this is Patricia Jennings from the Department of Social Services. It is imperative that you call me as soon as you get this. It is pertaining to your daughter's birth mother." She ended the call with her telephone number.

Bettye Jo stood there motionless. Francine nearly dropped her milk and had a stunned look on her face. Neither uttered a word for they knew not what to do. And everything was going so well. Now this. Bettye Jo gritted her teeth, angrily muttering, "Damn that woman! How dare she!" She looked at Francine, "You are my daughter. Now and forever!"

"Of course, you are, Mama," Francine affirmed. But she went on, "Let's see what happens. Give her a chance," she strongly suggested. "Perhaps she has changed. You do not have to worry, Mama, you are my mother, the only one. That woman gave me life and you gave me love and nurturing. I will not ever call her Mama. You are my mother, do not worry."

Bettye Jo smiled at her daughter. Always willing to give people the benefit of the doubt and a second chance. Look what happened with my sister and Philip's brother who are now dating regularly. Neither of them reverted to their former ways. Maybe this woman was truly sorry and wants to make amends. She will never be Francine's mother. She knew that. Francine will just meet her, that is it. Not anything more.

"Call her, Mama, call her now," she urged. "See what they have to say. It will not hurt."

"All right," Bettye Jo agreed flatly. How could she deny her daughter anything? Her loving, thoughtful daughter of whom she was extremely proud of. She picked up the receiver and punched in the numbers, waiting for an answer.

She heard the voice greeting her, "Mrs. Jennings, this is Bettye Jo Pennington, Francine's soon-to-be mother legally and formally," she enunciated precisely. "I am returning your call."

"Oh, good afternoon, Mrs. Pennington," she greeted brightly. "I called to give you some information about Francine's birth mother. I do not want to upset you, but I received a telephone call from her social worker. She wants to see Francine. She claims Leonora has been rehabilitated while being incarcerated during the past three years. She is doing very well. She is married to a very wealthy man, and they live in a big house, a mansion, you might say. They have no children." Bettye Jo continued listening. She really was not interested in those claims her birth mother's social worker stated were true. It did not matter. She was and always will be Francine's mother, thus she spoke, "I hear everything you are saying and if it is true that she has changed, that is fine and okay with me. But," she paused, then resumed, "Francine is my daughter. I love her and she loves me. Perhaps that woman feels a lot of remorse for her wretched, harsh treatment of Francine. I am not saying she has not made any progress during these years. People can change. I sincerely believe that. But I am the one who comforted, loved, and supported her, and I am not going to let that woman come between us. I promised Francine I will always be her mother, and she, my daughter. Francine has come a long way, and it has been a slow journey for her to trust anyone, and I am not going to disappoint her. She knows that. She is not going to spoil my relationship with Francine." She stopped to take a deep breath.

Mrs. Jennings pursued, "I understand and agree with you wholeheartedly. Perhaps we could arrange for a few days' visit at her home, to get to know her. Would that be all right with you?"

Bettye Jo replied, "I will be very frank with you, Mrs. Jennings. I am worried that Francine might regress back into withdrawal. I do not want that to happen. She has come this far into stability. But Francine is willing to give her another chance. That is the kind of daughter she is. Always willing to give people the benefit of the doubt and a chance to redeem oneself. And again, if this visit does work out, I am and will still be Francine's mother. If she wants to get to know her or have visitation rights, that is fine with me. It is up to Francine." She paused and gazed at her daughter, smiling with a nod.

Then Francine asked for the telephone and spoke, "Mrs. Jennings," she addressed her, "I will give it a try. Everyone deserves a second chance. I would like for us to get acquainted, and then we could take it from there," she stated decisively.

"All right, dear," Mrs. Jennings said agreeably. "We will start making arrangements for this week, being school is out. I will contact Mr. Carrington, Leonora's husband. Their chauffeur will pick Francine up this Monday morning, so she could start packing her stuff. So, please, have her ready."

Bettye Jo then took the telephone "As you might know, Mrs. Jennings, Philip, Francine's birth father unexpectedly showed up at my house just when I planned to finalize the adoption, but believe it or not, we fell in love, stranger than fiction, but it happened. We plan to get married this summer. He is coming over tonight, and we will talk. Is that all right, Mrs. Jennings?"

"Certainly," Mrs. Jennings smiled into the telephone, "Good luck to all of you."

The call ended.

6:00 p.m.

"I do not know, Bettye Jo," Philip began while eating the skirt steak Bettye Jo prepared. "I am worried. I may be a psychiatrist who helps people deal with their life issues, but Leonora was seriously disturbed back then. I would like to believe she has changed for our daughter's sake." He was doubtful. "I do not want her to get hurt since she has done so well and has progressed a lot doing these past years."

"I thought the same thing," she remarked. "She has worked so hard."

"My thoughts exactly," Philip continued, agreeing.

They both turned to their daughter. "Are you sure, princess?" He wanted to be reassured. "I do hope she has changed." He tried to sound convincing.

"Yes, I am. And as I told Mama before, no matter what, Mama is and always will be my mother and you, my father. You both are my parents." She smiled at them. Then she resumed her meal. Bettye Jo and Philip were jubilant and supportive. They were so honored to be her parents, and they were fortunate to have her in their lives, and she was in theirs, as well. Such a thoughtful daughter they have.

Monday, 7:00 a.m.

Everyone was downstairs. Francine was clad in a long-sleeved pink dress, her hair loose with a pink headband. Her bags stood by the door. Bettye Jo and Philip were with her to say goodbye. The chauffeur came and took the bags to the limousine. Francine hugged and kissed her parents. "Be sure to call us when you get there so we will know you are all right."

"Of course," she affirmed. They waved at each other with "I love you." The chauffeur opened the door to let her in. She was off and excited, hoping everything will work out. She will only be gone a few days. It was only a visit. She did remember Leonora's abusive behavior, but she was willing to forgive her. Perhaps she will apologize and explain it. She did not condone it, but she understood. Her father, the psychiatrist, informed her of Leonora's turbulent childhood. Thus, she did feel sorry for her anyhow. People can change. People do change, she reasoned in her mind. She had to. She wanted to believe it. Perhaps Bettye Jo and she could become friends—no, too far-fetched. Anyway, time will tell.

She looked out the window. She saw fresh green trees surrounded with different colored flowers. The sky was a bright, clear blue. The sun shone, beaming into her eyes. She gazed at it with a smile. It was going to be a great day, she surmised, her eyes bright and gleaming.

She reached for her backpack and took out a book and began to read. It was going to be a long ride. Leonora and her husband lived in the suburbs. Francine had never been in those areas where the wealthy people made their homes. Leonora's husband must be loaded, as the social worker informed her. *I wonder what he does for a living. Does he have his own empire?* she questioned curiously to herself. *Well,* she continued musing to herself, *he sounds a lot better than all those good-for-nothing loser deadbeat boyfriends she used to bring home.*

"Are you tired, Miss?" the chauffeur asked. "Would you like to stop and eat something now?"

"No, sir, but I do need to use the restroom," she mentioned.

"No problem, and, by the way," he added, "my name is Raymond. You may call me that," he offered.

At that, he turned into the parking lot at a rest stop. She got out and asked directions to the ladies' lavatory. She was leery at first, but was given specific directions, and she complied. "Thank you," she told the clerk at the candy stand, who smiled and wished her a good day. This way all new to her.

It was past 11:00 a.m. She returned to the limousine and Raymond asked, "Everything okay, Miss?"

Francine nodded.

"We should be there in about a half hour," he mentioned. And they were off. She went back to reading her book. Both were silent throughout the remainder of the ride. Her heart heavy with anticipation. *Here goes*, she thought to herself. *What is the worst that can happen?* Leonora would not want her. She would not apologize or explain her past abusive behavior and would not want to have any more contact with her, not even visitation rights. She would not hug or kiss her or show any displays of affection, never say she loved her despite all that had occurred over these last years. *I could deal with that. Anyway, I already have a mother who loves me unconditionally, and a father who always loved me though he had not, through no fault of his own, had contact with her for ten years. But it will only be for a few days.*

"We are here." Raymond turned to face Francine. He got out of the car, opened the door, and led her out. Then he took her bags. She walked up the walkway toward the entrance. The chauffeur rang the bell. A Hispanic woman in a starched uniform greeted Francine with a smile and let her into the house. A tall, thin, bald-headed man stood there. The maid told her he was Myles, the butler. Francine looked around mesmerized. It was such a big house; everything was fresh and new.

And there she was. Holding a glass of wine, standing by the server. Tall, slender, she had her dark hair carefully coiled surrounding her face, her eyes heavily made up with blue eyeshadow surrounded with eyeliner, her eyelashes curled, her cheeks with rogue. Her dark eyes piercing, cold as ice, nose erect, her lips pursed with bright red lipstick. Francine noticed bruises on both sides of her face and a black eye. She wore a sleeveless purple halter-top low-cut dress showing cleavage. It reached to her knees. As for her feet, they were high heeled, open-toe sling-back, shiny black shoes. She wore white pearls around her neck, bracelets on both of her wrists, and dangling gold earrings. Francine, saying not a word, stood as a statue. Well, she is well made-up and dressed impeccably. She looked like a lady, unlike when she lived in filth and poverty, always dressed in tatters and never clean. *Yes,* Francine thought. *She is a real lady, different now. She did well for herself.* Next to Leonora, a man stood, his back to her, inhaling cocaine. He turned toward his wife, offering her a joint. She put the glass down on the server and took it and put it in her mouth, smoking it heavily.

The she spoke chipperly at Francine.

"So, you are her." She paused. Still Francine said not a word, then she snapped, "Well, girl, are you going to just stand there?" Noticing her dress, she remarked snippily-like, "Doesn't that woman know how to dress you? That dress is disgraceful." Still Francine said nothing. Leonora walked up to her, eyes glaring at her. Francine extended her hand, which Leonora abruptly and roughly pushed away. Then she went on, "I will not, will not tolerate any displays of affection. I do not believe in it. You are not, are not to even try to kiss or hug or touch me. I will not allow it. Just because that woman does, I do not." Her eyes were cold, not a sparkle or twinkle of love shown. Francine began sniffing and her body shook. She looked down. "Look up, girl," she snapped haughtily. "Don't you dare cry. I will not stand for any waterworks." She paused again. Then she turned to her husband, who was dressed in a tan suit jacket and matching pants, clad in a crisp, starched shirt, and a matching tie. His thick light brown hair was impeccably combed at the side. He stared at Francine, his pale blue sizing her up from top to bottom. Francine felt uncomfortable. He glanced at her small, budding breasts. He smiled. She did not return it. He attempted to touch the side of her face, but she jumped back away from him. Then he took her hand and kissed it. Again, she pulled away. "You are very pretty," he complimented her. "You must have lots of boys chasing after you."

Leonora watched, her heart beating furiously, giving Francine a burning stare. Her black eyes glaring at her, boiling anger steaming up. She put her hand with her palm on his chest and stated arrogantly, "This is my husband. You are to address him as Mr. Carrington. Also," she added icily, "if you dare try to seduce him in any way or make eyes or smile or make any attempt to touch him provocatively, there will be consequences. As for your little performance just now, I will overlook it this time." Francine tried to defend herself and plead innocence, but Leonora paid no heed to her. "Hold your tongue, girl. I do not want to hear you." And she resumed, "I worked very hard to catch him, to love him, and he does me. You are not a little girl anymore when you did nothing but ruin all my relationships I have had with my men friends, especially your good-for-nothing son of a bitch of the man who claims to be your father. You stole him away from me by wrapping your fingers around him, cajoling him, batting your eyes at him. You are thinking he loved you when I know for a fact he loved me the best and foremost and he even said so to me. Well, girl, that is not going to happen again. And if you think otherwise, I will use the strap. You are not too big or old for me to have to use it. Do not make me have to for your sake," she warned sternly. "I gave you life and brought you into the world and I could very well take you out of it. Also, you are not to use your cell phone for any reason, including calling that woman whom you claim loves you. Every day I am going to check it to make sure you do not sneak in any calls. If you are good and you do everything I say and follow all my rules, we will get along fine. Perhaps, I will let you call her, but when you do, I will be there right next to you making sure you tell her no lies. You are not to speak to the help for any reason and they are not, likewise, to talk to you. You are not to ask questions and to only speak when I tell you to or need to ask you a question." She glanced at her watch, then asked Francine, "Did you have any lunch?" she quipped.

Francine sullenly shook her head. "No, Leonora," she answered.

Leonora snarled and enraged, her eyes burning into Francine's eyes. "You are not to call me Leonora! How dare you call me by my first name! I am not your friend, girl. I am your mother, and you are to address me as such, you understand?"

"Yes." She looked away. Leonora slapped her face. Francine touched the spot where she was hit.

"Don't you dare turn away from me, girl, yes, what?" she demanded.

"Yes, M-Mother," she struggled, trying to control the tears that formed into her eyes.

"I cannot hear you, girl," she demanded again, grabbing Francine's chin, her eyes on fire, glaring into her face.

"Yes, Mother!" she cried loudly, renounced and defeated and submissive.

Leonora smiled, satisfied. "Better," she announced triumph fully, letting go of her chin.

"You call that woman Mother?" she shook her by her shoulders. "Do you?" Francine was unable to answer. "Answer me!"

"No," she sobbed. At that, Leonora smacked her across the face again, "Liar!"

Then she turned to the maid and ordered, "Take her upstairs to the guest room and help her get settled in. You have ten minutes to do so. Then go fix her some lunch."

"Yes, ma'am," she complied

Leonora turned back to Francine and her maid.

"One more thing, I will be going out now, I do not know when I will return. Mr. Carrington will be leaving soon as well. Business," she said flatly, offering nothing more. "So, you will be by yourself. You like to read?" she asked, not expecting a reply. Thus, she continued, "You could watch television in the living room, or you could read, but nothing else. Remember what I just said, no funny business." She glared at Francine, her lips firm and tight. She reached for her purse saying nothing, not even a goodbye or a smile, slamming the door behind her.

The maid gently took her by the shoulders. "It is all right, honey," she soothed her. "My name is Agnes. I will show you to your room." She managed a smile. "That is just how she is. Do not worry."

Francine nodded looking into Agnes' eyes as they went upstairs. She felt some comfort. Agnes was actually very nice and kind, but completely dominated by Leonora and her husband, as were the other servants. Perhaps, Agnes will turn into a supportive friend, she hopefully thought. Perhaps, due to Agnes, there will be some brightness during her visit.

Agnes turned toward Francine. "I would let you use my cell phone, but she checks all of our telephones and as for the landline, she also checks the bills."

"I understand," she affirmed. "But thanks anyway."

They reached the bedroom and entered it. Old-fashioned worn-out oakwood furniture, walls painted pale green, lamps on both commodes, the bed in the middle, its headboard, off brown and rusty, two white pillows covered with pale green cases, bedsheets pale colored, but soft, the quilt, fluffy with a patchwork print. Dark green curtains flanking the windows and an off-white window shade.

Agnes watched as Francine opened her bags and put her clothes and accessories in the dresser drawer.

"I will go downstairs now, honey," she stated. "I will make you a baloney sandwich with mustard on toasted rye bread and tomato rice soup. Okay?"

Francine turned and managed a small smile. "Yes, thank you, Agnes."

Agnes turned and left. Francine continued unpacking.

"Dear God," Francine prayed, kneeling down by the bed, her hands clasped, looking up. "Please do not make her come home early. Not tonight," she implored. Then she thought of Agnes, "But, God, thank you for Agnes." Then she went on, "Make Mama and Daddy does not worry. It is not my fault I could not call them. You know that God. Do please find a way I can call Mama and Daddy to tell them I love them." She stopped, then mournfully resumed unpacking. *Just a few days,* she thought again, *and it will be over for good.*

She heard the downstairs telephone ring. Agnes picked it up and answered it. "Yes, Mrs. Pennington," she said into the telephone.

"It's Mama!" She jumped up with glee.

"I-I am s-s-sorry," she stuttered uncontrollably, sobbing and crying. "I know, Mrs. Pennington. S-S-She is sleeping. I-I-I c-can't," she bumbled. "I-I-I, p-please, u-understand," she said with tears in her eyes. "I-I k-know b-but," she hung up.

Francine came out of the bedroom and leaned over the bannister, looking pitiful.

Agnes looked up at her, tears streaming down her face. "I need this job. I have three children under the age of seven and a husband who is disabled and unable to work and the doctors offer little hope." She apologized profusely.

Francine stood there, saying nothing.

Both turned away from each other. Francine fetched a book from her bag and then came downstairs and began reading in the living room. Agnes went to the kitchen and prepared Francine's lunch. No one uttered a sound for the rest of the afternoon. Francine took refuge in her book. Agnes did her routine duties. *I must help her,* Agnes stared at Francine. *Poor little girl.* She sadly shook her head. *I just must, but how? I cannot go against the misses and her husband. I need this job. I do. But this child needs me.* She began to pray profusely, "Lord, tell me how I could help this poor girl. She does not deserve this treatment. She is just an innocent child."

5:00 p.m.

Myles stood by the entrance door. He heard Leonora come up the walkway. He opened the door and smiled. "Good evening, Mrs. Carrington. Can I help you?" he offered pleasantly. She was in disarray. Her hair, unkempt, dress torn on top, her shoe straps ripped off, her stockings dragging down, her face puffy.

"Are you all right, Misses?" he again attempted to be pleasant.

She glared at him, her face distorted. "Tell Alice to fix me a bath at once," she ordered indignantly. Alice was the part-time maid.

"Yes, ma'am," he complied and went to fetch her. She was in the back of the house.

When she appeared, Leonora arrogantly snapped at her, "What are you looking at, girl? I do not pay you to stand around. Now run me a hot bath. But first, help me up the stairs."

Alice nodded obediently and led her mistress up the steps. She, naturally, received no thanks, but she followed her orders precisely. Everyone watched helplessly but volunteered nothing.

Francine sat at the dining room table waiting for her dinner that Agnes started preparing.

About a half hour later, Myles heard a car roll up the driveway. It was Mr. Carrington. He had two girls with him. Myles saw them and opened the door. Mr. Carrington gave him his hat and coat. Then he ushered the girls inside, telling them to sit down in the living room and wait for him. They were not to speak to anyone. They looked no older than eleven or twelve years old. One girl had tousled shoulder-length blonde hair and bright blue eyes. The other girl had reddish long, brown, wavy hair that hung down her back. Her eyes were blue green. Silently, they obeyed and sat in the armchairs with their hands on their laps. They wore ill-fitting, shapeless dresses, knee socks, and scruffy worn shoes. They looked tired and hungry. Neither spoke a word, as instructed.

Mr. Carrington asked Myles abruptly, "Where is Mrs. Carrington?"

He replied, "She is taking a bath. She arrived home over an hour ago," he informed his master.

Mr. Carrington went up the stairs, loosening his tie, glancing at his watch.

When he reached the top of the stairs, he dashed into the bathroom. Everyone heard yelling and slapping sounds. Francine was stunned, but their employees were nonplussed for they knew exactly what was going on in that household. But no one thought to take a stand. They were at their employers' mercy, especially Agnes. They could barely pay their rent on their rat-hole apartments and barely had enough food and owed money on their basic living expenses as electricity and gas. The Carringtons offered them great pay, but at a price. They were to say and do nothing about what was happening in their house. They were sworn to secrecy. However, Agnes did not stop praying for Francine, that poor child.

"How many times do I have to tell you?! How many times do I have to say it? I need the money and I need it now. I have two girls I made promises to about becoming actresses and how can I do that if you cannot bring me the money I need?" He smacked her face again and again, and she did not stop screaming. "I am trying, Conrad, I am. I cannot get enough customers," she protested.

"Also," he continued, "you still did not buy the right drug, just like last week. I keep asking for a certain brand, but you defy me repeatedly."

He stopped yelling and hitting her, but he was still furious as a pot of boiling water.

"You are no good at anything," he sneered. "You cannot do anything right. You used to make such good sales. You are doing something wrong."

She pleaded plaintively, "No, Conrad, I'm not. Honest."

He stood and sneered at her.

"I don't know why I ever married you. You are a good-for-nothing bitch. The same with her, that brat you gave life to. You are both a couple of cunts!"

He went on, "Get up and put some clothes on," he ordered crumply. "I am going out." He turned and left the room.

The two girls still sat in their chairs. Mr. Carrington spoke to them, winked and smiled. "You're both so pretty. Men will pay a lot to love and be with you and to become famous. Remember what we spoke about before? But first you both need new clothes and be cleaned up and presentable." Then he motioned for them to get up and go out with him. "This way, girls." They obeyed and left with him.

Francine and Agnes watched Mr. Carrington with the girls. Agnes shook her head sadly. Francine did not understand what was happening.

Leonora came down the stairs in a low-cut, thick-strapped sour apple green dress that reached below her knees. She wore thick green heeled shoes. She managed to make her hair presentable. More bruises covered her face. She said nothing.

"Are you all right, Mrs. Carrington?" Agnes asked, concerned.

Leonora glared at her. Her face stonelike.

"Make me some pork chops and beans. I am hungry."

"Yes, ma'am." She turned to the kitchen.

Leonora took her seat facing Francine.

"Take that disgusting dress off!" she snarled at her.

Francine just sat and stared, not uttering a syllable. She loved that dress.

Leonora resumed her tirade, "You spoiled little brat!" she screamed in her face. Then she took a glass of water and threw it in her face. Francine was startled but silent. Then Agnes put a plate of skirt steaks with beans in front of Francine. Leonora pushed the table into Francine's stomach. She cried out, clutching it. Leonora got up and pulled her by her hair and smashed her face into the dinner plate and it cracked. Afterward, she pushed the whole broken dish on the floor. Still grabbing her hair, she demanded, shrieking, "Pick that up! Now, girl!" Agnes saw and had tears in her eyes. She felt helpless watching Leonora torture that child mercilessly. She came over to help her, but Leonora roughly pushed her away. Agnes nearly fell backward but managed to stand. Leonora arrogantly snarled at her, "I asked her to do it." Francine did so. She picked up all the pieces and Agnes brought the garbage pail over so Francine could discard the broken pieces. Leonor stood erect, proud, and haughtily over Francine, who looked up mournfully. Leonora resumed and pointed to the stairs. "Go upstairs and stay there and do not think of leaving. I will be upstairs soon." Agnes continued watching. She could not say anything. Then Leonora retorted, "What the hell are you standing around and looking at? I pay you to work and if you are not able to perform your few and simple duties, I assign you, I will go find someone who can. And then where will you be, homeless and destitute." Then with her hand in Agnes' face, she sardonically quipped, "Now, go." Agnes turned and went into the kitchen.

An Hour Later

Leonora finished her supper. When she got up, she snapped at Agnes, "Clear the table. Then you could have your break."

Agnes nodded, "Yes, ma'am. Are you all right, Mrs. Carrington? Could I do anything for you?" she asked, knowing quite well she would not get any sign of gratitude or appreciation. She just wanted to be polite and concerned regardless of the dismal, dire circumstances.

Leonora did not reply or display any sign of amity and headed upstairs.

Agnes saw her go into Francine's room. Myles, Raymond, and Alice joined Agnes at the kitchen table. They began to speak about helping Francine. She needed their support though it might cost them their jobs. But they decided to think about that later. Francine was in dire need of help. They were worried their employers might do terrible harm to her. As for their jobs, it is all in God's hands.

Leonora entered Francine's room. She lay on the bed facing the wall, still in that dress she loved, which Leonora demanded she remove and throw in the garbage. Francine refused to do so, though it would mean dealing with Leonora's wrath. Leonora stood at the foot of the bed glaringly, with her eyes afire into Francine's eyes.

"Get up, girl!" she snapped harshly.

Francine slowly faced her, unable to utter a sound. Her eyes, teary and wide, frightened, her face black and blue.

Leonora reiterated with deep anger, "I said, get up!"

She faced Leonora and was terrified. Leonora was holding a strap. Francine saw it and shivered as a leaf.

"You made me do it. I told you what would happen if you did not obey me."

She dashed over to Francine, grabbed her by the throat, and kept banging her head against the headboard. Francine screamed with all her lung power. Leonora yelled, "Shut up, you spoiled little brat!" Then she furiously ripped the dress off her, "I will teach you to defy me," she continued to yell while ripping off her dress. When she was through, she pointed to the shreds of her beloved dress lying on the floor by the bed. "Pick that up! Now!" Francine tried but was unable to. Her body hurt. Leonora went on, "All right, girl, you asked for it." She raised the strap and beat her on her back, then she forced her to face her, and beat her on her chest, all over her whole body relentlessly. Francine screamed in deep agonizing pain, tears streaming down her face, unable to defend herself. The beating did not stop for a few minutes. It seemed to go on and on. Finally, she put the belt down on the table. She smiled wickedly, her hands on her hips. She felt victorious. She did what she had to do. She sneered, "I had to do it. You left me no choice, just like when you were a little girl always wanting, taking, and demanding. Never giving, ever caring, always provoking me, destroying any happiness I had. Even in the womb, I could not handle you." She smirked, watching Francine cower and shake. Urine poured out on the bed. She was cold all over. It did not end. Leonora stared at her coldly, her eyes icy. Then Leonora left her on the bed and walked out the door in silence. Francine lay in bed in her slip, unable to move.

Two Hours Later

Francine sobbed quietly. She did not want Leonora to hear her. That would make the situation worse. She deeply feared that Leonora might kill her. She was that frightened. She continued lying down in the bed, unable to move her whole aching body.

Leonora was in her bedroom, brushing her hair, primping into her mirror, smiling into it. She felt triumphant and powerful. She disrobed and put on a long, hot pink, spaghetti-strapped nightgown. She pranced in front of her mirror, swaying with her hands on her hips back and forth. She continued to smirk with pride, her dark eyes gleaming. She was pleased. *I am the queen of the universe*, she mused pleasantly to herself. *I am the Almighty Goddess, the omnipresent and the great and powerful of them all. Nothing and no one can or will defeat me now. I am in charge.*

Then she heard footsteps up the stairs. It was Conrad. She wanted to look beautiful for him and for him to love her as she claimed he did before he married her. *He does love me*, she said, trying to convince herself. Thinking of today's earlier incident, she still thought to herself. *He was just having a bad day. He did not mean to hurt me*, she continued to tell herself again and again. *Those things happen*, she surmised, reasoning to herself.

When he entered the bedroom, she walked up to him and put her arms around his neck, smiling lovingly into his eyes. He roughly pushed her away, but that did not deter her. She was determined to make him love her. He ignored her and he loosened and ripped off his tie and undressed himself, saying nothing to her. She just stood watching him muttering under his breath. Then he stood in his white T-shirt and polka-dotted undershorts, then he put on his slippers. Leonora sullenly watched him. He said nothing to her as he left the room.

"Where are you going, Conrad?" He ignored her and growled. He was still raging, boiling as a steaming pot of water. She ran up to him, pleadingly, putting her hands on his shoulders. Again, he shoved her away. She just stood there as he left the room.

The staff heard everything. Luckily, Leonora and Conrad were clueless to their intentions, which they were going to follow through on. They were sure and would not back down now. Francine was in trouble. And they were going to go against their employers once and for all. They did not care about the consequences that would bestow upon them. They were going to take a stand. Now!

Mr. Carrington stomped into the hall, heading to Francine's room. The staff were aghast. Their hands over their mouths. Their eyes shocked. "Oh my, God!" they shrieked in a whisper.

He was in Francine's room and stood over her cowered form on the bed. Her eyes terrorized. He leaned toward her saying in a snarl, "You are very beautiful." He gazed at her chest, reaching to touch her breasts. She backed away, but he was relentless, "You stupid bitch! How dare you! You know you want it. All little girls do," he stated a matter-of-factly. "You're just a cocktease, but I will soon fix that." Francine stared, frightened, with a lump in her throat, unable to defend herself. He ripped off her slip, bra, and underpants. She tried to fight him off, pleading, whimpering cries. He pulled down his boxers, demanding she suck his organ. She tried to turn away, but he slapped her face, "Come on, you cuntface bitch!" He pushed her head down, but she refused to open her mouth. Then he pounced on top of her, spreading her legs apart, his hand on her chest, trying to enter her. She screamed. He smacked her again. He had no intention of giving up. Girls always did what he wanted. That is how he became filthy rich. Torturing innocent girls with false promises. Finally, Francine got up and kicked him between his legs with her feet. He shrieked, falling backward while grabbing himself. "Ow! How dare you!" He said nothing. He clutched his groin. He was in pain. *Finally! No more*, Francine said softly but with intense inner rage.

Meanwhile the staff were on the telephone with 911. Frantically, they spoke with panic in their voices, "Hurry, hurry, please. Please come right now. A little girl is being severely abused by our employers. They are totally insane!" They also mentioned the awful scams and schemes they did to obtain their wealth. "Thank you, oh thank you. Please!" They were hysterical and bitter, but they hung up the telephone, and stood there and smiled at each other. Mission accomplished! Francine was going to be just fine.

"Let us call her parents. They are probably worried as hell," Agnes advised strongly. She reached for the telephone and punched in the number, waiting for an answer.

"Hello, Mrs. Pennington," Agnes addressed into the telephone.

Agnes and the others were speaking into the telephone, informing them of today's occurrences. Francine was brutally abused by Leonora and her husband. Each employee took turns talking with her mentioning that their employers were rich and how they accumulated all their money. They listened to Bettye Jo's panicking, hysterical, tearful voice informing them that she and Philip will immediately drive down to pick up their daughter and take her home. Agnes hung up the telephone. The doorbell rang. "Thank God," Agnes stated, her hand on her heart. Myles walked to and opened the door, letting two policemen and one policewoman in. "This way," he motioned into the living room.

"What is going on?" Mr. Carrington demanded. He and Leonora leaned over the railing, ready to explode.

One policeman, Officer O'Connor, looked up, addressing them, "Mr. and Mrs. Carrington," he began.

"Get the hell out of our house!" Leonora sardonically and acidly demanded.

Officer O'Connor was not to be deterred and resumed, "Mr. and Mrs. Carrington, I strongly demand you get yourselves down here at once."

Leonora shrieked, "You have no right barging into our house."

Again, he ignored them, "Do not make me come up there and bodily force you. And I will if I must. We are not leaving until you do so."

"What are you talking about?" Mr. Carrington indignantly asked.

"I am not going to say it again. Now both of you get yourselves dressed at once and get down here this instant!"

Leonora and Conrad submissively and reluctantly went into their bedroom and put on the same clothes they were earlier. Officer O'Connor and his crew stood in the middle of the living room. They were determined and adamant. They waited. They finally descended the stairs in a disheveled, sloppy state. Their hair was unkempt, and their eyes were on fire bolting out of their sockets.

Quickly, both policemen grabbed them and pushed them down on two armchairs.

"You two sit right there. You are both under arrest. But first, certain procedures need to be taken care of."

"What are you doing?" exclaimed Leonora.

"What is the big idea? We did not do anything. We are law-abiding citizens; you have no right to do this," Conrad insisted arrogantly.

Officer O'Connor turned to the policewoman and instructed, "Go check on the girl." She nodded obediently and ascended the stairs.

Mr. and Mrs. Carrington continued their tirade, protesting their innocence. No one paid them any attention.

The policewoman was upstairs. She heard loud whimpering and went into the bedroom. She was appalled at what she saw. Francine lay on the bed, her body badly welted with scars, her face tear-stained, her hair wild, her head bleeding, her arms bruised, and blood dripping from between her legs. She was completely naked.

The policewoman walked over to her and introduced herself. "My name is Officer Klein." Then she asked, "Are you all right, honey? What happened?"

Francine said nothing though she faced Officer Klein, who gently touched her arm.

"Do not be afraid," she assured her. "We are going to help you. Can you tell us what happened?"

She stared mournfully at Officer Klein, her hand still on her arm.

"No one is going to hurt you anymore. We will definitely see to that."

Still Francine did not reply. But she was whimpering in a small voice as a little girl does, "Want Mama! Want Daddy!" She was still frightened, but Officer Klein reassured her that she will be helped and taken care of.

She heard the doorbell downstairs and left the bedroom and stood leaning over the railing.

Officer O'Connor announced to her, "The girl's mother is here. Her father is outside finding a parking spot. He will be here shortly," he informed Officer Klein. She thanked him and went back to tend to Francine.

She leaned over, comforting her. "Your mother is here. She wants to take you home."

At that, Francine turned and faced Officer Klein, still silent, but composed. Then she attempted to get up off the bed. She could not. She was in such pain.

"I will get you fresh underwear and a clean dress, okay?" she managed a smile. Francine nodded slowly, as she fetched her clothes from a dresser drawer. She struggled to put them on, so Officer Klein assisted her. When she was finally dressed, Officer Klein offered her hand and slowly led her downstairs.

Francine was clad in a puffed, short-sleeved pink floral dress with a sweater over it. She was in disarray, her slip showed, hanging down from her dress. She made no attempt to fix it. She wore no socks or stockings on her legs. She wore black flat slip-ons on her feet. She was struggling for she was in agonizing pain.

Bettye Jo looked up at her daughter. She was crying so bitterly. She could not help it.

When they reached the bottom of the stairs, Francine saw her mother crying, upset.

Officer Klein looked at Francine and said gently, "Go to your mother, now."

"Mama, Mama," she sobbed, tears streaming down her face as she staggered across the room into her mother's outstretched arms. She embraced her tightly, holding her to her breasts, patting the back of her head, keeping her close to her, never letting her go.

Leonora, seeing Bettye Jo comforting Francine, snarled with rage, "Shut that brat up, you fuckin' bitch!"

Bettye Jo faced Leonora, brewing, burning, boiling with fury in her eyes. Her face stoned and glaring. She screamed at this woman. "Don't you dare call my daughter a brat! And don't you dare tell me how to raise my daughter, you filthy, stinking piece of trash!"

Bettye Jo became bolder and more indignant. "You dare lay one hand on my daughter, I will scratch your eyes out. And with my bare hands, I will take you by the throat and thrust your head against that back wall, you see it?" She pointed to it. "And I will crack it open into a million pieces. And do not think I will not do it. I am not playing with you, Mrs. Carrington."

She was not through. Not by a long shot.

Then as she glanced down while comforting her daughter, she continued shrieking, "What the hell is wrong with you? What did you do to my daughter?" She saw caked blood on her daughter's scalp. She looked at Leonora and screamed, "You are a monster! You could have killed her!" She did not stop screeching. She was hysterical with rage.

"How dare you!" She was unable to stop. She was not finished saying what needed to be said to this vicious, evil woman. "You bitch! You are a crazy, stinking, stupid, little bitch! You have no right to hurt my daughter!"

Leonora jumped out of her chair, trying to grab Bettye Jo by her throat. Officer O'Connor pushed her down on the chair.

Leonora piped up and announced daintily as though she was stating the most remarkable, important, life-changing statement in creation, "I gave her life."

Bettye Jo retorted with anger, "So does a bitch in heat. And you are no better than an animal!"

Leonora was unable to say anymore. She was at last defeated. Now and forever.

Bettye Jo sat down, Francine's face on her lap. She stroked her head gently and patted her back. She was still weeping but was much calmer and composed.

Then she gently said to her, "Your slip is sticking out. Let us go to the bathroom where I could fix it. I know you cannot, but I will help you, all right, darling?" She smoothed the side of her head with her hand. Francine nodded solemnly. Bettye Jo took her hand and led her to the bathroom in the back.

First, she lifted her dress to pick up her slip. Then she sat her down on a stool beside the sink, seeing her tear-stained face, took a damp cloth and gently dabbed her drenched red bloodshot eyes. "Are you all right, darling?" She looked down with her hand under her chin. She slowly nodded. She was too weak to speak.

Then Bettye Jo took a towel to dry her face. She took her daughter's hand in hers and headed back into the living room and sat down. Bettye Jo held her tightly in her arms and stroked the back of her head softly. Francine had not uttered a word. She was drenched out and tired.

Bettye Jo was still furious, giving Leonora a dark, icy cold stare, a look that could split rock.

She continued stroking her head. "It is all right, sweetheart," she reassured her. "We are taking you home now, all right?" She soothed her. Francine looked up at her mother, attempting to smile. She then inquired, eyes tearing, "Where is Daddy?"

"He is finding a place to park. He will be here shortly," she answered Francine.

Again, Leonora leaped up, trying to attack Bettye Jo, her hands out. Officer O'Connor, angrily while pushing her shoulders down, threatened, "Sit down, Mrs. Carrington. I am not going to tell you again. If you get up one more time, I will pin both your arms behind your back! I am not playing around!"

Leonora piped up petulantly, "She ruined every relationship I have ever had. And she is still doing it. Causing trouble and heartache for me."

Bettye Jo glared at this woman, "My daughter did nothing of the sort. How could she? She is just a child. And furthermore, those male friends you claim loved you. They did not give a good goddamn about you. They used you for their own selfish purposes."

Leonora continued, "And that poor excuse for a father. She ruined it. He told me he loved me, but she," pointing to Francine, "stole him away from me. She is just and always was a cajoling, conniving, little bitch of a brat who never wanted me to be happy. He stopped loving me and left."

Bettye Jo retorted back, "You are a goddamn liar, and you know that quite well. That is not true. You threw him out of the apartment and prevented him from seeing Francine. Perhaps he did love you, but you never made it easy, and I could understand. He told me about your childhood. And I do understand. Your own mother did not or could not love you for whatever reason, but that is no excuse to blame Francine. You had a difficult birth, but she was just a baby, a child. She needed you. She would never hurt you. She is not like that. Some pregnancies are painful. But that is no excuse to abuse the one person who solely relied on you for her life and well-being, especially unconditional love, which you were unable to provide. So, she suffered for it." Also, she pointed out carefully, "That man," she looked at Conrad, her husband, "he is no better than the men you brought home years ago. You claim he loves you. The only difference is that he is a glorified son-of-a-bitch pimp who procures underage girls into prostitution to make you and he wealthy. These innocent girls were there for his pleasures only. You know that very well. And," she went on, "he put you on the streets to hook up with strange men and to deal drugs and provide booze. It was for himself only." She then looked at Leonora's face and arms. "How did you get those bruises and marks on you? Tell me! And you say he loves you. He hits you whenever you do not follow his orders to suit his selfish desires and needs. He used you, just like your previous male friends from a long time ago did. You have not changed at all, Mrs. Carrington. I am sorry to say. And believe it or not, I pity you. You gave Francine life, but I gave her love. I am her mother, not you. You do not know the meaning of the word and for that I feel sorry for you."

Then she faced Leonora's husband, "And you are no better," she staunchly stated. "Both of you disgust me. May you both rot in hell forever!"

Bettye Jo turned away from these people who were unable to love, feel, or care about others.

The doorbell rang. Myles opened the door. It was Philip.

"Hi, darling," Bettye Jo greeted Francine's father.

Philip walked up and kissed Bettye Jo. Then he turned to his daughter and asked, "How are you doing, princess?" He took her hand.

Managing a smile, slowly she answered, "I will be okay, Daddy."

Philip turned to Leonora with anguish in his voice. "You disgust me, Leonora, you always have. You have not improved at all one bit after all these years. I really hoped and thought by now, you would have changed. But you have not. You are the same as always just as you were younger. I should have known better than to think you have. The only reason Bettye Jo and I agreed to let Francine meet you was because she sincerely believed that you would be different and may have changed your ways. Francine believes in the good of all people, regardless of their circumstances. She believes in giving people second chances and the benefit of the doubt. For that, Bettye Jo and I are grateful and proud to have Francine as our daughter. Unfortunately, she was wrong this time, and she suffered for it. But she will not anymore, Leonora. No more."

Leonora sat there, bitter and stone-faced. "You were never much of a man anyway. All you cared about was your schooling that I worked for with three poorly waged jobs and for the bitchy brat you call your daughter." She glared at Francine, with burning hatred in her eyes.

At that, Philip stood erect and composed. He stated, "I am letting all that slide and roll off my back as water off a brook. You are very sick, Leonora, and you need psychiatric help now just as you did years ago. It is sad but true. You have never had any empathy for anyone but yourself." Then he walked over to Mr. Carrington and stared in his face. "And you, you sick, cruel son of a bitch are no better." He stepped back and concluded. "You both deserve each other." He turned to Bettye Jo and Francine. "We are done here. Let's go, my ladies."

Francine then chimed in, "Daddy, please wait. Just give me a moment. I would like to say something to Mrs. Carrington. She needs to hear what I have to say."

Philip and Bettye Jo allowed her and waited.

Francine walked up to Leonora, bold and brave, and no longer afraid or frightened. Calmly and softly, she began, "I do not hate you, Mrs. Carrington (she was no longer Leonora). I pity you as Mama and Daddy do, and I do understand. You had a wretched childhood, and I am sorry you did. You did not deserve it. But that does not give you the right to abuse me the way you did. I was just a little girl. Your past background is even more reason for you to give love to someone who is completely dependent on you. You knew how you felt being abused, so you should have had the decency and common sense to love me, but you were unable to. And for that, I do pity you. I did nothing to deserve your inhumane treatment of me. The only good thing you did was give me life, so that Mama and Daddy could give me the love I need and deserve. For that, I am grateful to you, and that is about it. You are not my mother and never will be."

Leonora stood raging and shivering inside herself. She was no longer able to hurt her again.

Francine turned to her parents.

Bettye Jo put her hands on Francine's shoulders, and Philip stood by them. Afterward, Bettye Jo smoothed the back of Francine's head and patted her back gently.

All the four employees were questioned separately. They told their stories to the police, who believed them, being they all witnessed their employers' goings-on even though it meant losing their jobs. They knew that the Carringtons gave them their jobs to silence and keep them quiet. They had to swear not to speak of their illegal activities to anyone, but they were reassured that they would get the help and compensation they needed. The police took their statements and rewarded them for finally taking a stand by helping an abused child who needed support from their employers' criminal, antisocial, and psychopathic behaviors.

Bettye Jo and Philip profusely thanked them for coming to their daughter's aid, knowing that they no longer had their desperately needed jobs to support their necessities. Bettye Jo reached into her bag and took out her checkbook. She made checks out to each of them to hold them over for a while. Bettye Jo and Philip told them that they might have employment for them for their experience and skills would be needed. The staff was speechless. They could not believe their luck. The Lord does provide. They were firmly convinced of it for it was true.

The policemen turned toward Francine's parents.

"We are taking Francine to the hospital. She has been severely hurt and needs help and treatment very badly, you understand?"

Bettye Jo and Philip agreed.

"There is an ambulance waiting outside. The paramedics will take your daughter to the hospital."

Bettye Jo piped up quickly, "Officer, I would like to be with her while she is in the ambulance. I will feel better and so will she, knowing I will be there for comfort and support."

Looking at Philip, she asked plainly, "Honey, you will follow us in your car, all right?"

"Certainly, sweetheart," he amicably agreed.

Before the paramedics came in the house, Francine stood staring at these horrible abusers and shook her head sadly. "We will be praying for you." Then turning to her parents, she said, "Isn't that right, Mama, Daddy?" They nodded with a smile. Then the paramedics came and led her to a stretcher. Bettye Jo followed.

While the policemen were putting Leonora and Conrad in handcuffs, they were fuming, raging and professing their innocence. Leonora, glaring at Francine, spat out, "You ruined everything, you fuckin' little bitch and spoiled brat. You ruined all my relationships with my boy friends and you did it again." Then to the officers, she screamed bitterly, "I brought her into this world. I gave her life, but she would not call me Mother!"

Then Conrad, with evil eyes piercing at Francine, said, "You are nothing but a little cuntface cocktease, just like the rest of them."

No one acknowledged them. The policemen pushed them out the door and into a patrol car. It was all over for them. They would never hurt anyone again for they were going to be put away for a very long time. They were no longer a threat to society or to Francine, who was safe now and loved as always.

9:00 p.m., Burnside County Hospital

The ambulance pulled into the emergency entrance. Quickly, they opened the back doors, first helping Bettye Jo out. The EMTs wheeled her daughter out on a stretcher. Bettye Jo took her hand and squeezed it tightly. They rushed into the waiting room. A lot of people were there waiting to see a doctor. It was going to be a long night, but Bettye Jo thought to herself, *I am in no hurry. Francine will get the help and care she needed.* She would see to that.

She went to the admitting desk, out of breath and panicking. She said, "My daughter." She pointed to the stretcher. "She has been hurt very badly. She could hardly move. She is in agonizing pain. Her birth mother beat her with a strap and her husband sexually abused her. Please help her!" Bettye Jo screamed in the receptionist's face, "Do something now!"

The receptionist looked up from her desk. "I understand and am sorry, but you will have to wait. There are others ahead of you," she explained quietly.

"She is in pain!" Bettye Jo shouted, which was so unlike her.

"Mama, Mama!" her daughter cried out clutching her stomach. "My stomach hurts. I cannot breathe." She was panting heavily. "I am sick. I have pains. I am nauseous. My head hurts," she wailed. "I hurt all over, Mama, help me!" She cried uncontrollably. She was breathing heavily and coughing up phlegm. Suddenly, she vomited all over the floor. "It hurts, Mama, it hurts badly. I am tired." Then urine poured out of her. "I wet my pants." Then, in a low voice, she whimpered, "I am hungry, Mama. She did not give me any supper." She rubbed her chest, which was growling.

Bettye Jo rushed to her daughter and put her arm around her while stroking her back gently. "It is all right, sweetheart. Mama's here. Don't cry. I am here for you."

Everyone was watching, but no one tried to help. Bettye Jo noticed two aides sitting around drinking coffee and chattering about, completely oblivious to their surroundings.

Bettye Jo shouted, "What is wrong with you? My daughter is in deep agony and no one is doing a damn thing to help. If any more harm comes to my daughter, I will have you all put away in a cell next to her birth mother. Don't try me," she warned arrogantly.

"Ma'am," an attendant walked up behind her, his hand on her shoulder. "You will have to calm down. You are not helping your situation."

Bettye Jo continued screeching, "Don't you dare tell me to calm down!" Pointing at Francine, she said, "My daughter was abused and beaten. And she is scared and frightened, so do not tell me to relax."

The attendant stood in his spot. "I will speak to a doctor, but you will still have to wait. I do understand, I really do."

Suddenly, Philip ran up to Bettye Jo and the attendant, demanding, "What is going on here?" He looked at Bettye Jo, asking, "What's wrong, honey?"

She began agitatedly, her body shaking uncontrollably. "No one is doing anything. Our daughter is in excruciating pain and no one cares."

Francine was still crying bitterly. Philip walked over to her and said, "Don't cry, princess. We are here. I am here. Mama is here. We are here for you. We both love you, okay?"

Francine nodded plaintively but said nothing. She was too weak, but she stopped crying.

Then two attendants rushed out and brought out a bed covered with a white sheet and pillow and a soft, thick blanket.

Francine was all worn out and tired. She threw her head back on the pillow and closed her eyes.

Bettye Jo and Philip looked at each other.

The attendant spoke to them calmly, but firmly, "I will get the doctor now, okay? But you will have to be patient. Do stay with your daughter in the meantime. I promise I will help you, all right?" He nodded. He turned to Francine. She was asleep. "She is sleeping now. That is a good sign. Stay with her. Tell her you love her. I know you both do." Then he saw the vomit on the floor. He looked at her parents and said, "Don't worry. It is all right. I will have someone clean it up. We are used to it. It happens all the time. We understand."

Bettye Jo and Philip managed to compose themselves and seemed to be all right, for now anyway.

"All right, sir," Philip confirmed. "At least she is fine for now. Thanks for your compassion. I am sorry for Bettye Jo's outbursts. She is really the calmest and subdued person I have ever known. She never gets excited or loses her temper. That is why I love her. She has been a good foster mother to my daughter. We plan to get married this summer and then formally adopt Francine. She is not at all hot-tempered and she rarely raises her voice or gets angry. It is that my ex-wife, her birth mother, is a deeply mentally disturbed woman who should have never been a mother. She herself was abused by her own mother, so she never knew how to love. Unfortunately, Francine paid the price, and she should not have had to. So you see why Bettye Jo acted out of character. She loves her deeply and just wants her to get the help she needs. She was frustrated and very frightened for Francine. She could not bear to see her suffer so, so she lost control and she overreacted. She definitely is my daughter's mother."

The attendant smiled at both. "I see, sir. You both are wonderful, caring parents." Then he glanced at his watch. "If you will excuse me, I am needed upstairs. Take care. I will get the doctor now." He turned and left them.

Bettye Jo and Philip looked at their sleeping daughter. They did not want to wake her because she was all conked out from relentless crying due to her ever-going, never-ending pain. They watched her in silence. Let her sleep, at least for now.

"Poor darling," Bettye Jo remarked mournfully. Then she leaned over her body, careful not to wake or touch her for fearing she would be in pain and cry out again.

Philip agreed, looking at his princess, their little girl. Then he faced Bettye Jo. "It is going to be a long night. We will probably not get any sleep worrying about our daughter. I do not want us to leave until the doctor arrives. So I thought, honey, would you like for me to bring you anything? I could use a drink. How about you?"

Bettye Jo smiled but weakly, as she was tired and stressed out. "That would be nice, Philip. I would like a Coke. I do need the energy and so do you," she affirmed.

Philip smiled back and headed toward the cafeteria. Bettye Jo stood by Francine's side, just in case she awakens. She wanted to be there, making sure she was all right, safe, secure, and tended to properly. She stood in silence, watching Francine sleep so peacefully. She thought to herself, *Oh, my darling little girl, I love you so much. And so does Daddy. It hurts both of us that you are in such agony and pain, but you will be okay. Daddy and I will make sure of it. You must believe that. No one will ever hurt you ever again, especially that horrid, vicious woman who brought you into this world and could not love you the way you deserved. You did absolutely nothing wrong to endure such brutal treatment. Nothing at all. You were just born to the wrong mother. But that is over now. I am here now, and I love you and always will. I am honored to be your mother. I could not love you anymore if you came from my womb and brought you out into the world. I do wish it were I who gave you life, but unfortunately, I cannot change that. And Daddy loves you very much. He always did. He never stopped thinking and wondering about you, although you knew it was through no fault of his own, he was unable to have contact with you or got to see you grow or be there and support you all these years. He missed a lot and he regrets it. But he is here now and always will be. We both will. For you are the light of our lives, the heart of our hearts.* She continued watching over her daughter.

"Honey." Bettye Jo turned. Philip was heading toward her with their two Cokes. They opened their sodas and began sipping their drinks. They felt refreshed and calm.

"Is she all right?" Philip asked Bettye Jo.

Bettye Jo affirmed, "She is still asleep. Let her rest. The doctor should be here shortly."

Both resumed their Cokes in silence, still by their daughter's side and refusing to leave her in case she needed them.

A few minutes later, they heard quiet, plaintive sounds. "Mama, Mama," she called. Then "Daddy, Daddy." She managed to open her eyes but did not move.

Bettye Jo leaned over. "Yes, darling. Daddy and I are here," she reassured her.

"I do not feel very well." While clutching her stomach, she went on. "It hurts, Mama, my stomach. I have pains, it hurts," she said, quietly trying to control herself.

Bettye Jo leaned over and took her hands in hers. "I know, sweetheart, I know. But we have to wait for the doctor who will take care of you."

Francine struggled to nod and tried to compose herself. The pain was unbearable, but she managed to stay calm, for Bettye Jo and Philip were with her and had no plans to leave until she was all settled in once the doctor arrived.

Bettye Jo brushed her daughter's hair back to the sides of her face and kissed her forehead. Philip watched them with interest. Francine became relaxed despite her present unrelenting pain. She was indeed his princess, now and for always.

"Dr. Marsowe, Mrs. Pennington," a voice from behind called. They turned around. "I am Dr. Paisley. I am here to help you folks," he announced with a smile.

Philip began, gazing at Francine, "It is our daughter. She was brought in around 9:00 p.m. She was severely beaten by her birth mother and sexually assaulted by her husband."

"I am sorry to hear that, sir, ma'am," he remarked sincerely.

Bettye Jo quipped, "Do not worry. The police came and handcuffed them and led them out into the patrol car. We were assured that they would be locked up for a very long time, and believe me, we are relieved. If it were up to us, those people would get the death penalty, and I would be there pressing the lever, watching them descend into hell. Anything for our daughter's safety. We just want her to get better. We do not care how long it takes. We want to be there for her and make sure she is all right, Doctor."

Dr. Paisley smiled and nodded agreeably. Then he walked up to Francine.

Before he asked her any questions, Bettye Jo, concerned, told him, "She just woke up from a brief nap. She might not be able to handle any questions that could trigger an upset and set her off."

Dr. Paisley stated, "I do understand, Mrs. Pennington. I will not stress her out now. She has had enough for tonight." Then he gazed at her and pleasantly stated, "You are going to be all right. Your parents told me what happened. You do not have to talk if you do not want to. I understand, but I need to speak with them, okay?"

Francine nodded politely, but slowly, not saying a word.

He turned to the nurse beside him and said, "Nurse Ruth, would you please take Francine into one of the rooms and get her cleaned up and fed? She is very hungry for she has not eaten since lunchtime."

Nurse Ruth smiled pleasantly and said, "Certainly, Doctor." Then she looked at Francine gleefully.

Francine held out her arms, and Bettye Jo embraced her and kissed her again on her forehead. Francine kissed her mother's cheek. Then Philip took her hands in his and squeezed them. Then he kissed her on the top of her head.

"We love you, sweetheart," Bettye Jo lovingly acknowledged.

Then Philip went on, "The doctor and nurse will make you better. We promise. He has questions we have to answer and matters to discuss and the required information to gather up to help you. Also, there are the necessary forms that we must fill out. It is standard procedure in all hospitals. Do you understand, princess?" He watched his daughter listening attentively but saying nothing.

"We will be back tomorrow morning to see you. We will bring you clothes and books, all right, darling? Do not worry," Bettye Jo stated profusely and lovingly.

"I love you, Mama, Daddy, all the way to Pluto and back," she said, attempting to smile.

"Goodbye," they said again a few times as they waved at her and she waved back. They then turned back to Dr. Paisley, and he led them into his office.

Nurse Ruth went up to Francine. "Are you ready for a ride?" she asked cheerfully.

"Okay," Francine replied quietly and calmly.

Nurse Ruth waved for two attendants to wheel her into the nearby room.

11:30 p.m.

Philip pulled up at Bettye Jo's house and then got out of the car to help her out. Both were exhausted. It was a long day. He walked her to her front door and faced her. "Honey, you must be very tired, and I do not feel you should be alone tonight. I think I should be with you to keep you company, in case you need anything." Then he paused as he watched Bettye Jo's expression on her face. "I do not mean it like that, honey, honestly. I love you, Bettye Jo, and you know I would never do anything to hurt or take advantage of you during this trying time. I am not asking for that. I am not like that and I hope you realize it. I do not want to make the wrong move for you to have that opinion of me. You know that. I just feel you need company just for tonight with no strings attached," he emphasized.

Bettye Jo put her key in the door and then put her hand on Philip's chest as they entered the house. "I know you would not try to take advantage of this situation," she mentioned quietly, "but you are right. I am tired and so are you. You can stay. I would like that very much. You are so kind and thoughtful." Then she turned toward the living room. "You may sleep on the couch. I will go get sheets and a pillow. Just give me a minute."

She took off her coat, hung it in the closet, and then headed up the stairs. Philip nodded and watched her. He began undressing for bed. He, too, was exhausted, thus he sat on the couch and started removing his shoes and socks. Then he loosened his tie, unbuttoned his shirt, and unzipped his pants. He sat on the couch in his underwear for about ten minutes, musing, in a daze. Suddenly, he heard patted footsteps behind him. He got up and walked to the staircase.

It was Bettye Jo with her hair carefully styled, her dark eyes twinkling, and her lips pearly. She was wearing a long, flowing, bright red spaghetti-strapped negligee, which were low-cut, showing her breasts.

Philip's eyes lit up bright and wide, his mouth gaped, and his heart beating. He was shaking with excitement, unable to speak.

She stood. He stood. Both stood. Their eyes gleamed at each other. Speechless.

She continued standing in her spot and lifted her index finger, motioning him to come to her while he was holding his clothes in his arms. He wanted her. She wanted him. They always did but were not always quite sure of each other's intentions and were worried about making the wrong moves and sending ambiguous signals.

He walked up the first step, still saying nothing. She extended her hand to him. Gently, he let it out to her. Both grasped each other's hands, their hearts facing furiously. Slowly, together, they headed to her bedroom.

She lay down on the bed. He was on top of her, tossing his clothes aside on the floor by the bed. He took her face in his hands and kissed her gently but ravenously. She put her hands on his face too and kissed him with fierce, longing love and desire. Then she lifted her gown up and spread her legs wide around his neck, and he masturbated himself. When he got hard, he orgasmed, and slowly he entered her gently, sliding his organ into her. "Ah!" they both sighed pleasantly. They stayed in that position for a while. Then they switched positions. She, on top of him with her hand on his chest, kissed his lips with utmost excitement, and he, her.

He took her face in his hands and said, "Oh, Bettye Jo, my darling."

Then she pronounced, "Philip, Philip," breathless and with deep anticipation.

"I love you, Bettye Jo, my darling, my love."

She responded, "And I love you forever and ever."

Tuesday, 8:00 a.m.

They lay in the nude, spread out across the bed. Their clothes were strewn on the floor. Philip got up, watched her sleep, and then slipped his pants on. She tossed to one side and then the other. He went up to her, stroking her hair. Slowly, she opened her eyes. "Good morning, honey. It is time to get up," Philip said.

With her eyes finally opened, she was in a daze, looking around. She saw Philip and smiled as she clutched the sheets over her. "Good morning to you, Philip, my darling." Both gazed at each other.

"You were wonderful last night," Philip complimented her.

"And so were you," she stated enthusiastically. He took her by the hand and led her out of bed. He finished dressing, and she put on a long, fiery, red duster with a sash.

"I will see you downstairs, honey," he stated. "I will put up the coffee," he offered.

She nodded with appreciation. He headed out the door, and she went to the bathroom, getting ready for today. Both were in deep excitement and planned to make it a wonderful, joyous day for them and their daughter.

A half hour later, she descended the stairs, face washed, teeth brushed, and her thick, blonde, wavy hair formed around her face.

She saw Philip at the kitchen table with a cup of coffee in front of him, gazing up at her with a smile. He rose from his chair and pulled out another chair from underneath, making sure she was seated comfortably. He went to the counter, poured her coffee, and placed it in front of her. She graciously acknowledged him. He responded automatically, "No problem, my lovely lady." They were sitting and sipping their coffee, saying nothing for a while. "I will call Kelly and tell her to cancel all my appointments for today. Our daughter needs us," he stated flatly but with glee. He dialed his office, and Kelly answered pleasantly.

"Good morning, Dr. Marsowe," she addressed carefully. "And how are you doing?"

Philip politely replied, "I am fine, thank you, Kelly. As I told you yesterday, my daughter was severely beaten by her birth mother and husband. She is in the hospital, and her foster/adoptive mother and I are going to visit her. So, please, Kelly, cancel all of my appointments for today."

Then Kelly piped, "Sure, fine, no problem, Dr. Marsowe. I am very sorry about your daughter. I hope she is okay. Send her my deepest regards," she stated.

Then Philip went on, "Thank you, Kelly. I will tell my daughter what you said. You are very kind and sweet. Goodbye, Kelly."

Kelly pleasantly reciprocated, "Have a good day, Dr. Marsowe."

The call ended.

Philip turned to Bettye Jo, who remarked while noticing, "Kelly seems to be such a nice, lovely girl."

"Yes, she is," Philip agreed.

Bettye Jo sipped her coffee and then looked at the wall clock.

"It is getting late," she pointed out. "We better get going. But first, I will call Danielle, my manager, to please hold the fort, since I will be at the hospital all day. She already knows about the situation. She has always been loyal and dependable. I know I can trust her to handle all that needs to be done. For that, I think she will be receiving a salary increase soon."

Philip added, "And so does Kelly, for she is honest and reliable. She deserves a raise for all the hard work and help she does for and gives me."

Bettye Jo punched in the number. Danielle answered promptly, and she recapped her situation patiently, "Sure, Mrs. Pennington, no problem. And I do hope your daughter gets well soon. Have a good day." Bettye Jo thanked her and hung up.

"Well, we best get started. Our daughter is waiting for us," Philip stated staunchly.

Bettye Jo went upstairs to dress. Philip stayed downstairs and straightened his clothes and hair. He called the hospital, informing them that he and Bettye Jo were on their way to visit Francine. They will have time to prepare her for their arrival.

10:00 a.m.

Bettye Jo and Philip waited in the lobby when Dr. Paisley and Nurse Ruth approached them.

Nurse Ruth said, "She is in her room reading. She ate all her breakfast. We gave her a mild tranquilizer after you left. She was out as a light and slept through until 7:00 a.m. We gave her supper for she was, as you both informed us, very hungry. Surprisingly, she ate as a lady should, being she had no food in her for about nine hours. We were not able to do much in examinations or treatments for she was so tired, and we felt she needed a lot of rest. She was calm when you left and is so now. She is not upset or agitated. She was up to answering some questions. She told me about how your relationship came about. I thought to myself, it sounds like a fairy tale, you know, unbelievable but true. I thought, how wonderful you two fell in love, stranger than fiction." Then Nurse Ruth paused.

Bettye Jo quietly and cautiously asked, "Did she mention, you know, her, what happened? What that horrible woman did to her?"

Nurse Ruth stood quietly before resuming. "As a matter of fact, she did, Mrs. Pennington. But she was not at all raging with anger. She was quite calm and stable. She has such maturity for a girl her age despite what she had just gone through. She said she forgave her and understood this woman's own tortured childhood. She did not hate her, but actually pitied her."

Bettye Jo smiled and said, "That is our daughter for you, Nurse, Doctor. Always forgiving and empathetic toward others."

Dr. Paisley remarked, "We have noticed it. She is lucky to have you as her parents, and you are both lucky to have such a lovely daughter."

Bettye Jo and Philip grinned at each other with love.

Dr. Paisley went on, "About treatment plans. Francine lost a lot of blood on her scalp. In about an hour, we will be sending her down to have stitches sewn in. In a week from today, you will bring her in to have them removed." He paused, and they nodded. "As for the bruises on her face and body, she will need massages down with cream twice a day. It will take some time. And most important, she will be examined by a gynecologist, who is scheduled to arrive at 4:00 p.m. He had been notified and he promised to check your daughter's genital organs."

"When do you think she could come home? We want to be there for her," Philip inquired.

Dr. Paisley pondered his question. He wanted to be precise and honest though, being aware of the parents' deep love for their child.

"Perhaps in two days. But for the massages, she will need someone to be there to do it, for it will be too hard for you, and Francine needs a lot of help now, so I will give you a list of qualified physical therapists for you to choose from."

Bettye Jo quickly piped, "Thank you, Dr. Paisley. But I happen to know someone qualified to tend to her care. She knows our daughter and happens to need a job now. She will be thrilled and pleased. She was very good to Francine and helped her during her ordeal. I promised her a job. I will call her, okay, Doctor?"

He smiled. "All right, Mrs. Pennington," he consented pleasantly. "So it is all set," he concluded.

Nurse Ruth offered, "Francine is in her room now. You may go see her now. She has been asking for you around breakfast." Then she led them down the hall to their daughter.

Francine sat in a chair reading, looking fresh and clean. Her face was bright, although with some faint marks. Her hair was hanging down her back with a part on the side.

"Francine," Nurse Ruth called, "look who is here!"

Francine looked up, her book falling off her lap.

Excitedly but cheerfully, she exclaimed, "Mama! Daddy!" as she tried to stand up but staggered a little. With a painful but steady gait, her arms flew wide open.

"Darling, honey," they greeted her, embracing her in their arms. They remained in that position for a while and never wanted to let go.

Both Dr. Paisley and Nurse Ruth watched their interaction with their beloved daughter. They could not help but smile. They were happy.

As they turned to leave, Dr. Paisley reminded them of Francine's schedule for treatment. They acknowledged him gladly, and he and Nurse Ruth left them to enjoy their visit with their daughter.

Bettye Jo reached into her tote bag and showed her something. "Look what I brought you. Your favorite book!"

Francine clapped her hands into the air with joy.

Bettye Jo again reached in and took out a puzzle book.

Francine jumped up and down, struggled into her mother's arms, and gave her a kiss on the cheek. "Oh, Mama, thank you, thank you so much." She took the two books and flipped the pages with great excitement.

Then Philip, who was carrying a suitcase, motioned toward Francine. He said, "Here are some clothes and accessories to hold you over. You will most likely be discharged in two days according to your doctor. All right, princess?"

She awkwardly leaped toward Philip and took the suitcase. "Thank you, Daddy!"

Then he took both her hands and swung her around and around. She laughed. She was so full of joy.

Bettye Jo watched, shaking her head back and forth and giggling. "My two precious babies," she remarked, "Silly, but I love them so. Honey," Bettye Jo began after Philip released her, "How are you feeling now?"

Francine answered, "Better. I just have a little pain my legs, but it is not as bad as before. I will be okay, Mama. Do not worry."

She smiled. "I know, honey. I am so happy for you."

Francine opened the suitcase and took out a pair of denim jeans and a puffed, short-sleeved, hot pink top.

"Can I wear this now, please, Mama, please?"

Bettye Jo smiled her approval. "Of course, darling."

Francine also picked a bra, a pair of underpants, peds, and dark blue open-toe sandals. She brought them with her to the bathroom.

Bettye Jo and Philip watched her pleasingly. She was becoming a very lovely young lady. No one would ever suspect that she had suffered severe, horrid abuse the day before. No one mentioned it. It did not pay. No one wanted to get upset and spoil the day. It was water under the bridge.

Five minutes later, she came out in her clothes, twirling and spinning with difficulty but nonetheless around and around, smiling, with her eyes as sparkling stars.

"Do I look nice, Mama?" She pranced in front of her.

"You look lovely, my darling!" Bettye Jo replied joyfully. "But please be careful. I do not want you to fall," she cautioned her lovingly.

"I will not, Mama. Do not worry," she assured her mother, chuckling.

Then she danced around her father with strained effort. "Am I a beauty, Daddy?" She battered her eyes coyly.

"You are simply a sore sight for sore eyes, princess," he replied lovingly.

Bettye Jo and Philip watched their daughter still prancing around the room. Though she did admit her legs ached a little and was in some discomfort, she was still in high spirits. She did not care if she fell. She would just pick herself up and proceed. She was going to be fine, she assured her parents.

Francine, still with excitement in her eyes, her body swaying although slightly limping, asked her parents. She knew quite well what their reply would be, but she wanted to ask anyway. She did not want the day to end. She loved and wanted to hear it nonetheless. They obliged.

"How much do you love me, Mama?"

Bettye Jo replied, "More than all the grains of sand since time began."

Then to her father, she asked, "And you, Daddy?"

He bent down, placed his hands on the sides of her face, and planted a kiss on her forehead. "Forever and ever, my princess."

"Let us take a walk," Francine suggested, and her parents agreed. She stood in between them, holding their hands and swinging her back and forth. She giggled. Philip and Bettye Jo looked at each other and said nothing. They did not have to. They were pleased and happy.

In between Francine's scheduled treatments, the three of them managed to find an activity during their visit. They met other patients and conversed with the staff. They ate hamburgers, french fries, and sodas in the cafeteria. They had such energy. They never got tired of performing an event. Sometimes, Francine would become tired since her legs have not yet healed, but that was fine. They understood that Francine was full of vigor, enjoying her parents' visit. Suddenly, an idea popped into Francine's head. She nudged her father and motioned him to join her by the right side of the corridor. Bettye Jo saw them and wondered what was going on between them.

Francine told her mother, "Mama, I need to talk to Daddy alone for a minute, okay?"

Bettye Jo shrugged her shoulders. "Why not?" She knew not what else to say. She was puzzled.

Philip and Francine walked down the corridor. She turned to face her father.

"Daddy," she began, "Mothers' Day is in three weeks. I would like to get Mama a card, and you should too." She urged gently, "I know she is not yet my mother legally and formally, but to me she is and always will be regardless of a piece of paper."

Philip remarked, "You have got a good point there, princess. Mama will be so thrilled and surprised."

Then she continued strongly, "You should too, Daddy. I know she is not your wife yet, but there is no law saying you cannot buy a card. After all, she is your daughter's mother. Certainly, you can manage to find an appropriate card to give her from you." She suggested continuously, "She will simply love it and will be definitely surprised."

Philip smiled and agreed, "You are so very right, my princess. Let's go to the gift shop now for they carry greeting cards."

Both father and daughter entered and walked to the card section. They took their time picking out appropriate cards for Bettye Jo. They were there for about fifteen minutes when they made their decisions on the cards. After they were paid for, Philip put them in his coat pocket.

"Boy, will she be surprised!" Both gleamed at each other.

6:00 p.m. The end of the visit

Dr. Paisley met with them in the conference room.

"Luckily, everything went as planned, but Francine needs to rest now. It was a pleasure meeting with you folks. We expect the test results tomorrow, and we will discuss them and further treatment plans when you come tomorrow."

Then he said to Francine, "You are a very lucky, young lady who is loved by your parents. But they must get back to work tomorrow. They promised they will visit you tomorrow late afternoon. You do understand that?" He asked rhetorically, and she replied in agreement.

She turned to her parents. She hugged her mother and kissed her cheek. "I love you, Mama!"

Then she took her father's hands and squeezed them. "And you too, Daddy."

Then she released herself and concluded, "Goodbye, Mama, Daddy. I love you." She blew kisses, and they waved back.

Francine went back to her room. Bettye Jo and Philip left through the front door looking into each other's eyes with love. And they were off.

Wednesday, 4:00 p.m.

Francine was dressed in a long puff-sleeved floral blouse with a multicolored beaded necklace and a pair of brown pants. She wore a charm bracelet on her right wrist and another beaded one on her left wrist. On her feet were flat brown shoes. Her hair hung loosely down her back with a tan headband in front. She sat curled up in a chair working in her puzzle book. She had started her massage therapy after lunch. She was given a walker to aid her until her legs were stronger. Her face appeared healed, as the scratches were faint. She applied cream for them. It seemed to make her face clearer and smooth. She was a little squeamish and sensitive during her Pap smear, but she took it in stride. She was told that she was very brave throughout her treatments, though at times somewhat uncomfortable and edgy, but that was to be expected given her recent ordeal. Now she was quiet and calm, awaiting her parents' arrival.

Nurse Ruth walked into her room and pleasantly informed her, "Francine, your mother and father are here waiting in the lounge. Would you like to go and greet them, or if not, would you prefer I have them come in here? I do not mind either way."

Francine put her book down on the table, attempting to get up. The nurse handed her the walker. Francine managed to reach for it, and the nurse held her arm to steady her. There was a little struggle, but when Francine saw her parents, her face glowed, her eyes grew wide, and her mouth opened. She put her arms out while being held and cried out, "Mama! Daddy!"

They walked up to their daughter, hugging her in their arms.

"Darling!" Bettye Jo called out. She kissed her forehead.

Then Philip automatically took her hands in his and gave her a kiss on the top of her head. "How is my little princess?" Francine reciprocated their greetings, but almost slipped.

"Be careful, honey," Bettye Jo cautioned. "You almost fell."

Francine chuckled, "I am fine, Mama." She assured her. Philip motioned his hand, leading them to the couch to sit down.

"Have a good visit, folks. Dr. Paisley will see you soon to discuss the test results and further treatment plans," Nurse Ruth reminded them and left.

Bettye Jo and Philip turned to their daughter.

Bettye Jo took her chin and said, "Your face seems to be healing nicely." Then she took her hands in hers. "You look simply radiant. And happy."

Francine laughed. "I do feel better."

Then Philip offered, "Would you ladies like a Coke? I know I would. I am thirsty".

They nodded in agreement, and he headed toward the cafeteria.

Francine had been thinking about her surname. She wanted to change it to Philip's name. Up to now, her last name was that woman's maiden name. That was the reason. She wanted no part of that horrible life with that cruel, abusive woman. Who could blame her? She wanted to start a new, fresh life.

"Mama," she faced Bettye Jo, "I want to change my last name. I want Daddy's surname to be mine."

"Of course, darling, why not?" It just never came up.

"Also, I want your middle name, Josephine, to be my middle name as well."

Bettye Jo's eyes lit up and she smiled. "Of course, honey. I would like that very much. It would please and delight me a lot." She was beaming. "We will discuss it when things settle down with your therapy, finishing school, and taking time to unwind. But I promise you, it will be arranged. After our wedding, not only will we formally and legally adopt you, but we will also do that. Daddy will be overjoyed."

"Francine Josephine Marsowe," she announced gleefully. She loved the sound of it. "But I want to be called Franny Jo like you are, Mama, okay?"

Bettye Jo happily agreed. She patted her daughter's hand.

"Of course I am keeping my first name. After all, I am named after my grandmother, Daddy's mother," she proclaimed.

Bettye Jo beamed. Her hands reached her daughter's hands and squeezed each of them tightly.

"Hello, ladies." Philip stood watching them. "Here are your Cokes."

All three of them began drinking them, glancing at each other while laughing.

A few minutes later, Dr. Paisley came up to them. "Folks," he addressed them, and they turned around.

"Hi, Doc!" Francine greeted.

"Hello, young lady," he acknowledged her and nodded to her parents. He was clasping papers on his clipboard near his chest.

"Come with me, please. We will go into the conference room. We will have complete privacy."

Bettye Jo and Philip helped Francine stand up and reached for her walker. Each stood on both sides of her, making sure she did not fall.

As they entered, they sat down. The doctor sat at the head of the long rectangular table.

"I have the results of your daughter's tests and recommendations for further treatment. We put stitches on the side of her head. I advise you not to have her wash her hair or touch that part of it for now for it must heal. If she goes out, she is to wear a hat to avoid infection. You could bring her back in a week from tomorrow to have the stitches removed. After that, we deeply feel that her hair will grow back, but it will take time. She could resume washing and combing it, but with care."

Everyone nodded in silence.

"Now, for the massages. She is to have them done in the morning and evening. It will take time. Also, I have been thinking that she will need the walker for a while. We want to avoid any mishaps that could lead to dislocation of bones or cause possible damage. She could try to walk with it at home a little at a time. As for climbing the stairs, she is to always have someone to accompany her. All this will take a lot of time and effort, but," he faced Bettye Jo, "you say you already have someone. I am pleased for Francine's sake."

"How about my school?" Francine inquired anxiously.

"At this time," Dr. Paisley started carefully, "I do not feel you are up to it. You are still a little weak and vulnerable, thus I do not advise for you to go to school. It would be too stressful for you. Though you are doing much better, you still need a lot of rest and relaxation."

Francine whined, "But I want to graduate with my class. I do not want to fall behind in my schoolwork."

"I understand and don't you worry. You will not fall behind. Your parents will speak to your teachers and counselor to inform them of your situation. They will be giving you your homework assignments, and a teaching assistant will be assigned to administer your examinations for you while you are at home. So do not worry," he reiterated, but this time with stress, "you will be able to graduate on time."

Francine sighed happily. "Yes, Doctor, I understand."

Dr. Paisley nodded. "Good."

"Also, Francine," the doctor warned pleasantly, "you are not to be dancing, twirling, and swinging around. I noticed you do it a lot, but for a while, do not do it. You could hurt yourself and you do not want that."

"Okay," she nodded humbly.

Bettye Jo faced her. "You listen to the doctor. We do not want you to get seriously hurt."

Again, Francine agreed placidly.

Then Dr. Paisley flipped through the rest of his notes on his clipboard. "To conclude, as far as her Pap smear test, I am pleased to say that she is a virgin. Obviously, that poor excuse for a man was unable to enter her. She told me that she gave him a good kick with both her feet in his groin and that he howled. It hurt so badly that he was in deep pain. Your daughter is quite a fighter and was very brave. The blood between her legs was just from inching and scratching her private parts."

"Thank God." Bettye Jo was relieved. She reached for Philip's hand, and he smiled at both Betty Jo and Francine.

Dr. Paisley looked at his watch and rose from his chair. "That is about it for now, folks. I will have Francine ready tomorrow afternoon for you to pick up. We are keeping her over one more night, just to be sure and to take precautions. Okay, folks?"

Bettye Jo and Philip extended their hands to the doctor and then ushered their daughter out.

"Enjoy the rest of your visit."

The three of them walked to the waiting room while the doctor left.

Bettye Jo told Francine that Agnes agreed to come and help her with her therapy. Also, she mentioned that she could use someone to perform some housekeeping and cooking duties, but for now, Francine was her top priority. Later, she will have a regular job with them. Agnes was naturally thrilled.

"Agnes will come over Friday morning. I gave her a list of instructions about your therapy and of the food you like. How does that sound, honey?"

Francine almost jumped out of her chair. With her hand, Bettye Jo gently motioned her to sit down. Doctor's orders.

At once, she did so, but brightly chirped, "Sorry, I forgot." And then she replied, "Fine, Mama. She is a nice person. And you and Daddy are wonderful to help her and the others."

"Also," Bettye Jo continued, "I told Raymond that I needed a delivery person, since the one I have at my shop plans to retire and move to Florida soon. He was very happy for the opportunity. He will begin work this Monday."

Francine sat listening to her mother as she spoke.

"Daddy said he needs a cleaning person. He feels Kelly does too much as it is and she deserves help for all her valuable work. So he called Alice and she, too, jumped at the chance." She stopped, facing her daughter. Both said nothing.

"How about Myles?" Francine inquired.

"I contacted an employment agency that specializes in finding maintenance positions. I referred Myles to them, and they agreed to help him. Myles happens to be very good with his hands. Though he knows it is only a menial job, he was nonplussed and keen on the idea. He does not mind sweeping or picking up the garbage. He thanked me profusely."

Francine clapped her hands while sitting in her chair. She remembered the doctor's orders about moving about.

"I cannot believe it, Mama. I simply cannot. You and Daddy are simply amazing and wonderful people." She threw her arms around her mother's neck and kissed her cheek. Bettye Jo laughed and returned her usual display of affection. She patted her daughter's back, and they held each other for a while. Philip watched them with pleasure.

Then he began, "Why don't we all take a walk?"

They strolled down the corridor with Francine in between them.

They spent the rest of their visit walking up and down the halls laughing and chattering about mundane issues. Bettye Jo and Philip eyed each other with gleam. Francine noticed but said nothing aloud. She thought internally, *What are they up to now?* She dared not ask for they would deny anything. And she left it at that.

6:00 p.m.

An aide walked up to them and announced with a smile, "It is time for Francine's supper now. Later, she will get her massage. I hope you all had a good visit." Then she eyed Francine and then her parents. "You have a wonderful daughter, so patient, sweet, and kind. She is simply a joy to have around."

Bettye Jo and Philip were ecstatic and beaming with joy.

Bettye Jo remarked, "She is the heart and joy of our lives." She patted Francine's head and pinched her cheek.

Philip added, "We have been blessed with such a loving daughter." She faced Francine and then the aide.

"You could all say your goodbyes now," the aide offered.

As usual, there were hugs, kisses, waves, and most importantly, the I love yous.

Bettye Jo and Philip thanked the aide for her support, smiled at their daughter, and then left.

The aide put her arm around Francine's shoulder and went for supper in the day room

Thursday, 5:00 p.m.

Francine sat in the waiting room, clad in a red puff-sleeved top and a peasant skirt. She wore her usual beads around her neck and wrists. She wore red flat sandals. Her hair hung loosely down her back. She had a red band in her hair.

She packed her suitcase with all her clothes, accessories, and books. She could hardly wait to go home.

Her parents were on their way in the car. Traffic was light and that was good. They wanted their daughter home where she belonged and was loved.

Philip's cell phone rang when a red light appeared. He reached for it in his pocket and answered, "Yes, Kelly? Is everything all right?"

Kelly assured him that it was, but she had to mention something not urgent, but he needed to be informed. "Wayne had a little car trouble. He is at the auto repair shop getting the problem resolved. It is nothing major. A gas leak, I think. He told me he might be late, so do not worry, Dr. Marsowe. Wayne always keeps his promises. That is why I love him. He is very dependable," she stated convincingly. "All right, Dr. Marsowe?"

"Of course, Kelly, it is okay. Thank you for telling me. Bettye Jo and I are headed to the hospital now. See you later and take care," he sincerely told her.

"I will and thank you. Bye now."

They both hung up.

Wayne was Kelly's boyfriend for almost a year. Philip met him and liked him. He had pleasant manners and treated Kelly with respect.

Bettye Jo and Philip planned to give Francine a new desktop computer. The one she had was antiquated and did not help her much anymore. Also, she will not have to go to the library to search for information or for homework. Philip knew Kelly's boyfriend was a computer expert. Thus, he hired him to purchase the necessary equipment and have it set up in Francine's bedroom. Philip intended to pay him back for all his work along with a generous bonus.

Philip told Bettye Jo about the call, reassuring her that the necessary work will be completed, but it might take longer due to Wayne's car problem. Bettye Jo was fine with it. She also knew that Wayne was loyal and true to his word.

Beep, beep. The car behind him honked impatiently.

Philip turned and smiled. "Sorry, sir," he apologized, and they were off.

When they reached the hospital, the parking lot was practically empty. They were lucky and grateful. They were eager to take their daughter home.

As they entered the hospital, they saw Francine sitting on a soft chair. Her eyes were enlightened, wide, and large. Remembering Dr. Paisley's orders, she did not jump up, but she cried out with her arms out, "Mama! Daddy!" They ran into her arms with the usual embrace.

Then Dr. Paisley walked up to them, handing her parents the necessary forms and treatment instructions. In return, they thanked the doctor for all his help with their daughter. They shook his hands. Then he walked up to Francine. "Good luck, young lady. Remember to follow my orders, okay? You were a very good and brave patient." Then to her parents, he went on, "Your daughter is a very sweet and lovely young girl. You are all very fortunate to have each other. Goodbye and good luck. I will have an aide carry her suitcase." He motioned to the porter near the entrance who obliged.

Philip and Bettye Jo helped Francine with her walker. She managed to stand up and walked between her parents out to their car. They were going home.

It was getting dark, but luckily, traffic was slow.

Francine sat in the backseat looking out the window. Bettye Jo turned and smiled at her. Francine smiled back. "Are you all right, darling?" she asked, concerned, but gleefully attempting a conversation. Francine assured her that she was fine. Bettye Jo turned back to the front. They rode home in silence, happy but somewhat tired, though every now and again, Francine witnessed her parents smiling and winking at each other. *What is happening? What is going on?* she wondered to herself while gazing up at the dark sky, the bright and round moon, and millions of stars twinkling brightly. She was mesmerized by them for they have always fascinated her ever since she was a little girl. But she was not a little girl anymore. She was now a fine and mature young girl of whom her parents were very proud of. That woman, that awful, horrible, and cruel woman and her good-for-nothing lowlife of a husband were never mentioned or spoken about or heard from again. They were put away and locked up for good. Francine was safe, loved, and no longer afraid for her life.

The three of them were now in their driveway. The house was dark. Philip got out to let Bettye Jo out, reaching for her hand. Both went to open the back door and help Francine out. They did it slowly, making sure they were careful not to intentionally hurt her. She stood up holding her walker, and they guided her to the front door. Bettye Jo fished into her handbag for her key and opened the door. The lights flew open.

Everyone yelled at once, "Welcome home, Francine."

She was aghast, with her hands over her eyes and her mouth in a wide grin. In the corner were words in bright colors that said, "Welcome Home."

On the living room table lay a very big bright colorful card that read, "Welcome Home, Francine." There were butterflies, hearts, and flowers on it. When she opened it, she saw that everyone at the party signed it. She was mesmerized, teary-eyed, and at a loss for words. It took some time, but she read everyone's greetings. She smiled at them and graciously said, "Thanks, guys!"

"Way to go," they shouted together.

First, she saw her three friends, Willow, Arlene, and Stephanie, who shouted out, "Hello, Francine!"

Unable to walk over to them, she went, "Hey, guys!"

Then they ran up to her, and they all hugged one another.

"Are you okay?" Willow asked.

Francine smiled gleefully, assuring them that she was.

Then she saw Aunt Ellen and Uncle Paul, who put his arm around her.

Francine threw her arms up in the air and called out, "Aunt Ellen! Uncle Paul!"

"Hi, sweetheart," her uncle greeted her. "How is my favorite niece?" Aunt Ellen and Uncle Paul asked, knowing Francine was their only niece, but it did not perturb her in the slightest. She was beginning to develop a sense of humor. Both walked up to her, pecked her cheeks, and patted her back.

Then she saw a young woman with long, straight blonde hair parted on the side. She was wearing a sleeveless white cotton blouse with a beige knitted vest over it, and on her legs were a pair of rustic brown sleek slacks. She wore low-heeled, sling-back brown shoes. She let out her hand and said, "I am Kelly, your father's secretary. It is so nice to finally meet you. Your father always has lovely accolades about you."

Francine piped up, "He says you are a valuable asset to his office." Then she shook Kelly's hand and smiled.

"Honey," a young male voice called from over the staircase railing.

Kelly turned and introduced him, "That is my boyfriend, Wayne."

He had dark blonde tousled hair and pale blue eyes surrounded with round, wired glasses. He had a boyish smile.

"Hi!" Francine chirped at him.

"He is the most, the utmost!" Kelly remarked.

Then another young woman with dark hair and short curls around her head, clad in a long burgundy sweater, black slacks, and owlish framed glasses, came up to Francine and extended her hand. "I am Danielle, your mother's manager, her right hand." She glanced at Bettye Jo. They shook each other's hands and nodded gleefully.

Bettye Jo announced, "Everybody, let us all have some refreshments. They are all on the kitchen table. Dig in!" They did so.

Philip and Bettye Jo helped Francine walk to the table and offered her a cup of Coke and three Oreo cookies. She sat down at the table, daintily drank her soda, and took small bites of her cookies. They all gathered around fussing over

Francine by cheering her on and making sure that she was all right and having a good time.

Francine acknowledged their pleasantries, "Thanks, guys!"

Bettye Jo and Philip were watching their daughter and everyone interacting. They were joyful and elated.

Then a voice called from the steps. It was Wayne. He announced, "Everything is ready, guys."

Francine just sat there speechless. She had no idea what was going on. Bettye Jo and Philip tied a blindfold across her eyes, helped her from her chair with her walker, and guided her slowly upstairs, saying nothing.

She asked them, puzzled, "What is happening?"

Bettye Jo replied evasively, "Let us just go upstairs, honey."

Her parents led her up the stairs quietly, saying nothing. Everyone was watching. They were all in on it.

"Careful," warned Bettye Jo as Philip opened the bedroom door leading Francine into her room. Then he ripped the blindfold off Francine's eyes.

"Oh my God!" she exclaimed breathlessly. There on her desk was a brand-new computer all set up and ready for use. "Oh my God!" she reiterated.

Her eyes were on fire, her mouth opened wide, and her hands were at the sides of her face.

"I cannot believe it!"

"Believe it, honey," Bettye Jo affirmed.

Francine stood in her spot, unable to say more.

"We went to a lot of trouble for you to have a brand-new computer, being the other was outdated and you would not have to use the library's computer anymore. And you are worth it, princess. You are a wonderful daughter. Everyone knew about it, and we had them swear to keep it a surprise among themselves. It was difficult and challenging, but everyone kept their part of the bargain."

Tears of joy ran down Francine's face, and her hands were on it.

"Thank you, guys," she attempted to embrace her parents but recalled Dr. Paisley's orders, so they came over to her. All three of them were laughing and crying while hugging and kissing profusely.

They heard voices downstairs say, "Let's go, you guys!"

"In a minute," Philip called out.

They composed themselves while descending the stairs, with everyone shouting at once, enjoying themselves immensely.

Friday, 9:00 a.m.

Bettye Jo was in the kitchen talking on the telephone.

"Hello, Danielle," she addressed her manager. "I will be coming in some time this afternoon to tend to some personal business. You understand, don't you?" She paused and then went on, "Good, I could always depend on you." She stopped again and then responded, "Yes, Danielle, she is just fine. All she needs is some rest for she is still weak." She paused again. "Thank you very much for your concern. You are the greatest." Still hearing Danielle, she reassured her that everything was being taken care of, and finally they said, "Have a good day and goodbye." The call ended.

Bettye Jo, clad in her long pink cotton robe, began preparing for Agnes' arrival, making sure that she completely knew what her duties were.

The telephone rang. Bettye Jo stopped to read the caller ID. It was Philip. He called to make sure that Bettye Jo and Francine were doing all right. He said he was sorry that he was not able to come over. He had patients that he felt needed him more so today than on some other days. Bettye Jo understood completely and was not upset. He said that he will call this evening and come to see how his two favorite ladies were holding up. She remarked on his sweetness and thoughtfulness. They bid each other the usual "I love you" and hung up.

Then the doorbell rang.

"That must be Agnes." She knew for sure. She wiped her hands with a dish towel and opened the door.

"Good morning, Mrs. Pennington," Agnes greeted cheerfully.

Bettye Jo returned her greeting and led her into the kitchen, showing her around and explaining her duties. Agnes hardly had to ask any questions. She picked up Bettye Jo's instructions to a T. Bettye Jo gave her a list of people's telephone numbers to call in case of an emergency. Agnes nodded with assent. Also, Bettye Jo wrote down all of Francine's favorite foods. Agnes glanced at the list and replied, "No problem, Mrs. Pennington," she assured her employer.

Bettye Jo looked up at the clock and then smoothed her duster. She pointed to the staircase, leading Agnes while mentioning, "Let us go upstairs and see how Francine is doing. Then I will give you the doctor's instructions for her therapy, since Francine's therapy is the focus on the agenda. And furthermore, she would love to say hello. She is so grateful to you for saving her life, and so am I and her father."

"It was no problem, Mrs. Pennington. She needed us, and we were glad to be there for her," she stated in a matter-of-factly way.

When they got upstairs, Bettye Jo gently knocked on Francine's door. Francine tossed and turned, opening her eyes. She did not answer at first for she needed to come to herself.

"Francine, honey, it's Mama. Are you awake? Agnes is here to see you," she stated softly.

At that, Francine sat up in her bed. Her eyes were wide open.

"Yes, Mama, I'm awake," she acknowledged her mother. Then she went on, "Please come in, Mama." And then she added, "And Agnes too."

Bettye Jo and Agnes entered her room. Francine, still tired but happy, managed a smile.

"Good morning, Francine," Agnes greeted her.

"Good morning, darling," her mother added pleasantly.

Bettye Jo resumed, "Agnes will be taking care of you now. You remember?" Francine nodded compliantly.

"I'll be getting dressed now. I must go to your school to speak with your teachers and guidance counselor. They will be sending over your classwork and homework assignments. A teacher's assistant will administer your examinations."

Francine listened to her mother. When she was finished, she asked curiously, "Where's Daddy, Mama?"

"Daddy had to go to work. He said today's patients had imperative issues and needs that he has to tend to, so they could get well," she explained. "He promised to see us tonight, okay, sweetheart?"

Francine understood that her father's work at times needed more consideration. She knew that her father loved her, so she did not have any qualms.

As Bettye Jo headed out of her daughter's bedroom, she mentioned, "Today, Agnes will be making you your french toast with bacon, just as you like it. I showed her how to do it. I wish I could do it as I always did, but I need to go to your school to pick up your schoolwork. You do understand, honey?"

"Yes," she affirmed, "I do."

"I will be getting dressed now. Then I have to go." She gave her daughter a kiss on the cheek, and Francine threw her arms around her mother's neck, tightly kissing her cheek. "Goodbye, darling."

Francine called out, "I love you all the way to Pluto and back."

Bettye Jo smiled pleasantly.

Again, she was compliant and unperturbed. She knew that she was loved, safe, and cared for.

They blew each other kisses.

She left Francine's bedroom and headed to her bedroom to start the day.

Agnes and Francine prepared for today's therapy. There was much to be done, but it was for the sake of love.

First, Agnes realized that she needed to make Francine's breakfast, so she went downstairs and promised to be up soon. Francine understood. She grabbed a book from her table beside her bed and started reading.

Mother's Day Morning

Bettye Jo was tossing and turning in bed all morning. She was tired and unable to find a comfortable sleeping position.

Agnes, Francine, and Philip were downstairs. Agnes was making their breakfast. Two floral bouquets, one was pink carnations and the other one was red roses, lay in the center of the table. Philip and Francine placed their cards near them. All three of them chatted away about nothing. They wanted today to be special for Bettye Jo. It was her day.

Bettye Jo was in still in bed. Francine and Philip were eager for her to get up and became impatient.

"I wish she would come downstairs already. I can't wait," Francine moaned.

Philip put his hand on her arm. "She will, princess. You have to be patient," he advised her gently.

"I know, Daddy, but she's taking too long."

Suddenly, they heard pattering of footsteps upstairs.

Philip and Francine lifted their heads up.

"Mama!" Francine clapped her hands together.

"What's going on?" Bettye Jo asked, clad in her long red nylon robe and fluffy red slippers.

Philip motioned to her. "Come down, honey," he eagerly stated.

Bettye Jo remarked, "Okay, just give me five minutes."

"Fine, Mrs. Pennington. We will be waiting," Agnes mentioned as she set the coffeepot back on the stove.

Philip and Francine leaned toward each other and gabbed between themselves with smiling faces. Agnes watched as she stood against the refrigerator.

Bettye Jo headed down the stairs gracefully like a gazelle. Her hair was combed and fluffy around her face, her face was clean, and her eyes were sparkling. Her lips were together and then broke out into a smile.

Philip got out of his chair, took her hand, and led her to a seat. He pulled out a chair, and after she sat down, he pushed it forward.

"Good morning, sweetheart." He kissed her cheek.

Francine leaned over. "Happy Mother's Day, Mama." She kissed her and put her arms around her neck. "Look, Mama." She pointed to the two bouquets of flowers.

Bettye Jo leaned over and put them to her nose. "Ah!" she sighed pleasantly. "They're beautiful!" she exclaimed excitedly.

Then Francine reached for the cards and handed them to her.

Slowly, Bettye Jo opened Francine's card and read the message. It had lots of hearts and flowers on the front cover. Francine wrote on it: "I love you, Mama, all the way to Pluto and back, Love and kisses, Your daughter, Francine Josephine."

Bettye Jo put the card down, turned to her daughter, and hugged and kissed her. "Thank you, darling."

She reached for Philip's card. It read, "To a very special lady on Mother's Day." Then he wrote on the bottom, "Thank you for being my daughter's mother. I love you forever and always." He took her chin and kissed her lips, and she, in turn, did so.

"Thank you, thank you both." She turned first to Philip and then Francine. She hugged both of them.

But she was puzzled and asked Philip, "When, how did you manage to buy these cards? I don't understand."

Philip piped up, "Remember at the hospital when Francine told you to excuse ourselves and we both walked away from you down the hallway?"

Bettye Jo nodded, trying to recollect the event in her mind.

"You had a bewildered expression on your face and shrugged your shoulders," Francine went on, hoping the moment would come back to her.

Bettye Jo tried to envision that day in her mind, thinking and thinking repeatedly.

"I nudged Daddy and told you I had to talk to him alone. It was on that Tuesday when you both visited me and spent the entire day with me. I had tests done that day. Remember, Mama? Please, please say it. You have to, you must," she urged her mother.

Suddenly, Bettye Jo's eyes lit up as twinkling stars. "Oh, yes! I do, I do, I do now. Oh, my darlings." She looked at Philip and Francine. "I remember very distinctly now. I can practically picture it quite vividly. Oh, yes, yes, I do, I do. I really do." She cried tears of joy. "I do remember."

Yes, she remembered that day. She rose from her chair and furiously embraced her daughter and Philip. Everyone shouted out with glee.

Agnes watched them with a slight pleased smile on her face. *It was going to be a good day,* she mused happily to herself.

A Month Since Mother's Day: Six Weeks Since Francine's Hospital Stay

Saturday Morning

Dr. Paisley looked at Francine's legs in silence for a while, and then at her arms. "I am pleased to say that she is completely healed. Not a sign of a scar or a bruise. The therapy worked well as I hoped. She will no longer need the walker." He looked at Philip and Bettye Jo. "You both did a good job keeping up with her therapy."

Francine smiled, clapped her hands in the air, and attempted to jump up, but the doctor motioned her with his hand. "As for you, young lady, you followed all my instructions, and I am proud. But I still want you to be careful. I know you are happy and feel like dancing around. I do too, but for now, you still must watch yourself. You do not want to have any relapses or repercussions, and neither do your parents."

Francine resigned but confirmed, "All right, you're the boss, but," she piped up coyly, "a cute one." She noticed his dark wavy hair and pale blue eyes.

Dr. Paisley smiled at her and then pointed out, "You seem to be acquiring a sense of humor, young lady."

Francine then popped up, "And what about school? I really think I am ready to go back."

The doctor pondered and then said, "You could, since you are practically cured, but still, I strongly advise you, no excitement, just your classes for now. No extracurricular activities for a while, okay?"

Francine pressed the palms of her hands together under her chin. Her eyes were bright and in her lips was a gleeful smile. She was fine. The doctor said she could see her friends but to take it easy.

Then he turned to her parents. "Just be sure she doesn't jump and leap around. She could forget, and you don't want that." He stopped for a minute. "Also, I nearly forgot. The spot where she had her stitches healed nicely. Hair is starting to grow back there, but again, do take care and be gentle around that area." Then he got up and faced Francine and her parents and extended his hand for them to shake, and they did so, likewise. Francine put out her hand, and he shook it and made a grin. "You're quite a girl," he remarked to her. The he said to Bettye Jo and Philip, "Take good care of her. If anything else comes up or if you have any questions, please feel free to call me." He gave them his business cards, which they took.

"Thanks a lot, Doctor," Philip said with a slight smile.

"You did a great job with our daughter. To that, we are grateful," Bettye Jo stated graciously.

The three of them turned and walked toward the door. Francine turned around, smiled, and waved to the doctor. He waved back, stood there for a minute, and then went back down the hall.

The sun shone brightly in the clear blue sky. Francine gazed up from the back seat. She leaned forward and put her hands on the back of the front seat.

"Mama, Daddy," she started, "may I see my friends later? It's been a while. Please?"

Bettye Jo turned to face her and put her hand on her daughter, gently saying, "Honey, I know you're eager to see them, but Dr. Paisley said you have to still relax, take it easy, and not get overly stimulated, and sometimes it could happen unintentionally. I will tell you what, you could call them and explain everything to them. They will understand. Okay for now, honey?"

She hated to disappoint her, but the doctor advised her to take it slowly. Francine was a little bit disappointed, but she knew her parents did it out of their love for her. Francine answered softly, "Okay, I understand. I will call them later." Then, as an afterthought, she suggested, "Why don't we go out for lunch to celebrate?"

Bettye Jo agreed and so did Philip, who stated, "Anything for our girl."

They were off.

7:00 p.m.

Philip stayed with Bettye Jo and Francine for a while after dinner. Agnes served Salisbury steak with white rice and covered in gravy.

Everybody was tired. Philip glanced at his watch and yawned. "It is getting late now, my lovely ladies. I think it is about time I started for home."

He stood up and kissed Bettye Jo on the lips and patted Francine's head and brushed the side of her face with his hand.

Bettye Jo and Francine bid him goodbye and waved.

"We love you," they said in unison.

"Me too," he automatically but sincerely stated with a grin and twinkle in his eyes. Then he was gone.

Francine and Bettye Jo sat down at the table facing each other.

"Mama," Francine began, "Father's Day is next Sunday. I would like to send him a card. You should too. And you know what else, Mama?" she paused to catch her breath and then resumed, "Why don't we visit Grandpa and Grandma and invite Uncle Paul and Aunt Ellen? You could have Raymond drive us. Daddy shouldn't have to. It's his day, you know, Mama." She stopped.

Bettye Jo put her hand on her arm and chuckled, "That's a simply wonderful suggestion, honey. I cannot believe you thought all of this by yourself. You are so considerate and loving. You are, darling, you really are."

Francine beamed up out of her chair. "So we'll do it, Mama, for real?"

"Of course," she replied, "but a lot of preparations have to be made. It may take a little time and patience, but I'm willing if you are."

"Oh, I am, I am." Francine smacked her hands together in front of her.

Agnes was by the sink cleaning up after dinner. She put the dishrag flat down neatly on the counter.

"I am all finished, Mrs. Pennington," she told her. "You need anything else?"

Bettye Jo smiled. "No, thank you. You did a wonderful job as always. You could go home now, it's getting late," she pointed out carefully.

"Thanks." She went to get her coat and grabbed her handbag. As she opened the door, she waved and said, "Good night."

Bettye Jo and Francine waved back and said. "Good night."

She went out the door, heading home.

Francine yawned. Bettye Jo suggested that she go relax in her bedroom since it was a long, big day. "We'll discuss your plans for Daddy tomorrow, okay, sweetheart?"

"Yes, Mama," she affirmed.

She got out of her chair to kiss her mother with a hug, which was naturally reciprocated with the usual "I love you."

Francine headed upstairs. Bettye Jo took the newspaper and began her usual routine of working on her crossword puzzle.

Sunday Morning

Francine and Bettye Jo sat at the kitchen table while Agnes made them their breakfast and coffee.

"What do you want to do today, sweetheart? Daddy will be here in an hour. We'll do whatever you choose, okay?"

Francine sat and pondered, "Mama, I have been thinking about this for some time now, but I hope you will not think it will be morbid."

"No, honey." She leaned over and touched her hand. "There is nothing morbid about you or anything you do or say." She was gentle and reassuring.

Francine looked down, her hands together on the table, pondered and unable to continue. Bettye Jo observed her, also saying nothing. Still, she wanted to hear what her daughter had in mind. She was sure it was something altruistic because that was just the kind of person she was, sensitive and understanding to other people's feelings.

"There is nothing you can't tell me. You know that, honey," she still reassured her.

With her head facing down, she began, "I would like to visit your daughter's, your other daughter's grave. It might sound foolish and peculiar, but I would like to 'meet' her. I feel like she's my sister." She stopped, worried that she would be chastised for her request.

Bettye Jo's eyes were wide open, and she smiled and squeezed her daughter's hand affectionately. "That's simply a wonderful and lovely thought to meet someone you never met or have not known. And I think it is cute that you think of her as your sister. I can't believe anyone could ever come up with such an idea, but with you, I am not really surprised because I know you and your gentle, caring nature."

Francine looked up at her mother and smiled. "You really think so, Mama?" She was a little doubtful.

"Of course, darling." Bettye Jo got up, took her face, and kissed her cheek. "It is a bit unusual, but in a good way."

"Daddy won't mind. I mean, Sherry Jo was not his daughter, nor did he know or meet her," she considered that point.

"Being the kind of man he is, he would not mind at all," she affirmed.

Francine jumped up and clapped her hands in the air. Bettye Jo grinned gleefully. She was pleased and proud of her daughter. It was all set.

12:00 p.m.

The doorbell rang.

Francine jumped from her seat. Bettye Jo stood by the counter.

"It's him!" Francine exclaimed joyfully.

She ran to open the door. Philip was standing erect with a twinkle in his eyes. He took her by both her hands and twirled her around. She giggled.

"And how is my little princess doing today?"

Her eyes shone brightly. "Oh, just fine, Daddy."

She looked at Bettye Jo, who smiled at them and shook her head. "My two babies," she stated with a chuckle. "That is enough, you two."

Everyone laughed.

Francine took her father's hand and led him to the kitchen table. Bettye Jo continued to watch them walk up to her. She leaned forward with her hands on his chest, and they kissed each other on the lips. Francine watched them from her seat and then remarked with a giggle, "Come on, you guys!" They turned and laughed joyfully at her. And then she added with a playful grin, "And now who's being silly?"

They all sat down at the table. Agnes, who had been dusting in the living room, came in and asked while putting the rag down, "Can I get you anything, folks?"

Bettye Jo popped, "Could you please bring us some coffee and a glass of milk for Francine?"

Agnes smiled. "Certainly." Then she went over to the counter to prepare her employer's request.

The three of them resumed their conversation.

Bettye Jo turned to Philip. "Philip, Francine wants to go and see my other daughter's gravesite today. She mentioned that Sherry Jo is like a sister, though they never met. She would like to talk to her and bring flowers. Is that okay with you, honey?"

Philip's mouth turned into a big grin. He looked at his daughter with such love. For all her past troubles, she managed to be sensitive and caring toward others. "I do not see why not," he stated agreeably. And to Bettye Jo, he affirmed, "I think it would be a great idea. Francine visiting her 'sister.'"

Bettye Jo plopped her hands on her lap. "Great!" she announced, "Let's all get ready."

She and Francine stood up. Philip sat, and Agnes handed him his coffee. He began sipping it gingerly.

Both Bettye Jo and Francine went upstairs to get dressed and refresh themselves.

Meanwhile, Philip and Agnes conversed in small talk.

"Dr. Marsowe, what a lovely daughter you and the misses have. You two are so lucky," she mentioned brightly.

He looked up and smiled. "Yes, I guess you could say that."

Agnes got up, went over to the kitchen counter, poured dish detergent on a cloth, and wiped the sink and then the counter. She stacked the breakfast dishes into the dishwasher.

Philip sat with his coffee in his hands and watched her. She was an excellent maid and most importantly, a loving, caring person. If it were not for her, God knows what would have happened to Francine. She was indeed a godsend. Bettye Jo, Philip, and Francine were extremely lucky to have her in their lives.

"By the way, Agnes," Philip asked with curiosity, "have you heard anything from Myles?"

Agnes was wiping around, but turned to answer him, "As a matter of fact, yes, I have. He got a maintenance position in some project development. He is happy, I am pleased to say. Also, Dr. Marsowe, how is Alice working out?"

"Alice is doing great. She is helping Kelly a lot. You know Kelly was always a hard worker, doing more than I ask her to do and without any complaints. They both have a good rapport, and I am glad. Alice is always eager to please others."

Agnes smiled at Dr. Marsowe. She then asked about Raymond.

"Raymond does whatever he has to and more. He came just at the right time when Bettye Jo's regular, longtime deliveryman was about to retire." Philip stopped, took a sip of coffee, and then tapped his fingers on the table. He looked up at Agnes and remarked sincerely, "You were all wonderful with our daughter. Every one of you. Bettye Jo and I are grateful, and you are all a big help and perform beyond the call of duty."

Agnes simply stated, "We did whatever had to be done. Francine needed us. She is a lovely girl, Dr. Marsowe."

"Thanks, we know," Philip affirmed.

At that, Bettye Jo and Francine were already at the bottom of the stairs, ready and willing to go. They had smiles on their faces. Philip faced them, got up, and said, motioning with his hand, "Let's go now, my lovely ladies."

They went ahead of him and bid Agnes a good day, and she waved back. "Bye now." Then Agnes turned toward the kitchen.

The three of them rode in the car, content and joyful. The radio was blasting with country music. Francine was swinging to it, leading the band with her hands in front of her in the air. They were singing off-key, naturally, but in perfect gleeful harmony and in a very good mood.

Francine was clad in a spaghetti-strapped floral red dress above her knees. Her hair was up in a bun as usual and surrounded by a matching scrunchie. She wore white stockings and red sandals. Around her neck was a string of red beads, as were on both her wrists.

Bettye Jo wore a low-cut bright red tank top, also spaghetti-strapped. Her red slacks were flowing down her ankles. She wore red open-toed sling-back shoes. Her blonde wavy hair, surrounded with a scarf, was fluffed up around her face. She was wearing a cameo around her neck and wore a charm bracelet on her right wrist. She wore dark, pearly sunglasses to keep the sun away.

Philip was dressed casually. Usually, he wore a suit with a white shirt and tie, jacket, and pants since he was in a professional occupation. Today, he was laid-back in a blue cotton short-sleeved shirt and dungarees. He wore loafers on his feet.

And to think they were heading toward the cemetery to pay respects to Francine's "sister," who was Bettye Jo's other daughter.

Suddenly, Philip, while removing his wire-rimmed sunglasses, piped up, turning first to Bettye Jo and then to Francine. "Hey, ladies, how's about we go out to dinner afterward? Chinese, anyone?"

Both Bettye Jo and Francine shouted out in the air, "Right on!"

Philip sped up the car and they were off. The three of them sang at the top of their lungs and chuckled while looking at the scenery. It would be a while until they arrived at their destination.

Francine leaned over and whispered into her mother's ear. Bettye Jo's eyes lit as she smiled at her daughter.

"Honey," Bettye Jo put her hand on Philip's shoulder, "Francine needs to use the ladies' lavatory. In fact, I could do so also. So, could you please stop in the next rest area? Francine and I would appreciate it." She turned to her daughter, her eyes bright and with a smile.

"Sure, ladies," he grinned.

"That's great," they both replied graciously as they slyly winked at each other. Francine bounced into her seat, still swaying to the music as they continued their ride.

Suddenly, Francine, while gazing out the window, pointed with excitement. "Mama, look, there it is," she exclaimed gleefully, trying to catch her breath.

"A rest stop and all those stores!" She could not contain herself.

Bettye Jo smiled happily. "Yes, there it is," she remarked. And then she instructed Philip, "Honey," she pointed out, "please let us out now. We really have to, you know."

"Of course, darling." He turned the car into the parking lot. Francine was still bouncing in her seat, squirming.

Philip parked and let them out. Francine and Bettye Jo strolled toward the stores. Philip watched them. *I know they are up to something. I just know it. But for the life of me, what is happening here?* he pondered to himself. A smile and gleam shone in his eyes, and his mouth watered.

While in the store, Bettye Jo and Francine browsed through the shelves. Suddenly, an item caught Francine's eye. "Look, Mama, look." She pointed eagerly. She walked up to a cup that read, "To the Greatest Dad." "I love that. I think that is a perfectly appropriate gift to give Daddy. Don't you think so, Mama? It says exactly what I want to say," Francine said.

Bettye Jo turned to her daughter agreeing profusely, "Yes, sweetheart, it certainly is."

Francine took the cup off the shelf, "I'm going to buy it right now, Mama, okay, please?"

She read the price tag $5.00 and she also wanted it gift-wrapped. Then she walked over to the card rack and nudged her mother and stated, "Let's get the cards right now," she strongly suggested.

Bettye Jo laughed while putting her hand on her shoulder. "All right, all right, honey." They headed toward the card stand searching for the perfect card. It took a while, but finally, they made their selections. They wanted to get just the right card.

Then Francine had a thought. She tapped her mother's hand. "And how about you, Mama? Don't you think you should also get Daddy a present? I mean, since we're already here, I don't see why not."

Bettye Jo replied, "I already bought mine last week while you were in school. It was hard to pick the appropriate one, but don't worry, honey, he'll love my present and yours too."

"Also, you know what, Mama," she thought as she pointed to a stand with flowers, "I'd like to bring some flowers to Sherry Jo's and William's gravesites."

Bettye Jo smiled. "Certainly."

Then they picked two floral bouquets, one for Sherry Jo and the other for Bettye's husband, William. They figured, "Why not?"

"Now, let us go pay for all of this. And you know what, I do, and I think maybe you also need to use the ladies' room. Okay, sweetheart?"

Francine agreed, and they both completed their mission.

As they walked to the car, Philip was watching them swinging their tote bags back and forth, staring and smiling at each other.

As they got into the car, Philip asked with loving curiosity, "What took you ladies so long?"

They were not going to tell him as it was a surprise. They giggled to each other, saying not a word.

"We had to go really badly, isn't that right, Mama?" Francine nudged her mother who, though surprised at her reply, quickly agreed, "Yes, that's right!"

Philip started the car, and they were off, still with the blasting country music on the radio. They sang throughout the rest of the ride. No one said anything, but they were all smiles.

A while later, they approached a sign near an entrance: Hill Side Cemetery.

"We're here," Bettye Jo announced, facing Philip and Francine.

They rode inside, searching for Sherry Jo's and William's gravesites.

Bettye Jo looked at the cemetery map where she marked their gravesites. She directed Philip and then reached their destination.

They all got out of the car and walked along the grounds. Then there they were, the two of them, Sherry Jo, and next to it was William.

Francine walked up quickly to where Sherry Jo was buried. The stone read, "Sherry Jo, Beloved Daughter, Loved by All, Our Angel, Always In Our Hearts." Engraved flowers surrounded the stone.

Francine stood in front of it, bowed her head, and clasped her hands under her chin. Then she slowly began to say as she lay the flowers beside the grave, "Good Afternoon, Sherry Jo, I am your sister, Francine Josephine, and I am very proud of it. Our mother loved you dearly, and she loves me and plans to adopt me. She told me what a wonderful, loving daughter you were. These flowers," pointing with her index finger, "are for you. Rest in peace, my sister that is always in my heart." Then she walked over to William's gravesite. Then she started, "I know you are not my father, but you are my 'sister's' father and Mama's husband. Still, I want to thank you for loving my mother. She loved you. In fact, you and Sherry Jo brought me to Mama and my birth father. You were a good father and husband. And for that, I am eternally grateful to you and my 'sister.' Rest in peace." Then she turned and walked back to her parents.

"A very lovely girl our Francine Josephine is." They smiled, agreeing with each other.

Then Francine suggested, "Mama, Daddy, why don't you pay your respects to Sherry Jo and William. I think it would be a nice gesture." Again, they consented pleasantly and strolled to the graves. Bettye Jo bowed her head to both her deceased daughter and husband. Though Philip had no connection to them, he stood beside Bettye Jo and silently said to himself, *Thank you both for loving Bettye Jo, whom I love dearly and plan to marry. May you both rest in peace always.*

The three of them were quiet for a few minutes. They smiled at the two gravesites and said, "God be with you." Then they left and headed to their car. Then they sped off into the highway.

Again, the radio blasted out the wonderful and gleeful country music, and they sang along, swinging their legs and arms to the music. It was a good day.

A Week Later, Father's Day, 8:00 a.m.

Francine and Bettye Jo were busily preparing for Philip's arrival this afternoon. He had called as he always did every Sunday. Bettye Jo warned him to dress casually, carefully avoiding ruining the surprise. Raymond promised to be there in a limousine that Bettye Jo rented. She and Francine finished putting their gifts and cards in the shopping bags on the kitchen table. Raymond was to come early, so they could put the presents in the limousine. They were to be hidden from him and not to be taken out until visiting and spending time with his parents, Francine's paternal grandparents. Aunt Ellen and Uncle Paul were also going to be there with them. This was a family day that Francine had thought up all by herself. They were more than happy to oblige in her thoughtful, altruistic, idealistic plans for others. She is a very special young lady who came into their lives and them into hers. Everyone was very fortunate and grateful.

11:00 a.m.

Both mother and daughter wore spaghetti-strapped sundresses. Bettye Jo's dress was a blue and yellow floral print. Francine's had red and pink flowers on it. Both wore open-toed white sandals. Bettye Jo's hair was put in a bun and Francine's was, as usual. Bettye Jo and Francine wore strawlike hats. Bettye Jo's was yellow and Francine's was red. Both wore lockets around their necks, and on their wrists were colorful beaded bracelets. They were all set. They heard a honk outside. It was Raymond, prompt and rearing to go.

Raymond got out of the limousine and, seeing them, tipped his hat, smiled, and greeted, "Good morning, ladies. You both look radiantly magnificent." They laughed at the compliment and thanked him.

Francine grabbed the presents from the kitchen table and handed them to Raymond, who then put them into the trunk.

"That's about it for now, Raymond," Bettye Jo graciously told him. She looked at her watch. "Dr. Marsowe should be here shortly," she informed Raymond. "Can I offer you anything, Raymond? A cup of coffee, perhaps?"

Raymond put his hand up. "That's very kind of you, Mrs. Pennington, but no, thank you, I'm good," he assured her with a pleasant grin.

"We'll just sit out here and wait for Dr. Marsowe, but first, I have to speak to Agnes for a minute." She excused herself and went back in to give Agnes some last-minute instructions. She did so and then later called out with the front door open, "You could leave early if you want. Dr. Marsowe, Francine, and I will be home late. Thanks, Agnes."

"Fine, Mrs. Pennington. Have a great day, you two and your wonderful man," she said with a chuckle.

Both mother and daughter sat on lounge chairs with their purses on their laps, waiting to begin the day. The sun was bright, so Bettye Jo reached into her purse for her sunglasses and adjusted them while putting them on.

"There, that's better," she remarked pleasantly to herself.

Both sat gazing at the clear blue sky in a happy and joyful mood, pondering loving thoughts inside themselves in reverie.

A few minutes later, they heard a car pull up. Getting out of their musings and looking up, they saw Philip getting out of his car. He was dressed in a light brown checkered shirt with brown dungarees. He wore beige loafers on his feet and on his head was a brown cap.

As he removed his shades, Francine cried out, "Daddy!" She ran up to him, putting her arms around his neck.

"Princess!" he exclaimed, kissing her on the top of her head and then taking her hands and swinging her around. She giggled.

Bettye Jo observed them, "Darling!" she called out. She dashed up to him. He took her face into his hands and kissed her passionately on her lips. They stood in that position for about two minutes. Francine watched her parents and laughed aloud.

Then Philip saw Raymond near the limousine. "What's happening here?" he asked puzzled. No one answered him.

Bettye Jo asked Raymond to park Philip's car down the block. Philip would not relent and kept inquiring what was going on. Raymond did as Bettye Jo asked of him. Philip did not stop wondering and looked about. No one would tell him anything. "Come on, guys!" he tried again.

Then Raymond walked back to the house. He motioned by waving his hand and said, "Let us go now, guys."

Bettye Jo and Francine went into the limousine. Philip stood transfixed. Raymond again waved and said to him, "You too, sir." At that, Philip began heading toward the limousine, hesitantly entering it. Still, everyone was still. And they were off. Philip looked around in wonder.

"Relax, honey." Bettye Jo patted Philip's knee gently.

Francine leaned forward and asked Raymond, "Please put on our favorite radio station."

Raymond did so, and everybody except Philip sang aloud.

Francine turned to her father. With a smile, she looked toward him and joyfully urged him. "Come on, Daddy, let us hear you sing. You love this station. It's our favorite, come on," she reiterated.

Reluctantly, he tried, and then everyone sang together, the three of them. Raymond smiled to himself as he drove them to the nursing home. *What a very happy family,* Raymond mused to himself. *So lucky.* Then another idea popped up in his mind: *I am also very lucky. It was this family who helped me out of a dire situation. My job may be menial, but it is honest work. Thanks to this family, I am happy and in a pleasant situation, not having to be frightened for my life, just as with Agnes, Alice, and Myles were.* All four of them could not thank this family enough for their lives and because of them, they were safe and content.

Raymond glanced in the front view mirror and asked, "Everything all right, guys?"

"Quite well, Raymond," Bettye Jo replied reassuringly.

"Good," he acknowledged.

They arrived at the nursing home. Raymond stopped the car and opened the doors, leading them all out.

Philip looked up. "This is the nursing home where my parents are residents," he stated.

"That's right, honey!" Bettye Jo remarked. She looked at their daughter. "It was all Francine's idea. We have planned all this for you as your Father's Day present. We thought you would like to visit them," she added.

Then Francine quipped, "Aunt Ellen and Uncle Paul will be here too, Daddy!" She beamed with delight.

He looked at his daughter with pride.

"I should have known, but I am not at all surprised. Thanks, princess." He kissed her on the forehead.

As they entered, they saw a doctor speaking with Paul. Ellen was with him. At that, a nurse approached Philip. His face showed perturbation as he faced her.

The nurse said, "Dr. Marsowe, I'm sorry to have to inform you, but the doctor doesn't have good news, and I really feel badly and so does he, being today is Father's Day."

Philip, though with a sad expression on his face, thanked the nurse and walked up to the doctor. Paul turned to Philip mournfully.

The doctor began hesitantly, careful in choosing his words. "Dr. Marsowe, as I already informed your brother, your father fell out of his bed and broke his back. Regretfully, surgery or any operation would not be feasible due to your father's present physical and mental states. He is in bed on a breathing machine and is being fed intravenously for he is not able to do so on his own. He cannot swallow either. I am very sorry, but we are not able to do much more than to keep him comfortable for the time being. It is just a matter of time. As I reiterate, I am very sorry since today was supposed to be a joyful and pleasant family visit. You can go see him now," he said and then walked away.

Bettye Jo and Francine looked at Philip, teary-eyed. Bettye Jo walked over to him, gave him a hug, and patted his back.

Francine, though upset for her father, walked up to him and sincerely said, "Daddy, I am so sorry. Today was supposed to be a special day for you. Mama and I took great pains to make today wonderful for you and we feel terribly unhappy, for Grandpa was a wonderful, supportive, and good father to you, though I do not remember, and I am sorry that I did not get to know him before he got sick. I know you loved him, but," she pointed her index finger up to her father, "think of this in a different perspective. Be grateful that Grandpa was a good man who loved you and your family and whom you also loved. You had a good father who will die soon, and you will be able to grieve for your loss, pay your respects, and be able to share your feelings about your relationship and his good qualities. He will be missed, and he loved and was loved by his family and friends. His life was worth living and valuable to all that knew him."

Philip slowly managed a smile at his daughter.

"Such a wonderful daughter I have. How did I get to be so fortunate?" Then he hugged her to his chest. "I am a very wealthy man, for you, my princess, are worth more than all the grains of sand since the beginning of time."

"I just don't want you to be sad," she stated. Then she turned to Bettye Jo and said, "And you too, Mama."

Philip and Bettye Jo gleefully gazed at their awesome, wonderful daughter.

Ellen and Paul watched the three of them. All of them stood motionless for a while.

Francine then strongly suggested, "Let us go visit them now and waste no more time. It's Father's Day!"

All of them headed toward their room. Grandpa lay in bed face up with eyes staring blankly. They gathered around him. Philip and Paul touched his hands gently and attempted a hug, which was hard but they did it. They murmured their "I love you" and planted a peck on his forehead. Of course, there was no reaction, but they felt that they should be loving and respectful to this wonderful man, their father.

Francine then walked over and gleefully greeted him, "Hi, Grandpa!" She touched his hand and kissed his cheek. "Love you!" She smiled at his blank expression, but was not at all upset at his lack of communication or awareness.

Grandma Marsowe was sitting up in bed observing her sons' and granddaughter's interaction with her severely sickly husband who will soon be departing from this world, but will do so as a good, upstanding, loving man. She was sad but was able to make peace and grieve for a man she loved and loved her.

Then she faced her two sons and began, "I know today is Father's Day and is a special one for Philip especially, but," she paused and turned to the two bouquets of flowers and greeting cards, "I'd like to thank all of you for remembering me on Mother's Day. I understand you weren't able to visit me then, but I appreciated your telephone calls, cards, and gifts."

"We are sorry, Mom, really," Paul apologized. "We should have been here for you, but could we make up for it today by giving you hugs and kisses and best wishes for a belated Happy Mother's Day? We feel terrible, and it was your day, Mom," he added.

"Of course." She smiled, struggling, she let out her arms. She was in pain, but she did not mind. Each son took his turn, and she softly patted their backs. Then they stepped away.

Francine came forth and eagerly hugged and kissed her. "I am sorry I did not bring my own present, so I made a belated Mother's Day card from a blank note card, sending you greetings. Look," she pointed to the card, "I made smiley faces and hearts just for you, Grandma."

She smiled at her only granddaughter, whom she had not known well but loved anyway. She patted her hand and squeezed it. Francine told her to take it easy, knowing she had arthritis.

"Such a sweet girl," Grandma Marsowe remarked to Philip and Bettye.

"We're truly blessed," Bettye Jo affirmed. "Isn't that right, Philip?" She faced him. He naturally confirmed that redundant but loving compliment, since they received it wherever they went and from whoever they happened to meet. Everyone was in accordance.

Grandma Marsowe turned toward Bettye Jo and said, "Philip is lucky to have you in his life. I could understand why he fell in love with you. You are great with Francine. She is lucky to have you as a mother. Unfortunately, due to circumstances beyond my control, I was not able to be close to my only grandchild. But now, perhaps it is not too late. Also, I would like to get to know you better before my time comes and perhaps you could be like a daughter to me."

Bettye Jo took her hand in hers and remarked, "I'd like that too." She stopped for she did not know how to address this remarkable woman, Francine's grandmother and Philip's mother. Mrs. Marsowe sounded too formal and distant. Calling her by her given name sounded too disrespectful and familiar.

"You could call me Mother Marsowe, dear," she suggested gleefully with a twinkle in her eyes.

"But Philip and I are not married yet," she pointed out.

Sternly, but while gently patting her hand, she said, "You're my daughter always, regardless of technicalities and formalities."

Bettye Jo resigned herself completely but was pleased and thrilled nonetheless. "All right, Mother Marsowe."

Both women held their hands tightly, though due to her arthritis, it physically hurt, but she did not care. She wanted to show Bettye Jo how she felt about her.

Philip witnessed their encounter. He smiled, put his arm around Bettye Jo, and said to his mother, "Isn't she the greatest? That's why I love her."

"I can see that," the elderly woman commented sincerely.

Then Bettye Jo turned to Francine and told her, "It's time now, sweetheart." She nodded, and Francine left the room.

Philip wondered for what but did not think to inquire, for he knew from previous encounters that no one would give him a straight answer.

Bettye Jo and Mrs. Marsowe engaged in a small conversation. Philip joined Paul and Ellen and chattered among themselves, motioning with their hands.

Then Francine appeared at the doorway holding two bags of presents for Philip. Bettye Jo waved her hand, motioning her to come by the bedside and put them down.

"Philip, look!" Bettye Jo instructed.

"What's this?" he was puzzled.

"Look, Daddy, look inside. See what Mama and I got you," she urged with perseverance.

He reached for a blue-wrapped box, unsure of what to do.

Still nudging her father, she said, "Open it, Daddy, open it now!"

He did so and saw that it was a coffee mug—To the Greatest Dad.

He was amazed. "How? When? Where?" He was in a dither.

"Remember while we were on our way to the cemetery, Mama and I stopped to use the restroom?" She did not go on.

Philip's eyes lit up and he chuckled. "Oh, yeah, that's right. I remember distinctly."

"But we did need to use the lavatory anyhow." She glanced at her mother. "Right, Mama?"

Bettye Jo nodded pleasantly.

He said to Francine, "You sly dog, you," and then to Bettye Jo, "And you too. My two lovely ladies." They all had a good laugh. "It's wonderful, princess. I love it." He bent to kiss her cheek.

He then reached in the bag and saw that it was a bigger box also wrapped in blue paper. He ripped off the blue paper and opened the box. It was a silky royal blue bathrobe. His eyes were on fire. He turned to Bettye Jo and exclaimed, "It's so beautiful, darling. I love it. It is exactly what I needed and in my favorite color." He walked up to Bettye Jo and kissed her cheek.

Then he saw two envelopes. The first one was from Francine. "Dear Daddy," it began, and Philip read it. "Love always from your little princess now and forever, your loving daughter, Francine Josephine." There were smiley faces, hearts, and xxxs (kisses). "I love it. What a lovely card, my princess." He bent over to kiss her again.

Then he picked up the second card knowing, it was from Bettye Jo. It began, "To my very special man, my daughter's father." She wrote in the card. He read the card, and Bettye Jo ended it with, "I love you forever and always. Thank you for being Francine's father and my wonderful man. Yours always, Bettye Jo." She put xxxs and ooos for kisses. Then Philip and Bettye Jo kissed on the lips.

Everyone watched in amazement by shouting, "Way to go, bro!" Paul slapped him on the back.

Then Ellen hugged her sister and remarked, "You're one heck of a lucky lady, sis!" Bettye Jo returned her hug. Everybody high-fived each other while jumping up and down. Such excitement.

Suddenly, everyone heard a knock on the door. It was an aide informing them that visiting hours were over. They could hardly believe it. They were having so much fun visiting the grandparents, but it had to end. It was 9:00 p.m., and they were tired from such a long day, though it was a very joyous one. Everyone said their goodbyes. Bettye Jo, Philip, and Francine gathered the cards and presents and left Philip's parents with smiles, kisses, and waves.

Raymond was waiting by the limousine and escorted them inside. It was dark out, but there were stars shining in the sky. Raymond asked them about their visit. They were tired but glad that they got to see Philip's parents, Francine's grandparents. They did mention about Mr. Marsowe's terminal condition, and Raymond was very sorry but knew that Mr. Marsowe had been a great man in his life and he will be missed by everyone who knew him. It was his time to join God in his final, eternal resting place. After that, everyone was quiet. The rest of the ride was uneventful for the roads were practically devoid of traffic, and for that they were grateful and eager to return home and retire for the night. They thanked Raymond for his service and promised him a bonus in his next regular paycheck at the end of the month.

After they entered the house, Philip and Bettye Jo sat on the sofa in the living room. Francine mentioned that she had something planned for Philip. Bettye Jo knew, but of course, Philip was clueless but eager and curious. Francine went upstairs to put on her new pink nightdress that Bettye Jo bought her a few weeks ago. When she put it on, she took a pink scarf and wrapped it around her shoulders. Also in her hand was a CD. She pranced down the stairs, entered the living room, put the CD in the digital tuner, and began batting her eyes coyly at her father. She put on the song "All Grown Up" sung by country/Western singer, Johnny Horton. She swayed back and forth, brushing the scarf from side to side on the back of her shoulders and danced to the music, trying to keep in step. She did not know all the words, but every time "Hey, Daddy" came up, she would mimic and act to it, motioning and galloping around. Bettye Jo and Philip watched their daughter in amazement for she was simply adorable every time she would say, "Hey, Daddy, I'm all grown up." She would laugh aloud as a hyena, her voice high-pitched. Mainly, her act was for Philip. It was his day. Then she fluttered around the living room looking at her father, who was beaming with love and pride. "Hey, Daddy, Hey Daddy, I'm all grown up." The song ended. Bettye Jo and Philip clapped. Then Bettye Jo turned off the digital tuner and gently but firmly stated to her daughter, her hands on her shoulders, "That was quite lovely and cute, and we loved it. But now that you are no longer a little girl, it is not proper to prance around in your nightgown in front of Daddy, showing off your certain body parts. You are a woman now and you must wear a robe or duster over you under clothes and nightdress. You do understand, don't you, sweetheart?" Then she turned to Philip, "Isn't that right, honey? She is not a little girl anymore. She must learn to act and dress properly."

"Certainly," he acknowledged. Then he turned to Francine and said, "Mama is right, honey. You are growing up to be a fine young lady."

Francine stood and listened to her parents. She knew they were right. She is not a child anymore. Those days are gone forever. But she asked her father, "Am I still your little princess, Daddy?"

"Of course you are. You will always be my little princess. That will not change. I'll always call you that, but let us just say you're my growing young lady little princess, is that okay?"

"I guess," Francine surmised.

Then he looked at Bettye Jo and asked, "Is she what I just said she was, a growing-up little princess?"

"Sure." She put her hand on his shoulder and said, "Forever and ever."

Philip smacked his hands on his lap. "There, it's settled." Afterward, Philip faced Bettye Jo. "Should I or should you?" he began.

"All right," Bettye Jo agreed, putting her hands into hers. "Honey, you know Daddy and I love each other very much and everything we do is for you especially." She stopped. Francine stared at her mother, saying nothing. She went on, "Daddy and I wanted to ask you a question and we want you to feel comfortable, okay? Would it bother you if Daddy spent the night with us? What I mean is, in our bed?"

Francine stood puzzled and asked softly and carefully, "You mean sleep together?"

"That's right, honey," she answered.

"But you are not married yet. When you explained the facts of life to me when I began menarche, you said people must get married first," she stated awkwardly.

"You're right. I did say it. But Daddy and I are grown-ups and have been married before. We have already lived through a lot. But when you are an adolescent, not a child anymore, but not yet a grown-up, different rules apply depending on circumstances. You know Daddy and I love each other, and we know how we feel. Young people as you are still getting their feet damp and just starting out and are wet behind the ears. Also, young people may think they are in love with the person they go out with or think vehemently that they are the one. That is how teenagers are. You have your whole life ahead of you. Do not be in a rush to grow up. Daddy is not sowing his oats with me. He is not a young boy trying to get into a girl's private parts. He is a man, a good and honest man. You know that, don't you?"

Francine nodded her head. "I do."

Philip then turned to Bettye Jo and asked her, "Do you think we should tell her about that night when we came home from the hospital?" He looked at her.

Francine observed them. "Tell me what? It is okay, you guys. I will not get mad. I love you both," she needed to mention.

Bettye Jo put her hand on Philip's chest and said, "It's all right, Philip. We should tell her."

"Let me, honey, okay?" Philip offered. "After we left the hospital the night you were admitted, we were exhausted. I suggested to Mama that I do not feel that she should be alone and that she needed company. I firmly told her that I was not suggesting anything and that I was not like that, and she knew it. I did not want her to feel that I put her on the spot. So she said that I could sleep on the couch, and I was in accordance with it. So Mama went upstairs, and I started removing my shoes and socks and then I unbuttoned my skirt. Minutes later, I heard something. I turned around. It was Mama clad in a long, bright red, low-cut negligee. She smiled at me coyly and motioned with her index finger to come upstairs with her. We stood for a while, not sure of how to proceed. So I walked up to her. She took my hand, and we slowly ascended the staircase and into the bedroom." He stopped and then added, "We did it and we loved it. She was great, I told her, and vice versa."

"Wow, you guys!" Her eyes enlightened, with her hands clasped in front of her. "You're amazing. I can't believe it!" She began jumping at the front of the stairs.

"You're not upset, princess?" he wanted to make sure.

"Not at all! Wow!" she said again.

Bettye Jo did have something else to say and she planned to, "Honey, your father and I have one simple request that you must comply to. What we did is personal and very private and just between us. And I need you to promise me and Daddy, do not, do not tell anyone, not your friends, not anybody, okay? Just because having sex is a universal phenomenon, it is still personal and is not meant to be shared. This is between the three of us. One for all, and all for one, all right?"

"Of course, Mama, Daddy, mum's the word." She put her finger to her lips and gave her parents a high five, and they did it back in return.

A week later, Philip's father died peacefully in his sleep. The funeral service was brief. Only family members and the nursing home staff came to pay their respects. Most of the family friends were either deceased or incapacitated. Philip recited the eulogy with admirable accolades about him at the cemetery. Those in attendance watched his father's casket go lower and lower into the ground.

During the past few years, Frances began her actual grieving when her beloved husband slowly descending into dementia, slipping away and sinking further and further away from the world. He did not even recognize her as time passed. But she reasoned, *now he is finally at peace and no longer suffering.* At least she had her two sons and beloved granddaughter, her namesake, to continue the genealogical line. She was blessed and thankful for that.

Burlington Psychiatric Center for Women

She stood in the middle of the dayroom clad in a gray shapeless dress, shuffling her feet and snarling expletives all around her. Her hair was messy and loose and her evil eyes blazed with fire.

"You see him," she said to no one in particular, pointing to the television. "He's mine, all mine," she announced staunchly.

The other patients watched her.

"Where's your boyfriend, girl?" a heavyset black woman jeered at her.

Leonora glared at her, fuming. All of them laughed while pointing their fingers at her.

She piped up, "He'll be coming soon. My man. He loves me. He will be here. Just you wait and see." She stood erect and proud. "And no one, especially that little bitch I brought into the world, will ever destroy my relationships. Never." Then she stated bitterly, "She didn't have the decency to call me 'Mother.'" Then she faced the others and said, "You're all jealous that men love me." She glared.

They laughed hysterically, and she fumed at them, her face contorted in rage.

A nurse walked up beside her and sternly stated, taking her arm, "Mrs. Carrington, it's time for your checkup. The doctor is waiting."

Leonora still eyed the man on the television and pointed at him. "You see him, girl, he's mine, all mine."

The nurse paid her no heed. "Let's go, Mrs. Carrington." Then she led her out.

"Where's your boyfriend, now?" Another woman grinned evilly.

Leonora jerked around. "Shut the fuck up, you bitch." Her eyes burned.

"Come on, Mrs. Carrington," the nurse reiterated firmly.

They left the dayroom and headed toward the examination room. The doctor stood and waited. Leonora saw him. *Those bright blue eyes and jet-black wavy hair*, she thought to herself.

"Mrs. Carrington," the doctor began, "please get on the table."

She ignored him and began to run her fingers on his chest, fluttering her eyes at him. "Call me Leonora." She smiled sensuously.

He gently removed her arms away from him and repeated, "Please, Mrs. Carrington." He turned to the nurse and instructed her, "Please get her medications." The nurse nodded and did so.

Leonora was furious. "You bitch, you fuckin' bitch." She screamed at the nurse, "How dare you steal my man!"

The nurse ignored her and quietly but firmly stated, "Take your pill, Mrs. Carrington."

"Come on now, Mrs. Carrington," the doctor ordered, trying to compose himself.

Leonora attempted to put her arms around his neck, gazing into his eyes.

"I'm not going to say it again, Mrs. Carrington!"

Leonora screamed at him, "It's Leonora, dummy! How many times do I have to say it?"

She jumped off the table, growled like a wounded animal, and pushed the table, with all its contents spewing all over the room. Then she kicked the chair and garbage pails around while throwing a desk lamp across the room and pushing papers off the desk. Lastly, she clawed her hands, attempting to scratch the nurse, who abruptly backed away.

The doctor turned to the nurse and said, "Get security at once. Have them put her in lockup."

The nurse obediently left the room.

"I'll show you a good time." Leonora looked up into his eyes with her mouth watering. "Let's have some fun. I promise to show you a good time. Tonight, Doctor?" she sweetly inquired, snuggling against his chest. Again, he gently pushed her back.

"That bitch! That killjoy! Still ruining my relationships, my happiness! She is still doing it! That spoiled little brat I brought into the world," she cried out bitterly repeatedly. "She wouldn't even call me 'Mother.'"

Two security guards entered the room, and the doctor indicated to Leonora. They took her away, yelling hysterically. "He'll come for me. He will. I know he will. Someday my prince will come. It's just a matter of time," she stated convincingly. "And furthermore, that cajoling bitchy brat will never ever ruin my happiness again! She would not call me 'Mother'!" she reiterated, spitting out vermin. "I gave her life. I did. Listen, everyone. He's coming for me."

The guard pushed her roughly in a cell and walked away. She grabbed the bars, shaking them furiously. "He'll be here. You will see. He loves me."

Washington Heights Psychiatric Facility for Men

Conrad and the other inmates were watching television in the recreation room. He saw a young woman in a sundress holding her daughter's hand. The daughter was also clad in a sundress.

"Ah, the life," he sighed pleasantly. "What a dazzler. I could make their wildest dreams come true—wealth and happiness. Oh, how beautiful, that woman and little girl. They're all mine."

"Shut the fuck up, Carrington!" another inmate demanded. "No one wants to hear your sick remarks."

Conrad turned, faced him, and stood up with his fist in the air, aiming at him. "And what are you going to do if I won't?" he dared him.

"Sit down, both of you, and be quiet," an attendant demanded of them.

Each one pointed at each other, protesting vehemently, "He started it." "No, you did." It went on and on.

"What's going on here?" a guard demanded.

Conrad smirked. "Nothing, I'm just having some fun."

The inmate insisted, "He's disturbing everyone with his deranged fantasies."

Conrad aimed his fist, but the guard stopped him and took him by the arm. "You're going back to your cell and you will stay there until you can learn how to behave as a proper human being should, Carrington."

"Come on," Conrad protested, "that woman and girl," he pointed to the television, "they're mine and mine only." He smiled, pleased with himself.

The guard jerked him toward the door. "Let's go," he continued, leading him away.

All the inmates watched with smirks on their faces, pointing at him. "Ha! Ha! Carrington!"

"They're mine, you shits. Get your own," he went on relentlessly.

The guard continued, heading him to his cell. He then opened it and pushed him inside. "Not another word, Carrington," he warned.

Conrad stood at the bars of his cell looking around for a few minutes.

He then saw a young woman, perhaps twenty-five or so, with thick ash-blonde hair in a long pageboy walking past the other cells. She was rolling a cart filled with cleaning implements.

He called, "Hey you, cutie," addressing her. "How are you doing?"

She turned to him briefly and nodded quietly.

"You know you could do better than working in here," he remarked.

The woman continued her duties, saying nothing.

"What's your name? Mine's Conrad," he offered.

"Elsie," she replied, not facing him.

He kept at it, "Pleased to meet you." He extended his hand out. She ignored him.

"Oh, come on, Elsie. Do not be like that. I am trying to be friendly. I could help you better your life. Do you have a daughter? I could make you both happier." He was relentless.

"I'm not married," she replied reluctantly, wishing he would just shut up.

At that, his eyes lit up. "Come on, honey, be nice."

She continued to ignore him, but he persisted, "You're very pretty. I bet you have a lot of boyfriends lined up in your front door." He still would not let up. She was his, he pondered in his mind, he would see to it.

"Do you like children? You know, I always wanted a daughter. Do you think you'd like to have them?" he inquired.

Suddenly, she volunteered, "I have a niece, my brother's kid."

Conrad was intrigued, "I'd like to meet her. Make you and her both mine."

Elsie felt her blood running cold and began to shake, rage building up inside her. "I'm busy, Mr. Carrington," she stated staunchly. "Now, leave me alone!" At that, she turned and left.

He saw her leave, but he was not giving up. He reveled pleasantly inside himself.

Feisty one, she is, he thought silently. He was not deterred. She was his, he kept insisting. Still, he was alone now, but not for long. He smiled at his own private reality.

The End of June, Beginning of Summer

Friday was graduation day. A happy time for everybody. A wonderful day. Francine was graduating from junior high school with her girlfriends. She would be receiving an award for the highest class average in English. Everyone was thrilled. Her parents were proud of her. She had been through so much, but she was resilient, at peace, and was not at all bitter or hurt. Not one complaint or rehashing of the past. She dealt with it as the mature young lady that she was. Everyone agreed. She was adjusting well.

Francine posed back and forth in front of her full-length mirror admiring herself. She wore a short puff-sleeved white dress with a V neckline. Red lacy trim surrounded its hem as well as her sleeves. Her hair was carefully styled in a bun on the back of her head, surrounded with a white scrunchie and curly tendrils dangling down the sides of her face. She wore short-heeled white sandals with straps across them. On her legs were white cotton stockings.

Bettye Jo observed her daughter. She was beaming with pride for she was just lovely.

"Honey." She walked over behind her. "Would you like to wear my pearl necklace that my grandmother gave me? I think it would look beautiful on you."

Francine nodded to her mother. "Oh, yes, Mama, yes." She was gleeful.

"Good. Also, perhaps you could wear some lipstick, a light pink color. I will show you how to apply it. Give me a minute, please." She exited her bedroom.

Francine stood there waiting. Lipstick and pearls, she envisioned.

Bettye Jo came in and put the necklace around her daughter's neck. She exclaimed with her hands on Francine's shoulders as they faced the mirror, "How beautiful you look, sweetheart!" Then she took her tube of lipstick and showed her what to do. Francine watched with curiosity. Bettye Jo then handed it to her, and she began slowly and hesitantly for a while. She did it. Bettye Jo was enlightened. "You are simply perfect, darling! You did it all by yourself." She turned her daughter around to face her, her hands on her shoulders. They looked into each other's eyes with smiles on their faces. Bettye Jo took her daughter's face into her hands and planted a kiss on her forehead. "Get that white-beaded purse I gave you the other day. Okay, sweetheart?" Francine went over to her top dresser drawer and got it. Bettye Jo spread her hands out wide. "Oh, darling! Wait a minute, I'll get my camera. I simply must take your picture. You're radiant!" She reached into her pocket for her phone. She could not wait to capture this precious moment. "Smile, honey!" *Click, click, click.* She took some more of Francine in different poses. "Now, you go downstairs and wait with Daddy. I need to get ready," she stated gently. Francine headed down the stairs.

As she did so, Philip looked up at her. "Why, if it isn't my grown-up little princess!" he remarked with a smile. He took her hands in his and spread out. "Just look at you, you are quite the dazzler!"

"You're not so bad yourself, Daddy," she stated. He wore a crisp white shirt, a silk black tie, a black blazer, and black pants. His shoes were of shiny black leather. His dark, wavy hair was perfectly parted. His eyes gazed at his daughter.

They stood there silently and looking proudly and lovingly at each other.

Then they turned and saw Bettye Jo descending the stairs gracefully, smiling at her daughter and Philip. She wore a long pink halter dress, her hair in a thick bun, a cameo around her neck, and slingback pink high heels on her feet. Philip gazed at her, and she and him both stood breathless and silent but joyful. As she reached the bottom of the staircase, Philip took her hand in his.

"You're beautiful too. Like mother, like daughter." He turned from Bettye Jo to Francine, who was observing her parents.

"Let's take some pictures now," Francine suggested excitedly.

The three of them did so. Then Philip reached for Bettye Jo's wrap and draped it around her shoulders. He then took Francine's spanking new white jacket and did so likewise. He opened the door to lead them out and locked it behind him. They were off.

Luckily, the sun shone brightly. The weather was not too hot nor too cold. The ceremony was held outside. Everyone was smiling, laughing, and chattering with one another.

Her parents met some of her teachers, who remarked on what a lovely young lady and student she was, and they shook each other's hands with a smile.

Francine went over to Willow, Stephanie, and Arlene, hugging one another and giggling and gabbing about mundane issues. Also, they waved to their other classmates.

Finally, Philip and Bettye Jo got to meet their daughter's friends' parents, which turned out to be successful. They got along well and were comfortable together. They knew about how Philip and Bettye Jo's relationship came about, just as in a storybook, but it was their real life. They were amazed. Plans were made to get together at each other's homes for dinner, movies, playing cards, shopping, ball games, movies, or just simply hanging out.

After the Ceremony

Francine and her three friends ran up to their parents, waving their diplomas.

She handed hers with a bright, gleaming smile and excitedly asked, "Mama, Daddy, may my friends and I go to the mall this afternoon? They have a new selection of DVDs. Please?"

The other three girls surrounded their parents with their diplomas, also asking for their permission.

Then all four girls turned toward each other, waiting in anticipation, all with imploring faces.

"Oh, all right!"

It was settled. The girls would spend the rest of the day at the mall. All four couples agreed to go out for coffee and a walk. They decided to be at Francine's parents' house early evening. Plans needed to be discussed. The girls jumped about, twirling around and around, waving their arms into the air.

"Thanks, guys," Francine acknowledged her parents.

And the girls were off.

The four couples got together, walking around and gabbing about nothing, but quite content nonetheless.

Early Evening

Agnes was busy wiping around the kitchen counter.

Bettye Jo, Philip, Francine, and her three girlfriends sat around the table.

"As you already know, girls," Bettye Jo began. Then she reached for Philip's hand. With their hands clasped together, she announced, "Philip and I plan to get married on the second Saturday in July. The wedding will take place outside in the nearby park. My sister, Ellen, will be my maid of honor, and Philip's brother, Paul, his best man." She glanced at the girls. "And all four of you will be my bridesmaids."

The girls jumped up and clapped their hands. "Cool!" They were enthusiastic.

"Next week, we'll go for an appropriate bride's dress for me, and you girls will all have knee-length pink gowns." Bettye Jo carefully informed them, making sure they were comprehending. "I also made summer plans for you girls, so you will not be bored and listless. I would like you all to work at my flower shop. Danielle, my manager, will assign you your duties. I will expect you to be prompt and do your jobs with the best of your ability. I am depending on you. This opportunity is not just to have something to do. It will teach you responsibility and prepare you for your futures. You will get paid, but it will be off the books since you are not of legal age to work. It will be just for the summer."

The girls listened attentively for they did wonder how they were going to spend their summer. They agreed that helping their friend's mother run her shop would be a great opportunity for them and would make them feel proud and have a sense of accomplishment. They all looked at each other saying nothing for a while. Suddenly, Willow jumped up and began a high five, and the girls obliged. Good, it was all set. Then they sat back down in their seats.

Philip then put his hand on Bettye Jo's arm and said, "Honey, is there something more you have to tell them, or should I do it? It's up to you."

Bettye Jo turned to Philip and said, "You could tell them."

Philip faced the girls and resumed the conversation, "Bettye Jo and I plan to go to Hawaii for our honeymoon for two weeks. And we are going to leave you alone during that time. We will expect you to behave yourselves accordingly. It is not that we do not trust you for you are all very nice, good girls, but sometimes, teenagers could slip up, not intentionally, of course. But like all teenagers, your hormones can act up and lead to impulsive behavior, and we do not want that." He turned to Bettye Jo and asked, "Right, dear?"

She agreed with him and patted his arm.

"We do have faith in you girls. You have been such good friends to our daughter." Then she faced Francine. "And you have shown us how responsible you are and we are glad that you are our daughter. But teenagers can, not on purpose, get a little bit sidetracked," she pointed out carefully.

"We won't, we promise," Arlene assured them.

Stephanie piped up, "We're nothing like that. You have our word."

Philip and Bettye Jo nodded in agreement and with slight smiles.

"Good," they said in unison.

"Agnes will be here the whole time and she is aware of our plans. She has our credit cards and she will give you one. But they are not to be used brashly, though occasionally you could treat yourself to something special but within reason."

Philip continued, "We spoke to all your parents to let them know what's happening, and they were in complete agreement. Bettye Jo and I spoke with them this afternoon while you were at the mall. They are all nice and lovely people. We consider them our friends. And by the way, we invited them to our wedding."

Francine clapped her hands. "Way to go, guys!" she exclaimed.

Then her friends leaped out of their chairs and shouted, "Right on!"

Bettye Jo nudged Philip with her elbow. "Honey, there's more."

"Right, dear," he affirmed.

"Francine," he began, "Mama informed me that you want to change your name, and I happen to agree that it would be a wonderful idea."

Francine sat silently with her hands clasped on the table, eyeing her father intently.

"After we return from our honeymoon, all three of us will be going down to the courthouse. We made an appointment during the second week in August for that and we are finally going to adopt you legally and formally. A certified document will be drawn up, saying you are our daughter, though you know you were and are always our daughter in our hearts."

He paused to catch his breath before resuming, "But first, the same judge will process your change of name. You will no longer be Francine Hawes, and we are not going to elaborate on the reason. That part of your life is over for good and there is no sense to discuss it. Mama says you want your new and forever name to be Francine Josephine Marsowe. But your friends could call you Franny Jo, okay, princess?"

Francine smiled gleefully, first at her father and then at her mother.

"Oh, yes, Daddy!" She got up and hugged him, and then he squeezed his hands into hers. "And you too, Mama." She threw her arms around her neck and kissed her cheek. Bettye Jo returned the embrace, patted her back, and smiled.

Philip glanced at his watch and yawned quietly. As he arose, he turned to Francine's girlfriends and said, "It is getting late, girls. I promised your parents I'd take you home. Also, I want to avoid any traffic that might come up." Then he said to Bettye Jo, "It has been a long day, honey. I need to get home, begin packing my stuff, and prepare for our future together, yours, Francine's, and mine."

The girls got up from their seats and all four of them bid their usual goodbyes and waved, concludingly stated, "See you!"

Then to Bettye Jo, Willow added, "Thanks for everything. You and Philip are simply awesome." Then to Francine, she said, "Your parents are so cool!" She smiled back at the compliment and agreed.

The Big Day, 9:00 a.m.

The window sign read Sheila's Beauty Salon. Both Bettye Jo and Francine rode up in the car near it. For years, Bettye Jo has gone to this beauty salon. The owner, Sheila, was always bright and cheerful, making her customers feel welcome and special. She wore her red hair up with tendrils hanging down on the sides of her face. She always dressed casually, claiming she wanted to feel comfortable. Today, she was wearing a short-sleeved black tank top and orange plaid baggy slacks. Her customers would tell her their problems and issues, and she would always lend her ear and show interest in what they had to say. They always felt better after their visits. They would refer to her as Dr. Sheila, and she would always laugh when they called her that. She said it was no problem. She never got married and thus had no children. She was not into it, though she did have some proposals. She had a brother and a sister whose children, her nieces and nephews, were like her own. She loved them so. She liked to tell her customers stories, and they enjoyed listening to her. Not once did anyone remember her uttering a negative word or complaint. That was her nature—cheerful and compliant.

As Francine and Bettye Jo entered, Sheila turned, smiled, and waved them over to two chairs.

"How're you doin', ladies?" she cracked happily.

Francine was wearing a three-quarter-length scooped neck black T-shirt. In its middle was a pink heart and in it read LOVE in big red letters. She wore blue denim dungarees and flat slip-on shoes. Around her neck was the locket that she received as a birthday present from her parents.

Bettye Jo was clad in a sleeveless red tank top with red creped slacks. She wore low-heeled open-toed red sandals. And around her neck was her grandmother's cameo.

Sheila remarked to both, "You both look so lovely today."

And to Francine, she took her chin and with gleaming eyes spoke gleefully, "You're quite a little lady now, your Mama tells me. You are so pretty and sweet. I bet a lot of boys are lining up just to ask you out on dates." Francine smiled but said nothing.

Bettye Jo smiled and had her hands over Francine's chest from behind. "I'm fine, thank you, Sheila." And then she looked down in her daughter's face, motioned to her, and said, "This is Sheila, sweetheart. She's going to do our hair, remember?"

Francine smiled while looking up at her mother. Then she faced Sheila and extended her hand. "Hello, Sheila. Mama always speaks very highly of you," she mentioned.

Bettye Jo laughed and looked up at Sheila. She gave her specific instructions about how to do her hair. Then she turned to her daughter.

"Remember what we spoke about?" Francine listened. Bettye Jo went on, "We're changing your hairdo. No more messy buns with scrunchies or uncombed stringy styles. You're a young lady now, all right?"

"Yes, Mama, I remember. I am not a little girl anymore. I am going to high school in the fall."

"That's right, honey." She patted her back and faced Sheila. "You can start on her now," she instructed.

Francine went over to an empty chair. Sheila put a smock over her and motioned for one of her assistants to wash Francine's hair, and she did. Glancing at Bettye Jo, she offered, "I'll wash yours now. Then we will get started."

Francine had her hair cut around her shoulders. A curling iron was used to make waves on the sides and on the back.

Sheila shaped her hair with a brush and sprayed it. She looked at her and pinched her cheek. Francine giggled.

She turned Francine over to Bettye Jo. "Show your mother," she instructed. "Doesn't she look nice?" Sheila asked her.

Bettye Jo replied, "My grown-up daughter." She smiled lovingly at her. She then continued, "You just sit in that chair by the door and read while I get my hair done. Today's my big day. Mine and Daddy's. And yours too, sweetheart."

She faced the mirror, and Sheila started working on her.

Francine sat, took a book out of her bag, and began reading.

"I bet you're excited about today, Bettye Jo?" Sheila started her conversation. "Philip is surely a lucky man, and so are you. Good luck. I wish you three all the best always."

Bettye Jo smiled and said, "We are definitely lucky." She turned to her daughter and added, "Right, honey?"

Francine looked up from her book and said, "Oh yes, Mama, yes. We are the luckiest people on the planet. Couldn't hope for anything better."

Sheila, Bettye Jo, and Francine laughed all in agreement.

Then Bettye Jo noticed that Francine was sitting with her legs spread apart and remarked firmly, but with a gentle, calm smile to her, "Honey," she started, "you are a young lady now, and ladies do not sit that way, okay?"

Francine looked up at her mother and said, "Of course, Mama, I'm sorry." She quickly clamped her legs together, crossed her ankles, and resumed reading.

"She's so lucky to have you as her mother, and she you," Sheila pointed out as she started on her hair. "She's getting to be quite a woman. You and Philip must be so proud. Francine will definitely grow up just fine."

Bettye Jo glanced with love at her daughter. "Yes, she is," she stated agreeably.

Sheila resumed working on her hair, telling her the latest news on her nieces and nephews. They were her pride and joy, though they were always up to shenanigans or harmless mischief. She admitted that they were so cute, adorable, and a lot of fun. She also described her new male friend as well as the others, cute and charming. She was not a fast or an easy woman, though she admitted that she loved every one of them. That was her pleasure. The men knew that it would not be a forever relationship, but they were satisfied and content with it. At least she was honest and felt that there was no need to lead them on and let them think otherwise. She did not want to be a tease or a temptress. Bettye Jo enjoyed listening to her stories, though Sheila's life was so different from her own. And Sheila loved listening to Bettye Jo's special and wonderful man whom she was marrying this early evening. Sheila was very happy for Bettye Jo deserved happiness in her life. She was a sweet, lovely lady. Also, she won Francine over for she was just like her mother in disposition and personality.

Also, she, like everyone else, knew how Bettye Jo and Philip ended up falling in love. Bettye Jo had planned to adopt Francine, but Philip, her birth father, appeared on her doorstep. He was indeed a loving, good father and loved Bettye Jo in an instant. She knew about the reasons why he was not in his daughter's life and how he persevered during those years. His vow was to be at her side, now and always. He loved that Bettye Jo was a warm, loving, and caring mother, thus he fell in love with her and vice versa. It was unreal at first, but it was very real how their relationship blossomed into love. It did happen.

Sheila was aware of Francine's turbulent childhood and recent brutal endeavor with that evil, mentally ill woman and her deranged husband. She could not help wondering how she managed to have such a positive, cheerful attitude and a forgiving nature and rose above it all and became a better person with character. She did extremely well despite of everything she had to contend with. *She was amazing*, Sheila thought to herself. Unbelievable but true.

She was setting and styling Bettye Jo's hair by fluffing and teasing it up at the sides, a thick bun on the back of her head, and tendrils on the sides. It took time, but Sheila always took great pains for all her customers. She wanted to make sure that they were completely satisfied. Sheila took a mirror and had Bettye Jo see how she looked, front, sides, and back.

"Oh!" Bettye Jo exclaimed joyfully, "it's perfect!" Then she turned to Francine and asked her, "How do I look, darling?"

Francine dropped her book as she jumped from her chair. "You look so beautiful, Mama! Simply radiant. Daddy will absolutely love it!" She ran up to her mother and hugged her neck.

Bettye Jo put her hands out on hers. "Be careful, honey. I do not want to get it messed up. And I also want your new hair style to be perfect for today."

"Today will be perfect, Mama. I know it. Everyone will have their eyes on you and Daddy, the perfect couple," she proudly stated.

Bettye Jo laughed and patted her arm. "I know that already." Then she leaned toward Francine and said, "And you're our perfectly, loving daughter forever and ever!"

Sheila watched them, mother and daughter interacting lovingly with each other. She smiled and was pleased.

Bettye Jo paid the cashier and gave out the appropriate tips with glee.

As they exited the salon, both had their arms around each other's shoulders. Francine turned and said with joy, "It was a pleasure to meet you, Sheila." Then she and her mother waved and said, "Goodbye, Sheila. Thanks for everything. Have a blessed and good day!"

Sheila smiled and waved back. They were out the door. Sheila walked up to her next customer and asked her usual, while smiling gleefully as always, "How're you're doin'?"

As Bettye Jo and Francine got into the car, Bettye Jo pointed out while glancing at her watch, "We better hurry home. We do not want to be late on this special, wonderful day."

"Right on, Mama!" she agreed.

They were off.

"Can we listen to some music, Mama?" she asked Bettye Jo. "I am in the mood. Are you?"

Bettye Jo grinned gleamingly. "Of course, honey," she consented.

Francine switched the radio on. Their favorite song, "In Love with Love, In Love with Life," played. Francine swayed to it, but was careful not to ruin her hair. Bettye Jo did not have to remind her. She glanced at her daughter with love.

They continued the ride home singing off-key but in harmony to their special song. Such excitement! And today's main event had not even begun yet.

12:00 p.m.

The house was filled with all women when Bettye Jo and Francine got back. Ellen, Kelly, Danielle, and Francine's three girlfriends were in attendance waiting for them. Everyone was chattering and fluttering around. Agnes made sandwiches and put them and some cold drinks on an extension table in the hallway. Bettye Jo was grateful to Agnes for all her hard work. Agnes said that it was no problem and that she always wanted to help all that she could. "Anything for my very special employers, who have been nothing but good and kind to me," she remarked.

Everyone sat at the table enjoying their sandwiches and drinks while laughing among themselves. Agnes watched them with happiness. *Everyone was having a good time and got along well together,* she noticed.

Little did anyone notice, but Agnes, Alice, Myles, and Raymond had a surprise for the happy couple. They had their duties, but they secretly managed to give them a gift though they were not invited. While everyone was sitting and socializing, Agnes called Alice, who called Myles, and then called Raymond, who was to drive all the ladies to the wedding. Wayne agreed to drive Philip and Paul. Willow's parents took Arlene's and Stephanie's parents in their car. It was all arranged.

Agnes and Raymond needed to leave, and that meant lying to their wonderful and kind employers. But in this case, lying was justifiable. They wanted to surprise this couple with a wedding gift.

Agnes and Raymond went up to Bettye Jo at the table. "Mrs. Pennington," Agnes began, "Raymond and I have to go out for about an hour. It is important."

Raymond added, "And it is necessary. I hope it is all right with you. We promise to be back in time."

"Certainly," their employer consented. "Do what you have to do."

Agnes and Raymond smiled at each other and left. They went to pick up Alice and Myles. They had to hurry back. They wanted to surprise this couple that helped them out of their previously horrible, terrible situation. They rode to Bettye Jo's florist shop and ordered a $100 huge arrangement of colorful and assorted flowers. The card read, "To the wonderful, happy couple, thank you for all your support." They signed their names. Quickly, they took the floral arrangement and carefully put it in the car, and then drove to the spot in the park where the wedding was going to take place. Alice and Myles stayed hidden near some picnic tables. Agnes and Raymond headed back to their employers, as they had promised that they would.

When Agnes entered the house, Bettye Jo saw her as she cleared the table.

"Is everything all right?" she asked Agnes.

Agnes smiled. "Oh, yes, couldn't be better." *It was not a lie,* she told herself. Bettye Jo did not persist as she went back to the table. Agnes went over to her and offered, "Let me, Mrs. Pennington. You've got a lot to do."

Bettye Jo thanked her, and she, Ellen, Francine, and her three friends went upstairs. Kelly and Danielle were in the living room. They were wearing spanking sequined dresses. Danielle's was purple and Kelly's was hot pink. Both wore sheer stockings and high-heeled shoes and carried their purses in front of them. Danielle had her hair done impeccably and was neatly in place. She wore a pearl necklace, white button earrings, and a silver band bracelet. Kelly's hair was piled up with wispy strands at the sides. She wore silver dangling earrings and a beaded necklace. Around her wrist was a charm bracelet. They waited eagerly for the big event. Agnes asked them if she could get them anything, a drink or a snack. They declined with a smile. Agnes then went to the kitchen.

While Upstairs

Bettye Jo was fixing and smoothing out her daughter's hair and put a ruffled pink headband on. Then she walked over to Francine's three girlfriends, making sure that they looked perfect. All four girls wore pink V-necked thin-strapped midi-dresses. They all wore their hair the same with a headband. Around their necks were leis. They all wore pale pink lipstick on their lips and their cheeks had blush patted on. They were to each carry a bouquet of flowers. They wore low-heeled, opened-toed white shoes. All of them had smiles on their faces. Their eyes were bright and wide. Bettye Jo was pleased. After she was through, she took them aside to give the necessary instructions to follow when they went to work in her florist shop. Danielle would give them assigned tasks and were to be prompt and not take longer than an hour for lunch. Three other female employers worked with Danielle and the four of them would meet and help them.

"Does everyone understand?" Bettye Jo asked them.

They quipped up and excitedly with gleaming eyes were in complete agreement.

"You could depend upon us," Willow chirped up.

Bettye Jo smiled. "I know I can, girls." Then she took her daughter's face in her hands, their eyes meeting. "And you're my special girl." She kissed her forehead. Her friends watched them interact. Francine was not at all embarrassed by her mother's open display of affection. "Now all of you, please go downstairs with Kelly and Danielle. I have to speak to Francine alone for a minute."

"Yes, Bettye Jo." And they headed down the stairs with their purses in their hands.

"And I have a surprise for you." Bettye Jo looked at Francine, smiling. Francine stood waiting. "Honey," Bettye Jo began, "Grandma is going to be there."

Francine's eyes widened. "Oh, really! I cannot believe it. How?" She knew not what to say.

"Daddy made arrangements for two aides to bring her in a chairbed in an ambulette. Your grandmother insisted on seeing her eldest son happily wed, and Daddy fully agreed."

"I want my friends to meet her. They know I am her namesake."

Bettye Jo again took her daughter's face and cupped it in her hands. "I know that, honey, and they will love her and she them."

Francine began to jump up and then became calm. "I know they will. Oh, thank you, Mama." She hugged her mother and gave her a kiss on the cheek.

Bettye Jo giggled, taking her hands in hers. "All right, darling," she concluded.

Francine took her purse and headed downstairs to join her friends. All of them were full of giggles and were chattering among themselves. They all had smiley grimaces on their faces.

Bettye Jo and Ellen left Francine's bedroom and went into Bettye Jo's room where their gowns laid on the bed.

Ellen's maid-of-honor gown was a pale pink scooped neck without sleeves. It reached a little below the knees. There were ruffles on the hem and around the waist. Bettye Jo helped her on zippering the back. Ellen smoothed out its front and straightened it with her hands. Bettye Jo went into her jewelry box and reached for a string of white pearls to clasp around her neck. Dangling down Ellen's ears were buttoned earrings hanging from a silver string. She wore a pale beaded bracelet on her wrist. Her yellow blonde hair was done in a round long page boy hanging a little below her shoulders. On her feet were low-heeled, slingback open-toed pale pink shoes. Her eyes were done with pink eye shadow surrounded with a black eyeliner, and her lips were a light pink color. Her face was covered with a beige foundation with powder, and on her cheeks a soft reddish blush. She posed her body facing the full-length mirror, admiring herself. Bettye Jo put her hands on Ellen's shoulders and was pleased. Her sister was beautiful and radiant. She smiled to herself. Then she remarked, patting her back, "There, you look simply divine. I am glad you are my maid of honor."

Ellen turned to face her sister. "I'm delighted to be your maid of honor. Today is so very important to you, and I only want the best for you." She paused before saying what she really wanted to say. She wanted to be careful to say the right statement. Bettye Jo stood with a smile but said nothing. "I want you to know, I'm sorry that I hadn't been such a good sister for most of our lives. I was very selfish and immature. I should have been there for you when William and Sherry Jo were killed and when Mom and Dad got sick and died. I'm deeply ashamed of my behavior and I want to make it up to you."

Bettye Jo patted both sides of her sister's face and, while looking into her eyes, she spoke, "It is all water under the bridge, Ellen. I am not angry with you anymore and I do forgive you and accept your apology."

Then Ellen chimed up, "I'd like for us to be close as real sisters should be. And I have been thinking a lot lately, why you and I do not go to our parents' graves. I have never even seen the site where they were buried. Also, I would like Francine to come with us. I am sure she would be delighted to see her grandparents, though she never knew or met them. If I know my niece, she will think it was a great idea. I want to pay my respects, to pray for forgiveness. I know you think it is too late now."

Bettye Jo interjected, "No, Ellen. I do not think that at all. I do feel that it would be a great idea for us to go see our parents' graves and we will, I promise. I will discuss it with Francine. I am sure she will agree to it. But right now, let us enjoy this special day and get through with finalizing Francine's adoption and her name change. It'll be for only a little while, but we will definitely do it."

Ellen smiled pleasantly at her sister, but added, "I'd also like it if we could meet perhaps some time for coffee and lunch to just chat and be close as sisters should be and even be friends."

Bettye Jo still stood smiling in agreement. She was elated. Then she hugged her sister. "Of course, I will. I'd love it." She patted her back tenderly.

Both spread apart, their hands stretched out, then burst into laughter, giggling as schoolgirls do.

Ellen then thought while looking at the clock, "Oh!" her hand over her mouth, "it's getting late. You need to get ready. You're the blushing bride!" Both were still chuckling. Then Bettye Jo walked over to her bed and began dressing for her special day.

Her deep pink dress was flowing and it reached to her ankles. It was low-cut, showing her cleavage, with spaghetti straps and lace around her waist and pale pink ruffles on its hem with tiny print rosebuds covering below the waist. Ellen carefully helped her make up her face while she sat at her vanity table looking into the mirror. She then reached for their grandmother's pearl necklace and clasped it behind her neck. She wore a band of white beads around her wrist. Then she reached for her tiaralike sterling silver band and put it in front of her bun with care. Then Ellen took her shoulders and stated, facing her to the mirror, "Look at you!" she exclaimed. "You're perfectly magnificent! You look just as stately as a queen! Philip will certainly flip when he sees you, so beautifully made-up. He is the luckiest man in the world and he will be the envy of all men! Just look at you!" she reiterated.

Bettye Jo remarked to her sister, "Thanks to you, sis, my made-up face is unbelievably impeccable. You should be a makeup artist. If I may say so myself, I do feel radiant." She put her hand on her wrist and looked up at her. "Thanks!"

"It is no problem. Anything for my big sister!"

Both squeezed each other's hands for a while. Then Bettye Jo announced to her sister, "It's time now," while straightening her dress smoothly.

Ellen, while standing ahead of her, motioned her hand and directed, "After you, sis."

Bettye Jo headed gracefully down the stairs with Ellen behind her.

Ellen called out, "Hey, guys, isn't she just ravishing?"

All six women turned to face Bettye Jo as she descended the staircase. Their eyes wide on fire and their mouths opened. "Aah!" they sighed breathlessly. They rose from the couch and walked up to her.

"How pretty, Mama!" Francine's face was glowing.

The others stared in amazement.

Agnes stopped what she was doing and walked up to her employer. "Wow! Mrs. Pennington! You sure are one big dazzler!"

Bettye Jo smiled at her and then at the others.

They heard the doorbell. Agnes walked up to open it. "That's Raymond," she announced. "Are you ready, ladies?"

They acknowledged her, and then when Raymond opened the door, he let out his hand, first to Bettye Jo. "You first, since you are the beautiful, exotic bride." She took his hand, and the others followed as Raymond opened the limousine doors, escorting them inside one at a time. Raymond looked up and winked at Agnes. She knew the cue. She would be waiting when he came.

An Hour Later

The sky was a clear blue, no sign of a cloud, and the sun shone brilliantly. It was not too hot or too cold. Just right.

A white trellis was situated on the perfectly mowed green grass. Colorful flowers surrounded it. On one side was an organist hired to play the wedding march. A minister stood at the podium. White chairs were placed on each side of the aisle.

Philip was clad in a black linen suit, a crisp white shirt, and a wide black tie. He wore black leather shiny shoes. He was a little nervous, his body shaking, mouth ajar, but he was overjoyed. It was his day.

Paul stood next to him, dressed impeccably in a black suit with a white shirt and a sporty tie. He wore flat black oxfords. He was so proud of his elder brother, who was so in love and willing to settle down. Regretfully, he was unable to change his past behaviors and told his brother, who said, "It's all right. You are here now and with the family. That's all that matters."

Wayne was seated in one of the white chairs. His hair parted on the side and also wore black apparel, a white shirt, and a black tie. On his feet were black comfortable sandals.

From afar, all three men saw an ambulette pull up. Two aides got out and headed to the back door. It was Grandma Marsowe sitting upright in a bedded wheelchair. Her white hair was short with teased-up curls around her head. Her bright blue eyes shone. She smiled and looked up everywhere. The aides let her out and wheeled her to the wedding site. She wore a royal blue jacket and skirt. Under her jacket, she had on a white blouse that is puffed up in the middle. She wore a string of white pearls around her neck. Her legs were clad in cotton stockings, and on her feet were flat white slip-on shoes.

"All set, Mrs. Marsowe?" one aide asked her.

She bowed down pleasantly, and they left her.

Also in attendance were the three couples, the parents of Francine's best friends and the newest friends of her parents, Bettye Jo and Philip. They spoke quietly among themselves remarking about the weather and, of course, mundane issues. They were all happy for the bride and groom. It was their day, and they were delighted to be part of it.

Raymond was heading up. He stopped and led all the ladies out near the lavatory to freshen up. All the ladies gathered around Bettye Jo as she gazed into the mirror, her eyes glowing bright and opened. No one could take their eyes off her for she was simply radiant.

Ellen motioned to Kelly, Danielle, and the four young maidens to take their places. All of them held small bouquets of flowers to their hearts. Raymond was going to walk Bettye Jo down the aisle. She was carrying a bouquet of pink carnations in front of her, her heart pounding, beaming with love. It was her day, and all her loved ones were present to celebrate this special occasion with her and Philip.

The organist began playing the wedding march.

Bettye Jo gracefully walked down the aisle, her arm linked to Raymond's. Everyone turned with amazement, their eyes on the bride.

Francine and her friends saw from up front, holding their bouquets down in front of them.

Ellen and Paul watched them with awe. They were extremely proud and happy to be their siblings. Then they winked at each other, their eyes met lovingly. Perhaps one day it will be their turn. But for now, their focus was on Bettye Jo and Philip. It was their day, and they were there to be a part of it.

As Raymond and Bettye were at the podium, Raymond bowed and politely excused himself. He took off in the limousine, and everyone saw and wondered but then turned their attention to the couple.

The minister read the vows, which Bettye Jo and Philip took graciously and with love in their eyes. They placed the rings on each other's fingers, promising eternal love and devotion. The minister concluded with the usual, "I now pronounce you husband and wife." Before he had a chance to say you may kiss the bride, they took their hands and placed them on the sides of their faces and kissed each other voraciously. Their kiss seemed to take until eternity, but they wanted it to be special and for all their guests to be there witnessing it. Francine and her friends giggled and remarked, "Come on, you guys!" Philip and Bettye Jo turned and smiled at them saying nothing. They thought it was cute.

Then, as an afterthought, Philip quipped up, having the urge to speak, "My wife." He gleamed at her. "And I have something very important to address to all of you." Both he and Bettye Jo faced their daughter with love and pride. "If it were not for our lovely, special daughter, none of us would be here today celebrating this joyful day. Francine has been nothing but a pleasure and a joy to us and for that, we are eternally grateful that she was brought into our lives. She is the heart of our hearts." He beamed at her as he bent over to kiss her. "We love you, our princess."

Afterward, Bettye Jo kissed their daughter as well. She looked up at Philip with love in her eyes, and they both gazed at their daughter.

"And most important," he said, reaching into his pants pocket, "is a card she made herself since there are no store-bought cards for children to send to their parents on their wedding day, as you all know. It has colorful hearts and flowers on it. She wrote, 'To Mama and Daddy on your wedding day. You guys are the greatest and I love you forever and always. Your princess, Francine Josephine.'"

Everyone *oohed* and *aahed*. "And one more thing, folks, her three best friends sent us a card they wrote and signed, 'To a wonderful couple on their wedding day.' My wife and I were ecstatic. Such lovely girls." He looked at them with a smile.

"Okay, everyone, time for some pictures!" their photographer called from afar.

Everyone gathered around him, each wanting to be a part of the action.

First, photographs were taken of the bride and groom in different poses. Then Francine joined them for pictures.

Everyone watched the newly happily wedded couple and their daughter posing in front of the camera, including Willow, Arlene, and Stephanie who were smiling among themselves. Then Francine joined them in their gleefulness and asked them, "Do you guys want to meet my aunt and uncle? By the way, they are actually dating each other and have been for some months now." She saw them from afar and told her friends, "Let's go over and greet them." She pointed and then waved her friends over. Francine called out, "Aunt Ellen! Uncle Paul!" who turned toward their niece. "Come meet my three best friends." She introduced each friend by name, and they extended their hands and brightly piped up.

First, Willow said, "Francine always talks about you guys."

Then Arlene chipped up, "It is so cool you two are actually a couple and are really in love."

Stephanie added a remark, "Just like a storybook romance, but so very real!"

Both Aunt Ellen and Uncle Paul, while holding a drink, smiled at each girl, their eyes bright and cheerful.

"What nice girls you all are," Uncle Paul remarked.

Then Aunt Ellen continued, "And such good friends of our niece. Glad you all came to see our siblings get married."

The girls laughed and, with a hand motion, they said, "It was a pleasure. Francine is such a great friend and her parents are remarkably awesome."

Then Aunt Ellen thought as she faced Uncle Paul, "Honey," she patted his chest, "they're taking photographs now. Let's head over there now."

Uncle Paul, while finishing his drink and discarding his and Ellen's cups, agreed. They took each other's hands and began walking away. Then, turning to the girls, he stated kindly, "A pleasure meeting you all." He nodded. Francine and her friends watched them.

Then they rubbed their brows with the back of their hands for they were hot and thirsty from the heat. They poured themselves a cup of fruit punch.

Then in the distance, two attendants came pushing a wheelchair bed. Francine saw it and at first said nothing. The wheelchair came closer. Francine got a clearer view. Then she cried out with her arms flung out, "Grandma!" She was so excited and ran up to her, throwing her arms around her neck. Mrs. Marsowe attempted to pat her back but was unable due to her arthritis.

"Darling!" she replied, happy to see her only grandchild, her namesake.

"I am so happy to see you. Mama and Daddy are too. And I'd like you to meet my three best friends." Francine turned and saw them a few feet away. They turned and faced her. She waved for them to come over, and they strolled toward their friend and her grandmother. "Grandma," she began, "these are Willow, Arlene, and Stephanie. We've been friends since the fifth grade."

Mrs. Marsowe smiled and nodded. "Such lovely girls," she remarked.

Willow piped up, "Francine told us about you."

Then Arlene continued, "I am sorry about your husband, Mrs. Marsowe. You really loved him."

Stephanie concluded, "Francine said he got dementia and wasn't able to care for himself. He remembered nothing, and for that we felt badly and deeply sorry for you."

Mrs. Marsowe smiled at the girls. She wanted to shake their hands, but they knew of her crippling arthritis.

Then the photographer called for them to join in on the picture taking.

Francine turned, nodded, and said, "In a minute. Grandma, let us go and get our pictures taken. I'll wheel you over."

They went.

Bettye Jo and Philip turned around. "Mother!" Philip hugged her and stated with a smile, "So glad you could come on our special day."

Then he motioned to Ellen and Paul, who walked up and called, "Mom!" Paul gave her a peck on the cheek.

"My two wonderful sons," Grandma Marsowe remarked. Then she faced Bettye Jo and Ellen. They grinned at her with joy.

"Mother Marsowe." Bettye Jo hugged her.

Next, Ellen piped up and patted her hand, "Nice to see you, Mrs. Marsowe."

Mrs. Marsowe was gleeful for she was with her family on such a joyous occasion. She did miss her husband, but then reasoned pleasantly to herself, "He's watching over us smiling and happy, free from sickness and pain."

The photographer continued with the picture taking of all the family members. All smiling, happy faces, in joy.

In the meantime, at a faraway table were Agnes, Raymond, and Myles displaying the floral arrangement they bought for their employers. They laid it on a picnic table. Now they said to each other, "How can we get them over here?" Everyone was oblivious and clueless to them. "What should we do?" They were ill at ease.

Suddenly, Wayne turned around and said to Kelly, pointing, "Look, honey, who are those people?"

Kelly turned, faced him, and then looked to the direction where he's pointing. "Why, I don't know," she was uncertain. "They weren't part of the wedding party," she stated in puzzlement.

There were four of them, two men and two women in uniforms. Then Danielle turned and cried out, "Look, guys." She motioned to them to come with her, and they did so as instructed.

When they arrived, Danielle gleefully exclaimed, "What are you guys doing here?"

They did not reply at first.

Then Kelly remarked, "Alice?" who nodded with a grin.

Danielle went on, "Raymond?" then "Agnes?" and finally, "Myles?"

All four employees grinned happily and turned their heads toward their wedding present to Bettye Jo and Philip. "We have a surprise gift for our wonderful employers. It took some time and planning. We wanted to show them our appreciation for all they have done for us," Agnes spoke for all of them.

Danielle remarked, "How very thoughtful of you all. Won't they be pleased at your generosity."

Wayne looked at Kelly and stated, "You and Danielle just wait here. I will tell everyone to come, but I will not give the surprise away. I'll think of something." He walked off.

"You guys," Kelly remarked excitedly.

"Are simply terrific," Danielle completed Kelly's sentence.

"After all they did for us, we should show our gratitude," Agnes affirmed.

"They'll love it!" Kelly was ecstatic.

They tried patiently to wait. It was getting very hot out, as the sun beaming down on them. They became a little on edge, but they were eager to see the newly wedded couple's expression on their faces when they see their unexpected gift from their devoted staff.

They then turned around and saw faint figures. Wayne was motioning them to come forward. He did keep his promise to not reveal the surprise. They approached closer and closer. Danielle and Kelly finally saw them nearer and nearer. Danielle walked up to Philip and Bettye Jo, with Kelly following behind her. Wayne put blindfolds on the couple's eyes and led them to the table. They were in such suspense but had smiles on their faces, though they had no clue as to what was happening. Everyone stood still. Wayne took their blindfolds off. Bettye Jo and Philip saw the colorful, diverse floral arrangement. Their eyes lit up and their mouths were wide open. Agnes, Alice, Myles, and Raymond came up to them. Philip and Bettye Jo were astonished, their hands on their mouths. They were speechless but joyful.

"How lovely!" Bettye Jo exclaimed.

Agnes began, "We wanted to show our appreciation for all you have done for us. Thus, we all chipped in and bought you a wedding present."

"Oh my!" Bettye Jo remarked with amazement.

Philip suggested, "We'll put this and all the rest of the gifts in the limousine." Gazing at Raymond, he instructed, "Please take all this to our home." Then to the others, he announced, "You could all have today off. You deserve a break for all your hard work. My wife and I thank you all."

Raymond stated, "It was our pleasure." Then he and the others said their goodbyes and good wishes as they began putting all the presents in the limousine. They waved to their employers and guests, and everyone reciprocated. They got into the limousine and were off.

Wayne motioned with his hand and piped up, "Time to cut the cake!"

Philip took Bettye Jo's hand and let her do it.

The cake was white with pink ice cream in tiers.

Philip cut a piece and then Bettye Jo did so too, and together they put it in each other's mouths. The photographer called out, "Hold it!" They stopped and he took a few pictures of them feeding each other. Everyone watched with their hands clasped together.

Then a young woman came up.

"What's going on?" Philip asked, curiously eyeing the woman.

Francine answered with a gleam in her eyes, "We hired her to sing yours and Mama's favorite song, 'Let your love flow.'"

"Oh, how thoughtful, honey," Bettye Jo graciously remarked.

"Are you all ready?" the woman asked.

They nodded as she sung. Philip took Bettye Jo's hand, and they did a small but graceful dance on the grass. Philip twirled her around and around. The photographer took more pictures. All the guests clapped for them.

Wayne then mentioned while looking at his watch, "Guys, it's getting late. We need to get to the airport soon."

The couple nodded in unison.

Danielle then lifted a finger and said, "One more item on the agenda." Then she turned to the others. "Ready?" she questioned them

Then everyone burst out in a song, "We believe in Bettye Jo, we believe in Philip."

Bettye Jo and Philip laughed, and tears of joy formed in their eyes. Bettye Jo put her hands to her heart, "Oh, you guys!" Philip agreed silently.

"I'll bring the car around," Wayne announced. Before he turned away, he added, "Let's all congratulate the wonderful couple and say our goodbyes now!"

All at once, everyone gathered around them wanting to offer their congratulations with hugs, kisses, and pat backing.

Francine walked up to her parents, hugging and kissing them in return. "I love you, Mama, Daddy, all the way to Pluto and back!"

They added together, smiling and waving, "We love you, too, our princess."

Then everyone waved and smiled, jumping up and down with happy tears in their eyes.

Philip led Bettye Jo into the car with his hand and then waved back. Everybody watched, still bouncing up and down. They were off on their honeymoon to Hawaii.

A Half Hour Later

Francine and her friends were chattering and giggling among themselves with drinks in their hands. The two attendants wheeled Mrs. Marsowe up to them.

Francine turned around and gave her grandmother a peck on her cheek along with a hug. "It was simply a wonderful day, Grandma," she professed. "And you were able to come. We were all so happy."

Mrs. Marsowe smiled while trying to pat Francine's hand, which she kissed. "Yes, it was, indeed, honey." Then she turned toward Francine's friends and complimented them, "You are such lovely girls. Such good friends for my dear, sweet granddaughter."

They smiled at her. Then Willow began, "Francine is a great friend to us, and her parents are wonderful."

Arlene went on, "It was a pleasure to meet you, Mrs. Marsowe."

Stephanie ended, "We're all so lucky. Thank you for coming."

Mrs. Marsowe smiled with a nod. An attendant mentioned, "It's getting late, Mrs. Marsowe."

The other attendant added, "It's time to go now. Say goodbye to the girls."

Mrs. Marsowe did so pleasantly, and they waved back. The attendants wheeled her into the ambulette and were off.

Danielle and Kelly watched the interaction. After Mrs. Marsowe left, the four girls walked over to them. Danielle needed to give them their instructions for they were to begin work in the florist shop on Monday. In the meantime, the parents of the three friends sat by a picnic table.

Danielle began, "Monday will be the first day on your jobs. I will expect you to be on time—9:00 a.m. sharp. That is when we open. As for the appropriate dress, you are not to wear tank tops, T-shirts, baggy pants, flip-flops, or open-toed shoes. You are to dress in a businesslike fashion. A clean blouse, a skirt, or long pants will do. If you choose a skirt, you must wear stockings. You may wear flat or low-heeled shoes. You will be dealing with the public, so you must present yourselves accordingly. You may wear lipstick. No fancy jewelry, but something plain and simple. You may wear your hair as it is. You are young ladies now. You must smile at the customers and to anyone who enters the shop. There are three other employees besides me, three young girls—Terri, Katie, and Rita. You will be assigned duties and assist them. They will show you what you must do. You will have an hour of lunch break. If you must leave your post, you come to me and let me know. I am depending on all of you, and please do not let me down. You are all lovely girls, but at times, teenagers do tend to forget themselves. It does happen due to their raging hormones and the transition from a child to not yet quite an adult." She paused while looking at them. "Any questions, girls?"

They all shook their heads no.

"If you girls need anything, please feel free to come to me or Kelly, all right?"

They agreed in unison.

Danielle then turned and faced Francine's friends' parents and motioned them over, and they did. Danielle informed their parents of their daughter's agendas. They were in complete agreement, and then they led them to their cars to head home. They all waved and bid goodbyes. The parents thanked Danielle and Kelly. Then they were gone.

Then Wayne pulled up in his car and called out, "Are you ready to go, honey?"

Kelly winked at him and said, "In a minute."

She bid Danielle and Francine goodbye with a happy grin. Then, waving to each other, Wayne got out of the car and bid goodbye and waved. Then he opened the door for Kelly to get in. And they were off.

Danielle turned to Francine and said, "I'll drive you home now. I will make sure you are safe. Agnes will come over tomorrow morning, okay?"

"Oh, of course. Thank you for being with my parents on their special day."

Danielle smiled and said, "It was a pleasure. Your parents are lovely people."

They headed toward Danielle's car and rode home in silence. They were exhausted but felt very elated for today was a very joyful and pleasant occasion.

Sunday, 9:00 a.m.

Francine tossed and turned in her bed, still sleepy but trying to get up. She heard a knock on her door. She sat up in her bed.

"It's Agnes, honey. Can I come in?"

Faintly, she replied, "Yes, Agnes."

She entered and stood by her bed. "Are you all right?"

Francine slowly nodded. She was not smiling. She had a mournful expression on her face, which Agnes noticed.

"Are you unhappy? You miss them, don't you? It feels strange without them here as they always are. I understand. You know they love you very much. And you love them. But they are on their honeymoon, you do understand. They need their time alone together. I'm sure they'll call, and when they do, you could speak to them and tell them you love them, wish them well, and hope they are enjoying themselves."

"Yes," she replied quietly.

"Would you like your usual breakfast, french toast with bacon? Why don't you get up, get washed, and dressed? I'll make it for you, all right?"

"Thank you. I'll be down soon," she mentioned softly but graciously.

Agnes left the room. Francine got out of bed. Both were ready to begin the day.

About ten minutes later, Francine quietly descended the stairs wearing a white spaghetti-strapped tank top with denim jeans. She had moccasins on her feet. Her hair flowed around her shoulders with a blue headband. She was carrying her puzzle and doodling books and placed them on the chair next to her.

She saw Agnes put her breakfast on the table, thanked her, and began eating. She did not say anything. Agnes watched her. *She is so sad*, she thought to herself. *I cannot make her smile. She will not even initiate any conversation*, she pondered sadly. *I will leave her for now. She will come around. She is very resilient. She understands and knows her parents love her, but they still needed their space.*

Agnes went back to the counter to clean up after making Francine's breakfast. She turned and faced her, "Are you all right, honey?" she was concerned and wanted to help her.

Francine looked up with a slight, small smile and replied softly, "Yes, Agnes.

I am okay, just tired and overwhelmed from everything. But I will be fine, Agnes. Thank you for asking. That is very kind of you."

Agnes grinned and said, "I understand. It was an exciting day yesterday. I want you to know I'm here if you need to talk, all right?"

Francine again thanked her for her support and kindness and then resumed her meal in silence. Agnes went back to her duties. She wiped down the counters and put the pan and spatula into the dishwasher. She went to open the refrigerator, took out a carton of milk, and poured Francine a glass. Besides the milk, there were three Oreo cookies next to it. After Agnes set them both down in front of Francine, the telephone rang. At once, Francine jumped up and dropped her fork and knife on her plate. Agnes went to look at the caller ID. She did not recognize the number. She had been informed not to pick up the phone if that were the case. However, she was confused and did not want to make a mistake. Perhaps it was important. Then she decided, *what the heck, nothing bad will happen.* She could always hang up. The telephone kept ringing. Resigned, Agnes answered it, "Good morning, P-Pen- Marsowe residence," she announced, almost forgetting that Bettye Jo was now married. Francine looked up from her plate, eyeing Agnes attentively. She saw a smile on Agnes' face. Agnes spoke into the telephone, "Oh, hello, Mrs. Marsowe." She was gleaming. "Yes, Mrs. Marsowe, everything is fine. She's right here eating her breakfast." Francine's eyes glowed, her mouth watery and wide opened. "She's been waiting for you and Dr. Marsowe to call." She went on, "She was a little sad this morning. But you know your daughter, very kind and understanding." Agnes listened into the telephone. "Yes, she does know that." She looked at Francine, whose eyes blazed while squirming in her chair. "You want to talk with her? She's dying to do so." Agnes handed the telephone to her. Both were grinning joyfully. "It's your mother (no fooling, Francine thought happily to herself)."

She took the receiver eagerly as Agnes looked on smiling. "Mama!" she exclaimed, jumping up and down.

"Darling!" Bettye Jo replied.

"I miss you. I was so anxious for you and Daddy to call. You did not last night to tell me of your arrival. I was worried. Are you both okay?"

Bettye Jo answered brightly, "Of course, and I am sorry we didn't call you last night. The plane was delayed for three hours, and we had a problem with our luggage, so do not worry. Fortunately, it was all taken care of with ease. We got to the hotel exhausted and we figured you'd also be very tired or asleep, so we decided to call you this morning just to check in."

Francine was listening. "I understand. I just was very sad. It is very strange with you and Daddy not being at home, but I am just fine. Agnes is simply great, a godsend. But I am not sad now. I will be fine, Mama. Can I please speak to Daddy?"

Philip had been washing up, brushing his teeth, and shaving. He took a towel to dry himself off.

Bettye Jo called, "Honey, you want to speak to Francine? She's been waiting."

"Certainly." Philip reached for the telephone. "Hi, princess!" he joyfully greeted her.

"Hi, Daddy! How are you doing?"

Philip replied, "Mama and I are fine. We are getting ready for breakfast. Afterward, we plan to go sightseeing and for a boat ride later."

"How was your first night of married life? Please tell me," she insisted elatedly.

Philip glanced at Bettye Jo, who gleefully grinned. He asked his wife, and they happily confirmed into the affirmative. "Simply wonderful. It was a blast!" they shouted into the telephone. They had tears in their eyes.

"I'm so happy for both of you. Do enjoy your honeymoon. It's yours and Mama's alone together, you two."

"Thank you, darling," Bettye Jo said chipperly. "And one more thing, Daddy and I will call you tonight and every night, just to say we love you."

Francine jumped up and down, almost dropping the telephone. She was ecstatic. "And I love you too, you guys. Adios!"

They reciprocated their greetings to her. She was no longer sad. The call ended, but everyone was joyful and satisfied.

Agnes smiled at her as she hung up the telephone. She went to finish her breakfast in contentment. It was the beginning of a very good day. Francine could hardly contain her excitement. Agnes looked at her with a grin and said, "I'm glad you're not sad anymore. I hate to see you like that."

Francine smiled at her. After she was through with her breakfast, Francine rose from her chair and brought her dishes, silverware, and glasses to the sink. Agnes chuckled and said, "You don't need to do that, honey. That's my job."

"I know, but I just feel like it. You've been so good to us."

Agnes laughed and took the dishes and utensils from her and put them in the sink to be rinsed off and stacked into the dishwasher. Francine took her books and went into the living room. She loved puzzles and delved into them enthusiastically.

12:00 p.m.

"Are you hungry, Francine? I'll make you some lunch," Agnes offered.

Francine looked up from her puzzle book. She smiled and said, "Yes, thank you. That is quite kind of you."

"Tuna salad on toasted rye?" she asked rhetorically. By now, she knew Francine's favorites.

She nodded, leaped off the couch, and went into the kitchen. Agnes began preparing the sandwich.

Francine sat at the table with her hands clasped in front of her. She was so lucky to have Agnes in her life, though it was through extremely unfortunate and horrible circumstances. Then she mused thoughtfully, *Things have a way of working out. Beauty stemming from ugliness. Love from hate. Good from evil. Triumph from tragedy. Stars from scars. Pleasure from pain. Halos from hurts. What does not kill one makes one stronger and gives one character.* Francine had a strong, loving character. Agnes knew it and so did everyone else who knew her. Agnes handed her the sandwich. She pleasantly thanked her and began eating it.

"Can I get you anything else in the meantime?" Agnes offered.

Francine grinned at her but pleasantly declined her offer.

The telephone rang. Agnes turned to answer it. It was Willow. Agnes gave her the telephone, and she gleefully greeted her friend with joy.

Francine was hopping around. "Yes, yes," she kept saying into the telephone. Then she covered the mouthpiece and asked Agnes, "Willow and the girls want me to go to the mall with them. Okay, her mother is driving us. Please?"

Agnes, while drying a glass, looked at her with a smile and said, "Of course you may. But remember, you girls have a job starting tomorrow morning. You need to get ready and go to bed early. You have responsibilities now."

"Oh, I know, Agnes. We all do. We promise to be home for supper."

Agnes put the glass down on the counter and said, "All right, honey."

Francine stood on her toes. "Good. Thanks, Agnes. You're the best."

Agnes continued smiling as she watched Francine tell her friend, "It's fine, but we have to prepare for tomorrow. Okay? Yes, I will be ready. Bye now." She hung up the telephone excitedly.

"Finish your lunch first, okay?" Agnes ordered gently.

She did so, though she was so thrilled to spend time with her friends.

"It's good for you to get out and enjoy your life. Life is too short to waste time being sad and unhappy," Agnes informed Francine carefully. "Your parents love you dearly and would not want you to be unhappy. They want you to live your life and have your friends," she added.

"I know that, Agnes," she agreed. "Mama and Daddy are wonderful parents. I'm very fortunate to have them." She got up from her chair, smoothed her hair and clothes, and then grabbed her bag and swung it around her shoulder. She asked Agnes, "Do I look all right?"

"You look lovely, dear," she replied sincerely. "But remember to be home by 5:00 p.m. Also, call me when you arrive at the mall, okay?"

"Sure," she affirmed. She turned toward the door and waved. "Bye, now."

Agnes stood and waved back.

Willow's mother pulled up, honking her car horn. Francine got into the car with Stephanie and Arlene. They were all giggling and high-fiving each other.

Agnes pulled the curtain aside and watched them from the window. *I am so happy for her, loving parents and good friends. To be young again,* she pondered to herself. She went back to clearing the table.

The girls strolled down the corridor eyeing the various diversified stores. They came to the store that sold DVDs and CDs.

Willow pointed to it and exclaimed excitedly, "Let's go in and check out some movies, okay, guys?"

Arlene popped up, "All right," and motioned to Stephanie and Francine.

"I hear Katie Perry has a new one," Stephanie mentioned.

"Really?" Francine remarked. "She's so cool."

They went in, glancing about. *So much to choose from,* they thought to themselves. Also, they noticed some boys hanging out in the back.

Stephanie pointed. "Look, you guys, those boys there. I think they were in our classes," she mentioned.

The others turned.

"Isn't that Mark Klineman?" Willow asked.

"Why, yes," Arlene answered.

"He's looking at you," Willow stated to Francine, who burst out into a giggle. Her face blushed.

"You like him!" Arlene stated excitedly.

"Oh, come on, you guys. He never even spoke to me," Francine stated.

"He's just shy," Willow said in a matter of factly. "He was in our science class last year, remember?" Willow nudged Francine playfully. "Why don't you go up to him and say 'hello.' He's not going to bite you."

Arlene then urged, "What's the worst that can happen?"

Stephanie poked her elbow.

Francine stood in her spot and hesitantly blurted out, "What if he doesn't like me and is snotty and mean?"

Willow kept on, "So? Give it a try. You do not have to marry him. Just try. You have never talked to a boy before. Now's your chance."

The girls looked at Francine. She was happy but still nervous and leery. She stood in her spot, not saying a word. They did not stop and refused to give in. Gently, they pushed her forward.

Willow exclaimed, "He's coming up to us!" She tapped Francine's shoulder.

Mark was clad in a blue T-shirt and baggy blue jeans with a denim jacket over it. He wore Reebok sneakers on his feet. His eyes were a pale blue and were surrounded with silver-wired rimmed rectangular lenses.

He stood in front of her. Francine wanted to be friendly but was still silent. He smiled at her, and then she managed to smile back.

Her friends watched her. "Do it!" they urged to themselves. "Come on!"

Mark began, "It's a very nice day out. Don't you think so?"

The girls continued, "Go for it!"

Francine was still hesitant. "Yes, I guess so." She doesn't know what else to say.

She glanced at her friends for support. "Help me out here, you guys." Then she thought, "Do you like Katie Perry? I hear she has a new DVD out," she stated.

"Oh, yeah, she's so cool," he replied.

Francine suggested, "You want to check it out?"

Mark shrugged his shoulders. "All right." They walked together down the aisle searching for it. They were silent.

Her friends were still watching with their hands together in front of them and eyes sparkling in amazement. "Atta girl, Francine," they mused, chuckling among themselves.

Francine piped up excitedly as she lifted the DVD from the rack. "This is it." She was so happy.

Mark remarked, "If I had the money, I'd buy it for you."

Francine was speechless. He spoke to her. He really did. She then continued, "That's very sweet of you, but I'm paying for it with my mother's credit card."

He nodded nonchalantly. "All right."

They walked up to the cashier and she rang it up.

Mark watched her with awe. "She's so beautiful," he was breathing heavily, unable to say more.

When they left the store, Mark asked the girls while glancing at three other boys that were friends of his, "You girls want to join me with my friends? We could stop at the food court for a soda. I do have the money for that, at least."

Francine stood with her friends as Mark motioned for his friends to join them. All of them looked at each other, unsure of what to do.

Mark introduced his friends, "This here is James, then Richard, and that one, finally, Tom." They all winked at the girls. Then Mark adamantly stated carefully, "If you think we are here to try anything or pull something, don't worry. These guys and I were eyeing you girls. We just want to be friendly and become better acquainted. We promise our intentions are honorable. We think you are all nice girls. Not like some other girls in our school who look to get it on. You are not like them one bit."

The girls listened. They wanted to believe him, but they were so young and inexperienced. They were never with a boy before, even as a casual acquaintance.

"We promise to be perfect gentlemen and we are not all talk, not like some other boys who have the gift of gab."

The girls shrugged their shoulders, looking at each other for support. They were still somewhat leery.

"Okay," Willow decided, "let us do it." She gazed at her friends and then at the boys.

Stephanie then said, "You boys do seem nice. It is not like a date or anything. Just for some talk and sodas."

The girls agreed and they casually walked with the boys. Everyone was excited. So much was happening unexpectedly, but it was a good day.

When they arrived at the food court, the boys each pulled out a chair for each girl to sit on.

Then Mark mentioned to them, "You girls just wait here. We'll be back with the sodas."

The girls smiled pleasantly at them, and when they left, they began laughing and nudging each other. *What a day,* they thought under their breaths. They turned to watch them go on line for their sodas. It's their first time they had any encounters with boys. They were a little nervous but joyful.

The boys came back with the sodas for the girls and themselves. Then they sat down and began small talk with each other mostly about their summer plans. Francine and her three friends mentioned working in her mother's florist shop where they would get paid, though off the books. They were to begin tomorrow morning. Willow told the boys how cool Francine's parents were. Francine did not think to speak about the relationship between her foster mother and birth father. She did not think that Mark would understand being it was a unique but quite a wonderful situation. She wanted to, but not now. Maybe he would think she is queer and strange and might lose interest in her. So the conversation went to other topics. Francine sat there silently observing her friends with the boys. They seemed all so comfortable with each other.

Willow was never shy or awkward with people. She always attempted to be sensitive and kind to how others felt and thought, and she would never put anyone down. One can say she is a leader, a good take-charge person, for it was she who befriended Francine when her classmates tormented her. Stephanie and Arlene always agreed and sided with Willow, and they also took a stand with Francine. And they had been together since then.

Francine glanced at her watch. "Guys, it's after 4:00 p.m."

She turned to Willow, who acknowledged her. She took out her phone to call her mother to come and pick them up. Francine promised Agnes that they would be home by 5:00 p.m. Tomorrow was going to be a big day.

Mark turned to Francine with breathlessness excitement and asked, "Can I call you tomorrow night? If you give me your telephone number, I will put it in my phone, okay?"

Francine's eyes lit up and she smiled at him. "Of course you can." She gave him her telephone number, which he punched into his phone and then snapped it shut.

"I had a good time, Francine. I'm glad I got to meet you," Mark stated hesitantly but with a slight grin and a wink.

"Me too," she acknowledged him sincerely but softly.

Willow finished speaking to her mother and told her friends, "Mom is coming soon."

As they got up, the boys pulled their chairs out for them and they smiled brightly. "How kind of you all."

The boys brushed off their gracious remark and said, "It's been a pleasure meeting all of you. Please give us your telephone numbers and we will call you soon, we promise."

The girls did so. Everyone was happy. It was a very wonderful day, though it had to end. They all waved their goodbyes as the boys strolled down the corridor and the girls walked to the mall entrance waiting for Willow's Mom to pick them up. They were laughing, giggling, and tapping each other's shoulders playfully.

Francine punched in her home telephone number to let Agnes know that she was on her way home. Meanwhile, Agnes was in the kitchen preparing supper. She glanced at the clock. It read 4:45 p.m. She heard the key in the door. Francine entered her house. Agnes stood waiting with a smile.

"Hello, Francine," she greeted her. "Did you have a good day?"

Francine beamed up, clapping her hands, hopping up and down, "Oh yes," she replied, but she said nothing more for she wanted her parents to be the first ones to know of her day at the mall. She could hardly wait until they called. She was a little edgy and impatient, but managed to be composed.

Agnes nodded pleasantly. She did not want to press her if she did not feel like talking. She needed her space.

"Very good. I am glad you had a good time. Now, go upstairs and wash up. Supper will be ready soon. I am making skirt steaks and ravioli. I know you like that."

"Yes, thank you, Agnes," she replied as she climbed up the stairs to her bedroom.

Agnes went back to preparing dinner. She was humming to herself. *I bet it is a boy,* she pondered pleasantly to herself. *My, she is growing up. Dr. and Mrs. Marsowe are so proud. I just bet she met a boy. I just know it. I know that look. I had it when I was about her age. It happens to all girls. My, she is quite a young lady now and always was.*

Francine came downstairs and sat at the table. Agnes took a plate and set it down in front of her. Francine smiled graciously and began eating daintily, as she always did. Agnes watched her and said nothing, but she was still in suspense. She could not help herself.

Francine looked up from her plate and asked her, "Are you all right, Agnes? You have been watching me since I came home without saying a word. Is everything okay?"

"Yes, honey, everything is fine. I just can't get over what a fine young girl you've become." That was true, sort of, but she did not want her to know what she was curious about. She did not want to pry and make her feel uncomfortable.

Francine finished her meal, excused herself, and went upstairs to prepare for tomorrow. She had to be up early. She laid her clothes out and made sure that they were appropriate and in good condition. Then she reached for a book, plopped on her bed, and began to read.

Two Hours Later

Francine took a shower, splashed water on her face, and washed her hair with three soapings. She put talcum powder all over her body. She smelled like a rosebud, all fresh and clean. She tweezed her eyebrows and filed her nails. She put on a fresh long pink nylon nightdress with long sleeves. She slid her feet into her fuzzy pink slippers. She felt refreshed and rejuvenated. She was ready. Again, she pounced on her bed and resumed reading her book.

"Francine!" she heard Agnes call out. She dashed off the bed and opened her bedroom door.

"Yes?" she called from upstairs.

Agnes held the phone. "It's your mother."

Francine leaped out of her room, bounding down the steps in such excitement. She eagerly took the phone from Agnes.

"Mama!" she called into the mouthpiece.

Agnes looked at her. "Take it easy, honey!" she cautioned.

"Sorry," she apologized to Agnes.

"Hi, darling!" Bettye Jo exclaimed. "What's up?"

"Put Daddy on. I want you and him to hear my news," Francine said to her mother, who asked Philip to come to the telephone.

Philip did and called, "Hi, princess! What is going on? What happened?"

"Guess what?" she gleefully shouted into the telephone so loudly that her parents had to back away. Her voice was so high-pitched.

"We went to the mall this afternoon. You know, with Willow, Stephane, and Arlene. And you know what? We met four boys from our junior high school class. They treated us for sodas. One boy, his name is Mark, he asked for my telephone number. He promised he'll call tomorrow night."

Bettye Jo and Philip listened attentively. Francine was perky and bubbly with excitement that she could hardly contain herself.

Bettye Jo turned to her husband and said, "Philip, she met a boy. Philip, our little girl is growing up. I cannot believe it. Can you, Philip?"

He smiled and said, "As a matter of fact, I can. Our daughter is simply a joy and a pleasure. Any boy would be lucky to be her boyfriend." Then he said with caution, "Mama and I are very happy for you. I do not want to be a killjoy, but you be careful, and don't do anything you don't feel comfortable with. I was a boy once, you know."

Francine laughed and said, "Don't worry, Daddy. He and his friends swear they are not like other boys. They promised us."

Bettye Jo then took the telephone and said, "I heard what you just said and I believe in you, but you're very young. I want to believe what you said this boy vowed—to be kind and behave as a gentleman should. But you are too young to date. You could be friends with him. Daddy and I would like to meet him. Okay, honey?"

"Oh yes, Mama," she cried out gleefully.

Agnes stood listening as she rinsed some plates in the sink. *I knew it,* she mused triumphantly. I *simply did. She has a boyfriend.* Agnes smiled to herself.

Suddenly, the conversation of Francine's day ended and it led to her parents' day. They spent the afternoon at the pool swimming and sunning. They got suntanned. Later tonight, they planned to go dancing. Tomorrow, there was going to be a show with a movie and a stand-up comedian. Francine listened to each word. She was joyful that her parents were having a good honeymoon and they were ecstatic. Their daughter was growing up. Their conversation ended by saying the usual I love you and goodbyes. Francine hung up the telephone.

Agnes saw her and said, "I'm so happy for you. I knew you met a boy, but I did not want to nag you. I figured you'd tell me in time."

Francine smiled at Agnes, and she did so in return.

"I'm getting ready for bed now. Good night, Agnes." Then she ascended the stairs.

"Good night, honey," she reciprocated.

The Next Day, 7:00 a.m.

T he alarm clock rang off—7:00 a.m.!

Francine tossed over to the clock and pushed the button down. *Time to get up!* she thought to herself. The first day of her first job! She pounced out of bed to wash her face and brush her teeth. She was ecstatic and could not wait to start the day. She threw off her nightdress and put on her fluffy pink robe and headed downstairs.

Agnes arrived before 8:00 a.m. to see her off. She prepared Francine's usual french toast with three strips of bacon, a glass or orange juice, and another glass of milk.

"Good morning," Agnes began. "Excited about your first day?"

Francine sat in her chair, returned Agnes' greeting, and then gleamingly replied, "Oh yes, quite so." She was very chipper. Then she began eating her breakfast. Agnes then wiped around and put the pan and other utensils in the sink. She poured dish detergent in, rinsed everything, and then piled it all in the dishwasher. She scrubbed the stove, making sure there was no grease. Francine observed her work. She is so efficient and diligent. She does not have to be told or reminded of any of her duties. Francine noticed this as she was thinking to herself.

"Raymond will be picking you and your girlfriends up around 8:15 a.m.," Agnes informed her.

"Sure, fine," Francine acknowledged her as she sipped her milk.

"I bet you can't wait for tonight, honey. Your first boyfriend," she remarked. "But first, your priority now is this job. You have responsibilities. I know you will not fail or disappoint your mother, though she knows you are capable and diligent, and I know that too. I'm just making a light but pleasant conversation."

"I know," she stated. She was finished with her breakfast. She rose from her chair and mentioned, "I'll be getting ready now. Thanks for the delicious breakfast. As always, you did a superb job."

Agnes smiled at Francine as she cleared the table. "Just doing my job."

Francine headed upstairs.

She remembered that she had laid out her clothes the night before. She wanted to look and act professional. She was starting her life in the business world, a new venture for her and her friends.

She chose a white puff-sleeved blouse with a bow in front. Her skirt was flowing and its color was navy blue. She made sure they were clean and apropos. She put rogue on her cheeks and applied a pale pink lipstick on her lips. She ran a brush through her hair and put a lacey white headband on. She smiled in the mirror. She was pleased with herself.

She threshed off her robe and put on fresh underwear and a slip. She took a pair of low-heeled black pumps and slid them on her feet. Finally, she dressed herself in her work clothes, smoothing out the creases. She walked over to her full-length mirror, swaying to and fro, admiring herself. Her eyes gleaming bright and wide. She wanted to make sure that she looked her best and make a good first impression.

Today is the first day of the rest of my life, she sighed voraciously. A new start, a new beginning. And at the same time, she would be with her three best friends all summer. She could hardly contain herself. So many events occurring all at once. She could not believe that all these wonderful events were happening all at one time. Tonight, she would be receiving her first telephone call from a boy. Her body shook at little, but she was composed and in control of herself. She heard a knock on her bedroom door. She got startled out of her pleasant reverie. She turned and saw Agnes open the door.

"Raymond's here, dear," she informed her. "Are you ready?"

Francine grinned gleamingly, grabbed her new black shoulder bag, and replied quickly, "Yes, yes."

She left the room with Agnes behind her descending the stairs. She greeted Raymond and then bid Agnes goodbye and waved.

Agnes stood watching her leave. "Good luck!"

She thanked her and she was off.

The girls rode in the back seat glancing at one another and chattering away gleefully. They simply could not believe they would be working for money, their own money that they would be earning on their own. It was very unexpected. Usually, children want to be laid-back and carefree without a care or worry in the world during the summer, after ten grueling months of examinations, papers, homework, and assignments. But thanks to Francine's mother, those plans were not to be. They were to learn responsibility and the rewards of hard work to prepare them for their future. Success is the reward of toil. They were to feel good about themselves and to have a sense of pride and ownership in addition to being of service to others for their hard work. They were going to be dealing with the public every single day. It would be a challenge, but a good and positive one. All four best friends working together for the common good, joined for a wonderful cause. They could not be happier. Sitting with their bags on their laps, they gazed about. It was their first day in the business world.

Raymond turned right at the corner. The girls gazed out the window. There it was, the flower shop where they would be working together during the summer.

He stopped in front of the shop, got out, and opened the doors for them. Then they entered the shop. Danielle was waiting for them. She had a big smile on her face. She extended her hand to each of them, and they returned her acknowledgement of "Good morning."

Danielle turned her head and motioned for the three young girls in the back who were rearranging flowers, sweeping the floor and counters, and watering the plants.

Danielle called, "Girls!" They turned around and Danielle continued, "These are the four young ladies who will be helping us during the summer. Could you please come here and introduce yourselves?" They obliged as they strolled up to them.

"I'm Terri." She had short wavy black hair in layers and her dark eyes were framed with black rimmed oval-shaped lenses.

A girl with long thick wavy red hair, green eyes, and a face covered with light freckles announced, "I'm Rita."

Lastly, a girl with long blonde straight hair styled in a pageboy and with sparkling bright blue eyes gleefully stated, "I'm Katie. We're all very happy to meet you all."

Terri chimed up, "Welcome aboard!"

Rita added, "We're looking forward to working with you."

Then she faced Francine and remarked, "Your mother is a simply wonderful, marvelous woman to work for. She is very kind to us."

All four girls smiled at their coworkers and extended their hands while stating their names proudly.

Danielle turned toward them and then to Katie. "Could you please show them around? Later, I'll assign them their duties."

Katie went, "Certainly." Then she motioned to the girls and said, "This way," and they followed but with pleasure.

Danielle watched them with awe. She was pleased. She knew it was going to be a great summer. Then she turned around. A customer was waiting. She took her eyeglasses that hung from a chain in front of her chest and put them on and pleasantly greeted her, "Good morning, ma'am. How may I help you?" She led the customer down the aisle.

Katie continued to show the girls around the shop, informing them of what she, Rita, and Terri were doing. All of them were in accordance and pleased to be of service.

After the tour, the four girls were led up to Danielle, who gave them their work assignments.

"Willow," she looked at her, "your job is to sit at the front desk and greet the customers by saying 'good morning,' and if it is afternoon, 'good afternoon,' and introduce yourself with a smile. Also, you will oversee the answering of the telephone almost as if you are greeting a customer, but you will add, 'Bettye Jo's Florist Shop, how may I help you?' Then say, 'Just a minute, please.' Try not to keep them waiting. And if you do, please say 'Sorry to keep you waiting.' Okay?"

Willow nodded accordingly.

"Also, you will have filing to do, customers' accounts and creditors, as well." She showed Willow the drawers for them.

She responded gleefully, "I get it. Do not worry. I understand."

Danielle nodded and said, "Good." Then a customer walked in. "There's your first customer, good luck." She motioned to Willow, who then walked away.

Danielle then walked up to Arlene. "You will help Terri with arranging, sorting, and taking care of the flowers. She will show you what to do, okay?"

Arlene replied with a cheerful grin. Danielle looked at Terri, who smiled at her young coworker, and they went to work.

"Stephanie," Danielle called to her, "you'll help Rita wipe down the counters, sweep the floors, and empty the trash. The bags are in the back." She pointed. "Okay?"

Stephanie replied, "Yes, ma'am."

Danielle walked to a shelf and took down two smocks. "Arlene and Stephanie, here are two smocks to wear so you will not get your clothes dirty."

The girls took them and put them on and proceeded to do as they were instructed.

"As for you, Francine, I need someone to take care of the supply closet. You will take a count of any item that goes out." She showed her an inventory sheet with each item listed. "You will help Katie keep track of any items that get removed from the closet. At the end of the day, you and Katie will give me the complete list of supplies left. Also, I need you to make labels and price tags of the flowers and tack them under each array of flowers. You understand?"

"Yes," Francine brightly responded, "you can count on us. We will not let you down, we promise."

"Good." She smiled. "If any of you have any questions, please do not hesitate to ask me."

Everyone jubilantly and gleamingly went to work. Danielle walked back to the cash register. A customer had a bouquet of pink carnations that she wanted to purchase. Danielle gleefully rang up the sale, wrapped the carnations in green paper, and then handed them to the customer. "Thanks for shopping with us. Have a good day."

The customer nodded with a smile and left.

"Oh yes," Danielle thought to herself out loud. "Girls," she called, and they turned to face her.

"Lunch is at 12:00 or 1:00 p.m. It is your choice, but do inform me when you take your break. There is a small refrigerator at the end of this corridor for you all to put your edibles inside. There are tables outside in the yard for you to eat and do what you want during that time. Everybody clear on that?" She wanted to be reassuring.

The girls, in unison, said, "No problem." And they went back to their duties.

The day resumed. Nothing imperative or of relative importance occurred, just a usual, typical workday. The girls did what they had to do with no casualties.

5:00 p.m.

"Girls," Danielle called, "that's all for today. You all did a very good job. It was a good first day, if I may say so myself. You are all off to a fresh new start. I am pleased with all of you. Raymond will take you all home soon. He just has to finish up."

The four girls bid her good night with waves, and she did so likewise. They waited on the bench outside the shop.

6:15 p.m.

Agnes smiled as Francine entered the house. She was preparing meatballs and spaghetti for supper.

"How was your first day on the job, honey?" she asked as she stirred the spaghetti in the pot of boiling water.

Francine gleefully answered, "Oh, it was so great. Everyone is so nice there."

"Good, honey, I'm glad. Now, go wash up. Dinner will be ready soon."

She scooted upstairs enthusiastically. She could not wait for tonight's telephone call from her first boyfriend. Agnes watched her with a grin and then began pouring out the contents in a bowl, stirring it while added Prego spaghetti sauce in it. She wanted it to be good and hot. Francine loved spaghetti and meatballs very much. Bettye Jo used to take great pains on Saturday making it just right for her daughter.

Then Agnes heard Francine bounding down the steps giggling. She sat herself down and began eating her dinner.

"Just the way you like it, dear." She watched her enjoy it. She went back to the sink and scrubbed the pots and pans; the faucet was running.

As Francine ate, she kept glancing at the clock. *Tick, tock, tick, tock.* She could not wait, but still ate her supper in a ladylike fashion. It was scrumptious. Agnes was getting to cook just as her mother did. She knew all of Francine's favorite food and dishes. Francine appreciated Agnes and always thanked her for her delicious meals. Agnes stated that it was a pleasure for such a wonderful, loving family. One hand washes the other, both Francine and Agnes would think to themselves. Agnes helped Francine and her family, and her parents came to her and her three coworkers' aid.

Finally, Francine was through. She put her fork in her bowl, lifted the sauce under it, and handed it to Agnes, who took it and put it into the sink to rinse off.

Francine wiped her hands with her napkin.

"Would you like some Jell-o for dessert?" Agnes asked. "I made you cherry."

"Oh yes, please," Francine piped up.

Agnes went to the refrigerator and took out a cup of Jell-o. Francine held her hands out and thanked her.

The Agnes went to the sink to tend to the dinner plates.

Francine ate each spoonful with delicacy and chewed each piece a few times before taking another. Still, she was anxious. *He will call,* she was certain. When she was through, she brought the cup and spoon over to Agnes near the sink. Agnes took it and began to clean it.

She also noticed Francine eyeing the telephone. With a chuckle, she remarked, "The telephone is not going to ring if you keep looking at it."

"I know, but, you know," she began and could not go on. Then she came up with a suggestion: "I think I'll go get a book and read in the living room."

Agnes agreed silently, watching her. She went back to her duties. Francine headed into the living room. She found a book on the table near the couch and began reading.

"Finally," Agnes thought to herself. "She's preoccupying herself and not glancing at the telephone. Maybe she will get engrossed in her book. She always does," she reasoned silently.

The clock went *tick, tock, tick, tock.*

The house fell silent. Agnes busy in the kitchen. Francine involved with her book. Too much quiet, they both noticed. It was deafening. They could not stand the suspense.

R-R-Ring, r-r-r ing!

Both Agnes and Francine jumped at the sound. Agnes nearly dropped a plate. Francine sprang up, her book falling to the floor. They both stood in their spots.

Francine heard Agnes pick up the receiver. "Marsowe residence," she introduced. "Yes, she's here." Agnes turned toward her and handed her the telephone. She was smiling.

Francine flew into the kitchen and eagerly grabbed the telephone, almost knocking Agnes back against the counter. "Easy, honey, easy," she warned gleefully. Francine apologized and then spoke into the telephone. Agnes went to stack the dishes and silverware into the dishwasher. Then she walked out of the kitchen to leave Francine alone for she needed privacy.

Composing herself, she greeted, "Hi, Mark! How was your day?" She knew not how to begin.

He, too, was unsure but managed. "Fine, you know, same old, same old." Then he thought, "How was your first day at your job?"

Delightedly, she replied, "Great! Everyone is so nice there. They say my mother is a wonderful employer to work for." Then she felt the need to ask him, "And what did you do today?"

Mark said that he was with his three buddies on Elm Drive at the arcade playing video games.

Then Francine wanted to talk about her parents, whom she was so proud of. She told him they were awesome. But she wanted to tell him the whole story that began with her abusive birth mother, her fifth-grade teacher coming to her aid, being in a children's shelter that led to Bettye Jo becoming her foster mother. And when she planned to finalize the adoption, Philip, her birth father, unexpectedly appeared. They fell in love and are now on their honeymoon. So she did so, slowly, quietly, and gently.

It took a while for Mark to absorb. He was absolutely astonished and amazed. "Far out!" he shouted. "Your parents are definitely the utmost, unbelievable, but in a good way. I do admit it's an unusual story, but wow!"

She smiled into the telephone and felt great. He understood and had no problem with it since he agreed on how super her parents were.

"I mean, mine are great too, you know. Average, but they're okay. I mean for parents. They're not abusive or harsh, just the run-of-the-mill sort."

They both laughed with each other.

"I told them about you. They did say we could be friends and they do want to meet you. My mother says I am too young to date. I hope you understand."

Flippantly, Mark said, "Sure. I'm not allowed to date yet either."

Both agreed.

And they went on talking about mundane issues, the weather, summer plans, television shows, the latest DVDs, and pop stars.

Suddenly, Francine heard a muffled, plaintive voice on the other end. Then Mark's voice asked, "What is it, Mickey?" Still whining. Mark called, "Mom!"

Then she heard his mother's voice say, "Come over here, Mickey. Leave your brother alone. He's on the telephone." His mother took Mickey's hand and led him away.

"Sorry, Francine, just my six-year-old brother being a pest!"

"That's okay, I understand," Francine stated nonchalantly.

They went back to their conversation.

Agnes watched her. Francine was so happy. She was full of joy and pep, enjoying her first boyfriend. But it was getting late and her parents would be calling soon. So Agnes walked up to Francine and gently motioned to her and said, "It is getting late, honey. Your mother and father will be calling soon. Do please tell your friend that you have to go now and hope he understands, all right?"

"Yes, Agnes." Then into the telephone, she stated gently and softly, but still gleeful, "Mark, I really, really enjoyed talking to you. It was great. But my parents will be phoning me, so I must go now. You do understand?"

Mark went cheerfully, "Oh, sure. I must also. My parents want me to spend some family time with them watching some sitcom on television. You know, why not? It is my family. We are both lucky that we have good parents. How about I call you at the end of this week? I do not want to monopolize your time and space. All right?"

"Oh fine, of course. It was nice of you to call. I enjoyed our conversation. Have a good night."

"You too. Talk to you again at the end of the week. Looking forward to it. Good night!"

It was the end of the call, but the start of Francine's new and exciting life with her first boyfriend. There will be more to come. But for now, it was getting late. Mama and Daddy will be calling shortly, and she had news to tell them. She could hardly wait.

Agnes pointed out to her, "I'm so happy for you, honey. I am glad he called as he said he would and that you enjoyed your first telephone call with your first boyfriend. But it is getting late. Why don't you put on your nightclothes, wash your face, and brush your teeth? Then you could come down and read or just sit and talk with me until your parents call. Okay, honey?"

Francine happily agreed with her and thus she galloped up the stairs. Agnes watched her. She was quite a young lady and growing up so fast, so joyful and full of life. *Ah, to be young again,* Agnes sighed pleasantly to the air. She went back to the kitchen and made herself a cup of tea. Seeing a newspaper on the counter, she reached for it and started to read while sipping her tea.

R-R-R-ing R-R-R-ing!

Agnes sat the paper and her cup of tea down and went to the telephone to answer it with the usual, "Marsowe residence." Then she went on. "Mrs. Marsowe," she addressed gleefully, "how are you and the doctor doing?" She smiled into the telephone, replying, "Yes, yes," to Bettye Jo's questions. "She's been waiting for your telephone call. She's so excited. No, I'll let her tell you both, okay?" She covered the receiver and called, "Francine!"

Francine bounced down the stairs wearing her pink thick-strapped nightgown smiling with glee.

Agnes handed her the telephone. "It's your mother. Go speak to her and your father."

She eagerly took the telephone. "Mama! Daddy!" she cried joyfully.

"Hi, darling!" Bettye Jo greeted her. Philip was lying on the bed next to her. She handed him the telephone, and he, with excitement, spoke, "Our princess," as he watched his wife's facial expression. "You sound so happy. Is everything all right?" He did not have to ask for he knew. Then he guessed, "He called, didn't he?!"

"Yes," she shouted so loudly that both had to back away from the telephone.

"Honey," Bettye Jo said into the telephone joyfully, "that's wonderful! I'm so happy for you." Then she faced her husband, who already knew their daughter's news. He grinned lovingly at his wife.

"Tell us everything, our lovely princess," Philip asked eagerly. He and Bettye Jo held the telephone between them.

Francine told them everything about the telephone call. She was breathless due to her excitement that Bettye Jo had to say, "Slow down, honey. Take a few deep breaths. You are talking too fast; it is hard to understand you. Do tell us everything."

Francine went on and on. She could not stop herself. Then she remembered what her mother just said, to slow down. She did so finally. It went on for about fifteen minutes, yet no one was the least bit tired, though it was nighttime and it was a very long and eventful day for everyone.

Then Francine changed the subject and asked her parents about their day. They mentioned strolling down the boardwalk gazing at the sun in the clear blue sky. Their plans for this evening were to go to a movie and then attend a show that featured a stand-up comic.

She went on about her first day on the job. "Everybody was very nice, and they said Bettye Jo was a joy to work for." She spoke of the other employees, the three girls—Terri, Rita, and Katie. Her job was to assist Katie in the stockroom and make up labels and price tags. Danielle was very pleased with her and her friends' job performance. "She's real nice, Mama," she stated.

Bettye Jo smiled into the telephone and said, "She's a godsend, but at times she tells me what to do. But I laugh and take it in stride."

Then Philip took the telephone and mentioned, "Honey," he addressed his daughter, "when you get a chance, could you please call Kelly? I would like to see how she is doing. I hired a temporary doctor so my patients would be able to get any help if they need it. Okay? I'd appreciate it."

Francine nodded and replied, "Sure, certainly, Daddy. I'll do so tomorrow after work."

Philip confirmed, "Thank you, honey. You're very kind and sweet." Then he glanced at his watch. "It's getting late now. We need to get ready for tonight, and you have work tomorrow, young lady."

"I know, Daddy. But could you please put Mama on? I want to say good night and I love you to both of you together."

Bettye Jo and Philip held the telephone together. "Good night, our darling angel. We love you all the way to Pluto and back."

And Francine responded with the usual greeting and blew kisses into the telephone, and they did so likewise. It was the end of another good day. Agnes looked at her with sheer joy. Francine bid her "good night," and as she galloped up the stairs, Agnes replied without having to think twice, "Good night, honey."

A Week Later: Monday, Lunch Break 12:00 p.m.

The four friends sat at the table in the backyard eating their sandwiches with cold drinks. They talked about their first boyfriends. Willow spoke of Tom, Arlene of James, and Stephanie of Richard. All of them along with Francine and Mark met at the mall on Saturday and Sunday just to sit and talk, drinking their sodas. Most importantly, Francine's parents were the main topic of discussion that continued during their lunch break. They were thinking of chipping in to buy them a wedding present. Willow noticed a personalized couple's heart mantel clock for $50. The money for it would come from their earnings from their summer job. Francine could not believe it. She did want to get them a special gift but she did not have the money. Yet her friends thought about it, and she was eternally grateful to them for their generosity. She saw that clock and she fell in love with it. Each of them would give $15.00. As for personalizing—there would be engraving to: Mama Bettye Jo and Daddy Philip. While they had been in the mall, her three friends past a store that had it, but they were being secretive. They wanted to surprise their friend and her parents with this great idea. So they made plans to order it while Francine was at the food court with Mark and his friends. Her parents would be ecstatic for they were not expecting such an expensive present. They knew that their daughter did not have that kind of money, but her friends brought up the suggestion, which they all agreed upon. At the end of the week, they would go to the store to pick it up and have it wrapped. Her parents would be back from their honeymoon on Sunday. Everyone would gather at Francine's house where the gift would be waiting for them.

Also, a welcome-home party was being arranged for the happy couple. Everyone would be at the house celebrating the joyous occasion. There's so much to be done, so much happening, but no one complained. It was for a good cause.

Monday Night, 8:00 p.m.

Francine was on the telephone with Mark. She was discussing her parents' homecoming from their honeymoon and the surprise party that was being planned for them. She also mentioned the wedding present that she and her friends were going to give them. She did ask him if he could come to the party, and he agreed to. He did say he was sorry that he did not have the money to chip in for the present but decided on a card. Francine thought that that was very sweet of him. He would then meet them. Francine could hardly wait. They chattered for a few more minutes. It was getting late. She had work tomorrow, plus awaiting her parents' usual nightly call. Mark, being understanding, bid her good night, and she did so in return. The call was over. Both were content.

Agnes watched as she wiped the kitchen counter. She was happy for Francine, for she was enjoying her life, which was going quite well—loving parents, a job, girlfriends, a boyfriend, good physical and mental health, and a stable, secure home. Yes, she was indeed fortunate.

Francine then told Agnes, "I think I'll go get a book and read in the living room while I wait for Mama and Daddy to phone."

Agnes agreed and went back to her cleaning.

A few minutes later—

R-R-R ing, R-R Ring

Agnes picked up the telephone and said, "Marsowe Residence. Oh, hello, Mrs. Marsowe." She handed the telephone to Francine.

"Hi, Mama! Hi, Daddy!" she greeted her parents brightly, leaping up and down, with a smile in her voice.

Sunday Afternoon: The Homecoming

Everyone gathered around in the Marsowe house busy preparing for the happy couple's return from their honeymoon in Hawaii.

Raymond informed Francine, "It's almost time to pick up your parents at the airport."

"Yes, thank you, Raymond." She nudged Mark. "It's time to go meet my parents," she announced cheerfully.

"Right on!" Mark leaped up, and they gave each other a high five.

Both Francine and Mark piled into the limousine. They were off.

Francine wore a pink floral sundress and white sandals. A white sun hat lay on her head. Mark wore a light blue short-sleeved T-shirt with denim dungarees and Reebok sneakers. He wore his blue baseball cap backward.

They sat in the back seat poking each other's arms playfully, giggling with joy. Raymond was watching them through the front mirror and smiled with a chuckle. "Cool it, you guys."

They knew he was only teasing. Everyone was so excited, and the main event did not even begin yet.

Francine and Mark looked out their windows. The sun was beaming down in their eyes. The sky, a light blue. There were shopping centers and movie theatres on all the streets. The scenery was breathtaking, but they could not wait, especially Francine who was desperately eager for her parents to meet her first beau, Mark. And he also could not wait to meet who he said was the utmost, fantastic couple.

Raymond turned a corner leading to the airport. "Here we are guys," he announced as he stopped the limousine.

Mark got out first and extended his hand to help Francine out of the limousine. She took his hand and thanked him. They walked over to the gate and saw people claiming their luggage. Francine searched for her parents. There were crowds of people gathered around the stations. Francine kept craning her neck, hopping up and down on her toes trying to locate them.

There they were, bending over to get their luggage. She jumped up gleefully with a smile.

"There they are!" she exclaimed. She turned to Mark and waved him over with her hand. "Come on," she ordered eagerly. Both ran toward the couple, and she cried out, "Mama! Daddy!"

Bettye Jo was wearing a bright floral yellow sundress. She had white open-toed sandals on her feet. On her head was a yellow beach hat. She wore her usual black sunglasses to keep the sun out of her eyes.

Philip wore a long Hawaiian shirt and khaki short pants. On his feet were flat beige-colored sandals. He wore a tan cap on his head. Rectangular shades framed his eyes.

Both were deeply suntanned. Leis surrounded their necks.

Bettye Jo and Philip turned and saw their daughter with Mark beside her. An attendant came and picked up their bags and asked if he could bring them to their car. Philip told them about their limousine, instructed him on what to do, and gave him a tip.

Francine threw her arms around her mother's neck and kissed her cheek. Bettye Jo removed her sunglasses and patted her back. "Darling!"

Then she did so with her father. "Our princess." He smiled at her. Seeing Mark, he asked, though he knew the answer quite well, "And who is this fine gentleman? As I didn't know."

Francine put her hand on Mark's side. "This is Mark."

Philip piped up, "Your young gentleman friend stealing my daughter's heart?"

They all laughed. Philip had a sense of humor.

Mark smiled while extending his hand. "Pleased to meet you, Sir, I mean, Dr. Marsowe. I hear you are a psychiatrist. That is interesting, for I have only heard tales about what you do. Your daughter explained it to me. She says she wants to be one when she grows up. She'd be really good at it for she has such a warm, compassionate nature for people."

Francine playfully patted his chest with the back of her hand. "Oh, Mark, you say the sweetest things."

"It's true," he stated. "You do. That's what I like about you."

Then Mark turned toward Bettye Jo, her eyes wide and bright. "And you, Mrs. Marsowe, are so beautiful just as your daughter described and much more so." He shook her hand, and she laughed at him, a little embarrassed but very pleased.

"You're very sweet. Francine is so lucky to have you as a boyfriend."

Philip chimed in, "Where is everybody?"

Francine and Mark knew and giggled to themselves and each other. They were not going to let up, so they said nothing. Both motioned to Bettye Jo and Philip. "Let's go. Raymond is waiting for us."

They went.

Philip escorted Bettye Jo into the car. Then Mark took Francine's hand and led her inside. They rode off. Everyone was a little tired but very cheerful, chattering among themselves.

While at the Marsowe Residence

A big sign reading "Welcome Home, Bettye Jo and Philip" hung across the hallway. A large table with food and drinks were put out. Francine's and her friends' present along with Mark's card lay on the table. Everyone was jabbering about with excitement. They could not wait to see the happy couple enter the house.

Agnes walked over to the window and pushed the curtain aside. "They're here!" she called out facing all the guests. "Quickly, someone shut off the lights."

They heard a key turn in the lock. Slowly, the door opened. Bettye Jo and Philip stared around in the dark. They heard noises. "What is going on? What is happening?" They looked at each other puzzled. No one said a word. The couple was in deep suspense. The lights went on.

Everyone yelled, "Surprise!"

The couple was in shock but joyful. What thoughtful great friends and family. Francine took both her parents by the hands and led them to a table. The personalized couple's heart mantel clock with the inscription, "Mama Bettye Jo and Daddy Philip," laid there. Francine pointed and exclaimed, "Look!"

Bettye Jo's eyes were afire. Philip's eyes seemed to pop out of their sockets. "It's beautiful, honey," Bettye Jo bent down to kiss her daughter.

"There's more." She reached for Mark's card and gave it to her. It read, "To a great couple always, on your wedding day. May you experience all the love and joy you deserve." He signed it, "Your friend, Mark." He explained that he did not know exactly what to do for this new and special occasion, but Francine was special to him and her parents were wonderful people. Bettye Jo and Philip thanked him, and he hesitantly shook their hands. Looking at her parents for approval, Francine gave Mark a peck on his cheek. He shook her hand and smiled.

Over in the corner was Grandma Marsowe with her white hair fluffed up and clad in a white blouse, gray skirt, and jacket. Two attendants were at the side of her chair.

Francine exclaimed, "Grandma!" Her eyes lit up. She turned to Mark and motioned him to meet her, and he did. She flew into her arms and kissed her cheek.

She laughed. "Darling!"

Francine introduced him, "This is Mark." He took her hand carefully for he knew of her arthritis.

"What a fine young man." Then to her granddaughter, she said, "You little minx, you! A boyfriend! What a sweetheart." Francine giggled. Then back to Mark, she said, "You treat my granddaughter well, you hear me, young man? Or you'll answer to me!"

They laughed.

"See you later, Grandma." She kissed her and then took Mark's hand and went to join their friends.

So much gleeful noise. Such excitement and thrill for the happy couple with all the guests digging into the refreshments and drinking heartily.

Later That Night

Bettye Jo and Philip sat up in bed laughing. Philip squeezed his wife's hand. She gleamed at him with love. They heard a knock on their door.

"Hey, you guys!" It was Francine. "May I come in?"

They consented pleasantly as she entered her parents' bedroom.

She wore a long pink thick-strapped, low-cut nightgown. Over it was a matching nylon robe.

"I missed you guys, but I'm glad you're home now. Also, I am happy that your honeymoon was spectacular. You both look so radiant."

They both smiled at their daughter's compliments, listening attentively. But they were very exhausted, though it was a good tiredness. They had their family and friends with them celebrating their joyous occasion, but it was time to retire for the day.

"What did you think of Mark? Isn't he simply nice?" She eagerly waited for them to answer. "Grandma likes him," she mentioned as an afterthought.

Philip agreeably replied, "He appears to be a very fine young boy and he is lucky to have you as his girlfriend. Mama and I are very happy for you."

"I'm so glad you are. I think so too. It is getting late," she said as she walked over to her parents to hug and kiss them good night, as usual. "I love you, guys." She blew them a kiss.

They looked up at her with pride. "We both love you too. Good night."

Francine smiled and nodded, and then turned and left her parents' bedroom.

Everyone went to bed ecstatically.

Monday Morning

Agnes was standing by the counter making coffee. Bettye Jo and Francine sat at the table. Philip came up behind his wife, put his hands on her shoulders, and kissed her cheek. She squeezed her eyes shut, surprised but joyful. He sat down beside her.

"Good morning, ladies," he greeted.

Agnes turned and bid him, "Good morning, Doctor. So glad to have you both home."

He nodded at her and then smiled at his wife. Agnes handed him his coffee, and he took a sip and then set it down on the table. He clasped his hands together in front of him on the table.

"Francine," he began slowly. Then he reached for his wife's hand. "Mama and I have some important matters to discuss with you. Nothing bad, not at all, honey, so just relax, all right?"

Francine sat and agreeably nodded.

"First of all," he said, reaching for a package under the table, "this is for you for being such a wonderful, caring, good, and thoughtful daughter. Your mother and I are very proud of how respectful and honest you are to us." He handed her the package.

Francine ripped off the bright red wrapping paper and thrusted it on the floor in haste. She saw a large heart-shaped jewelry box and lifted it up. On it was an inscription, "To our lovely daughter with much love always, Mama and Daddy."

Her eyes glowed. "It's beautiful! Thank you, Mama, Daddy!" She excitedly hugged and kissed them. "I love it!"

Both smiled at her pleasantly.

Philip then mentioned, "That was a lovely gift you and your friends bought for us. We were very surprised." He looked at his wife. "Weren't we, dear?"

She smiled agreeably. "We were indeed."

Francine mentioned, "We wanted to get you guys a very special gift. It was Willow who picked it out. We all chipped in, and I know it is a little late, but better late than never. We wanted you to have something from us for being wonderful people to all of us."

Both of her parents sat gazing at their daughter. She was truly amazing.

Then she added, "Mark wanted to get you something, but he apologetically said that he did not have the money, but he got you a card. I think that was very sweet of him."

"He is definitely a fine boy, honey," Bettye Jo remarked as she looked at her husband.

"He is," he affirmed. "Now, furthermore," Philip continued, placing his hands down on the table.

Raymond walked up to the table and mentioned, "It's getting late, Doctor." He looked at the clock.

Philip stated, "Raymond, Francine will be a little late this morning. There are some matters we need to tend to. Tell Danielle I will drop her off later."

Raymond bowed and said, "Yes, sir." Then he left.

"This Saturday will be just for family. I know you like to spend time with your friends at the mall, honey, but not this Saturday. You could explain it to them that it is for family. They will understand. All right? I do hate to disappoint you."

"It's okay, Daddy. I'm not upset at all," she responded nonchalantly.

"Good," he was pleased. He went on, "Your Uncle Paul and I will be spending the day discussing some major changes. As you know, he has done a complete turnabout with his life, I am happy to say, though I was a bit surprised. And it is all thanks to you, honey."

Francine remarked, "I really didn't do anything."

Philip put his hand on hers. "But you did, sweetheart."

Francine smiled and shrugged her shoulders. "Okay."

Then Bettye Jo quipped up, "Also, honey, you, I, and your Aunt Ellen will be spending the day together. It was her idea for us to visit my parents, your grandparents' gravesites. She said she knew you would agree to it. She has apologized for her past behavior and wants to be a better sister to me and an aunt to you. Okay, sweetheart?"

"Of course, Mama," she cheerfully announced. "It'll be great. Just us girls."

Bettye Jo smiled affirmatively. She was content and satisfied.

"Honey." She leaned over to Philip.

Then he continued, "Also, after we all go out for Chinese dinner, we'll pay a visit to Grandma. How does that sound?"

Francine jumped out of her chair and clapped her hands into the air. "Cool!"

"All right, it's all settled." He faced his wife, who avowed pleasantly.

Then he had some more information to mention to Francine: "Mama and I are staying in today just to unwind and relax. I will inform Kelly that I will be in tomorrow. She'll notify any patients scheduled for today to hang tight just for one more day." Then he faced Bettye Jo and said, "You will call Danielle now, all right? Today is just the two of us, darling."

He took his wife's face in his hands and gave her a big smack on her lips. Excitedly, she returned it, and they embraced each other, gazing lovingly in each other's eyes, completely enthralled with each other. Francine and Agnes were watching with smiles on their faces.

Sunday Afternoon: The Homecoming

Agnes was clearing the breakfast dishes from the table and began rinsing them in the sink. Francine sat at the table with Ellen. Philip sat across from them, waiting for his brother.

Bettye Jo came down the stairs with her hair pulled back at the sides in a bun and the front fluffed up. Francine wore her hair in a round shoulder-length pageboy with a lacy band on top. Ellen wore her usual hairstyle, a long pageboy.

Bettye Jo, like her sister and her daughter, wore knee-high halter dresses. Hers was lilac, Ellen's was yellow, and Francine's was red. They wore open-toed slingback sandals and wide beach hats with a sash around the rims.

Philip rose from his chair, kissed his wife, and pulled out a chair for her to sit down.

The doorbell rang. Agnes put the dishrag down on the counter and went to answer it. It was Paul. His hair was neatly parted at the side. He was dressed in a short-sleeved light blue T-shirt with long linen beige pants. He wore flat beige sandals and a beige beret. He carried a pair of gold-rimmed sunglasses in his shirt pocket.

He extended his hand and gleefully greeted his brother, "Hi, bro!"

His knuckled hands tapped Philip's hands. They engaged in a bear hug and patted each other's backs fervently. Philip's eyes had a twinkle in them.

"I'm doing just great!"

Then Paul asked, "How's married life?"

Joyfully, he replied, "Couldn't be better."

Both men smiled at each other. Paul walked over to Ellen, and they gave each other their usual kiss on the lips.

"Hello, sweetheart," he greeted her.

Ellen smiled at him. Paul then went over to Francine with a big high-fiver, which she eagerly acknowledged.

"How's my beautiful, gorgeous niece doing?"

Francine giggled, her eyes aglow. "Okay, Uncle Paul. You're so silly," she remarked.

Everybody joined into laughter.

Then he remembered Bettye Jo and apologized, "Oh my God, I nearly forgot. How about a kiss from my new sister-in-law?"

They briefly pecked each other's cheeks and simply grinned.

Philip stood up, his dark wavy hair combed perfectly. He was clad in a short-sleeved white shirt with long dark brown pants. He wore flat brown leather shoes. His sunglasses were in his shirt pocket. He straightened himself erect. "All right, everybody," he began. "Paul and I will be at the park, and then we plan to go to the café for lunch. You ladies already know today's agenda. We intend to call you when we are through for the afternoon. Remember, Chinese tonight, everybody. And afterward, we visit our mother." He turned to his brother, who gleefully acknowledged him. And then to his daughter, he said, "Your grandmother!"

Francine's bright dark eyes were afire with love.

Agnes called from the counter, "Have a good day, everybody!"

She waved, and they turned and waved back. They were gone. Agnes went back to her work. *A very happy family,* she remarked, smiling to herself. She was fortunate to be employed by such a lovely family.

Afternoon in the Park

The two brothers strolled down the walkway near the grass saying not a word at first. *How to begin?* each thought to themselves. *So much to be said, but how?*

Paul turned and faced his brother. "So married life really agrees with you. Bettye Jo is very pretty and nice."

Philip interjected, "That's not what we came here to discuss, and you know it quite well as I do. So let's give."

Paul looked down on the ground and admitted, "You're right. I do need to talk with you about something important and it does concern you and me. And for the record, I do plan to continue to better myself. I have so far, haven't I?"

Philip agreed, "I must say you have changed a great deal of your past irresponsible behavior immensely. But, Paul, I know there's more."

"All right." He stopped and faced his brother. "I want to move out of that rat hole of an apartment and I can afford a better place. I know I was just some assistant in a hardware store, but the owner was thinking of making me sort of his partner for now. It would mean more money."

Philip pondered before answering and then stated, "That's a very good idea. A better job, a better place to live. But do you have anywhere in particular that you would like to live? Do you have any place in mind? Did you consider any possibilities?"

Right away, Paul piped up, "Phil, you know your apartment you had before you got married? I thought that perhaps that could be mine, and you would not have to worry about getting rid of it to some stranger. I am your brother, and I know I am no saint but I have become responsible. You've seen that."

"Yes, you have, and your suggestion is very feasible, and it would help me as well, as you say. But you must take very good care of it. Fix things that need to be repaired, clean up any messes. Do not be neglectful, and turn off the stove and appliances when you are not using them, okay? You think you can handle it? I want to believe in you. Also, if you need any advice, just call me and I will be glad to help you. Okay, bro?"

Paul put his hand up, and so did Philip. They high-fived each other. It was all settled. They could not wait to tell the girls of their decision.

Paul put his arm around his brother's shoulder, and as they walked together, he happily suggested, "Let us go to that café on Elmwood Place. I hear they have great corn beef sandwiches." Philip smiled at his brother, and they were off.

While on the Way to the Cemetery

"You know, girls," Ellen began as she was driving, "I decided to settle down and not travel so much. I would like to start an online business at home. This way I can see other places while I am in my own home. I plan to tell Paul. I think he would like that. We'd be able to see a lot of each other more."

"It does sound reasonable, but before jumping into this, you should discuss it with Paul first to see how he feels about it," Bettye Jo advised carefully.

The Francine quipped up, "You really like my Uncle Paul, don't you, Aunt Ellen?"

Slowly, she nodded. "I do, honey. I do. Very much."

Then Francine went on, "And he likes you. I know he does." She stated without reservation.

Bettye Jo interjected and said to her daughter, "They do like each other a lot and appear to be happy together. But, honey, having a serious, committed relationship is new to them. They need to get to know one another better and need more time. You do understand, sweetheart?"

"Of course, Mama. But both have come a long way. You know that, Mama, you do!" she persisted earnestly.

Bettye Jo shook her head. "Yes, I do. They did. They have made great strides to better themselves. But they need more time, all right, honey?"

Renounced while shrugging her shoulders, Francine affirmed her mother's heedful advice. She was right, her aunt and uncle did like each other. They all agreed they did, but it was too early in the relationship. Then she piped up, "Let's enjoy the rest of the day."

Both Bettye Jo and Aunt Ellen smiled affirmatively, and they drove off.

They noticed some stores on the way. Francine pointed to a flower shop. "Look, guys, look," she cried out excitedly. "Let's get flowers to put on your parents' gravesites!"

Ellen stopped the car. "That would be a wonderful idea, honey." She turned to her sister and asked, "Don't you agree?"

Bettye Jo was in accordance. "A splendid idea!"

All three of them jumped out of the car. Ellen and Bettye Jo held their large bags over their shoulders. Francine swung her small purse in front of her with excitement. She began dancing around, twirling her body up and down. Both sisters watched her as they strolled behind her.

"Francine," Bettye Jo called out, "walk as a lady ought. Remember what we spoke about? You are not a little girl anymore. Right, honey?"

Francine stopped dead and gleamed at her mother. "Yes, Mama." She turned and walked gracefully to the store. The sisters both smiled at her and then at each other.

Ellen remarked, "She's quite a young lady. You and Philip are raising one special daughter."

Bettye Jo smiled hesitantly. "Yes, we are truly blessed."

They all went into the shop and were mesmerized for there was so much diversity of floral arrangements to choose from. All of them were bright and colorful. But they could only pick three—one big bouquet from each of them—to put on the double gravesite. Each picked their selection. The cashier wrapped each bouquet in its own crepe paper and handed it back. Bettye Jo took out her credit card. It was all paid for. The cashier smiled at them. "Have a good day, ladies. Thank you for shopping with us." They turned and waved with a cheerful grin and then headed back to the car.

Farmingdale Cemetery

The three ladies strolled delicately to the double gravesite. Each carried their own bouquet.

They were finally there. The stone read "Clarke" in the middle, and on the right was "Amelia, Loving Wife, Mother, and Grandmother." Engraved roses shaped in a heart surrounded her side. On the left was "Gerald, Loving Husband, Father, and Grandfather." Twinkling stars surrounded his side. On the bottom across read, "In our hearts always and forever. Loved and was loved. R.I.P." Tears filled their eyes as they read the stone. They were silent for a while, just gazing at it.

Ellen made the first move. She turned to her sister and niece and quietly asked, "May I go first, please? I have much to say and I need to be alone. After all, I was not there for them and want them to know how deeply sorry I am for my self-centered, insensitive behavior, though I know I am very late and cannot change the past. You do understand?" She asked of them, "Please?" She implored with mournful eyes.

Bettye Jo grinned with deep compassion for her sister. "Of course, Ellen." Then she turned to Francine, "All right, honey? Aunt Ellen needs time alone."

Francine nodded. "Certainly. Take your time, Aunt Ellen."

Ellen laid her bouquet of red roses down slowly. She grasped her hands together. With tears in her eyes, she began, "I know I'm too late to be with you when you were alive. And for that, I am deeply sorry. I was selfish and immature. You needed me, and I let you both down. I wish I could undo my past misbehaviors, but unfortunately, that is not possible. Though your physical bodies are no longer here on earth, I know your spirits are, and I hope that you can forgive me. You both had beautiful souls that will last forever in mine, Bettye Jo's, and Francine's hearts. I do love you and I want you to know it. I plan to be a better sister to Bettye Jo and a good aunt to Francine, Bettye's adopted daughter whom she loves dearly. Goodbye, Mom, Dad. I love you always and forever. Rest in peace." She kissed both sides of the headstones, wiped her eyes with a handkerchief, smiled slightly, and walked away.

Bettye Jo walked up to her and patted her shoulder. "That was beautiful, Ellen. I'm proud of you." Then she turned to Francine and asked, "You want to go now?"

She nodded and went up to the double headstone. She stood erect, gazing at it. Her grandparents, whom she never knew and who did not know of her existence. She started carefully and slowly while holding her bouquet of lilacs to her chest: "I do not really know what to say or what to call you. You never knew me, and I did not know you both either. I do know that if I did, I would love you and you would love me. You raised a wonderful daughter, whom I am honored to call my mother. She was there for me since I was twelve. She was my foster mother at first and then she planned to adopt me. The funny thing is, my birth father, whom I did not remember but did so later, showed up. He explained that he had tried relentlessly for ten years to locate me, but she, that woman, made it nearly impossible. But he never gave up. And you know what else, he and your daughter fell in love and just got married. In a few weeks, they plan to make my adoption legal, formal, and official, although I was always their daughter in their hearts, and they are my parents forever in mine. I wish I got to know you both, but the funny thing is, I love you for bringing a wonderful, caring, loving daughter into the world. She said she could not love me more if I had come from her womb. She is and always will be my mother, and you two, my grandparents. R.I.P. Grandmother," then she kissed that side and then, "Grandfather," she planted a kiss on his side. "I love you both." She knelt and put her lilacs in the middle of the stone. Francine's eyes were wide and bright. She smiled, first at the double stone, then to Ellen, and lastly to her mother, who let out her arms, and she flew into them. They stood, hugged each other, and planted kisses on their cheeks.

"That was a wonderful, loving speech you did for the two people you never knew but do happen to love nonetheless. They would be so proud of you as I am."

She patted her daughter's head, and she looked at her mother with loving eyes.

"Mama, it's your turn now. Do go over and say how much you love and miss them," she urged while nudging her mother's elbow.

"All right." She smiled. And she did so. She laid her bouquet of pink carnations down and knelt in front, her hands in prayer form. "Mother, Dad, I miss you both. We all do. I am so proud of my family. I know you would be too. I am adopting a wonderful little girl. I married her birth father, a wonderful man. You would love them. Francine shows such a rare maturity for a girl of her age. She tries to understand people, always looks for the good in them, and loves them unconditionally despite all the abuse she had suffered and endured from her mentally ill birth mother, whom she forgave and does not hate. She is truly amazing. I am proud to be her mother, and you would love her as much as I do. We all love you both forever and always." She also planted kisses on both sides. Bettye Jo walked away and up to where her sister and daughter stood. All had smiles on their faces. The sun was beaming down on their faces. They walked to their car, waiting for the promised telephone call from Philip and Paul. It was getting late for it was nearly time for their special family Chinese food meal.

Crestville Nursing Home, 7:00 p.m.

All five family members sat in the waiting room. The nurse came over and announced, "Mrs. Marsowe asked to be seated up and wheeled around during your visit. We got her ready. Is that all right with you folks? She's been looking forward to seeing you all."

"Oh sure, we've been eager all day," Francine piped up. "I can't wait to tell her about our day."

The nurse smiled at her and then at the others. "All right, I'll go get her." She turned and left.

Everyone waited in anticipation while standing around looking at one another, not knowing what to say.

Then Francine faced the hallway. Excitedly, she pointed. "There she is." She twirled around, swinging her purse into the air. Suddenly, she was facing her mother. She had a stern look but a slight smile on her face. Francine remembered. *Walk as a lady*, Bettye Jo thought to her daughter without having to say it aloud. Francine stopped in her spot.

The attendants wheeled Mrs. Marsowe into the waiting room. Francine walked up to her with her eyes beaming. "Grandma!" She gave her a hug and a peck on her cheek.

"How's my little minx? And your gentleman friend? Hope he's treating you right."

She laughed with her granddaughter, who replied, "He's just great, Grandma, just wonderful."

She attempted to pat her back, but it was too painful, thus she grinned with pleasure. "That's my girl." Then she looked up at the other family members. "How are my boys?"

Philip stepped up first and gave his mother a kiss on her cheek. Then Paul gave her one on the top of her head.

"My fine sons!" she stated proudly. She looked at Bettye Jo. Her eyes sparkled.

"My lovely daughter-in-law. My son treating you well? He'd better." Everyone laughed at her joke. "You're simply radiant, my dear."

Bettye Jo smiled and put her hands out to her mother-in-law. "Philip is a wonderful man, Mother Marsowe. I am so lucky. Married life is simply bliss. We're truly blessed."

Paul and Ellen were watching the encounter with happy grins on their faces. Then Mrs. Marsowe saw them standing by the window. Paul's arm was around Ellen, and she winked at him and he gazed into her eyes.

"And you, Ellen?" the elderly woman inquired, "my son treating you right?" Again, she joked, and everyone burst out giggling.

Ellen looked at her. "You're so funny, Mrs. Marsowe. I mean for a woman your age. And yes, Paul is great and is making a new life for himself. And I am as well. We're doing fine."

Paul squeezed her arm.

Mrs. Marsowe was pleased. Her family was doing well. Sometimes she became sad that her husband was not here anymore to enjoy and witness his family and share into their happiness. Then she mused to herself, *he is here in spirit and is looking down on us with a smile on his face.*

"Grandma." Francine leaned over. "Let us all go for a walk," she vehemently suggested. They were all in accordance and strolled down the hallway together, chuckling and grinning up at each other.

9:00 p.m.

After dropping Ellen and Paul off, Philip, Bettye Jo, and Francine rode home in silence for they were exhausted. It was a very long day, but a very joyous one. The whole family had been together. Francine sat in the back seat gazing out the window. The sky was pitch-black, but the stars were twinkling—her usual pleasant and favorite view since she was a child. It still filled her with awe, and she was completely mesmerized by it. Philip's eyes stared straight ahead, fixed on the road, though he was tired. Luckily, there was no traffic. Next to him, Bettye Jo laid her head back to the side and was asleep. He gazed at her, so beautiful, so sweet.

Then he glanced in the mirror. "You doing all right, princess?" he was curious.

She quipped up, "Oh yes, Daddy!"

He nodded. "Good." And then he and Francine rode on in silence.

Finally, they were in the driveway. Philip turned off the ignition and put his hand on his wife's cheek.

"Honey," he called her, "we're here."

Then Francine tapped her shoulder. "Mama, we're home."

Bettye Jo awoke in a daze, in a bewildered state.

"You were asleep, honey," Philip stated.

Bettye Jo managed a tired smile. "Oh my!"

Philip got out of the car. First, he let Francine out, and she walked to her front door. Then he walked around, opened the door, extended his hand to his wife, which she took, and let her out of the car. Philip put his key into the lock and led them inside the house. On the kitchen counter, the light on the answering machine was flickering. *Who could that be?* Philip and Bettye Jo looked at each other.

Francine walked over and pressed the caller ID button. Her eyes blazed and gleamed. "Mama! Daddy!"

They both stood and smiled at her.

"It's Mark! He called!"

Francine pressed the play button. "Hi, Francine. It is Mark. We missed you today at the mall. I will call you tomorrow morning. We decided to go to the park and we want you to join us. Good night."

Francine clapped her hands in front of her. Tears of joy filled her eyes. "Can I go, Mama, Daddy? Please, can I?" She was so eager.

Bettye Jo smiled. "Of course you may, honey. But Daddy and I need to tell you something first." She turned to her husband. "Honey?" She nudged him.

Philip started, "Tomorrow afternoon, Uncle Paul and Aunt Ellen will be coming over for lunch. It will be just the four of us. We need to discuss some important matters with them. I'm sure you might be aware, but for now, it's just between us. Okay, princess?"

"Sure, Daddy, whatever."

Philip looked at his watch. "It's getting late and we're all tired. So how about giving your Mama and me our usual kisses and say good night?"

"Of course," she cheerfully agreed and did so.

"I love you guys." She turned to face them before heading upstairs.

Bettye Jo and Philip smiled. "All the way to Pluto and back. Our princess, our darling, precious angel."

The Night before the Big Day

Bettye Jo and Philip sat up in bed going through their wedding and honeymoon album pictures. They laughed as they turned the pages while looking at them.

There was a knock on the door. Naturally, they knew it was Francine coming in to say good night.

"Come in, darling," Bettye Jo called, and Francine entered the room wearing her long pink low-cut nightdress with a matching robe over it.

"Excited about tomorrow?" Philip asked.

"Of course, how can I not be? We've all been waiting forever for it," she replied without conviction.

Francine noticed that her parents were looking through a photo album. "What's that you're doing?"

"It's our wedding and honeymoon photograph album. Do you want to look through some of the pictures with us?" Bettye Jo asked her daughter.

Francine plopped on the bed in between her parents and they began.

Bettye Jo pointed and said, "This is a family portrait taken at our wedding. That is Daddy and me in the middle, of course, Aunt Ellen beside me, Uncle Paul next to Daddy, and Grandma Marsowe on your father's side, and last but not least is you, in the middle, seated in front of us. All of us smiling. It's such a beautiful family portrait of us." She looked at her daughter. "Don't you agree, honey?"

Francine shook her head affirmatively.

Then she showed one of them feeding each other a piece of the wedding cake. Bettye Jo's chin had crumbs. Francine giggled. She thought it was funny.

"Of course, honey, there's one of us kissing. Well, that's to be expected."

Then she showed one of Philip behind her, his hands on her shoulders, and kissing her cheek. She was surprised at his gesture, but loved it. Francine laughed again.

Another picture showed Bettye Jo putting her hands on Philip's face and giving him a kiss on his lips.

Another photograph was of him also kissing her on her lips.

Both smiling, gazing into each other's eyes. Francine could not take her eyes off the photographs of her parents. She was simply awed and enchanted.

"Let's see your honeymoon pictures," Francine piped up excitedly.

Bettye Jo turned a page and pointed, "That's Daddy and me at dinner." She was wearing pearls around her neck and dangling earrings. Her hair was fluffed up in a bun. She wore a sequin dress. Philip was dressed in a crisp white shirt, a black dinner jacket and tie, and black linen pants. His wavy, dark hair was combed perfectly apart. Both smiled at the camera.

Another picture showed them dancing cheek to cheek across the floor. Everyone was cheering at them with applause.

One photograph was with Philip hugging her closely but clad in swim clothes.

Next to it was one of her grabbing his chin and giving him a peck on the lips. His eyes lit up.

One photograph showed Bettye Jo asleep on a lounge chair. She appeared embarrassed, but she smiled at Francine. "Daddy sure has a sense of humor."

Francine agreed with a giggle.

There were others, but Francine was getting tired. Bettye Jo closed the album. "That's all for now. We will go through the rest on a day when we have nothing planned. We could spend a whole day. Okay, darling?"

She smiled, and Francine nodded accordingly. Everyone was tired and eager for tomorrow. Francine kissed and hugged her parents, bidding them good night—as usual but with great joy.

The Big Day in August

The three family members headed up the stairs to the courthouse, their daughter walking in between them. Both wore business attire. Bettye Jo in a white blouse, gray jacket, and a skirt. She had low-heeled gray pumps on her feet. In front of her, she held a small gray beaded purse. Philip wore a white shirt, a gray jacket, and matching pants. He wore gray oxfords. Their heads were covered with gray hats due to the beaming sunshine. Francine wore a navy skirt with a puffed, short-sleeved white blouse while carrying a small purse. On her feet were gray open-toed flat sandals.

They were seated inside by a desk clerk in the waiting room. They glanced around the huge room and saw people coming and going about their business.

Then a tall, thin, austere-looking woman with brown wavy hair surrounding her face, brown rimmed glasses fastened to a chain around her neck, and her eyes a hazel color, walked up to them and spoke with deliberation, "The judge will see you now." They all rose, and the woman, saying not another word, led them into the judge's chambers and closed the door behind her.

The judge sat at his podium sorting through the necessary documents. The three sat in the court room observing him and saying nothing. Then he banged his gravel down and presumed, "All rise," and they did so immediately.

He began, "I hear you are all here for two legal purposes, right?" he asked rhetorically, for he knew that quite well.

He glanced at Francine. "Young lady, I hear you're requesting a name change. Am I correct?"

Francine spoke with a smile. "Yes, sir, that's right."

The Judge resumed, "Also, you are here to become officially, legally, and formally adopted by these two people, your foster mother and your birth father."

Again, Francine affirmed it. "Yes, that is right, Your Honor."

"I'll be more than happy to grant you both since you've been waiting quite a while due to past issues and obstacles. But everything seems to have been resolved, and I see no reason not to proceed as promised." First, he glanced at Bettye Jo and Philip and said, "I need your daughter's birth certificate."

Bettye Jo reached into her bag, retrieved it, and handed to him. He looked at it.

Bettye Jo began explaining the circumstances but with weary reluctance for she wanted to forget and move on once and for all. She was tired of rehashing it. Hopefully, she will not have to after today.

"Your Honor, Francine had lived with her birth mother, Leonora Hawes, from birth until she was ten years old. Being this woman threw her birth father out of the apartment when she was three, Francine had no recollection of his existence. Her birth mother was mentally ill and abused Francine relentlessly. Thus, she never thought to ask about her father. When she was ten, her fifth-grade teacher decided to take a stand, reported Ms. Hawes to the authorities, and had Francine placed in a children's shelter. She remained there for two years. That is when I became her foster mother and I made plans to adopt her. Then Dr. Marsowe appeared at our doorstep claiming to be her birth father. At first I was angry and indignant and said on no uncertain terms was I going to renege on my promise to adopt Francine, and he said he understood. He did explain that through no fault of his own, he was not able to have any contact with his daughter, for Leonora was always moving around, dodging landlords, and not paying the rent. He never gave up, and he contacted Francine's teacher and the children's shelter, and he found us. And though it had not even been a whole day, Francine, through a flashback of her wretched childhood, remembered her father, and she understood why he had not been able to have contact with her all these years. However, surprisingly to all of us, we fell in love and got married a few weeks ago, and we just got back from our honeymoon. And here we are."

Both she and Philip stood up with pride, their hands on their daughter's shoulders. She looked at both gleefully with her eyes twinkling. And they returned her smile.

The judge sat and listened attentively with patience and understanding. He was pleased and satisfied.

He stood up and took a form from a clerk, who walked up and gave it to him. It read, "'This is to certify that Francine Hawes' change of name is to be legally Francine Josephine Marsowe, aka Franny Jo to her friends.' You, young lady, are no longer Francine Hawes, never, ever again."

He signed, sealed, and stamped the document and handed it to Francine. He extended his hand to her, which she took with joy, and they shook. "Thank you, Your Honor."

Then the Judge faced Philip and Bettye Jo while moving some documents on his podium.

"Now, for the adoption, I need you both to swear that you are and will always be Francine's legally adoptive parents, to love, nurture, support, and provide for her."

They raised their hands and placed them on the Bible, vowing to be the official parents of Francine Josephine Marsowe legally as well as in their hearts. They were given a document stating, "Certificate of the Adoption of Francine

Josephine Marsowe to Bettye Josephine Clarke Pennington Marsowe and to Doctor Philip Winston Marsowe." Again, the judge stamped, sealed, and signed it, handing it to the proud parents.

"And you, young lady," the judge added, "are now the legal, official daughter of these two kind people. You be good and listen to and appreciate them for they took great pains to adopt you. I do know you are a wonderful, caring daughter, but I just thought I would add a little humor to the situation. It cannot hurt."

"Thank you, Your Honor, for everything." Bettye Jo graciously beamed, and Philip did so too. Both smiled in agreement.

"Have a great rest of the day, folks." He waved, and they did so and then left the building.

As they headed down the courthouse steps into the sunshine, Philip suggested, "Ladies, how about we celebrate?"

Both mother and daughter nodded gleamingly as they all headed to their car.

September: The First Day of High School

The Marsowe family was busily preparing for Francine's first day in her new high school. She wore a red floral print dress that Bettye Jo purposely bought for her first day in high school. She wore white flat sandals. Her hair was around her shoulders and a red-laced headband was placed in front. She packed her supplies in her book bag, zippered it up, and flung it over her shoulders. Bettye Jo touched up some strands in her daughter's hair and took her chin in her hand.

"How's my girl?" She put her arm around her shoulder.

Philip got up from the table after he finished his coffee. They planned to take Francine to school. Bettye Jo and Philip were clad in their business apparel. Philip was wearing a beige suit, a crisp white shirt, and a tannish tie. On his feet were shiny brown leather shoes. Bettye Jo wore a pale blue skirt reaching her knees along with a matching jacket and a white blouse that had ruffles at her throat and buttons down her chest. She wore low-heeled white pumps.

They had businesses to tend to but were glad. The summer was over. Fall had approached. But it was a happy time for everybody. A new start.

Agnes watched them from the kitchen counter while wiping a glass. She smiled at them.

Philip glanced at his watch and then looked up. "I think we better get a move on, ladies." He led them out the door and into the car.

The sun was shining down on them. The sky was a clear blue.

While heading to Francine's new school, Bettye Jo then remembered that she had something to say to Francine. "Honey, don't forget Aunt Ellen and Uncle Paul are coming over to dinner tonight."

"Right," their daughter knew quite well.

"I know, but I just thought to remind you, sweetheart, just to make sure. That is my job," Bettye Jo stated gently.

"And you do it quite well, Mama!" she acknowledged gleamingly.

They both laughed from sheer joy and love.

The Marsowes rode in the car with cheerful expressions on their faces. As they reached the high school, Francine pointed with glee. "There's Mark!" He was wearing a denim jacket and jeans with a blue T-shirt and holding his books on a satchel by his side. He waved and smiled at her. She smiled back.

Philip stopped in front. All the teenagers were laughing, jabbering, and poking each other's arms playfully.

"Here we are, our princess." Philip turned to face her.

Bettye Jo faced her. "Our precious, darling angel."

They both smiled as she first kissed and hugged her father. And then her mother, who removed her sunglasses. She was wearing a scarf around the front of her hair that was loosely knotted under her chin.

"I love you, Mama! Daddy!" she stated lovingly to them as she waved goodbye, and they did so likewise.

Francine got out of the car and blew kisses at her mother and father.

She saw Mark, who took her hand. "Hello, Franny Jo. You look nice today," he complimented her.

"So do you," she stated back to him.

They walked up the steps. Their friends were waiting for them. Bettye Jo and Philip watched their daughter with deep love, both saying harmoniously, "Our daughter, our love, our light, our joy, our pleasure, heart of our hearts forever."

Philip looked at his watch and stated to his wife, "I have patients waiting."

And then she announced, "And I have a shop to open. Danielle and the staff are waiting for me. We are expecting a lot of customers today."

Philip took Bettye Jo's face in his hands and his in hers, and they kissed each other for what seemed a long while. "And I love you, darling," he proclaimed.

And she in return said, "And I love you too."

They drove off and switched on their favorite country/Western station that played their song—"Let Your Love Flow."

About the Author

Beth Carol Solomon has worked in classified advertising in New York City. She has volunteered her time at the Clove Lakes Nursing Home and at the Silver Lakes Nursing Home for senior citizens, P.S. 16 and WIllowbrook State School for special needs individuals, the Snug Harbor Cultural Center, the Alzheimer's Foundation, and at the Staten Island University Hospital. She has a B.A. in psychology, a B.A. in English, a B.A. in history, a double B.A. in women's studies and sociology, and an M.A. in English. She has graduated with honors, and as magna cum laude and dean's list student. She took adult education classes in bookkeeping, astrology, short-story writing, and computers. She has appeared in several Who's Who publications. She published her first book, *Collected Works*, which consisted of several personal memoir accounts and two novellas. She had stories and poems published in several anthologies. Her hobbies include reading, writing, country/Western music, meditation, self-help, creative visualization, and family life. She lives in Staten Island, New York.